BOOKS → BEER → MORE → PEOPLE →

Koushik Banerjea

Category Unknown

KOUSHIK BANERJEA used to peddle vintage jeans and theory. Now he makes do with fiction. His shorts have appeared in *Minor Literatures*, *Writers Resist* and *Verbal*. His debut novel *Another Kind Of Concrete* was published in 2020. *Category Unknown* is his second. He deejayed as one half of The Shirley Crabtree Experience, survived the Hatfield train crash and once had dinner with legendary vibesman Roy Ayers, having originally only popped out to get some groceries, proving that in South London perhaps there is such a thing as a free lunch. He is still scribing, paying lip service to convention.

To Khuthaza,
Super fine!
With love
+blessings,
Ko.

Koushik Banerjea

Category Unknown

LONDON BOOKS BRITISH FICTION

LONDON BOOKS
39 Lavender Gardens
London SW11 1DJ
www.london-books.co.uk

A catalogue record for this book
is available from the British Library

ISBN 978-0-9957217-8-4

Printed and bound in Great Britain by
CPI Group (UK) Ltd, Croydon, CR0 4YY

Typeset by Octavo Smith Publishing Services

This one's for all the bouncers. Nah, not really.
It's for all the kids they never let in,
the ones whose faces never fit.

This book would not have happened without the following people. In years to come, I hope they don't hold that against me. A big shout out then to: George Dyer, a gentleman and a scholar, but also a natural mystic with needle and thread; Simon Smith, for the forensic editorial eye, the equal in sharpness to any bespoke stitch; John King Esq. and all at London Books, for actually 'getting it' and then for staying classy throughout; family & home, grateful for both, and frankly lucky to have either, especially in this day and age.

'Will this story someday become my own
congealing? How do I know.'
Clarice Lispector, *Hour of the Star*

'You're the problem! You're the fucking problem,
you fucking Dr White honkin' jam-rag fucking spunk bubble!'
Don Logan in *Sexy Beast*

PROLOGUE

LONDON, 1978. A teenage boy called Denis is about to undergo an epiphany on his way to school one morning. Blondie are riding high in the charts, but everything else is going pear-shaped. The unions, the economy, race relations. On the streets a winter of discontent, rats the size of dogs mingling with commuters near the uncollected mountains of rubbish. It's the rodent hustle, fur on plastic. A new sound, restless and furtive. And if those rats could speak, they'd have told Denis they were already part of the underground culture of this city. Its subterranean conscience nibbling away, throwing fresh shapes against the older cabling. Avantgarde, scene stealers in the way only rodents could be. Punk (plastic, making use of 'found' materials, riffing on outrage) – check. Funk – the hustle (see above) but also the smell of something lived in leaking from the city's arteries – check. Pop, reggae and the ultimate scavengers of hip-hop, feeding around in sonic cast-offs – check. The true arbiters of something from nothing, burrowing ever deeper for snapshots of a different future. Sound boxes and deerstalkers, Farahs and Trimm Trabs. In years to come the rats would have hipped young Denis to the joys of early Luther (Vandross), swishing their tails in the dark recesses of soul and funk all-dayers. The various recs and leisure centres tricked out in Adidas, Fila and the irresistible strains of Lonnie Liston Smith. 'Expansions' inviting the serious dancers to go to work, the rats, as ever, doing their own thing in the shadows. They'd have pushed open the fire exit and smuggled young Denis inside, past the self-appointed guardians of this invented demi-monde. Into Crackers, into the Blitz, into Gullivers. And into a hundred disused warehouses where the stink of work, of tanning, processing, canning had long since given way to the reek of pleasure, rising from the stink, casting its spell from the old Thurston Road industrial estate in Lewisham to the Mutoid Waste parties in King's Cross, to the dust and dread frequencies at Jamestown Road in Camden. The posh kids and the black folks they worshipped, at Shake And Finger Pop. Sound scripting another story to the one the Westminster politicians were peddling. The rarest of rare grooves, black, white, Puerto Rican, well not quite, it *was* still London after all. Buckingham Palace, Tower of London, curry 'n' chips for tea. The rats, who'd seen it all, from Balearic to bhangra, but still had a soft spot for the perfect pop creations of Edwyn Collins; they'd have told Denis to stick around, 'you might like the next bit'. Smiley faces and cramped arches, Millwall soulboys returning to the Old Kent Road 'converted' from their MDMA holidays in Ibiza. The football tribes now the best of frenemies. Bushwackers and the ICF swapping Stanley knives for plastic bananas, and a new summer of love ushered in under the strobe lights. Denis' old muckers from the neighbourhood, Bermondsey boys, at first playing ball but then, like the scorpion on the frog's back, reverting to their true nature once the rumour of profit began to waft up like a bad smell. The wrong funk. Pills to poppers to snood, and the rest, as they say, is history. But every now and then the music itself would still break through the greed, and for a brief, poignant moment, man and rat could once more stand and marvel in unison at the acid-fried genius of 'Voodoo Ray' or the first, glorious bars of 'Spliffhead', which, as far as the rats were concerned, was the most exciting sonic development they'd been privy to since 2 Tone, from 'back in the day', when Denis was still himself and London was first waking up to its 'rat problem'. They've been through a lot, the rats, and they've probably seen more than us, occluded in the dark corners of our social experiment. This story then is as much theirs as it is ours, shadow boxing something beautiful from the guts of their nescient host. And Denis? You'll have to read on to find out what happened to him.

PART ONE

PART ONE

ERROR OF JUDGEMENT

London 1992

6.30AM, AND SHE was up before him, coffee on the go, the ingredients for a fresh ploughman's laid out on the chopping board. I have to tell her, he thought, adjusting the no-longer-compulsory tie. Moments later, though, when she asked him what the matter was, all he could manage was an unconvincing, 'Oh, it's just work stuff.' And he let her kiss him as if nothing had changed.

All this even though it had already been a week since he was made to clear his desk, chaperoned off the premises by security.

The whole charade, he suspected, deliberately set up to make him feel small and weak: the 9am appointment with HR, the pep talk, the decision to 'let him go'.

Then the pause, security on hand in case he turned out to be a shouter. But all he'd done was just sit there, stunned. And in the end, perhaps taking pity on him, the ex-army stalwart on security detail had at least kept a respectful distance from the condemned man as he passed by former colleagues, an occasional nod but mostly with eyes averted, the box of goodies his only prop on that long walk of shame to the lifts. Only after he'd left the building did D loosen his tie, but the charade resumed when he got home and just couldn't bring himself to tell her. I'll shower first, he thought, but reconsidered when all he could see looking back at him in the mirror were little flecks of doubt mixed in with the salt and pepper. I'll tell her after dinner then, he thought, but when that didn't happen either he simply sat in front of the television quietly absorbing the news that England had been knocked out of the European Championships by the hosts Sweden. For all the pre-tournament bluster, there they were, first-round failures. The

13

economy tanking, boom definitely turning to bust, but, through it all, the national football team, as regular as clockwork. Some things never changed. He was glad of the distraction, then chided himself for not having had a punt on the wearily predictable tournament exit. Money for old rope, always handy in a tight spot, which for the time being was where he appeared to be.

So it was that he found himself only a week later heading down the park with his freshly cut sandwiches and a copy of the paper, the odd listing circled but with no great conviction. Perhaps it hadn't properly sunk in yet, and that was why his efforts to find another position had been so half-hearted. As yet he felt no great urgency. Something would turn up, and when it did he'd be able to look back and wonder what all the fuss was about. But if it didn't, well, the truth was, he hadn't really thought that far ahead. He'd cross that bridge when he got to it. *If*, not when, he corrected himself. Positive thinking, that was half the battle. In his head, nothing had really changed except that he was no longer having to put up with the nose-to-armpit commute twice a day. It was still him, though, with his sarnies and the paper. Yeah, it was still him.

But if this kept up much longer, he thought ruefully, he'd have no option but to tell her. The park, library, café circuit already felt stale, and he had no intention of spending the winter on the benches with the jakeys.

He hated it when they tried to speak to him. Especially the Irish ones. For whatever reason, something to do with word order and a tragic poetic quality, their pleas would really get under his skin.

'Can you find it in your heart to spare some change for a lost soul?'

To start with, he'd try and ignore them, pretend he hadn't heard. But they would persist.

'You seem like a gent. Could you find it in your heart to spare even a few coins?'

At which point he'd look up, feigning surprise, though mainly because the lilting brogue sounded closer, and indeed the man in the overcoat would be hovering around the edges of his bench.

His bench! Fuck. A matter of days, and already he was staking a claim.

'I'm no gent, pal. What do you think I'm doing here?' D replied, immediately regretting it as the Irishman took this as his cue to settle in alongside him. He should have just ignored him or told him to 'get a job', which just a week ago would have seemed as natural to him as squashing a spider or stepping over the homeless. Instead, he'd end up sharing his lunch with a stranger and giving him the change he would otherwise have used to buy himself a cup of tea in the café near the station.

After a while, following up the listings started to feel a bit like chasing circles.

Too young, too old, not enough experience or too much of the wrong kind.

And on his CV, like in the mirror, he started to sense the catch in his voice when they'd have it in front of them at interview and pick out a little detail.

'I notice you spent time in the peace corps. Would you like to tell us a little more about that?'

Or later, when his credibility was truly shot, the less trusting, 'It says here you did a stint in…' followed by something unbelievable. He'd sense the note of borderline desperation then and really it just made him want to give up. Let go, drop his kecks and do his business on the floor before getting up and leaving, the steaming pile of waste the one memorable detail from an otherwise under-whelming interview performance. Something at least for the panel to discuss.

'What about the last candidate, then?'

'What, you mean the shitter?'

'Yes, I mean the shitter!'

'Highly original, I'll give him that.'

'Well he certainly left his mark.' (Laughs all round.)

'A contender, though?'

'I don't think so. Not really a team player. We're not Lloyd's. There's no shitting forecast here.'

'Quite.'

'And what was all that stuff about the peace corps?'
'Exactly.'

It took D just over a month to tell his missus. In the end what convinced him to come clean was that in that whole time there wasn't a single interview. He'd been hoping to land another position in the industry by now. He'd tell her about it eventually, but really, so long as the salary kept coming in, what did it matter whether he was with so and so over there or such and such over here? Anyway, for whatever reason it hadn't happened, but now there were bills due and an account about to slip even further into the red. So he cleared his throat and spat it out, detail by horrible detail. HR, the pep talk, the jakey, even the imaginary shit, though by that point he was babbling like a fool and all the regular kitchen sounds of chopping and cutting had stopped. With hindsight, of course, he wouldn't have told her, or at least not then. Looking back, D recognised it wasn't the smartest move breaking the news to her at that particular moment. She came at him with the Japanese fish knife, and though he was able to disarm her fairly easily his second error of judgement was in thinking that the threat had passed. Once the knife had been put away and her breathing appeared less fevered he slowly let her up from where he'd been holding her close next to the sideboard. It took a moment longer to register the fork attached to his leg like a fridge magnet. But afterwards, when he didn't press charges, she decided to go ahead and ask for a divorce anyway. He found it funny when her lawyer informed him they would be 'aggressively pursuing his assets' as if they were Yanks on some legal drama. And it was almost sweet, the poor, deluded soul evidently still believing D was a corporate somebody rather than the middle-management nobody he'd always been. 'Good luck with that,' he'd told the lawyer. 'I'm sure she'll be very happy with 100% of fuck all.' And with that as his parting shot, he'd walked out, metaphorically at least, on his old life, which when he thought about it, as he tended to less and less these days, was no life at all.

The Taint Of Refusal

TO START WITH it hadn't been easy. The lowering of expectations, the gradual realisation that this might be it, the land of no quick fix. That perhaps there *was* no shortlist or appropriate – by which he meant equivalent – job in the pipeline. That it wouldn't be back to the station any time soon for the daily grind, those unspoken courtesies for the regulars – the dedicated platform space, a barely perceptible nod indicating an acceptable presence, the shared dislike of interlopers. No executive benefits (then again had there ever been?) and in all likelihood not even the dubious privilege of desk-bound, open-plan drudgery. At least the bleary-eyed rituals could be put on hold now that there was no need to rush any more, though equally, when he rose in the mornings no longer would he find his clothes neatly laid out, tie, shirt, trousers, socks, all colour coordinated, the detail its own window. Her holding up her end of a domestic bargain he'd never asked for, him drinking in the adulation, while knowing full well it wasn't that anyway. Different now. No breadwinner's privileges anywhere to be seen.

She'd left, fucked off in every which way. And really, given the opening salvo with the knife, and then the fork, he'd even started to believe he'd got off quite lightly.

After a while he'd stopped circling specifics on the appointments' pages of specialised broadsheets and had begun to internalise instead the details he'd previously never believed applied to him, or to someone like him.

The loser's small print, already designed to lower expectations, soften the expected blow. There it was, the '*only successful applicants will be contacted*' stipulation; or the ones placing a time limit on his optimism. *'If you haven't heard back from us within X weeks, assume…'* And while he might have made a note to himself *'on this occasion'* and moved on, the difficulty lay in the time it took for hungry digits to stop circling and dialling and find something else to nurse instead. Before long even the briefest break in his attention seemed to pre-empt a stray hand (always the left) on his tackle. Somehow he always managed to drum up horniness from the boredom, no matter how disengaged the rest of him might have felt. Anything: his ex's fashion catalogues, which carried on arriving long after she left, the personals section of the local rag, even the increasingly angry colour scheme of the overdues, began to have the same effect.

Gas, electric, the water rates.

Red. Angry. Strict.

He could picture some severe-looking librarian type at the council mailing him his final warning. And then his inability to pay, and then her fixing him a particular look, and then, well, there he was again, more alert than he had been for months, and the next thing he knew it wasn't really the job search he was focused on any more.

It didn't take long for this shift to occur, the only real surprise being how tenaciously D initially held on to the fantasy of a quick return to action, the surrogate vacancy always about to hove into view. Until it didn't and stayed out of sight each time he went looking for it. At least that's how it was to start with, the stubble kept at bay by long-held habit. Until one day it just happened, on his way to the library to carry on with the pretence of the job search. A selection of the papers, computers, 'careers advice'. The benchmark lowered just that little bit further, toes dipping into uncharted waters now. His fellow travellers, perhaps other refugees from his previous life or maybe nothing of the sort. But every face carrying the taint of refusal: *'Sorry'*, *'Not at the moment'*, *'Try another time'* and, worst of all, *'We'll keep your résumé on file'* the regular hymn sheet for this tribe. The library at least somewhere warm and relatively quiet for all of them to ponder just what it was that had happened to their lives.

SOMETHING VAMPIRIC

Handyman required.

Private tuition.

Domestic cleaner.
References supplied on request.

HE'D ORIGINALLY ONLY stopped to tie his shoelace. That was when he realised he never stopped anywhere on the high street. It had always just been a straight run to and from the station, the interim details reserved in his mind for the service sector, not a high flier like himself. He rarely paid attention to anything other than roadworks or snow or the occasional faulty paving slab. (To be fair, those municipal seesaws were the one thing he always paid attention to in that cranial department of his that would be forever 'risk analysis', the bit that skipped past the hazard and instead of thinking 'Phew' was suddenly consumed with weighing up another type of seesaw: what price a personal-injury payout versus the pressing need for further council cutbacks?)

Now, though, as if for the first time, he suddenly became aware of shop windows advertising a whole different social stratum to the one he still felt some attachment to. The cards in these shop-fronts magic markered or biro'd up with the requisite information, somehow keen not to parade the desperation behind the unfussy scrawl. The problem, of course, being that the entire transaction between newsagent, advertiser and potential client was, at first glance, held together by nothing so much as its desperation. The cards jogged some distant teenage memory in D's head of other services being offered in shop windows, but what struck him most was how few of these openings he was qualified for. All those management seminars and team-building days on the company coin, but he'd still have to call someone else to deal with the electricals or the pipes or any kind of practical emergency. It was one thing shitting on a carpet, quite another clearing up afterwards.

As for the cards themselves, he couldn't decide which were more lacking in class, the ones with writing straddling more than one line, as if the whole thing was a terrible imposition for the reluctant author, or their rivals, spidering away against a plain background. It all smacked of indiscipline, shoddiness. No wonder they needed a handyman. Lazy sods couldn't even write straight.

One stood out, though. It bore the familiar gnarled shadow of Nosferatu hovering above the details of the community hall where the auditions would take place. Some thought had at least gone into the advertisement, and he was briefly impressed. Here at last was some evidence of craft, a hint of German expressionism amid all this local tat. The placeholder had clearly taken some time over the Count Orlok outline. He made a note of the time and place and headed on to the library, where his attention kept shifting from the job advertisements to something vampiric elsewhere in his mind.

Later, at the hall, he felt tired and wet and cold. Heading there on foot he'd been caught out by a late downpour, cursing the endless prevarications which had seen him turn back several times en route while the skies were still friendly. In the end he was one of the last to arrive, unkempt and flustered, barging in with his brolly turned inside out and a barely suppressed 'shit' as he tripped and nearly fell by the entrance. After the sniggering had died down, he began to study the faces of his fellow thesps. In the main these were good, honest faces, an optimism and an openness about them which took him by surprise.

Of course, he was soon feeling less generous when, in spite of his dishevelled appearance, the marquee role went to a fresh-faced self-starter, as did the other front-of-house openings to various local good sorts, their expressions somehow inoculated against the two-day-old-paper smell that covered his hands. But when even the lighting gig went to some school leaver he decided to cut his losses and head down to the well-known high-street pizza outlet before the 'all you can eat' sign was replaced by something less inviting, the evening version designed for the gainfully employed.

'Are you OK there, sir?' the waiter asked, hovering nervously as a number of croutons tumbled from the summit which D had lovingly constructed in the unfeasibly small bowl. D looked up, took in the anxious looking Asian kid who was obviously new to the job. Give it a week, he thought, and this youth would be grateful for the 'all you can eat' recidivists sat in mid-afternoon silence by their gastric ziggurat before being gently chaperoned towards the exits so the place could be prepped for the evening crowd. Who'd look at him as if *he* was the loser.

'Depends what you mean by OK?' D replied, squeezing the cod philosophy past the sweetcorn now lodged in his teeth and gesturing for the kid to join him at the table.

'Thanks, but I can't really,' said the kid. 'The manager won't like it.'

'The manager?'

'He says he wants us "looking alert at our stations", otherwise it gives the wrong impression.'

'The wrong impression, you say?'

'He says it looks "slovenly", and if the customer thinks we're not fully alert front of house then maybe we're cutting corners in the kitchen, too.'

'Front of house, eh?'

'About that. I never really –'

'Listen, son,' D interrupted, enjoying the conceit as he was barely old enough to be the boy's elder sibling, 'you seem like a good lad, so I'll let you in on a little secret. Your manager hasn't been playing fair with you.'

'What do you mean?'

'Think about it, son. What do you think he's been doing all that time he's had you running around picking up croutons?'

'Croutons?'

'That's right, son. Croutons. Right now I bet he's got his feet up, taking his time with a copy of today's papers and a nice cup of tea, having a bloody good laugh at your expense.'

The kid kept looking around nervously as though expecting his manager to spring out at any moment from wherever he was hidden. But when this didn't happen, D could tell that he was thinking on what he'd been told.

'How do you know that?' he asked D, his voice betraying a certain amount of doubt even if he was doing his best to appear nonchalant.

'Look, son,' said D, thoroughly addicted already to his self-appointed role as mentor to the young man, 'he's got you running around for no good reason while he's doing all sorts round the back.' He paused for dramatic effect, enjoying how the kid was hanging on to his every word as though it was anything other than garbage. Well, filler mostly, but with more than a hint of rubbish about it. 'How can you even tell whether those are croutons at all? For all you know he might be mixing in bits of French toast for a laugh, or worse. Something from the end of the biscuit tray and,' he paused again as though genuinely troubled by what he'd just come out with, but not so much that he couldn't carry on with a, 'No I can't say. I've said too much already. Don't want to get you into trouble.'

The ploy worked, just as he'd hoped.

'Oh, that's not fair. You can't just stop now. What were you about to say?' asked the kid, definitely interested now, but with the same gormless look on his face which had inspired D to make stuff up in the first place.

'Look, son, all I'm saying is that whatever's in those croutons, he's adding a little extra if you get my drift.'

Predictably enough the gormlessness stayed put on the kid's face.

'Do I have to spell it out for you, son? He's picking it out from one of two places, and really you're better off not knowing which one.'

With that, D got up to go to the toilet, successfully flicking the bogey he'd been cradling in his left palm straight into the salad. He'd make sure to point it out to the kid as 'Exhibit A' when he came back. It'd be all the 'evidence' he required to point the kid like the Manchurian Candidate at any middle-management scum hiding behind company guidelines and team-building exercises. Anyway, all that could wait. Right now it was the deep pan churning in his gut which led his decision making.

He liked this time of day, untroubled, unhurried, room to breathe, to think and with no one demanding files, reports, graphs, projections, all that shit that used to pass for work. As if houses were held up with bar charts or cars with monthly stats. The only reason for any of it, as far he could tell, the money – yet more numbers really but ones which kept everyone off his back – and which assured the bearer their socially appointed prestige of being an earner. Fair enough, he thought, squatting over the bowl firing pellets as outriders to the main event. But what about all those times he'd raided the stationery cupboard, the half-inched staplers, all those HB pencils, biros, paper, envelopes? An old habit really, picked up at school but somehow not yet discarded even though money was no longer an object. Where was the prestige in that?

Still, the sense of shame crept up on D, caught him unawares, literally with his pants round his ankles. What if someone else was to walk in now? He'd be made to 'own' the stench, there'd be no nose wrinkling at some phantom menace, and, to be fair, if there was eye contact he'd either have to exit the entire establishment without ceremony or ask the stranger what he was looking at, in a dress rehearsal for some needless face-off, the urinal cakes just another baleful reminder of school and how far he clearly hadn't come since then. No learning, no distance, all that stuff with numbers and a fancier pay grade just a comic interlude, treading water before the comedown. Ah well, making haste with the mop up would avoid such unpleasantries, so he did just that, and moments later he was back at the salad bar, the spray-can art on cracked porcelain already a fading memory.

'As I was saying, son, it's this kind of thing you need to be worried about,' he said, fishing out the dried bogey with the plastic tweezers. 'Not exactly croutons,' he added with a triumphal sneer, the offending object sat in full view on a crinkly bed of lettuce.

This time the manager was on hand to offer advice, though. 'Everything OK?'

No 'sir' from the higher pay grade. It just added to the growing sense of outrage.

'No, everything's not OK. I mean, does this look OK to you?' he replied, pointing at the non-crouton in the salad.

'I'm not sure what you mean,' said the duty manager, and, in truth, he did look genuinely confused.

'You're not sure what I mean?' repeated D, allowing the manufactured grievance to roll around his teeth. 'I show you *this*, and you're not sure what I mean?'

'Look, I'm not –'

'That's right, mate, you're not... at the races. I've got a good mind to take this to the papers.'

'Take what? I'm not sure I'm following you.'

'No you're not, are you? Let me spell it out for you then. When I come to the salad bar I don't expect to find *this* in the salad. And before you ask, no, it's not a crouton. So the question's not so much "Are you following me?" as "What are you going to do about it?".'

'I can assure you that –'

'Uh-urgh,' D interrupted, mimicking the Dalek-like failure noise he'd heard on that television quiz show when contestants gave the wrong answer.

'Now look –'

'No, mate, you had your chance, and you fluffed it. So *you* look, and if I were you, this time I'd listen very carefully.' D paused, had a quick look around to make sure the Asian kid was within earshot. The show was as much for the kid's benefit as his own, with the key element being the management take-down. He'd show the kid there was no mystique to the half-sleeve shirt and clip-on tie, the name badge, the whole ragged notion of being a company man. 'Work station!' The neck on this cunt, as if the deep-pan outfit was some hi-tech aerospace project. The kid seemed unsure about what he should do, either wait in the wings until summoned or pitch in on someone's behalf. 'Conflicted' seemed to describe it best, all the options – have-a-go hero, potential dismissal proceedings, the relative discomfort of finding another job – whirring around under that gormless exterior. Still, the kid would work it out, they usually did. It was the so-called adult D was keen to set straight.

'I've only gone to the bathroom to wash my hands, and what do I find when I get there? It's not what I was expecting, I can tell you that. It smells like something out of Dickens in there. And last I looked, it's not the H-Block, so why you've got filth smeared on the walls is anyone's guess. It's not exactly conducive to the dining experience, if you catch my drift. So when I get back to the salad bar, the one thing I don't want to see sitting on my lettuce is *this*.' And with that, he deftly employed the tweezers to push the bogey from one side to another. 'Anyway you can imagine my shock, and coupled with what I've just seen in the bathroom, it starts to look like a pattern around this place. It kind of sets the tone, don't you think? And you've got the nerve to stand there and ask me if everything's OK? Well I'm telling you, squire, no, everything's not OK, and now I want to know what you intend to do about it?'

The commotion, if it could even be called that, had attracted the attention of the other waiters, and in this distracted environment at least one of the other 'all you can eat' patrons slipped away unnoticed, though when he spotted the move in his peripheral vision, D suspected it was the subsistence rather than managerial wage packets which would later take the hit. It just made him want to redouble his efforts on the shop floor.

'I wonder what Health and Safety would make of this?' he mused, enjoying how the employees seemed captivated by his every word. 'I mean, it's not every day they get to tear apart one of the bigger chains. Can't see them turning down an opportunity like this. The easy headlines. Makes them look good, like fearless crusaders. But when they've finished digesting the news, the public might see things a little differently, though. Don't you think?'

'Look, sir, I can assure you –'

The first whiff of Health and Safety and this clown suddenly remembered his manners. 'Sir'. A bit more courtesy from the get-go, and perhaps this whole tawdry little charade could have been avoided.

'It's not your assurances I'm after,' said D, meeting the manager's eyes with a knowing look. The company man's hesitation told D they both knew the game was up. A deal would need to be struck, or the inspectors would eventually troop in, negative headlines trailing in their wake. The company might not like it. Every chance they'd promote from within, and then the manager would be joining him on Income Support.

D enjoyed the complimentary meal, replete with ice cream and coffee, and just to show there were no hard feelings, made sure to shake the manager's hand afterwards. Smiling as he walked out, heavier of belly but for once no lighter in the pocket, the shake-down didn't feel petty. This would count as a good day, one of the few he'd enjoyed of late. Harmless fun. It's not as though the manager could tell D hadn't washed his hands.

'Sir! Sir!'

There was no way he could tell. People just didn't notice that type of thing. Terrible really, when he thought about it, how quickly the whole country had gone to the dogs.

'Excuse me, sir!'

Louder this time, as though he was being followed. Still, he didn't wait to find out. Mid-afternoon, and there were leads to pursue and jobs to actively seek.

Beyond This Funk

H-BLOCK! WHERE had that come from? He'd barely been five minutes on the benches with the jakey, and here he was carrying on like the actor who supplied the voice of top IRA dissidents any time the BBC came knocking. Still, the look on that manager's face when he'd mentioned 'Health and Safety' in his little rant pretty much justified everything. D knew what that man was, and, if he had any kind of integrity, the man must have known himself. A bean counter, if not quite the dictionary definition then at any rate a stooge co-opted by the enemy (management), so as good as in D's books. Then again, once he'd had a chance to reconsider the day's events with a late-afternoon brew, something else settled over him. Unwelcome, like dandruff, but very much there, no matter how hard he tried to ignore it.

These days he viewed the seven-minute timer as more of a guide-line than a precise measurement. Sometimes a little bitterness on the tongue was just the tonic for another futile job search. So the brews got stronger, tea more in the manner of tar, but the bags defiantly niche, a refusal to stock the builders' favourite one of the few remaining concessions to his former life. All those aspirational tics – the exposed brickwork, the coffee-maker, something about the wife – now razored to the bone, everything pared back, the living circum-stances, the daily routine, the cancelled subscriptions. Everything, that is, except for the tea. He wouldn't be throwing in the towel just yet; Yorkshire still no match for the foothills of the Himalayas.

The first sip was always the best, causing him to close his eyes in half-remembered ecstasy, taste buds reminded of an elsewhere, beyond this funk.

The way he held the mug, though. Well, old habits again. Thumb to the left circumference, the other digits to the right, gently throttling the life out of the vessel. Oh, he'd tried the dandyish affectation, legs crossed at the knee, right hand nursing the cup at the handle, left poised with saucer as safety net. Tried it, but it just hadn't felt right or comfortable, the posture borrowed from some other projection of himself: office hologram, social butterfly, the D that never was, a bit of a beast under all those mannerisms. A projection maybe, but still with a nod to the ten-minute presentation, or lives, futures and any kind of doubt banished to the tea break, which as far as he was concerned was the only acceptable time and place for a lack of conviction. Small talk for small minds before it was back to the real business of 'analysis'.

His devolved shtick the psychobabble of numbers, figures, caressed, massaged, the spokes made to fit, the stats in place, an army of willing dupes just the other side of the spiel. And all this so he could sit and nurse the mug (ah, what a man of the people) with the mien of a leader. A winner, whose rotten luck it was to be the last on his trading floor to punt a sure thing just as the foundations were coming loose, and the hairline cracks started to appear, and the whole Mithraic temple began to crumble. So that when the rubble was cleared and the post-mortem began, it was to his blushingly guilty screen that the internal investigation was drawn. Numbers, letters, risks, timecoded, the ether no kind of disguise. In plain view, for anyone who cared to look. *His* doing, *his* risks, the only numbers which really mattered the time and the date. Which is how, for perhaps the first time since he'd been there, this dedicated follower of the winning routine started to hear the alien sounds of defeat pressing down on his neon-lit terminal.

Reckless. Liability. Unsustainable losses.

Weird, alien sounds which he'd never expected to hear. At least not in relation to himself.

Cutbacks, regrettable, no other way. Probably for the best. Syntax error. Full stop. Security.

No, those were not words he'd ever thought would be

addressed to him, so in that sense (of being a novelty), at least it counted as an 'experience'.

'It'll be the making of you, son,' chirped up his old man, the voice lodged in his mind, though he hadn't seen him in what felt like far too long. Or at least it's more than likely what he would have said if D had opened up to him. But, of course, being more buttoned up than his hologram, and never having been a butterfly, D just couldn't spread his wings, bring himself to confide in his dad when it mattered most. Yet he couldn't quite shake that voice either, and not for want of trying.

His father had staying power, he'd give him that, lying dormant in his imagination all this time while the prodigal son made ever fewer trips home. The template forged once D had left to go to university. The calls, once so regular, then intermittent and now rare enough that they constituted a genuine event.

'It's D,' he could hear his mum saying, then an awkward silence, his dad shifting on the armchair, thinking of something to say. Then, 'How are you, son?' The embarrassment (mutual), though only D suffered from the self-absorbed skittishness which even he would admit seemed to be the prerogative of the young.

Jumpy, touchy, not like his dad at all.

Not generous in the way his dad was, feeling out the good in each moment, past the ache in the bones or any lingering regret that this was what life had become.

A distant son, an occasional voice, some unspoken kindnesses, not quite what his father would have chosen. You didn't really choose life, but you chose how you dealt with the one you'd been given. He knew that much. So when the receiver was handed to him, curdling dead air, his father didn't act surprised. Or hurt. Spivs had stitched up this area before. It's just what they did, the irony being they felt they were offering a service. Would never have seen themselves as parasites. And like his son they maintained some bizarre sense of attachment to the area, even as they leeched the very dust out of the brickwork.

The father knowing why the son couldn't speak, ambition pressing down hard on his tongue. 'You do what you like, son.

We'll back you all the way. Now you go out there and knock 'em dead.'

His exact words.

That's what his dad had said to him in the first place, back when he'd been hoovered up in the milk round of potential employers who cherry-picked what for them was presumably the cream of the crop. D remembered handing out his CV, touting for trade like a lonely brass, all the other bright young things shuffling around in identikit suits. This would have been around the mid-eighties in his final year as an undergraduate. The man he'd eventually spoken to seemed more impressed by his vintage threads – all very Steve McQueen in *The Thomas Crown Affair* – than by anything on his résumé.

In the way of these things, it turned out that in another life before debentures, the recruiter had a cousin who was a client of a famous Savile Row tailor, so the cloth caught his eye more powerfully than any personal statement. D played it straight, only minor Estuary in his accent and serious about his future, and the recruiter seemed to like that, too. But D also made sure to intersperse their conversation with a snippet he recalled from a recent article on fashion he'd read as preamble to a typically pretentious student dinner party down in Royal Leamington Spa.

Third-year English lit, unimpeachably Home Counties, but even as students still not quite able to relinquish the well-appointed comforts.

Hence the big Georgian terrace, the stucco front, the well lubricated meal. *Champers, darling. It's what the Bloomsbury set would have wanted.*

As for that snippet, it concerned 'kippers'. No, not the fish, but the slang term for a female tailor, which, as D explained to the recruiter, had come about because they sought work in pairs so as to avoid unwelcome attention. Clever girls, and he was a clever boy. At least he was *then*.

That had more or less sealed the deal, though there was still some cursory bobbing and weaving to do with the finer points. Projected degree status, key skills, availability, that sort of thing.

An official interview was set up, though in the end it was more or less a formality, with the written confirmation waiting in the wings. And that was when he'd finally called his father to let him know the good news, but in no small measure because he also craved his approval.

D was nervous beforehand. And he knew why.

He knew the old man used to swear by braces, mohair parallels, knitted long-sleeved polo shirts, brogues. The whole nine yards, basically. He'd been a modernist, probably still was in his outlook, but right up until D and his brother had started school, their father had kept his threads. He still had the holdall where he used to stash his towel and the talc and even the occasional record.

He'd been one of the lucky ones, so they said, coming of age after the war. Always had work, married young and married well. The day they'd met, he'd been particularly dapper, a one-button Huntsman coat with an in-house check. *She'd* been impressed by that, he could tell, and it wasn't long after that that they'd got together. But what she really liked was his temperance. He wasn't coarse the way some people could be, didn't need to overdo it. She felt safe with him, and round here that was something.

He was steady and present, and again not everyone round this way could say that about their fella. He must have been happy enough with her, too, because he'd never taken to drink or straying or any of the other wayward things she would sometimes hear about from the less fortunate on their street. He'd been employed as a delivery driver, first for Hartley's and then the other canneries which were all nearby, so the work was regular, and while she was at Peek Freans the money worries and tetchiness that often came with never blighted their early life together. If the area itself was better known as 'the larder of London', then they, too, felt blessed in the abundance of their lives. No more rationing, no memories scarred by the Blitz and even an ecclesiastical nod from the nearby Southwark Cathedral on those rare occasions they'd venture within. Best of all, nothing changed when the boys arrived, and if anyone asked about them, about her, he'd always say *he* was the luckiest chap in the world. Of course, it didn't hurt either that he'd always known how to dress, without being too flash.

Mohair suits, single vents up the back, and a taste for the black-American sounds released by Atlantic Records at the same time that everyone else was messing around with scooters.

So he was nobody's fool, D's old man. Everyone knew that. He could see what was already happening to the place he'd grown up in. And he had a fair idea where D might see himself fitting into this picture. That's why his son was a little nervous that day when it came to making the call.

Long before numbers and projections fell like a shroud on the whole area, red-figured calculations then demands then eviction notices had been served up as sacrament for the old timers. Spooned in like cod-liver oil by smart-suited boys and girls, medicine for the neighbourhood's growing pain. The old men in high-backed trousers, held up over string vests with button braces, tea and fig rolls on a side plate, watching the world they'd built dismantled brick by accursed brick.

Fibre glass, per square foot, clean lines and exposed brickwork the new alphabet around here.

Its lettering found the condemned, tracing the bitter secrets between fathers and sons, the accelerated pace of change. They described what happens when speed becomes the new drug. Not Dexys or the gift of Northern Soul all-nighters. This was a different kind of speed. No need for a holdall now. Barely an echo in this empty chamber, the buttons clinging on, Frank Wilson reduced to a whisper, a dying croak peeping out of the brickwork. This was on the hoof, high-velocity theft, in plain view but with numbers and stats and graphs to make its case. The old timers choking on the bitterness, their own flesh and blood the source and the system. Stakeholders and servants, the spoils divvied up by boys like D, history barely even stretching to their own memories. Childhood, innocence, place, locality, not much left of that, of any of it, really. Just something fetid, unrivalled, in the water. Shad Thames.

THE FAVOURED
LOCAL OPTION

AT FIRST WHEN his boss had called him in and those alien sounds had started up, he'd checked to see who else was in the room.

No one.

Those words, the ones bemoaning failure, were meant for him, and the shock of that must have strangled whatever cry was building up inside him.

That would have been the time to call out, yell out, reach out. Do something, say something, to someone, anyone. Starting with the genius who was 'letting him go'. Management, kitted out in Moss Bros like the other Square Mile clones, maintaining eye contact to (i) establish dominance and (ii) as a mark of sincerity, the 'this is hurting me as much, if not more, than it is you' gambit clearly approved during some training seminar. In D's mind, another version of events. The bit the seminar never quite spelt out. He pictured himself bending said manager over the desk and parking an indelible marker up his harris, on the point of whispering sweet nothings into the stricken man's ear, but settling instead for grabbing his head back and looking him straight in the eye. *Yeah, mate, this is really hurting me – more than you can imagine.* That's the message his eyes will convey before he leaves the more senior man bunched over the desk like a head-office question mark, silently weeping into the midweek mid-morning.

Instead, of course, nothing. Not a sound. And he's led off the premises by something chunky, ex-army, no trouble at all, his meekness shocking (even to the ex-army man) in its involuntary ease. Desk cleared, a minor history boxed up, the whole operation over in minutes. In the weeks and months ahead, this would become a familiar enough sight, the debacle of Black Wednesday not far from anyone's lips that September. But again, that parade of bewildered City workers belched back on to the streets with their boxed possessions had yet to happen, and even when it did, he felt only the briefest vindication and, in any case, utterly without joy. It was still painful even now to contemplate those first days, the ignominy of being an outlier.

Early summer, 1992

The cold air does nothing to sandblast the silence, and for a week it hangs over him, invading every thought but slipping back into the shadows each time he tries to pluck up the courage to say something. It would indeed have been the time to reach out, to his wife, to his dad, to someone. But no, the words won't come, so it's routine he makes do with in their place. The shirt, the suit, the tie, the commute.

'I've left your tie out, the one you said you couldn't find,' he hears his missus say, and if he wants to tell her, his desire, his need to, is stymied by her sense of routine.

Sarnies and socks, the pressed uniform, her devotion to the routine, all of it leaving him shamefaced and silent.

When should he tell her? Whenever he does, it's going to hit her hard. This routine, he thinks, in some ways, it's all she has now.

There are no kids. Miscarriages, ectopic pregnancies, but beyond the spotting and the bleeding and the tears, little else to show for the years of marriage. (In reality, it has only been several years, but he knows this feeling of intensity is something to do with all those theories of space/time compression that have been doing the rounds in the fancier postcodes, especially since the Berlin Wall came down.) The truth is, he's felt for a while now that lifestyle has been a factor in all this. She could give up work, he's told her that over and over. Let her know how well he's doing, how they could easily manage on just what he brings in. But she won't budge, still wants to hold on to some semblance of parity, which, given what she makes, should have been discarded long ago. Press officer for some environmental organisation. All a bit hairy as far as he can tell, but there's no reasoning with her. Not around this. And it's that stubbornness, he reckons, that's been getting in the way, blocking her mind, her tubes, everything. She's a strange one, though, he thinks. Totally adamant about the work but still insists on making his lunch and picking out his shirt and tie. Yet another detail he knows he can't, he mustn't, share with his father. A man dressed by his wife. Dear oh dear!

But they've both been tested, D and his missus, and it's not him. His swimmers are fine. D feels rotten for even thinking it, but he's glad it's not him. Not that he would have minded seeing himself in miniature, but when it didn't happen, couldn't happen, and she didn't want to adopt, he'd be lying if he said he wasn't just a tiny bit relieved. Of course, there was sadness, some regret there, too. When he saw other men out and about and how they were with their children, an occasional pang would surface, but then he'd catch the snippets of conversation floating over from where they were, in cafés or museums or just out in the parks, and it would be all 'Daddy, I want this' or 'I don't like this' or 'I want that' or just 'No!' And just as quickly any regrets he might have harboured would evaporate.

Some people would call that selfish, but he'd always been that way. Was perfectly happy not having the responsibility.

She was different, though, had always wanted them, just never really expected it to be so difficult.

After the first miscarriage she was briefly soothed by the knowledge that her mum had been through the same before she'd arrived.

'Nothing unusual, sohni. And I know it's horrible, but it won't last. Sadly it just happens sometimes, but you'll see, it'll be fine after this. You'll see.'

Except it wasn't. Other miscarriages, the freakish cruelty of ectopic pregnancies, more spotting, more bleeding, more bundles wrapped in failure until finally the terrible realisation that she must somehow be marked.

Not for her the joys of feeding, clothing, entertaining her own little bundles of fat and tissue and miracle.

But for all of that, in her eyes D is a good man. He even initiates the conversation about adoption, though she couldn't possibly know that it came about as an extension of the day job.

Risk analysis. What he was good at. Weighing up the variables and identifying the safest course of action. Or at least providing a cost/benefit ratio for those in the market for something more adventurous. Which is how he came to the conclusion that a failure to have said conversation would be inherently more damaging to the marriage than the outside chance that his wife would actually want to adopt. He banked (correctly, as it turned out) on her holding dear some pathological attachment to her 'cultural roots', which had been fostered in a comfortable, middle-class immigrant upbringing far away from the Klondike speculators of his inner city. She was proud of her roots in a way he just couldn't quite bring himself to share, yet conversely this made her far more resistant to the idea of adopting. Something alien. Not hers. Not actually of her blood. And she was done with that really. Something alien implanting in blocked tubes. The dizzy, faint spells. The pain in the tips of her shoulders. The constipation. All that crap, just blocked up. An industrial dispute in the tubes. A work to rule. Something alien which refused to become part of her. Yes, after the ultrasound, the tears, any amount of kind words, she was done with that. With aliens.

The art of the accurate forecast. It was why work paid D handsomely for his predictions, why he was able to live without the monthly fiscal dread he'd grown up with, maybe even why his dad still nurdled the receiver whenever D called rather than declining it in disgust. The boy had his odd ways, that was for sure, but he never asked them for anything, and on the rare occasions that he would visit, it was never empty handed like so many other relatives. An odd sort but not a parasite.

'I was just in the area,' about the daftest thing he'd ever come out with during one of those visits.

His father tempted to add, 'Well why wouldn't you be, with all the art and culture and other local attractions?' but somehow managing, as ever, to sit on the words instead, finding a conciliatory, 'Well that's good, son. We're pleased you came.'

There's tea and fig rolls, and no one asks where D has been all this time. What he's been doing that is so bloody important that he can't even manage the odd call or pop by after work. It's central here, barely a stone's throw from his fancy workplace. Tower Bridge just round the corner, London Bridge up ahead. He could even have walked it if he wasn't wearing those poxy shoes. Looking down, his dad is not impressed by D's footwear. Leather all scuffed up like some sort of amateur. Though his girl doesn't seem to mind. Her eyes drift beyond the footwear and settle on the decor, a world away from her semi-detached origins. His father can't be sure, but he gets the sense that she finds it 'reassuring'. The flock wallpaper, the fig rolls, the tea. Her eyes soak it up, some kind of a primal fix, and she passes his dad the plate of fig rolls, pausing first to take one herself. She likes his parents, and they're fond of her, too.

When she'd come round, that first impression, well, she'd really made it count. A box of chocolates and all dolled up, but nice, like in the old films.

His folks had liked that. She'd made an effort, and she spoke nicely. Complimented his mum on the tea. Took an interest when his dad dusted down the photo album. Good manners on her, and, to be fair, these days even those were in short supply.

D saw how she was with his dad, and he had to admit it made him happy, her occasionally pointing him out in his latest incarnation, a Polaroid capturing the moment when the suedehead morphed into something else, first a fringe then a wedge. Her and the old man enjoying the makeover, but his father keen to remind her how smart D always looked, just in case she got any ideas about taking the mickey. That wouldn't do in this household, no matter what. You had to have some sense of loyalty, else you were no better than the spivs.

'Is that a Pringle sweater?'

It was indeed. D tricked out like a golf caddy at one of those ridiculous soulboy conventions he used to swear by. The other boys in the photo a predictable mixture of swagger and inebriation. Fast-mouth Charlie Nicholas clones, nineteen to the dozen back then, with their black mates favouring the Viv Anderson, Linx wet look. It must have been one those Chris Hill 'Family' events, because there, in the next snap, was the master of ceremonies himself, kitted out like some sort of Butlin's Nazi, complete with a very camp leather cap.

Hard to believe now, D thought, but for a few brief moments at the fag end of the 1970s and into the early part of the 1980s, soul, or, more precisely, jazz-funk, had been *the* thing for ordinary kids like himself. Kids whose older brothers might have been punks or skins, or in D's case fencing moody gear down the Walworth Road when he wasn't hiding out under D's bed waiting for Officer Dibble to start making inquiries in someone else's house, to someone else's dad. At any rate, these kids didn't seem all that interested in what was going on outside of their bubble. So long as they got to meet up down the pub or the record shop after a week of dead-end jobs and have some laughs in what they rapidly came to view as 'their' clubs playing their kind of music all over London and the Home Counties, they seemed happy enough. Froggy, Chris Hill and later Robbie Vincent their heroes, plugging the underground black music they were into.

At first he'd enjoyed the camaraderie, all the tribes peacock-strutting their little bit of the soul nation. A bit of a scene, something to distinguish them from their scruffier, whinier peers. A way of letting the world know they might not be students, but their tastes were every bit as sophisticated. Socially, too, things were a bit easier than D remembered them being when he'd first started school, when the assumption was made by almost everyone that, as a white English boy from that area, he would be Millwall. No one bothering to ask whether he actually liked football. Or, for that matter, whether he had a head for figures or something other than the ball. No one asking anything much. That was the thing back then, no one ever made the right kind of inquiries.

For D the critical moment at one of these soul conventions was the first time the entire dancefloor broke out into a rendition of the *Ovaltineys* song. It was a bridge too far, the girls hooked up like Lady Di at a wet-T-shirt competition, the joy unconfined not quite filtering through to the young man with a head full of numbers and a gift even back then for prediction. Right at that moment, scanning the faces in the crowd, he knew his future lay elsewhere. No amount of enforced jollity, even if peppered with the occasional half-decent tune, was going to change that. He wanted more for himself than these embarrassing party games. *The Family*. Fuck off. His wasn't here.

'And is that seriously your hair?'

D felt himself bristle at the question, but not because the layered wedge wasn't deserving of ridicule. No, it was something else. The fleeting sensation that he was being studied, like some creature in a zoo or an ancient tribe in a book. No one else he knew spoke like that, the words curling into a sneer when a simple question would have sufficed. Or, better still, no question at all, as in the favoured local option, the salon-styled detail in any case overly familiar and so not worth commenting on. Then again, not being from here, she couldn't know that. He knew it was unintentional, she meant well, but all the same he had to fight the urge to blurt out something about her parentage (foreign) and accent (posh). Not that he particularly cared, but those were the details which seemed destined to get under the skin, really rile someone. He thought better of it, though, more worried about what his dad would say (to him, not her).

In the end it didn't matter anyway, his father piercing the moment with something typically wry. 'That's what they called "fashion" back then, young lady.'

They both laughed, the moment passed, and girlfriend and Pops were able to resume with the visual odyssey through D's past.

Had that been the moment when he knew? Back at the Royalty, or was it Frenchie's, he couldn't be sure? Sardined on to a heaving dancefloor, everyone else carrying on like the *Ovaltineys* was the funniest thing ever. D just thinking, what a bunch of idiots. Hope that's not how people see me.

Marked Out For Special Attention

London, early 1980s

PERHAPS HE'D ALWAYS known, feigning ignorance at school so as not to stand out as a swot. Pretending he was as mystified by the shapes and figures on the board as the rest of his class. Never really sure how many others there were in on the charade, processing boredom on the cusp of mutiny. Multiplication, long division, vectors and velocity. None of it especially challenging for a brain like his, weaned on counting shadows under the door those days that his brother would hide out in his room, a job lot of tom in the bag and the long arm not far behind.

He'd hear the knock on the front door, his parents' raised voices and then the thud-thudding of feet as they stormed upstairs.

And he could tell each time, just from the shadows they cast, what sort of nonsense his brother was mixed up in. Feet apart, shadows spreading out like searchlights, and he knew it was serious. Otherwise, feet closer together, the allegations, like the shapes, would be more circumspect. Either way, his dad always made sure to catch D's eye when berating his brother, the implication – 'You're better than this, son' – as clear as anything within earshot of the docks.

'You're better than this, son.'

And it was true, he was. It's just that no one apart from his father seemed to know. Plus, it wouldn't do to point it out. Bad form.

But when he'd mumbled the answer to some verbal reasoning problem in class the next day, the teacher had just yelled at him to 'speak up', and with the rest of the class now turned to face him, the words simply died in his throat. The Marshall twins, Sandra whose mum was a dinner lady and once met the Queen, Conrad the kid from the 'suicide' tower block up nearer New Cross, whose stunted size nonetheless belied his status as the head bully, always taxing people for their lunch money. There they were, just staring at him, as if aware of his presence in that classroom for the very first time. Making mental notes. The swot by the window, or was he just a bit slow? It made little difference. Either way, he'd be marked now. Marked out for special attention.

Some crap about John having 15p and Mary having 17p more than John, so how much money has Mary got?

The only reason he'd tried to say anything was that he just couldn't bear the silence any more, and what it said about him, his peers, about all of them. It simply wasn't possible for such a large group of people to be consistently this stupid. He knew he wasn't alone in thinking that, but the others in class who shared his misgivings seemed happy enough to play the long game. The teacher, one of the few in this school who didn't seem scared of his young charges, just shook his head, his boredom and unhappiness at least the equal to any of the kids in this class. That was when the 'thirty-two' had slipped out, the mumble as much an involuntary spasm as it was a considered response.

'What was that you said?' the teacher asked, unerringly picking D out from the cannon fodder arraigned in front of him. He'd felt the burning in his cheeks even before the not-so-collective adulation of his peers was trained on him. But the mumble refused all attempts to revive it.

'Oh for God's sake, speak up, boy!' yelled the teacher, his initial surprise now outweighed by an entirely predictable disappointment. This bloody school, he thought, yet another 'social experiment' that should never have seen the light of day. As soon as something better came along, he'd be off. Not like those bloody scruffs in the common room, pretending they knew the first thing about teaching or geography (it's always bloody geography) or kids in a school like this. This kid wouldn't be speaking up any time soon. It was a miracle he'd said anything in the first place.

Things hadn't really improved after that either, occasional

mutterings of dissent the only peer-approved classroom response to straightforward number sequences, and every simple shape somehow rotated in the silent imaginary as an obscene diagram. Anything to alleviate the boredom.

The coup de grâce, to no one's great surprise, an utterly point-less question about volume and bathtubs. There was just some-thing very suspect about the question. Why not mention if it's a man and a woman filling the bathtub? Why leave it open? Why take that risk? And, worse still, why keep adding more people to the equation? 'If it takes two people twenty minutes to fill a bath-tub measuring... then how long does it take four people to fill two bathtubs?' Again, D didn't particularly care, but, marked as he now was, he knew some attempt would be made to lump him in with the class fairy, Michael, who the other boys called 'Quentin'. As far as the class was concerned, the question had a bit of a homo subplot to it. Away from the bathtub, D had his own reservations. This puzzle showed bad form. It was a snide question, just the sort of thing his brother, or any of the other rogue traders down in East Street Market, would instinctively know the answer to. It wasn't honest, and he had to wonder what kind of underlying message it was sending out to impressionable young minds. Believing his cards were in any case marked, D now felt he had nothing to lose by yelling out, 'The same time. Twenty minutes.'

Maybe that was the moment, he thought, long before Frenchie's. Perhaps that was when he decided to look more care-fully at those number sequences and turn what used to be simple into improper fractions.

'Oh my God, that's so gay!' said Conrad, much to general amusement.

No one really knew why, but the little bastard was right. All those 'people' in bathtubs. Only queers did that.

Even Michael was looking D's way now, wondering how he could have missed something so obvious before.

'You're so gay!' added Conrad, evidently on a roll now.

'Well you're a blubba mout, but you don't hear me com-plaining,' replied D a split second before his brain had had a chance to process his instinct, the words tumbling out to collective gasps.

Though they were both sent out of class, predictably enough only D's parents were contacted by the school. Which got him to thinking, this numbers game, it really gets people's backs up. I might need to look into that.

Conrad kicked his head in a little later on, before himself falling foul of some old-fashioned coppering not long after. So there was *that* at least. In the manner of these things, he recalled, there was usually some kind of a silver lining if you waited long enough. And in this case it took a familiar shape and form. Conrad himself.

The silly sod was so used to getting his own way at school that he must have forgotten the most important thing. The cardinal rule of extra-curricular life. That outside of school hours the same rules rarely, if ever, applied. So when the plod asked him what he was doing hanging around outside the shop (which one was never specified in the retelling) one Saturday, and he'd replied, 'What's it to you anyway?' without even thinking, he was genuinely shocked to hear the words, 'Don't get lippy with me, Rastus,' volleyed right back at him.

'What?!'

'Oh, so you *do* understand English then?' the plod added, enjoying the unexpected bonus of some civil liberties' trespass to get the weekend under way.

'Don't talk to me like that!' said Conrad, the habit of talking back to his pathetically weak teachers now serving him poorly in the decidedly non-LEA environment of 'community' policing.

The copper smiled. Some of these kids made it so easy for him. Especially the IC3s, or, as they computed in his mind, 'fat lip and crime' on account of all that mouth and all those collars.

D laughed when he heard about it, and he couldn't lie, he was glad the little cunt had copped a hiding. Evidently plod didn't go in for the same sort of crowd-control techniques – i.e. non-existent – favoured by the crusading, long haired Marxists who pretended to be teachers at his school. For all the interest they took in Conrad's depressing back story – suicide tower, no mum or dad, hostile environment – they never seemed to notice what a complete louse he was, pockets unusually heavy with change for someone on free school meals. They ignored his lip, too, and, in fairness, that had only encouraged more of it. Perhaps it was for his own good then, thought D, as Paul, the little suedehead also from the suicide tower, relayed the details, which he himself had only heard about second hand, to the rest of the class.

So when Conrad walked in, his lip still bruised and the after effects of a black eye very much in evidence, D felt bad for earlier finding it funny. Right up until the moment that Conrad issued the challenge, 'What are you looking at, gay boy?'

That was the problem with this place. No learning.

It Doesn't Mean They're Blackshirts

D SOMETIMES THOUGHT about where they had met.

College.

Funny word that, not one that D would ever use himself, as he preferred to let people know he was part of the minuscule elite that attended one of Britain's top universities. College, to him, still inferred sixth form, which meant the locality and sitting in class biting his lip, pretending he didn't know the answers, the faint whiff of prospects overwhelmed by the presence of fresh linoleum. College meant still being stuck a stone's throw from the factories, pinched faces in the street but an oddly enduring self-love swelling the streets on Millwall match days.

But he'd hear that word used to describe universities, and it annoyed him. As though that whole 'not for us' mentality passed on from generation to generation in his neighbourhood meant that no one could quite bring themselves to say the word 'university'. It somehow stuck in the craw, people pretending not to be interested when they'd spot D back in the area during holidays, crossing the road or pretending to be busy with their shoelaces just so they wouldn't have to listen to him going on about 'university'. Not that he was fooled. He'd learnt to spot the signs. There it was contained in a look which they probably didn't even know they were giving him. But it was there alright. And he knew what it meant, what it had always meant round this way.

Mr La-di-dah, turned your back on the area, think you're better than the rest of us.

Above all, he saw it in the glazed-eyed mask so many of them still wore, a relic from school, the past never really discarded. An apparent lack of interest still not enough to muffle the question, sourness dripping from every letter.

So why did you bother coming back then?

And most of the time, when he saw his old classmates still patrolling the same beat, having a skinful with the other troglodytes on match days or pushing prams or, in Conrad's case, something a little stronger, he was almost prepared to concede that they might have a point. But in the end it wasn't about them, not that he ever expected them to see that.

His folks still lived there, however, which was the only reason he bothered. And though they wouldn't go on about it in front of him, he knew they were proud of him.

University. The old man loved that word, enjoyed seeing the almost indiscernible flinch it induced in some of the people he knew whenever they asked him about the boys.

'The eldest has straightened right out, ever since the twins. And my youngest, well, he's really thriving now at university.'

Then again just being at university hardly meant that D was exempt from having to be around strange attitudes.

He'd noticed the oddest thing when he'd first arrived at Warwick. All those Fauntleroys bidding fond, sometimes tearful, farewells as one top-of-the-range Merc after another disgorged its well-bred cargo on to the campus catwalk. A whole retinue of mothers, fathers, darling little brothers and sisters to help transport all those suitcases, crates, boxes the short distance from parking lot to hall of residence. It made him laugh, his own journey by comparison a straightforward one with the old man, on the train, then the bus, just one suitcase and a rucksack to tide him over. Dad joking that D was 'all made up for a quick getaway' but not exactly hanging around himself once he'd made sure D registered at reception and picked up the key for his room. A hug, a 'be well, son', and then he was back on the bus, proud, for once, of a Bermondsey export that didn't garner red-top headlines for something antisocial and football related.

What really caught D's eye, though, was how scruffy these kids were. Even in the suicide tower people didn't dress this badly.

Slashed jeans, grubby T-shirts, but in spite of that a certain confidence in how they stepped out of the cars. To be fair, anyone stepping out of the suicide tower in such shambolic gear would at least appear shamefaced. Being poor was no excuse.

And if the parents of these shabbily dressed kids were bothered, they didn't let on. His dad would have been mortified if D had left the house looking like that. What would it say about them if their own flesh and blood wasn't properly attired for his first day at university? What sort of people let their kids loose on society with a rip in their jeans?

He surprised himself by how quickly he got used to their accents. Truly, there were young people here who pronounced the 'off' after 'get' or 'piss' (though rarely 'fuck') as 'orff'. But what was weirder still was the speed with which those accents declined, glottal stops suddenly all the rage for well-spoken boys and girls. Perhaps it wasn't that surprising, everyone here to study, even if it was just each other and the social etiquette of the human zoo.

The funniest of the lot were the class warriors on campus, invariably from up-to-do backgrounds nowhere near a pit village. The disappointment coming off them palpable when D refused to be the token working-class standard-bearer in their midst.

They'd made a real effort to court him, he'd give them that. Usually whenever he'd pass their stall and they'd call him 'comrade' and press some flyers into his hands, which, in fairness, were every bit as soft and untested as theirs. Once or twice he'd even listen to them, especially if the punky-looking Asian girl with the nose stud and the pirate rings on several fingers was part of the sermon. When she wasn't scowling or ranting on about the means of production, D would occasionally get what he thought was a mildly interested vibe off her. She had a tendency to drone on, though. Actually they all did.

For the amount they went on about black people, he thought, it was as though they'd grown up in the Congo or in some bit of south London. But, oddly enough, they never seemed to have met someone like Conrad or any of the other thieving, scamming bastards he could recall all too clearly from school, a sizeable number of whom were also black.

Actually, those earnest boys and girls with their revolutionary slogans reminded him a bit of his old teachers, the Marxist ones who were always making excuses for the Conrads of this world. The same overly concerned expressions, that familiar catch in the voice, the tell-tale split-second delay whenever the word 'black' couldn't be avoided any longer.

It was all a bit puzzling to D. He couldn't really see why they were so obsessed. It wasn't as though they were in Deptford. There *were* hardly any black people here anyway, and the ones he saw definitely didn't hail from that part of the world.

Quite early on he'd noticed a black guy who'd regularly turn up on campus for his law lectures by cab. This man who would be king wasn't unique either. There were others just like him swanning around like country squires in their Harris tweed, the tribal markings on the face and briefcases held with an ease which D wasn't yet to know they'd mastered in various prep schools. He'd never heard black people speaking that way either, the ripest of plums in the mouth, and beyond the colour of their skin no discernible link to any of the black people he'd ever known. It almost made him nostalgic for a Conrad, but then he remembered the number of times he'd suffered a shakedown at the hands of that scrote, and the feeling soon passed.

Most of these RADA-clipped Tundes or Olas appeared to be law students, but there were several on D's course as well. And, unlike himself, they seemed to have no problems blending in. That was one of the first things he'd picked up on, self-tutored as he was, as an aspirational (and therefore in the eyes of his peers, suspect) white, working-class boy from southeast London: to record mentally even the micro-currents of black presence in and around his everyday existence. If anyone had ever bothered to listen he'd have explained to them it was as much a question of self-preservation as casual anthropology, but, of course, they never asked in the first place.

These well-spoken fellow students were quite chirpy in the seminars, though he got the feeling that was more for effect than anything else. Anyway, the lecturers seemed to enjoy their contributions, and if they had any doubts about the integrity of what was being said by the precocious budding economists, then they kept it to themselves. For instance, that time during an economic theory class when a chap called Celestine launched into an impassioned defence of Keynesian economics, though everything about him positively screamed Milton Friedman. D just couldn't picture this guy as a stalwart of the public sector, but here he was intoning the virtues of massive inward investment in public-infrastructure projects.

He noticed the easy rapport which existed between these high-born Africans and their English peers. In class it was as though all of them were just paying lip service to the idea of a disagreement, whereas in reality they were already sizing one another up for future collaborations. His English classmates certainly didn't act as if it was the first time they'd ever seen a young black man in Harris tweed or carrying a briefcase.

Though he rarely spoke in class himself, when he did he soon learnt the trick was to bookend whatever he was saying with something a little obscure. And while he lacked the visual props of black skin and a designer briefcase, he more than made up for that with unexpected references to Hobbes and Weber, on one occasion even Nietzsche, throwing a massive spanner in the works just as his classmates were getting their heads around his earlier espousal of Leo Strauss. Of course, by this point he'd begun to revel in the discomfort some of his views seemed to cause them. Again, that all-too-obvious 'disappointment' which he'd first sensed emanating from the revolutionary benches now writ large on the faces of these Timothys and Charlottes, though not so much on Celestine's haughty boat.

D had really enjoyed the gratuitous introduction of Nietzsche into a discussion about economic rationality. It was a handy addition to his repertoire and, already displaying an impressive ability to predict outcomes, he had memorised the quote beforehand for maximum effect: '*Objection, evasion, cheerful mistrust, delight in mockery are signs of health. Everything unconditional belongs to pathology.* So you see this idea that consumers behave rationally and will always do so is a bit of a non-starter. How can you accurately predict that, and what do you even mean by "rationally"? Put it this way,' he went on, 'There's people who only do stuff to get a rise. You run an SWP stall, and they'll goose step around it, just to get a reaction. It doesn't mean they're blackshirts, but it does mean they don't recognise your authority, and for some people it's worth it for that alone. I reckon that's what Nietzsche is saying, and, to be fair, he's got a point.'

'But people don't act against their own self-interests, do they?' objected one of the boys in his seminar group who D had barely even noticed until now. Grandad shirt, messy barnet, prominent konk, baton-twirling his biro like some Home Counties' majorette.

'Well that depends, doesn't it? If you mean Mummy or Daddy have promised you a car, then you're not exactly going to go around slagging them off beforehand, so I suppose you've got a point. Then again, let's say you're on the way to the football and you see someone you know getting a hiding near the ground, well, you're going to get involved, aren't you? Even if there's plod everywhere and you stand a good chance of getting nicked. So you might say that's not in your self-interest either, but you get stuck in anyway. You want to know why? I'll tell you why. It's better to get nicked than have word filter back to everyone else that you did a runner, left your mate in the lurch. Know what I mean?'

Not all his lecturers seemed to appreciate his uniquely customised input, but on this occasion the expected word (of admonishment) in his ear after class never materialised.

Instead, D found himself invited by his tutor, Dr Thornton, to an informal workshop followed by refreshments at his, Thornton's, house.

'It's just a little group of us who get together every so often, trying to figure out the bigger questions. Keynes versus Friedman.

Monetarism versus social contract. Why don't you come along? I think you might enjoy it.'

And so, the following Thursday, there he was, standing across the road from a very tasty Georgian terrace in a part of town mercifully free of students, kitted out in Lois jeans, a navy-blue Puma kagoule and a pair of Stan Smith trainers.

Back home this would have made him a bit of a wally. Frightfully passé, or at any rate embarrassingly last season.

Not here, though. They didn't have a clue, that much was clear, every other bloke thinking a grandad shirt and some ripped jeans made them into Morrissey, whereas in reality the one thing it *did* achieve was to transform them into instant targets for the perennially disgruntled locals with their time-honoured recreational pursuits. An unappealing roster of 'tache, slacks (not quite Farahs, never quite right), beer, student, blood on kebab. Often in that order.

D paused for a moment, observing a couple of other invitees, older students, who he'd seen around on campus, and the confident way they approached the door with their bottles of wine neatly wrapped.

He felt stupid then, thinking how long he'd spent in his room picking out the outfit like some deluded social butterfly, imagining it lent him an aura of authenticity.

And, of course, there was the small matter of the beers, a four-pack, ring pull, Holsten.

He took a deep breath, attempted to calm himself down, by which he meant pep himself up, before he reached the front door.

'*No Conrad, no Millwall. Listen, you dozy sod, there's no one here who even cares. Now get in there and give them some supply side.*'

That was the mantra his inner voice kept repeating, at least until the door opened and, faced with Dr Thornton, D panicked, blurting out in spite of his best efforts, 'I brought these. Hope you don't mind,' while he held up the four-pack like the chancellor's box of tricks on budget day.

'Why would I mind?' asked Dr Thornton with what appeared

to be an indulgent smile, ushering D inside to the sounds of civilised murmur, somehow amplified by the lack of carpeting.

The black Keynesian was already there, holding court in the living-room to a coterie of interested English nationals. He tipped his half-full wine glass in acknowledgement as he spotted D walking past in the corridor.

Once in the kitchen, D's natural instinct was to keep ahold of the beers, but somehow feeling he was under scrutiny, he reluctantly separated one for himself and placed the rest in the fridge. Then, of course, the question of glass or no glass? This was where it all started to get a little tricky for a self-starter like D.

Drink straight from the can, and he'd instantly become an all-too-easily placed IC1, the casual get-up pointing right at that category labelled 'hooligan'. But that wasn't quite the effect he was after here. Too obvious, and frankly a bit limiting for a young man looking to experiment with social as well as economic theory.

Then again, pour the contents into a glass, and someone, somewhere, would inevitably mark him down as an iron. It wasn't even that he particularly cared, but then there'd be a protocol to be observed, the need for over-emphasis, and he knew he'd louse that up. Would make himself look silly into the bargain with some over-compensatory nonsense which in the end would fool no one, least of all himself. Tiring and time consuming, with diminished odds of a repeat invitation to one of these soirées.

Fuck it, in for a penny, he thought, admiring his handiwork as the liquid settled into a perfect pint, the decision made easier by the surprising presence of a pint glass in one of the cupboards. He hadn't figured Dr Thornton as light fingered, why would he? The good doctor was, after all, his first-year guide to 'Economic Theory'. Then again, the presence of the pint glass, and of several others nestling behind it, raised another set of questions. This was not the kind of object to be readily found in any high-street shop, and most certainly not in the kitchen cupboard of a promising young academic. No one was saying they'd been half-inched from some local establishment, but there was clearly more to Thornton than met the eye.

D made sure not to be greedy with his first slug. Granted, it wasn't wine, but that was no reason to let people think he wasn't cultured.

Also, the pint glass would act as a prop. To stop him fidgeting during any conversational lull or as a subtle form of emphasis if he happened to be holding court. The act of putting it down on a table or work surface would certainly stress that whatever he was about to say was worth paying attention to. He'd seen countless chancers with something to sell use that very trick on the markets back home. Whether it was moody perfume or a job lot of polo shirts with 'le croc' looking a bit fatter than usual, it was always the same routine. Hold it up admiringly, as if unable to fully comprehend the value of the object, then put it back down, making a mental note of the gullible, the plant and the not-so-easily afflicted. Next, rehearsed banter with the plant, passion building up from an entirely fabricated reluctance to let the item go at such a scandalously low price to the not-so-silent partner, and then barely a moment to set the imaginary timer before the expected deluge of Walworth Road hands and queen's heads. But it always seemed to work, no matter how many times the assembled crowd must have witnessed similar scams, equivalent routines, before. That was the bit that never ceased to amaze him. People knew, they must have known, but still they went along with the farce. 'Bought as seen', an exaggerated shaking of the head and the flat denial of all responsibility the standard response to any disgruntled punters after the event. And then, more often than not, the chancer and the plant would decamp to the local for an elongated session on the freshly fleeced punters' coin. Pints, shots, chasers and a damn good laugh at how easy it was to play some people for a fool.

'You just going to study the glass all evening?'

D looked up. His eyes must have been swimming in the flatlining bubbles from the German brewery.

'Sorry, what was that?' he replied.

'Are you just going to stare into your glass all evening?' repeated the girl, a faintly amused expression on her face.

'No, I was just thinking,' said D, immediately annoyed at

himself for coming up with something so conversationally lame. Just thinking?! Barely a month around the Fauntleroys, and here he was greedily sucking away at the teat of middle-class am dram.

'About what?' said the girl, now looking genuinely amused.

'Oh, nothing much. Just random stuff,' said D, realising even as he did so, how unconvincing he sounded.

He paused for a moment to look at her.

Some kind of a Gypsy/flamenco get up, but he was fairly sure she was Asian not Spanish.

Soft hands, like his, barely a hint of work about them. He liked that. It should at least mean there'd be no sermonising, not about *that* anyway. He wondered if she'd noticed his paws, too. Or was the surface detail, the pouring of a pint, *enough* by itself? Was that who she'd see, a young man with all the trappings of a sportswear casual? White, presumed working class, soft hands notwithstanding.

'I haven't seen you around campus,' she said, choosing to ignore the inanity.

'That's because I'm not a student,' he replied, immediately surprised by his own rash choice of lie.

Why had he said that? What could he possibly have to gain from telling such a porkie? He knew eventually he'd have to backtrack, and doubtless there would be otherwise entirely avoidable recriminations, so why had he done it? He knew why. The same reason he'd sprinkled their Keynes with his Nietzsche. Doused more like. A desire, on both their parts (his, the working-class charlatan; theirs, presumably, the dilettante Byronic socialist) for some clean lines, some boundary markers to help redefine their burgeoning interaction. He'd already seen it on campus, in classes, the way their ears pricked up at the mere hint of conviction. In an idea, a look, a statement, anything to disrupt the cosy consensus where all roads seemed to end up at the same dreary set of destinations. Home Counties, no economic downturn, Daddy most certainly not a bank robber, at least not in the eyes of the law. And just as he'd predicted, he saw it again now on this girl's face, a look of mild incomprehension muddled with a little frisson.

'Really? So how do you know Dr Thornton then?'

'What do you mean?'

'Well, it seemed like you knew him earlier when he opened the door.'

Think, man, think, the time for retractions, apologies, is later. D's mind was racing, the whiff of attraction spurring on ever greater lies.

'He sometimes drinks in town. Says it helps him unwind, get away from all the work pressures. We got talking one time, and it turns out we have a shared interest in philosophy.'

Again, the utterly pointless falsehood, or at any rate it would be if D didn't manage to make it count, following up on what he at least perceived to be clear mating signals coming off the Asian girl. Throwing in the towel now would just confirm him as a feeble liar as well as a grassroots fraud. In his own way worse than Conrad or any of those other friendly Samaritans he thought he'd left behind back in Bermondsey. At least in their case there was no pretence. They weren't fooling anyone; in fairness, they weren't trying to. What you saw was what you got. A lot of gyp, hardly any couth and no apology for any of it. Sex just something else that happened, when it did, in between a ruck and a job lot of moody gear which might have started off 'up west' but always ended up on one of the stalls down south. D, on the other hand, well, he wasn't like that. Even before he came to this place he was already indecisive, dithering away – 'just thinking' – not entirely unlike his newly acquired, expensively educated peers.

For all the advantages they'd grown up with, there was just so little about those peers that convinced in a social setting. Not in the sense of not having views – oh, they had plenty of those. No, he was thinking more about the stuff that *actually* impressed people. Decisiveness, conviction, a bit of neck. He'd seen that down the markets, seen it at school. The front to just say 'That's bollocks' or 'What? That was never me! I forgets where I was, but that weren't me.' Or some such. And he'd seen how well it played with girls, with women. His own problem not so much that he couldn't reach a decision but more that he'd take too long getting there, so that by the time he'd weighed up all the permutations or the possible consequences, what had formerly seemed straightforward now appeared fraught. Which made him handy at chess and eventually a lot more than handy at what they called 'risk analysis' but not so great in the pulling stakes. And definitely not in the kind of place he'd grown up in.

Bermondsey was full of that inner-city flash, people who were tannery smart, large even when they barely had two coins to rub together. By which he meant the snap, crackle and *pop 'em out for the lads, love* which had always left him cringing, struggling in its wake, his own industry by comparison a dull appreciation of numbers which just didn't appeal to the weekend seekers in his manor. Hard-faced funsters with little patience for the presumed la-di-dah of improper fractions.

Here, though, a world away from the spivvery, he was suddenly the real McCoy, at any rate the closest thing for a lot of these kids to an endangered species. On campus he practically belonged in a glass cabinet. A living, breathing product of an inner-city environment. And in the raw calculus of his loins that ought, he felt, to make him catnip for the many Hannahs and Beckys, Imogens and Alices also on display in this human zoo. Boldness its own aphrodisiac, class just something else to be pimped out for carnal exchange.

He saw her looking at him, really looking at him, then. Flamenco girl. Taking in his clothes, the sovereign ring, the classic trainers in one greedy sweep of the eye, and, in truth, understanding little of it beyond the gut-level sense that sex, hopefully something a little raw, might also be lurking beyond the philosophy.

'But you don't sound like you're from here. I mean your accent's not exactly local, is it?' she said, supplying him with just the kind of 'in' he'd been hoping for.

'You don't miss a trick, do you? Actually, you're right, I'm not from here, this is just where I work. On secondment from head office.'

Encouraged by her silence, D ploughed on. 'It's all a bit hush-hush,' he said, borrowing the phrase from some crap he'd recently seen on telly. 'I could tell you, I suppose, but then I'd have to kill you.'

'Oh well, in that case you'd better keep it to yourself,' she replied, smirking.

Good, he thought, at least she's got a sense of humour. Later that would come in handy when D, unwisely also ploughing on with the lager, failed to raise a salute in the bedroom. Don't worry about it, she'd said, and, of course, that just made him question his manhood, his whole being, in unspeakable detail, the only silver lining being that none of it was actually spoken. But she must have had a sense of humour anyway because when they tried again in the morning, and he fumbled his way through it, there were no complaints, whatever she might actually have been thinking. And all this even though both of them knew they should probably have waited. Well they hadn't, so it was a bit late for that now.

For whatever reason, though, it wasn't one of *those* mornings, where the only thing she could actually feel beyond the regret and the embarrassment was some vague sense that she'd let herself down again. OK, so they'd had a false start, and even when they had managed in the morning it wasn't exactly memorable. Yet this boy D was funny, at least to her he was, those odd little anecdotes about work, and there was something in the way he said 'mind', it must have been the Estuarine stretch of the 'i', which seemed to make her forget all about chronology. So in the end it was more impatience than desire that meant it had all happened too soon, eyes to fumble to an odd kind of shyness, which was what she was feeling now. Odd because they'd already seen each other with no clothes on, and some kind of an encounter, albeit of the fumbling kind, had clearly taken place. Still, here they were, already sizing up the breakfast options.

She brought the tea back to her room, quickly working out that he was too embarrassed to show his face in the shared kitchen at the end of the corridor. Perhaps it was because he wasn't a student here, she thought, and therefore somehow felt exposed in her hall of residence? Even so, he seemed happy enough with the brew.

'Oh, that's blinding,' he said, cupping both hands around the mug, his mood evidently improved by the morning's minor exertions.

'You must be hungry?' she asked, hoping against hope he'd answer no or, better still, suggest going out to eat. Her cupboard was bare; it had been all week. She hated stocking up only to see the staples – bread, milk, cereal – whittled away by light fingers. Even more galling, the looks of innocence from her flatmates any time the subject was raised. Yet if so much as a cream cracker went missing from one of their cupboards, a 'group meeting' would be called and faces would cloud over at the indignity of it, a thief in their midst. So now she didn't bother any more, limiting her groceries to non-perishables which could be safely stored in her room and only really making occasional forays into the kitchen to put the kettle on or use the toaster. In a way she didn't mind too much either; it meant less time spent in the kitchen, the only really communal area in the flat, and this kept random meetings with her flatmates to a bare minimum. It wasn't even that they were particu-larly bad people or difficult to get on with; more that they reminded her so much of the eager, pleasant and utterly bland kids she'd grown up with; ironically enough the very type she'd come to university to get away from. Not that she was so different, but that was the deal with this place, one of the first things she'd noticed. How everyone, after a fashion, seemed to be trying to get away from something.

She liked that he hadn't tried to slip away first thing, especially after the embarrassment of last night's false start.

D wasn't at all like the boys she was used to, and thinking about it as she took a sip of her tea, maybe that was why she hadn't minded too much at the time. He'd gone 'bollocks', then a bit moody, but before too long he'd drifted off, and when he event-ually did wake up he'd got on with it without too many frills and then seemed pleased with himself. There had been no desire to talk about any of it, and that suited her just fine. None of those Byronic pauses or awkward silences after some terribly polite boy from the Home Counties had just professed his undying love for her, or worse, commented on her 'exoticness', thinking he was paying her the ultimate compliment when really all he was doing was reminding her just how safe and unadventurous her life was. How much she was appreciated in this settled landscape. Noticed for the right reasons, that hair and those eyes and, yes, a hint, just a hint, of somewhere hot on that skin, nothing *too* toasted mind, but just enough to get the white boys pondering. And best of all with D, none of that fawning Esperanto delivered through reed-thin lips which always seemed on the verge of either a sneer or a tremble.

'I tell you what,' said D. 'Let's go out to eat. Don't ask me why, but I could murder a fry-up.'

She could have kissed him then, the mysterious man/boy about town, all sportswear and indignation and a very funny line in self-aggrandisement.

WINTER/SPRING
(1983-4)

THEY WENT OUT for a couple of months, which in those days was a lifetime. It carried them through the worst of winter and into the first, desperately craved days of spring. But it was doomed, as he'd always known it would be, once she spotted him on campus, clearly on his way to a lecture.

'What are you doing here?' she'd asked.

'Oh, hi,' he'd replied weakly, knowing the game was up. Then, prompted by her silence into offering something more, he'd added, 'I was going to tell you, but it just never seemed the right time.'

She just stood there staring at him, unmoved.

'Look, I can't talk now,' he said, seeing the lecturer appear in the corridor, notes in hand. 'I'll meet you afterwards. 4pm in the bar.'

And they'd talked, and he even felt he'd done a fair job of explaining his actions. Nerves, feeling a bit out of place, not really comfortable yet with the other students, with how they looked at him when he'd speak up in class.

At this stage his instinct appeared to serve him well, the detail about 'moral economy' and how that look he'd mentioned became really noticeable then, as though that accent and those words didn't belong together. It found its mark, at least that's what he thought, her eyes visibly softening at the merest hint of a largely phoney class warfare.

She listened patiently, at one point even doing that thing with her eyes, which he wasn't to know she'd perfected over countless family meals long before this clear-the-air session.

'Sohni, we only want the best for you, and maybe you're spending too much time now with those other girls when you could be studying. This year is so important for your future. You know me and your baba, we do special puja for you. For your exam. It's such an important year for you, sohni. Your success is our success.'

The gesture, widening then hinting at water behind the eyes, made her look attentive and somehow moved by her mum's advice, when the truth was she'd already started hanging out with boys unknown even to the girls she was supposedly busy hanging out with. Better still, it had the happy knack of defusing whatever trouble might have been brewing, allowing those closest to her to really look into those big brown eyes and imagine she was holding on to their every word. And though this boy sitting opposite her now wasn't exactly a rerun of the clear-skinned, upwardly tilted prototype she was used to, he still wasn't entirely immune to the subtle messaging of her body language.

So D remained blissfully unaware that she'd already seen him several times on campus before today; that this was, in fact, the only occasion he'd been spied alone, when he *hadn't* appeared to be joking and laughing with his classmates.

Of course, she should have ditched him then, right there in the bar that looked like an airport lounge, patterned mustard vomitus diamonds performing some kind of an optical illusion where the carpet rolled out endlessly, swirling around her feet as if alive, a distant relic mindful of elsewheres. Like her uncle's place, colourful off-cuts, no two rooms alike, cousins with furry dice and Ford Capris, gorees somewhere in the background, and the whole house subsiding with a hint of disgrace in its posture. Yet when she looked down, feigning hurt as this boy fumbled from one excuse to the other, much as he'd blundered his way through their first night together, what really struck her was how the vomitus neatly set off the near-turmeric streaks on his trainers. 'Trimm Trabs,' he'd proudly told her when he'd caught her staring at his feet, with no way of knowing that for her his Chaplinesque stance was weirdly evocative of the bharatanatyam dancers she'd been encouraged to emulate for far too long during expensive and largely futile private lessons. She never could get that turnout right or hold it for more than a few seconds, yet here was this gora who'd probably never even heard of bharatanatyam, just stood there, feet splayed apart, beer in one hand, like it was the most natural thing in the world.

They reconciled, of course they did, the occasional arguments and histrionics just part of it. She had her moments, too, matching his every hissy fit glottal stop for glottal stop. At any rate keeping up with the exaggerated Estuarine vowels by throwing down a gauntlet of her own. Bold statements, all wheeze and bluster, daring him on to his own forms of contrivance, the two of them riffing on the sheer neck of it.

'All men are rapists.'

'What, all of them? Even your dad? I suppose that includes me and all?'

'You wanker!'

'Yeah, that's right, love, twice a day and more at weekends. You should know. I mean, it ain't just me who's there.'

'You're horrible!'

'Yeah, yeah, yeah, I know, I'm horrible. It's all my fault. Is that why you're still with me then? And by the way, is it just my imagination or are those nipples getting hard?'

'Shut up! You're a pig! You'll never understand, not until –'

'What? Go on, say it.'

'I don't know what you're talking about.'

'Oh, really?'

'Yes, really,' she lied. 'I don't know what you're on about.'

'So the wandering digits, the probing, I've just imagined all that, have I?'

'Seriously. I don't know what you're talking about.'

'You must think I'm an idiot?'

'No, D, I *know* you're an idiot.'

'Am I going to have to spell it out for you?' he asked her, already knowing where this was headed and not entirely unhappy about it.

'Looks like it, because I haven't got the faintest what you're talking about.'

'Alright then. Here's what I reckon. You think I'll never fully get it, not until I've been violated in some way. What's wrong with you? You can't wait to stick something up my harris, can you, girl?'

'You're disgusting!' came the expected reply. Though to be fair, that was a more seasoned response. The first time he'd used that word, 'harris', she'd just looked at him bemused, the phonetics more or less entirely unfamiliar.

'I know. Shall we go then?'

Of course, that was an abridged version, the real thing lurching forwards and backwards through the full gamut of provocation, denial, shame and anger until one or both of them felt sufficiently riled or just horny enough to acknowledge how dull the whole charade was. She said, he said, Punch and Judy for the chatterati in training.

Still, it *was* funny, all these hopelessly sensitive girls on campus with their split loyalties to dungarees and the Bloomsbury set. Barely a term in from their debut, stepping out of expensive German motors, paterfamilias dutifully at the wheel while mother's powdered cheeks are streaked by the expected water-works. Just as quickly wiped away, though, something by Tiffany's briefly visible. *We'll miss you terribly, darling. It won't be the same without you. You won't forget us, will you?* The unspoken. *Your father is a bore, darling, and there's some doubt as to whether you're even his, but look, you're young, you've got your whole future ahead of you, and I know you won't make the same mistakes I did. I love you so much, darling. We both do. And we're only ever a phone call away.* Daughter barely even listening, already escaping to the clean slate of modern languages or the history of art or, at a push, something in politics.

A fresh start and a new look, all country lesbian, a denim romper suit with no frills up top; prison cut, army cut, angry vowels. Nothing remotely suggestive of a cul-de-sac, well not that kind anyway.

The spirit of Ginny Woolf sneaking under the tarpaulin of Greenham Common. And even if the wardrobe went default goth

– longer hair, a need for the crimper – the bit which remained the same was the big statement. *All men are this, coal not dole, abortion on demand, no nukes.* At least until the silver, the piercings, made their own kind of statement.

No Tribal Affiliations, None Of That Nonsense

PETE MURPHY CROAKING about bats leaving the bell tower, and *oh, Bel-la, Bela*, of course, Bela Lugosi, a gnarled cipher planted in D's head while he stretched out on his narrow hall-of-residence single bed, the trainers and the wedge somewhat at odds with the louche goth soundtrack tipping out of the speakers.

'You don't have to go,' he says to Lisa, almost meaning it as well, unsure if her nipple twisting antics have impaired his judgement or whether he is just a sucker for more punishment.

She turns to look at him, a wicked little grin on her boat. So the cocksure soulboy liked a bit of slap and tickle then? Not at all what she'd imagined when he'd sidled up to her just after the seminar which found them once again arguing over the pros and cons of monetarism versus Keynesianism.

He'd been fervently free market amid a chorus of disapproval, and that, along with the wedge and the trainers, had stood out for her, accustomed as she was to timid boys referencing Robert Smith and not a lot of sunlight in lieu of actually having opinions. Or, at any rate, ones that might actually contradict hers and thus scupper what in any case were their negligible chances of some kind of romantic liaison with her. She knew that full well but enjoyed stringing these sensitive gothic souls along anyway, letting them have their fantasy, teasing them with a pout here, a stroke of the hand there. Encountering some resistance was a novel experience for her, and if it took something Friedmanesque to keep it going, then so be it. It made a welcome change.

Actually, the whole thing had been a bit surprising, curiosity as much as anything driving her to check out what a soulboy, especially an upwardly mobile one with (for this place at least) such unusual vocal phrasing, kept in his grant-funded lair. The country at large seemed to be with the soulboy, she thought, opting once again for Thatcherite laissez-faire when presented with the choice to do something different during the recent election. But really, there's no argument, and she knows that, assumes he does, too.

Economics is just the pretext. The necessary tango for all those hormones simply part of the experience.

University.

It's just preamble before an (again, to her) surprisingly expert tongue is inside her, prepping her like a hungry gila. Later she takes this as a hint, twisting his nipple in one hand while cupping a fistful of wedge with the other, and is not at all surprised when he grows even harder in her.

It's only afterwards that the Bauhaus twelve creeps out of what she *had* thought was a box of magazines but which on closer inspection turns out to be a stack of vinyl, mostly stuff she doesn't know, black singers in soft focus, but with the occasional more familiar record tucked away among them, the dead giveaway being their largely monochrome artwork and a tendency to focus on the tormented image. Anguish, monstrosity, the long dark night of the suburban white soul. Wire, Bauhaus, The Sisters of Mercy, even something by The Smiths. The soulboy was full of surprises, she'd give him that, and he was right about one thing at least. She didn't have to go. Plenty of time for more *white on white*, with or without Pete Murphy croaking away in the shadows.

The Ls. Lisa gives way to Laura, pronounced Loww-ra, as she keeps reminding him the first few times he says it the English way.

'No it's Loww-ra. Why you never say it right?'

'Laura.'

'No, Loww-ra. Who is this Laura?'

'Just some girl I know. Nice girl, Spanish. To be honest I think she's only with me for my accent.'

They'll both laugh and that will be their thing, any time they're out and stuck for things to say. That tends to happen if they're out with other people (usually off her course, or from her hall, very rarely students of *his* acquaintance), and the conversation turns to how they'd met or what their plans were for the rest of the afternoon, the weekend, the summer. He liked her easy smile, about as far from the expressions he'd grown up with as it was possible to get in a young life of limited experience. He liked the way she invited people in to their conversations, removing the conspiratorial element that would have taken over had it been left up to him.

Really, though, there was no mystery to it. No wonder people liked her. She made the whole business of spending time appear so effortless, a wave, a smile, the sharing of confidences with her girlfriends one moment as if they were the last secrets on earth, the unflustered interest she took in D's random little-big-man trivia the next. *This campus sit-in, that rare record. Some idiot running the Marxism Today stall, and get this, Laura. Loww-ra.* That's when she'll roll her eyes in mock outrage, and from where he sits, it all seems so easy. She just doesn't have to try so hard to be liked, to make herself interesting. Something else he notices. She seems to manage this by making herself listen to what other people are saying.

If he was being honest, D would admit the contrast with himself was less than flattering. More often than not his only interest in what anyone else told him went no further than trying to work out if they liked him or not, whether there was some clue in the words as to a potential physical attraction. And if there wasn't, if they really *were* just keen to explore Schumpeter's theory of creative destruction or International Monetary Fund austerity programmes, then he would find himself going through the motions, not wishing to appear impolite but at the same time weighing up his impoverished time/hook-up ratios and looking for a way out. In the cold light of day it was the sort of detail that a certain type of campus inmate might have found a bit suspect. But D paid them little mind, sensing somehow that his ambition, his desire for something more than Bermondsey, less the architecture and more the mentality, would in the end damn him in their eyes anyway, the well-appointed undergrad socialists. They reminded him a little too closely of his teachers at school, the LEA hairies who went along with any old shit the black kids would come out with just to avoid looking racist. With the hairies he'd seen how it was all about the ideology, right up until the moment they got into their cars and drove back to suburbia, leaving D and the other unscrubbed urchins to fend off the freshly emboldened demands of their black classmates.

'*Jus' gi' me yuh money, white boy! Reparations!*'

Or, '*Racialist!*'

Or, on a really bad day, '*Enoch! Enoch! Enoch! Gi' me yuh money NOW!*'

Conrad always in the thick of it, evoking an out-of-date name and a not-quite patois to carry out shakedowns more or less in full view. And knowing full well that no one would intervene. Least of all the teachers, held back by guilt or whatever it was that made them such a liability, and evidently assuaged by the all-day sermon they'd been peddling on 'injustice'; the self-same one which Conrad and others had taken as a green light. In any case, the hairies were always too busy driving away from the scene of the crime to notice that in this place, as opposed to wherever it was they were driving back to, it was all about setting the tone. Get it right, and peace might even break out. On the other hand, keep mentioning words like 'harassment' and 'prejudice', and it'd be like handing the local pyro the nearest box of matches.

D had worked hard to leave those associations behind, and yet here he was, once again surrounded by visionaries who saw everything in ideology bar what was actually going on right in front of them. So again, on campus, a black skin seemed to automatically confer some kind of moral authority upon its owner, no matter how many of his countrymen had been rendered destitute to pay for his fancy foreign education. *His* shakedowns taking place out of sight, with no English hippies harmed in the making of the princeling. In truth, D had no proof of any of that, it was more a hunch, the sense he'd got of something very high born, from a throwaway comment by Celestine about 'mischief makers' during a conversation they'd been having about Nigeria.

'What's it like when you go back?'

'Oh, it's a beautiful country.'

'What, all of it? I mean it can't all be the Lake District. Come on, man, don't tell me you've got no Middlesboroughs.'

'Middlesboroughs?'

'Yeah, really ugly bits full of inbreds.'

At which point they'd both laughed, even though at the time he'd suspected the irony of his own upbringing among a diminishing dockside gene pool was most probably lost on the expensively educated Nigerian.

'Ah, I see what you mean. You're talking about troublesome sorts. I think that's who you meant, isn't it, D? Well, of course, we have our mischief makers, too, but, in truth, they don't get to make too much mischief.' And a broad nose had been tapped and the impression left that the key to a happy life back among the chieftains was not to make too much mischief. A bit like Bermondsey then.

One need neither venerate Marx, or for that matter any of the great economic thinkers, nor remain blind to their shortcomings. Purport, inspect the virtues of their theories and methods.

His talk with Celestine had made D revisit the key readings from Thornton's class. They were full of this type of guff. Really just a fancy way of saying 'on the one hand, on the other'. But somehow it rubber-stamped any amount of dithering – 'prevarication' – in the seminars. He'd witnessed that first hand, something else the rest of his English and African peers seemed to share, an ability to sound balanced when really they were anything but. Keynes made to hold hands with Smith, Marx with Malthus, the entire debate removed from anything remotely concrete. Butting heads no longer a literal enterprise, the important thing being the ability to demonstrate 'breadth of knowledge', ideas unfurled like a fan, the connections between them offsetting any potential rancour. At any rate, redesignating it as flirtation. And when he thought about it in those terms, perhaps this place was not like Bermondsey at all.

Debates here would typically unfold along the lines of, 'Are you seriously saying that it all starts with Adam Smith? What about the mercantilists? Don't tell me they weren't interested in economic theory. They knew what a surplus was and how to get it. I'm sure we can agree on that much.'

'No one's saying they weren't interested, it's just they didn't exactly produce a theory to go with it, whereas whatever else you might think of Adam Smith, he certainly *did* do that. Of course, I don't want to remain blind to the shortcomings of his theory, but in a way you have to say, wow, he did all that way back in 1776.'

'Still, you can't get away from how imperialism was the driving force. Acquiring gold and silver and yes, let's be honest, slaves, enriched one state at the same time as it impoverished another. One man's meat, so to speak, was another's poison. And it still is.'

Throughout the exchange he'd noticed how the speakers seemed to enjoy the abstract quality of the joust. The key thing, it seemed, was to keep sparring but with one eye on a mutually agreeable stoppage. He'd watch as, more often than not, the participants continued their discussion after the bell, without rancour, and on this occasion – Ola/Lucy – with a look only a hound like himself would pick up on, suggesting something more than a debate to be reconvened at a later date.

'What are you doing?' asked a familiar voice.

It was Laura, who'd been standing next to him undetected for a few moments.

'What are you looking at?' she asked, following his eyes to the debating couple, whom they seemed to be fixated on.

'Who are they?' she asked again.

'Just a pair of debaters,' D answered, admiration and bile simultaneously rising in his throat.

'Debaytas?' Laura said, repeating the word as if there was some kind of a clue in the vowels.

'That's right, debaters, alligators, see you laters,' said D, sensing the alliteration would somehow please her. His instinct was correct, though any joy was shortlived.

'Tower of Power for Loww-ra from How-rah,' she replied, laughing.

'What was that?' he asked, temporarily caught off guard.

'Tower –' she began before he cut her off.

'No, that last bit.'

'What, you mean Loww-ra from How-rah?'

'Yeah, where did that come from?' he asked, only half wanting to know the answer.

'It's funny, no?' she said, glad she'd finally got his attention. 'Some boy in my class, he say it to me, and I like how it sound, so now I say it to you.'

D looked at her, telling him with that innocent expression about 'some boy', and he knew right then what that boy was after. Knew nothing about him but could already picture some leering Forest cunt in a Slazenger jumper. Just a hunch, he'd seen a few of those hanging around, playing out their own version of the posh blacks. Something a little different for the campus army of middle-class girls to ponder. All very John Lennon-meets-sportswear-casual, the whole mess solidly congealed on a management science degree. They tended to favour that horrible bar that looked like an airport lounge, the one where he'd had the 'clear the air' talk with that Asian girl, Roxy. *Rukhini, but everyone calls me Roxy.* Actually there'd been one or two of these casual types floating about that day, and D had been surprised by the strength of his aversion to them. The shock that his weren't the only faded pastels on show, that his vowels weren't the only ones mangled by a regional dialect.

He suddenly felt the need to stress the accent, remind Laura of his niche status here on this achingly modern campus. It was pathetic, and he knew it, but there was nothing he could do about it. The shrunk-fit persona just took over.

'Funny? Nah, not so much. Laura, sweetheart, I don't know how to say this really, so don't take this the wrong way, but I think

71

that boy might have been mocking you. You know, like taking the piss.'

'Why he want to take my piss?' Laura asked him, her eyes suddenly serious.

'I don't know, sweetheart, I really don't. Why would anyone do that, especially to someone as lovely as you?'

'Stop it. Now *you* mocking me,' she said, playfully pressing D's arm.

'Look, Laura, what does he look like, this boy?'

'Why you want to know that? What difference it make?'

D grimaced inside. His dad would have hated that, answering one question with another. What was it the old man used to say? Oh yeah, that manners were the first thing to leave the manor.

'Well, I'm just saying, someone ought to have a word, is all.'

'What for? He no doing no harm. He just friendly.'

'*And* I rest my case,' D blurted out, instantly regretting it, the sarcasm a dead giveaway.

Her expression changed again then. He saw a flicker of laughter in those big brown eyes, a smile spread out across her Iberian peninsula.

'Oh, Dios mío! You're jealous. Just because some boy talked me for five minoots, you're jealous! I don't believe it. Is very silly.'

'Don't be daft, girl. I'm just looking out for you is all. When my girl comes to me telling me someone's been making fun of her, of course I'm going to react. Anyone would, or at least anyone proper would. That's not jealousy, that's concern. I mean, would you be happier if I just said nothing? Of course you wouldn't. If looking out for you somehow makes me jealous, then, yeah, I'm jealous. Guilty as charged,' D said, holding out his hands in the appointed fashion, thinking that at least would soften the tone. Of course, it only made things worse.

'But I never say he make fun. *You* say that, I never say that. I just tell you something simple from class and you make it into this big thing. *You* do that, I never do that. I think you jealous because I talk to other boy, but what I supposed to do in class? Sit there like Mona Lisa, wait till I see my boyfriend before I open mouth again?

Is what you think I should do? I'm Spanish, D, not stupid. No seas borde, tío. No eres mi jefe.'

He tried to laugh it off, but it wasn't so easy, knowing full well that he'd been sussed. Thinking about it, it seemed unlikely that Slazenger was, in fact, Slazenger. The disturbing familiarity of the made-up rhyming slang – 'Loww-ra from Howrah' – suggested something far closer to home, in all probability kitted out in Diadora Borg Elites and one of those horrible knock-off Tacchini tracksuit tops. Invented vowels, with a persona to match, the whole thing about as authentic as those late-flowering 'imports' of Adidas Dublins down East Street Market. Yep, the more he pondered, the likelier it seemed, 'the boy' from class was no Notts Forest supporter – there wasn't even a hint of northern kagooligan in the slang. Also, there was just something about the 'Howrah' detail that D found troubling. He wasn't sure what that was a reference to, but it sounded foreign, and not Marbella or Freddie Laker foreign either. This aitch, those vowels stretched beyond Miami, spanned an ocean or two and then fetched right back up in the heart of his beloved London. And no amount of Cerruti 1881 velour tracksuit tops in his faux-sartorial locker was going to change that basic fact. Everything suddenly seemed horribly clear to D. Without even needing to meet him, D knew already that the boy from class was a boy just like him, a cardboard cockney trying his luck among the less casually appointed. And this boy was snouting around his bird, the lovely Loww-ra, who most definitely was not from Howrah. This did not please him at all.

They made a point of going their separate ways after that, at least for the next few hours, to show just how wronged each party felt about the other's *faux-pas*. In D's case for the apparent slight to his fragile ego, in Laura's because she could see that the situation demanded a certain indulgence of his weakness but also because his manner had left her feeling mildly irritated. It was all so familiar.

Boys, from one place to the next, usually strutting about, putting on a show, but then at the merest hint of doubt so easily wounded. Silly boys, this one no exception. She felt it was pointless trying to reason with him when he was in this kind of a mood; she knew that every attempt to do so would be batted away by a mask of surly, his charade fooling no one, least of all her, but that it would still somehow be upheld as a form of rehabilitation. She'd learnt from previous wasted afternoons that it was best just to leave him be. An hour or two was usually enough for him to see sense, and then he'd wander across campus, past the library, through the Arts Centre, strolling past the bar that looked like an airport lounge, carrying on into the Union building, basically anywhere they'd ever hung out, pretending he was going for a walk but with none of the genuine stroller's randomness on his itinerary. The best-case scenario that she'd be there, in one of their haunts, reading a book or having a coffee or just sitting around aimlessly but full of remorse for their earlier row. The reality more often than not that she'd be with friends looking anything but unhappy or, if alone, then with her head in a book or an article, biro to hand, effortlessly slipping back into scholar mode. All the same she knew the drill, they both did, recognised how it would save time in the long run, and so she played her part. In any case, as was already clear to her, D's wasn't an entirely unfamiliar male-pattern brittleness, and far from the worst she'd encountered.

Unusually, though, today she was nowhere to be seen, and before long the diamond Pringle was holed back up in his cell trying to figure out why, in a space of higher learning, he couldn't even work out the basics.

When he'd eventually caught up with her she was in the library canteen, and Slazenger was with her.

He knew the moment he spotted them. Actually not Slazenger, but something far more niche and therefore troubling: a cream Le Coq Sportif zip-up top. D knew straight away *this* was the boy from class. A wedge, early-season bum-fluff hovering above the lip, and right there in the eyes a look that had sized him up in much the same way as he had, though perhaps drawing a more comforting set of conclusions: Pringle, rival, the unspoken ('so this is the prick?'). As far as D could tell, Laura not much more than one smart quip and a Styrofoam cup of coffee away from being chatted up.

Le Coq Sportif! The neck on this cunt. Though it had been a while, D remembered enough rudimentary French from school to know what that motif signified. The Gallic colour scheme on the collar wasn't exactly helping the mood music either. So Le Coq fancied himself as a bit of a cosmopolitan then? D wasn't entirely unfamiliar with the concept. There'd been a few of these types back in sixth form, dining out on the area's older mythology, thinking a pair of Adidas Malagas would divert attention away from the sheer smallness of their ambition. Not even to be the best-dressed chicken in Bermondsey but instead its bastard offspring, squawking away in a shit-filled coop, and even when it finally did come up for air, holding aloft nothing more than yesterday's worms in a stained beak.

These lads, often Spensers, Garys, Bradleys, though every now and then a Carlton or an Ercan, too, forever smuggling an *entente cordiale* or *déjà vu* into their everyday observations (presumed witty, mainly by themselves) but always with one eye on the talent (pasty, local, familiar) and the other on each other, the greatest linguistic coup ultimately measured by the winning of peer approval just a stone's throw from where their old men had given their best years to the tanneries or the docks or pissed it all away in one of the spit-and-sawdust establishments the area favoured.

D had always loathed that faux-sophistication, its orbit limited to a few narrow streets enclosing some obsolete wharves. *That* was never going to be enough for him, to keep him here with all the other little big men. He wanted something more, something to take him away once and for all from the less than challenging verbal reasoning puzzles, the lunch-money shakedowns, the shitty local football team who, it was true, no one liked, though they really didn't care. So when he'd got the offer, then the grades and became the first in his family to make it to university, the last thing he'd expected once he'd got there was some kind of a throwback to that classroom long since left behind.

He remembered how proud his folks had been that day the results came through, the brown envelope waiting for him on the kitchen table, still sealed, him feigning nonchalance – poorly, one might add, having been up all night in a state of nervous excitement. Both of them looking at him, then each other, furiously sipping cha with no thoughts of scalded tongues. He'd done his best to hold the excitement down, style out a poker face, keep the tension going as long as possible. But it just wasn't in him, the Anglepoise of the 'A' shooting straight from his gut to his face. And once the first hint of a crack appeared in the plaster the game was up, the old man virtually snatching the printed note right out of his hands, all their eyes now brimming.

'I'm proud of you, son,' said his dad, planting a kiss on top of his head.

'My boy's going to university! And he's as smart as any of them,' said his mum, throwing her arms around him, kissing every part of his face as though it was hallowed ground.

He'd done his best not to cry, felt nobody would have been too impressed with the waterworks, but when he'd seen his dad welling up himself, that's when the dam had burst. Afterwards there had been a celebratory tipple of ginger wine and a slice of fruit cake, though it was nowhere near Christmas, or even midday.

Seeing his son this excited about the prospect of yet more study was a first for his dad. But he was pleased his boy wasn't one of those stone-faced ne'er do wells the area seemed to specialise in. The ones whose faces only came alive when the Black Marias showed up on match days. The older one, D's brother, oh, he'd given them all a headache, flirted with that nonsense for years before the long arm and short shrift finally caught up with him. To be fair, though, he'd done alright since, the entrepreneurial skills picked up as a hoister put to good use as a trader. Not only that but in a great big office with loads of computers. And, of course, he now had Angela and the kids to add some much-needed ballast, an ongoing reminder that transferable skills were one thing but youthful misdemeanours quite another. Feeling a little tipsy from the cheeky tipple, the old man reflected with no little satisfaction that, yes, his boys hadn't turned out so bad, so he must have been doing something right all these years. And before he knew it, he was breaking out the Peek Freans, hoping to sprinkle yet more stardust on this most unusual of weekday mornings.

A quick scan revealed stonewashed Lois jeans and a pair of Adidas Sambas. This is what the opposition looked like, thought D, and in those surrounds, full of the expensively educated but poorly dressed, it came as something of a shock. Also, Le Coq was Asian, rare enough on this campus, though he crowed away in a very familiar brogue.

'Hello, mate, I'm Ravi,' he said, offering his hand without waiting to be introduced.

It blindsided D, leaving him with little choice but to reciprocate the gesture.

'Alright,' he said, 'I'm D. I see you've already met my other half,' he went on, hoping to restore some order to proceedings.

'Oh, right. Laura. Actually, I didn't know that,' lied Ravi, enjoying the fact that his presence made D sufficiently anxious to have to spell out the nature of his relationship. This was going to be easier than he thought. Fun, too, once Pringle had got his shapes and styles all mixed up as he surely would the moment he, Ravi, headed back into the bowels of English literature on the third floor. And this, even though he was an engineering student, with very little need for Ginny Woolf to help him understand how bridges got built.

'Anyway, got to chip,' he lied again, gathering up his biro and the solitary piece of paper he had out on the table. As ever, after the first lie, the rest was child's play. 'Good to meet you, mate, I'm sure we'll run into each other at some point. See you soon, Loww-ra,' Ravi said, pronouncing it the Spanish way, again enjoying the involuntary wince he'd spotted on the English boy's face as he did so. And with that he was off, the classic three-stripe

Sambas disappearing up the stairs in a time-honoured Lambeth shimmy.

After that D kept spotting Ravi out and about, always in the company of some white girl. Also spotted, in no particular order: Gabicci crew-necked jumper, lace-up Stan Smiths and a Fila velour Bj tracksuit top, the rarity of which, D had to admit, seemed wasted on some, if not all, of these girls. The next time he spied Ravi with Laura, though, it was the light-blue Tacchini tracksuit that really caught his attention. There was definitely something about Ravi, maybe it was the Chaplin walk or perhaps it was that salon-layered wedge or something else entirely, which just screamed London particular. As in a particular kind of London fraud. And it bothered D immensely.

To the uninitiated the whole casual shtick probably just seemed like a load of sportswear framing a fast mouth. Style and patter or something along those lines. But D knew it was more than that, each fresh incarnation of Ellesse or crew necks or stripes or tank tops a personal affront, another one in the eye for the competition. This bastard was just like him really, no tribal affiliations, none of that nonsense holding him back, just a clear sense of style and marketing and its pay-off in sex. So where D felt he should have been cleaning up on campus in the cod-anthropological battle of the sexes, Ravi, as far as he was concerned, was taking a highly unwelcome, if stylish, one-man wrecking-ball to the entire operation. And for D it was that, rather than the gear, which made him into the opposition.

Bare Minimum
Protocol

SHE SEEMED TO like the gear, Laura, that is. Any time he'd stay over, he'd get up the next day to find her already poring over her engineering manuals with nothing standing between her and the early-morning chill but one of his Pringle jumpers or plain white Lacostes. He got to like the smell of her in those clothes, began leaving choice items with her, would drink in the aroma one last time when she'd give them back before they'd join the pile of sweatstink destined for the launderette.

Actually, that was how he found out, the day an unfamiliar Ellesse polo shirt got mixed up with the other loaned laundry items. To his shame he'd even thought about pocketing it, not mentioning the top again; after all, it'd be spotless once it came out the wash, and with a bit of luck there'd be no traces of betrayal left on it.

It was at moments like these that he fully understood the real reason he'd been so desperate to leave Bermondsey behind. There was nothing instinctive in his reaction to finding out his girlfriend had been two-timing him. Had he been anything like the other boys in his class, the ones getting worked up about the homoerotic undercurrents of a verbal reasoning problem, he'd have been screaming blue murder. In one or two cases it might even have come to that. At the very least there would have been a confrontation, a dressing down of sorts and then payback of his own, most likely a fumble with a stranger up the Old Kent Road, nothing to write home about, but equally nothing to be ashamed of. And, according to local wisdom, some kind of parity would have been restored.

But that type of guttural response just wasn't in him, nor the idea that these things happened, and when they did, you wiped your mouth and moved on, but only after you'd got even.

Instead, he was that other kind of boy, the type to weigh up all the variables before arriving at some coldly rational conclusion. Utterly devoid of frenzy or spark or any of those things which made people so wary of the dead-eyed chancers pouring out of the towers and the terraces. No, he was nothing like them. Implacable herberts with a gift for the antisocial gesture. Belts and verbals and a specific pathological weakness often getting mixed up in the business of 'straightening her out'. Nasty, brutish even, but, to a certain kind of mentality, not entirely unwarranted. Domestic violence. The sound of it all wrong to his ears. He'd barely ever seen Dad even raise his voice let alone his hand at home.

Not the way to do things. You're better than that, son.

But there were plenty who didn't see things that way, whose rages and weaknesses easily got the better of them. So he knew domestic violence lurked in those streets, too, along with its kindred, assault and battery. And everyone else seemed to know as well, especially those who weren't even from the area. The finger-pointers who saw it as something else to file along with the underpasses, the poor lighting, the tight warren of streets feeding off the trading estates, just another detail in that mental inventory – 'Millwall' – which was really just a site-specific charge sheet. He could see, even if no one else could, that if it lent the area rep, what this inventory actually achieved was to supply everyone else with some much-needed moral high ground to scramble back up. And once they had they could get right back to doing what they did best. To pointing those fingers and muttering those slurs – *What do you expect? Dirty dockers. Southeast London* – without a care in the world for their own shortcomings. But it was true, when he thought about it, that word 'rep'. Reputation, notoriety, they were about the only things the neighbourhood *had* managed to hold on to once most of the work had dried up. And, in all honesty, he had none of it, the rep or the work.

Now a shining example of local manhood like Conrad on the

other hand, *he'd* have known how to handle things, and no doubt something bad would have happened as a result, but at least he'd have been decisive. Not like D, a ditherer, always working the balance of probabilities like some petrified bookie. Which is why, as he sat in the launderette admiring the classic red-block, fine-stripe polo, any thoughts he might have had of confronting Laura soon dissolved into an unexpectedly erotic cuckolded frisson. One that arrived intact with its own rationale.

Act outraged, and it would just confirm her suspicions about his ongoing jealousy. And given that it was most likely *that* which had driven her to playing away in the first place, a repeat performance would only make her more bold. Do nothing, though, while giving the impression that he knew, and she'd think he didn't care so would have no incentive to stop straying. Play dumb, on the other hand, act as though nothing was wrong, and he'd get to bone her *and* keep the shirt, maybe even wear it on the job. *Though on the balance of probabilities* he'd surely be wiser to not mention the shirt again, let alone have his Ron Jeremy moment in it. That way, when and if Le Coq ever came back for it, *she'd* have some explaining to do, and then *they'd* be the uncool lovers (she and Le Coq) with all the unresolved issues. The other advantage of not letting on was that Le Coq would more likely than not trip himself up in the interim, given the rate at which he seemed to be working his way through the English Department. Laura was bound to cotton on to Ravi's antics sooner rather than later, and D very much doubted she'd put up with the kind of pro-rata crap he was currently trying to justify to himself. So he decided to play innocent, have his polo and eat it, too, so to speak.

Valladolid, Spain, Easter 1984

'No. Como éste, tío: borracho,' said Laura, rolling her 'r's, letting them burr that way he liked. Best of all if they were lying down somewhere and she started whispering sweet nothings about 'la guerra civil' or 'el perro con sus asuntos arreglados'. The more random the phrase, the better the roll, something about the illogicality of it all playing well to D's ears; the good feeling, probably the tickle of the burr, heading further south, too. But they were in public, in a bar, and that meant observing at least some bare-minimum protocol. So for the time being a roll in the lobe didn't mean one in the grass.

The barman, whose demeanour suggested he was also the owner, looked on decidedly unimpressed. Bloody kids, no decorum, no respect for their elders. A couple of desgraciados. This would never have happened in Franco's day. But business was business, he reasoned, and in any case it might be a while yet before he had another customer.

'Boratcho,' said D, deliberately squashing the burr, enjoying how she winced at the sheer Englishness of it all.

'No, D,' Laura cut in, unable to help herself. 'De nuevo, colega: borracho. As in, like, eres borracho, tío. Muy, muy borracho. Eres completamente –'

'Beratcho. Yeah, I know, I get it. Take the piss out of the foreigner time,' said D, the after-effects of a favourable exchange rate and an all-day drinking culture beginning to catch up with him.

They'd barely been here two days, and already they seemed to have settled into a familiar routine. Late nights, even later mornings (in reality, early afternoons) and then the bleary-eyed rush to the discount supermarket – 'el hipo' – to stock up on some basic provisions before mainstream society closed down for its daily siesta. A big pot of Russian salad, some pork chops and an uninspiring, but cheap, selection of non-brand-name yoghurts the unfussy and highly effective stomach liner before venturing out again to the tight cluster of bars near the university and a repeat performance of the previous night's foolishness. The flat they were staying in handily vacated by an older friend of Laura's, apparently away in Madrid 'on business'. What he knew of Laura from the short time they'd already spent together in England meant that D had his doubts about this mysterious 'friend', but the default analyst in him could see that the flat was free, the friend was absent and really there was nothing to be gained by making a show. Best to keep shtum, let nature run its course. After all, that was an approach which had served him well enough up to this point.

Actually the decision to come to Spain had been taken in a hurry. She'd burst into his room, highly agitated, and D was just grateful she hadn't caught him in the act with the Linda Lusardi centrefold he'd not long returned to its marginally more socially acceptable housing inside the latest copy of *The Economist* on his desk.

'Vámonos, D. Vamos a España por Semana Santa.'

'¿Qué?' he'd quipped, doing his best Manuel impression, pretending he didn't understand exactly what she'd just said to him.

'Let's go to Spain, D! I got place to stay and we have fun there. Just for holiday. What you say, D?'

'Well, I don't know, Laura. It sounds lovely, but the thing is, I've just got so much work to do,' D replied weakly, loathing himself almost immediately for his lack of impulsiveness.

'We all got work to do, D. But I think it do you good, do me good, to have break from this place. I sick of this place now. Same people, always same face, always moan, moan, moan. Sick of it. We go Spain, friendly face, every day nice and hot. And we with each other, not like here, with all other people. Vámonos, D. We have fiesta over there.'

He didn't like the sound of her 'with all other people', didn't like it at all, so for that reason as much as any other, he surprised himself with (for him) an almost unprecedented boldness and agreed to go.

Laura's mood seemed to change almost instantly. She no longer felt quite so desperate and was inwardly relieved that for this boy, at least, her charms remained intact. Only an hour or so earlier her confidence had been severely dented when she'd walked in on Ravi nose deep in Patricia from Burgos. She'd suspected that puta of having designs for a while now, ever since she'd innocently started sitting next to him in the lecture theatre on the flimsiest of pretexts.

Can't hear properly from over there. Hard to understand when English not first language. Much better here. Oh me, I'm Patricia. Where I'm from? Oh, Spain. A little norte of Madrid. Burgos.

Even so, she'd been surprised by just how angry it made her feel seeing the familiar layered black mane bobbing up and down between that puta's thighs. It was no fun being second or third or wherever she was on Ravi's list. But when she saw how little her unexpected arrival meant, Ravi hungrily lapping away, Patricia not even embarrassed when she became aware of Laura's glowering presence in the doorway, she wasted no more time on that scene. Only after she'd bawled and screamed the worst of it out under a pillow in her room did her thoughts turn to D, whom she felt certain would not be doing anything to humiliate her, or himself, if she called in on him unannounced.

FIRST TIME ABROAD

AT THE AIRPORT she paid for the tickets in cash. She'd done the same at the train station earlier, seemingly untroubled by the full fare for two to London. If he'd even been paying attention, D might have been surprised by the fact, and the fat, of the roll she produced from her pocket. In truth, it barely even registered, his thoughts consumed by gratitude that his passport had been here with him on campus rather than back home. But for some issue with his yet-to-be-agreed overdraft facility and the requirement that he bring several forms of ID into the campus branch, the little black book would still have been languishing next to a book of Panini football stickers in a shoe box under his bed round Mum and Dad's. Gawd bless that lank-haired, Burton-tie/half-sleeve-shirt-wearing bank manager and his insistence that 'it's no problem, a passport is every bit as good as a driving licence'.

It was D's first time abroad. That much became obvious during the rabbit-in-the-headlights routine he pulled at the airport. Once the tickets were bought, as far as he was concerned, that was that, they could just stroll up to the plane and jet off. Clearing passport control and customs came as something of a shock, in no way lessened by the way the official was looking at the admittedly laughable pudding-bowl haircut on the document and then back at the gormless idiot stood in front of him. He seemed amused.

'So this is you then?' he asked D.

'Well it's not me mum, that's for sure,' replied D, instantly regretting the sarcasm.

'No need to make this any harder than it needs to be,' said the official, giving D that finger-up-the-bum-anytime-we-want look regrettably familiar to the seasoned traveller but clearly not to a virgin voyager like this.

'Yeah, that's me,' said D. 'I was having a bad-hair day.'

The attempt at humour fell predictably flat. This was neither the time nor place. He knew that *now*. These weren't like the teachers from school, not at all. You'd think twice before mouthing off in this place, or at least the seasoned traveller might.

'A simple yes or no will do. Is that clear? So, first time abroad is it?'

D was outraged. He sensed the official was deliberately goading him. This cunt had probably worked out by now that the girl hanging about nearby who'd already cleared passport control was with him and was determined to humiliate the novice with his spectacularly bad passport photo. In any case how did he know this was his first time?

'Look, I –' he began to protest before he was cut short by the local Stasi.

'A simple yes or no will do.'

'Er, yes, but how did you...?'

'No stamps, son. You've got no stamps on your passport. That means you've never left the country before. Well, now you know. *Bon voyage* and all that. But a free bit of advice. From now on, keep it simple.'

Once he knew it was free, he'd got pissed on the plane. It made everything easier, or at any rate took the edge off his embarrassment. He really did know nothing about flying. Still, by the time the third whisky kicked in with the altitude, D was already halfway to slumber, the plane within touching distance of Madrid.

Yet more tickets, paid for in cash, to Valladolid, and several hours later there they were, Laura wasting no time undressing, kneeling on the bed with her buttocks in the air. Luckily the after-effects of the whisky had by now worn off, and the first thing they did was a time-honoured doggy within full view of anyone who happened to be looking out from a balcony in the adjoining block of flats.

Not long after was the first time he heard that word, the one they would keep hearing over and over again for the rest of the week. *Desgraciados!* On that occasion the voice clearly belonged to an old lady, but at various times it could be male, too. Often husky, soaked in its own kind of muscle memory, but almost always an older voice. *Desgraciados!* Whatever else it was, this wasn't the calling card of the young. Lying there in a giggly naked clinch, D had the sense that Laura wasn't entirely unhappy at the old lady's disapproval.

'Escucha, tío. Listen to the bruja. She no like what we do, but she still watch.'

'Just as well we put on a show then,' said D, both of them breaking into peals of laughter.

And again, right on cue, desgraciados! This time, though, followed by the sound of a window being forcefully shut.

They lay there like that for some time, not saying much, Coventry, Warwick, campus already a world away. When the early-evening breeze turned into something a little sharper, a sense of urgency was suddenly returned to the lovers. *The lovers!* What kind of a cunt thought, let alone said, stuff like that? D pondered his mental flight of fancy and felt momentarily disgusted by himself. This is what happens, he thought, when you spend too long around the Fauntleroys. He looked at Laura, one arm stretched out over the pillow, her tufty armpits a welcome change from the stripped clean English girls he was more used to. One thing for sure, though, this was in a different league to Schumpeter. 'Creative destruction' – my arse!

As the light changed and more voices became audible at street level, he found himself listening out for that word again, *desgraciado*. But what he heard instead was laughter and lipstick and the sounds of a neighbourhood waking from its own slumber.

Still, *the lovers*. What a prize Toby. A good job no one here knew what that was. Reason enough, if they did, to think of him as a desgraciado. But, of course, in this place at least his boat carried the cachet of not being from here, and even in his limited experience that usually equated to some kind of pay-off. At which point the thought of much-needed food and coffee and a first peek (for D) at the local pond life didn't seem like such a bad idea.

'Lorrra, Lorr, Lorrra,' he kept repeating in his most exaggerated English accent, knowing that was about the only thing which could goad her out of her half-sleep. It worked. She took the bait, protesting 'Loww-ra, Loww-ra, Loww-ra' all the way to the bar at the top of the street and right up until the first mouthful of the ham-and-cheese bocadillo she ordered for both of them.

He liked the place as soon as they walked in. A neat, circular bar, not too many tables, room for about thirty punters tops, and an old-style menu board not exactly overrun with choice. Several older men were sat on raised stools, facing away from the bar, staring intently to one side where a football match was showing on the large but bulky television which had been set up on a makeshift Formica table. Every now and then an 'Oouieee' went up from the bar when one of the players went close. Though while they were waiting for the bocatas and chips and coffee to be brought over, D noticed that this enthusiasm only extended to goal-scoring opportunities for the team in white. Whenever the other team, kitted out in yellow, so much as stitched three passes together, some other word would get muttered. 'Soothio' or something along those lines. Another one he kept hearing was 'maricón', but when he asked Laura what that meant she just looked embarrassed, though she tried to act casual, popping chips in her mouth while pretending to follow the game.

The floor was covered in sawdust, and when he bent down to tie one of the laces which had come loose on his Adidas Sambas, D saw that smuggled in with the sawdust was an army of discarded shells. Only then did he spot two of the bar-stoolers, who must have been regulars, taking handfuls of pistachios from the bowls being constantly replenished on the bar, the shells expertly dislodged in the mouth and either spat out directly on to the floor or placed in a stubby hand and dropped there more deliberately depending on how compelling the live action was.

'¡Son esos unos maricones! Te lo juro, están jugando como Atleti,' complained one of the regulars, clearly incensed by what he was seeing.

'No tiene cojones, colega. Es la cultura de hoy,' added his mate, a few more shells hitting the floor.

Again, D asked Laura what they were talking about, but this time, fortified by the food and the coffee, he was more persistent. Eventually she relented, the last of the chips hoovered up with another splash of tabasco.

'They calling these players gay like, how you say, 'omosexual? The short one, he say they play like Atlético de Madrid.'

'And that's not a good thing?' D asked her.

'No, not good. Atleti not good team. Always play like gay.'

'What about the other one then? What was he talking about?' D asked, somewhat surprised, though he didn't really know why, at how Spanish football fans appeared to be every bit as progressive as their English counterparts. Then again, this was a bit of a spit-and-sawdust effort, and in fairness he wouldn't even have set foot in its Bermondsey equivalent, let alone stayed for an evening.

'His friend, he say it a bigger problem than football. It's the cultoor. How you say, kulchoor. He say it weak. No balls. Bollix,' she explained, briefly wondering why D was so interested. It was just a game, some pijos kicking a pelota, at the end of which the team in white usually won. But, if there was one thing she knew, it was that boys, silly boys, would always find a way to get worked up about this little drama when really there was so much else, and rarely all that far away, to be worked up about. Things they never seemed to see, even when they were happening right in front of them. Ten years on from the death of the not-so-great dictator, and it was clear in the shell casings, the lack of respect, in the untroubled but coded curses – well, to her at least, it was clear that franquismo was still in good voice here in the heartland. Fachadolid.

As long as she was in England, at Warwick, on campus, Laura could play another role. And for a while she almost believed it herself. Maja, simpática, the kind one, the bright one, on her engineering scholarship at the prestigious English university. It was easier there, where no one knew her; where she could be just another face in the international crowd. The university administration had thoughtfully even placed her in International House, the special hall of residence for all the foreign students, and she doubted it was coincidence that there was another Spanish girl on her corridor. The thinking behind it easy enough to fathom, even if it made certain assumptions about both of them. But it was all fairly benign really, and from a bureaucratic point of view she could see how it made sense. *Both from the same part of the world. Will help with the process of settling in. Mutually supportive.*

From the beginning, though, something about this girl just didn't sit right with Laura, even when she found out they were on the same course. She hoped it wasn't something as superficial as the hair (big, salon-styled) or their very different ways of dressing, as much for what that might say about her as for any principled aesthetic objection.

Chalk and cheese, though.

Laura's standard uniform of black jeans and whatever T-shirt she had to hand, the informality well enough suited to the persona. The other girl with what could only be described as the pija trappings of jodhpurs and leather satchel or matching tweeds; or the impression she sometimes gave in a look, which lingered on Laura just a moment too long, of being one of those spoilt bitches from every major city in Spain, prepped and styled in El Corte Inglés. Also of note: how she always wanted to know what Laura was doing, where she was going, who she was seeing, the intrusions starting off as an indulgence but quickly becoming a habit.

At first Laura felt sorry for her, thought it must be because they were both Spanish and far from home. The poor girl was probably homesick, she thought, or maybe she just missed the familiar comforts of hearing Spanish, of rolled 'r's and shared confidences, something as simple as that. So Laura would share her plans with her, sit with her for lunch, invite her to join in with her own burgeoning group of friends if she happened to be passing between lectures and they were sitting around having a coffee or sharing their own confidences. In practice, of course, what this meant was that Laura would have to listen to her constant complaints about the food, the weather, the campus, the lecturers or some other aspect of life at a prestigious university, not bothering to point out that much the same, if not worse, could be said about the life that awaited them back in Spain. By this point, of course, Laura was already fully immersed in the role of maja, so it was too late really to approach things a different way, certain expectations in place, the pattern set. Else she might not have been so accommodating the day this girl spied her sitting in class with a handsome moreno, and decided that *this* was the day she was going to come over and sit with them, citing the poor acoustics in every other part of the lecture theatre. Pouting and feigning like she was born to it. Patricia, from Burgos.

The match ended in uproar, two players sent off for what barely even constituted handbags. But then an injury-time penalty, which seemed dubious at best, and an ill-tempered victory for the team in white.

At the bar, Derek and Clive carried on dropping shells, and insults, more or less until the final whistle, though the penalty right at the death seemed to lift their spirits. Normal service resumed, the team in white triumphant, and they could get back to slating queers and Gypsies.

D sat there increasingly entertained by the double act, the match itself something of a sideshow. He felt better, the earlier plate of food topped up with regular sides of mushrooms in garlic sauce and bread and olives. It took a while for Laura to explain the concept of tapas to him, or the idea that they'd settle the bill afterwards. He just couldn't imagine such an arrangement back home, everyone too wary or crooked or perhaps both for the idea to get off the ground.

Hard to see any of his old classmates going in for this type of set-up, the unfamiliarity just one part of it. Even if they could have been persuaded that this way of doing things actually worked, he doubted they'd ever embrace it. There'd still be resistance, not least because it largely dispensed with hustling or preening or the sharp one-liner or anything really which helped stave off the need for thought or reflection or a passing resemblance to a proper conversation. He knew what they'd say. *What was the point of a night out if you couldn't buy bar presence by flashing the cash or scope the local talent with a string of one-liners? And what's with all this sitting-down-to-eat malarkey? I tell you what it is eating into, though, and that's valuable drinking time. You want contemplation, they would have told him, go and join the church. You've gone soft in the head, son. It's those lah-di-dahs, D, you've been around them too long.*

'Gitanos. Maricones. Qué puta mierda,' Derek, and then Clive, seemed to be saying to no one in particular, even after the final whistle.

The bar was a little busier now. Some younger lads had come in for the second half, and they seemed to be making a lot of noise about the result. A couple of them were looking over at Laura, and then at D, but it all seemed harmless enough. He found it hard to get too worked up about people who dressed this way.

They were wearing those slightly too short hybrid Sta-Prest/chino efforts that a lot of the lads round here seemed to favour. He'd already spotted a handful of them at the airport and then on the train but hadn't really given them a second thought. Here, though, he took the opportunity to scan the whole outfit. Exposed ankle (a bit gay), tasselled loafers, moccasins and in one case yachting pumps (still quite gay), pastel-coloured polo shirts and light cashmere jumpers draped over the shoulders (again, nothing to dispel the gay rumours). The whole thing came over very Cappuccino Kid-meets-Risky Business but maybe that's inevitable, he thought, in a slightly warmer climate. They picked away at the olives generously provided by the bar and occasionally looked over in his direction, muttering something, probably about the two of them, before just as quickly returning to the post-match inquest on the television being conducted by some lairy cunt in a

Miami Vice suit. It was all a bit incongruous, and when Laura tapped him on the arm saying 'Let's go', he was happy enough to follow her. Hard to tell whether it was just his imagination, or the caffeine working its magic, but on his way out he thought he heard the word 'puta'.

Nothing Like The Girls He Was Used To

PEOPLE STARED OVER here, and he quickly realised that he didn't mind at all. After the initial surprise he was disappointed if they went into a bar or a café and no one clocked them. Best of all it was the women who really stared, and when he plucked up the courage to hold their gaze, he saw that they weren't afraid to look back. They were nothing at all like the girls he was used to; for one thing, they didn't have that sour expression as if they were constantly tuned in to the lowest common denominator. The outlook always a bit severe even when there was no need. Then again, he could hardly blame them, having to deal, as they did on a regular basis, with such charmers as Conrad or any of the myriad local chancers who made the fun palaces of the Old Kent Road their own once the working week was over.

Still, these girls seemed somehow friendlier even when they weren't saying much. D had already noted the rarity of the perma-scowl which came so easily to their English counterparts. The difference this made was amazing. Where ordinarily he'd expect to be blanked, if not outright belittled, in a bar setting, the absence of hostility here dramatically raised his expectations, and D found himself smiling and nodding at a group of girls when Laura went to the bathroom. If she suspected anything when she came back, she didn't let on, though in his mind D largely put that down to guilt. Hers. They'd never spoken about the Ellesse. He doubted they ever would.

Though she was roughly the same age as these girls, Laura came across as older. She projected a confidence in how she went about everyday things. So whether she was buying tickets or drinks or just suggesting an idea, more often than not it rang true. Actually, that was one of the first things D had noticed about her and liked about her. Along with that accent and the straightforward style, it was yet another detail that set her apart from the Beas and the Allys, the Chars and the Emms, and pretty much anyone else who'd arrived on campus with expensively assembled baggage.

She'd even asked him once, 'All men are this, all women are that, what they mean by that, D? Girl in my class she tell me this, say, Laura, come to our meeting. I think you like what you hear. We want girl like you at our meeting. What she mean by that, D? Girl like me? She doesn't even know me.'

'I know, Laura. It's this place. Everyone here acts like they know everything, but the truth is no one knows anything.'

It's what his dad used to say whenever anyone accused him of having 'airs' just because his boy was going to university. It nearly always had the desired effect, casting a philosophical aspersion without actually needing to mention the two-stretch or the gambling debt or the pickled liver or whatever filial exploit it was that got in the way of their own 'airs'. And D was happy to note its transferable value in the largely untested area of fledgling romance.

'You right. That's so true. You really know what to say,' she told him, placing a hand on his surprisingly soft fingers.

It happened fairly easily after that, all the hanging out and coffee inevitably leading back to hers and the kind of sex he just wasn't used to. Where nothing was expected of him, and it was as though she knew that that was the one thing he dreaded more than any other, being expected to perform, and not only that but in a particular way befitting his status here as a kind of endangered species. *Bermondsey Man*, the missing link between Godalming socialite and her superannuated future of basement excavations and yearly invitations to the Cartier polo event. His dick apparently the divining-rod for south-London bohemia, another notch on dearest Bea, Ally, Char or Emm's socially diverse bedpost. A totem of what, and who, they did in the interim, in that vague, unspecified period between Ginny Woolf and Ayn Rand. Proof positive of their liberal credentials, of how much they'd transcended the straitjacket of their privileged upbringings and of their overbearing social assumptions. A memory stick. His dick, and the priority access it was being afforded, evidently somehow an emblem of *their* bravery. 'Come on, D, fuck me till I fart,' apparently the ultimate compliment from a certain type of seeker.

With Laura it was different, quieter, her touch more experienced than his. And in the absence of hostility, of the unspoken passive/aggressive upper-middle-class kind, he developed the kind of boner that thus far only a soft-focus Linda Lusardi had been able to tease from him.

The Old Way of Doing Things

'WHORE-HEY.'

'Or-Gay?'

'No, hombre. Whore-Hey. Like Georgie.'

'Georgie, like Georgie Porgie?'

'No, tío. Whore-Hey.'

The barman sounded fed up. He'd been trying, and failing, to explain to the guiri how his name was pronounced. Not his idea, but, as so often in these situations, drink had loosened the foreigner's tongue, and inhibitions were quickly cast aside in an entirely faked bonhomie. The girl the guiri was with hadn't spoken until now, but Jorge did at least feel that she, too, was bored by the entire farce.

'Díselo, D. Jorge. No seas bobo.'

'Jorge,' said D finally, sensing her irritation, realising he'd overplayed his hand.

For all sorts of reasons, Jorge regretted the presence of the girl. Something about her tapped into a deep melancholy, at least in him. Perhaps it wasn't that surprising, he thought. Probably it was the same for anyone, any father with a daughter her age; more so one who'd long since made her disappointments clear. In life, and its ability to surprise. In the neighbourhood and their flat and her room full of things he'd have loved to have had at her age. Well, maybe not the lip liner, but definitely a room of his own. Kids, or at least his kid, only ever happy when she was finding fault.

There's nothing to do here, Papá. Why do we have to live here?

All this, so bored and tired of life already, even though she'd barely touched the sides of two decades. The only consolations to be found apparently away from home and what she made clear were the stifling routines of family, appearance, study. Which he'd have to hear about from Marta, his wife. A constant litany of complaint detailing their daughter's unexplained absences, her silences at dinner, the monosyllabic the rest of the time. *And, Jorge, have you seen her? Always in dark colours as if there aren't already enough shadows hanging over this town. (Well, of course I haven't seen her. I've been at work.)*

Still, that was a shroud he just couldn't seem to break free from. In its own way the whole thing – 'family' – every bit as much of a sham as this little 'cultural' exchange taking place right now with the guiri. His wife, sad, his daughter, angry, and himself, barely even there.

It made him wonder where *he* was in all of this? What about himself and his business, this little forgotten bar? The only good thing about it, as far as he could tell, the way it formed a buffer between the distant man he'd become and all that disappointment, that unhappiness he'd supposedly left in his wake. It puzzled him, though. The only thing he was doing was making a living, putting nice things on the table for them. Not that they ever seemed to notice. In this brave new world of drunkenness and juerga, he was the villain, apparently. The bad man with the old ideas, the old way of doing things. His daughter had once told him that decorum and respect were no different to parades and power. *And that practically makes you a fascist, Papá!*

At the time she'd seemed so angry with him there didn't appear to be much point in telling her her own abuelo had lost everything under Franco. Gone to jail, lost his job and his health, nearly lost his family, too, and for what? For being a trade unionist. Which was why he, Jorge, had always wanted his own business and whatever security that provided. Didn't want his family to go through what he had as a kid. What should have been the best years spent without a father, the time for play taken up instead by any work he could find. Poverty, and the shame of it, dripping off him like slumstink. That's what his daughter couldn't understand, or wouldn't. Everything he did was to keep that stink far from her.

It was also why he steered clear of politics, just wanted an easier life without the sectarian divides.

He didn't ask much, only that people respect him in his bar. He didn't ask for, nor did he expect, miracles. His life away from the bar would doubtless remain a car crash. It didn't take a genius to see that. But here at least, here he was somebody. El Dueño, El Míster, and definitely El Hombre not to be messed with. So, as far as he was concerned, he had every right to take the insult personally. In any case who was this marica the girl was with? Inglés, by the sounds of him, and he looked like one of those hooligans who'd sometimes come for the football but always end up in the puticlub anyway. Or running rings around the Guardia Civil. Coño, one more Or-Gay from the guiri and he might have been reaching for the bate he kept under the counter. This cagón didn't know how lucky he was.

BLINDSIDED

D WOKE UP rubbing his jaw. It still felt sore from where he'd been punched and then kicked a little earlier. The whole thing had happened so fast he hadn't had time to react, at least that's what he was telling himself in between 'Oh, shit, why?' on his way down, felled by a single punch. Moments before they'd been soaking up the sweet apple liqueur, one chupito after the other, the warm, sickly buzz resting just below something familiar. He recognised those voices before he saw the ridiculous boating pumps. (Turquoise, for crying out loud!) The liqueur made him slow, one beat after the event, so even as voices were being raised and he could make out Laura's among them, the first slap (hers) was being delivered. He was slow to rise out of his seat and never even saw the carefully telegraphed punch about six feet above the turquoise. That word again, 'puta', and then he was being kicked in the head, with all the mixed messages that an exposed ankle in a brawl could transmit. The voices trailed off then, the sweet sickly in his gut spilling out from one side of his mouth. He vaguely remembered being helped to his feet and spirited away past a wagon wheel of enquiry. Lots of faces, Spanish faces, not English ones, staring at him with no great anger. And then nothing.

'What happened?' he asked Laura, who had come back to bed as soon as she heard him stir. He had no idea how long she'd been sitting by the window in just a T-shirt.

'Hombre, te pegaron una ostia,' she said, making no effort to translate, somehow knowing the state of him made that unnecessary. Indeed, as D rubbed his jaw, it wasn't so much the what as the why which troubled him.

'You don't say,' he added sarcastically before remembering his manners. 'No, what I meant was, what was that all about? Who were they?'

Laura shook her head. 'I don't know, D. Just some gilipollas who want to act like tough guy. But they just silly little pijos. Vaya, colega, no pasa nada,' she said, trying to reassure herself as much as D. 'You feel better with some coffee. I make you some coffee. Anyway, I glad you not like that,' she went on, trying to make him feel better about being blindsided.

In truth, she couldn't think of anything else to say to him at that moment. She knew his silly pride was wounded. He'd been no use in the fight, and she'd had to take care of him. He didn't seem to mind when she took charge in bed, but out there, where people could see, he wanted to play another part, be the big man, defend her honour. Even where he barely knew when it was being called into question. If he'd just stayed in his seat it would have been fine, she was handling things. But it was that familiar male pride, all puffed up and misguided, which got the better of him. It was why he had a sore head now and why she found herself wondering whether this trip was actually a mistake.

D vaguely heard the sounds of air spurting out of the top of the pot. He could feel some bruising around his jaw, but other than that he appeared to have got off quite lightly.

'Oh, this is good,' he said, complimenting Laura on the strong, sugary coffee she'd handed him in what looked like a shot glass.

She nodded, not saying anything. Perhaps it *was* a mistake, she thought again, coming back here, assuming things would be different this time.

'Just what I needed,' said D to no one in particular, replaying the incident in his mind, trying to work out how he'd managed to get back up and beyond the range of the swivelling boat pumps.

'Feeling better?'

'Yeah, a little. A bit bruised on one side, but I'll live,' he quipped, hoping to make light of his embarrassment. 'Look, Laura,' he said, putting the glass down for a moment. 'I feel bad I didn't see it coming. Wasn't much use to you back there, was I?'

'Well we both still here, colega, so no worry about it,' she said, betraying no hint of the annoyance she'd been feeling for some time now. What the hell was all that Or Gay nonsense? Una tontería. It might have cost them dear, too, had that very same Jorge not waded in to the pijos with the wooden baseball bate. He barely said a word either, but several full arc swings of the bat later and the pijos were gone, clutching at legs and a weak-sounding promise to 'come back'. And once they'd gone he'd wasted no time pointing the two of them to the exit as well, even helping D back on to his feet to speed things up.

'No, I mean I didn't even realise there was a problem until it was too late. If I'd known, Laura, I mean if I understood what was being said, I could have done something.'

Laura looked at him, sitting up trying to work the angles, and briefly felt bad for him.

'Mira, hombre. It's no problem. We still here and the coffee taste good. Everything good.' Then, casting a lascivious eye at his shorts, she went on. 'When you finish coffee I make sure everything else working OK. ¿Vale?'

She saw the gratitude in his eyes, and in that moment knew that it was finished between them. Not right now, of course not. They still had a couple of days left before heading back to England. She'd show him the Semana Santa floats as they went by and the hooded-up devotees, and they would eat traditional pastries and D would no doubt comment on the Ku Klux Klan aesthetic of the pointy capes with the eye slits. Perhaps she'd even pretend that was the first time she'd ever heard something as witty about the costumes or she'd laugh just the way everyone liked, a warm, maja invitation to join her in her fragrant landscape. The way she'd been laughing when they first met, open and happy, no hint of trouble anywhere in the mask.

She'd carry on fooling him for a couple more days before their return to England with all the necessary solemnity, the better to convey the gravity of their situation. Of what they'd shared, a common but special bond, and claro, hombre, one which had now also been strengthened by the white heat of conflict. But a situation nonetheless which could no longer be about them *together*. She needed something more, an attitude to kick against, and there was just too much gratitude on display now. This boy could never seem to resist her charms, and a part of her hated him for it, saw it as weakness. It was challenge she craved, something hard won, not this wide-eyed wonderment of a child. Those were the lines she found herself rehearsing even before her hands snaked down his shorts. She couldn't help it (with the lines at least, and hated herself for thinking this way), but, as even the pijos had pointed out, once a puta...

Also, a promise was a promise.

D slept on the train for most of the journey down to Madrid. The bruising was still there and his left eye remained partially bloodshot, but Laura suspected (rightly) that he wasn't entirely displeased by this state of affairs. Campus life was all about the surface, and, at least while she wasn't around to contradict him, there was a war story or two in those blemishes. She saw no reason to spoil the fantasy. After all, that was the closest thing she knew to a cast-iron guarantee. Let a boy feel like a man, and his mind would start to play tricks on itself. It would lose its focus, revel in its newfound freedom.

She knew it was a filtration process, siphoning away negativity, and more than that she knew how it allowed for lapses in memory. Let him dine out on the fantasy, and all those things which reminded the boy of his inexperience would start to drift away. Well, maybe not permanently but at least long enough for a fresh set of possibilities to come flooding in. In that state, sad, flaccid managers became guapos and nobodies found their voice. And *that's* when this boy, when any of this army of lost boys who always seemed to be everywhere, would become putty.

Strangely enough, on this occasion she felt no joy at that knowledge. If in the past it might have been one way of gaining leverage over clients, who were always older than her and potentially a threat to her, she now felt a tinge of regret at how her mind processed data. She observed weaknesses, stored them away for future reference. Straying spouses, limp dicks, early finishers, all of the details useful, particularly in this country which had such a jones for appearance.

Coño. She'd even starting using that word after some frat boy with sandy hair and a prickly tongue, on a language exchange, who she doubted had ever been near una negra back in Boston but *had* been with her, tried to impress her with the worldly wisdom of his 'street' persona by telling her he had a 'jones for her pussy'. (Though she also noted how, as an early finisher, he never mentioned its evidently short-lived nature.) For all his brevity, there was still an arrogance about the yanqui. As though she should be grateful he'd chosen her. The money she took while he slept serving as only partial recompense for the inconvenience.

The bruised boy sleeping opposite her now couldn't have been more different, inasmuch as his vulnerability made her a little sad. And it was true, it was sadness not opportunity which she saw before her. She could just as easily take what she needed. But no, not from this boy, not this time. There *was* no need. He was only here at her behest; she'd seen just how many seconds he'd needed to agonise over that decision. And if there was gratitude in his eyes then it was for some other reason. Those weren't the hungry eyes of a predator or even the sad ones of the lonely. No, this boy just wanted to see and touch and feel without limit, and in those eyes was the wonder of a boy/man who was being allowed to do just that as if for the first time.

As she watched D sleep, the thought passed through Laura's mind that maybe none other than she, *Loww-ra from Howrah*, was finally losing the taste for the grand gesture, for the screaming and shouting, the dipping of pockets as if *that* was politics, was what made her an outlaw, thumbing her nose at the manifold hypocrisies of this place. The scholarship had certainly lessened the need for self-preservation. For working the angles and hugging the margins. In one way, though, the pijos were right. It was precisely the working of those angles which made her a puta in their eyes, and no amount of fancy foreign letters after her name was going to change that any time soon.

THE BOSS MAN

Valladolid 1982–3

ACTUALLY THE SCHOLARSHIP had in part come about through the working of those angles. Academic ones but without any of the trappings. School, high school, though she preferred to call it 'college'. Colegio, colega.

A boyfriend, his papá, un profesor en el instituto, and a random conversation one day over at this boyfriend's place. El Profesor home unexpectedly early that particular afternoon, his wife with relatives in Segovia. The boyfriend first blaming nerves then the ecology for an earlier reluctance to perform.

'No, Laura. Es que hace un calor que me está matando.' (The heat's killing me).

'¿Verdad?'

'¿Qué dices, Laura? No me cae bien.' (What are you saying, Laura? It just doesn't sit right with me.)

'What, me or the heat?'

The happy upshot, of course, when the key unexpectedly turned in the door, that Laura and the boyfriend could pretend that they'd been studying together. El Profesor, suspicious but knowing in these liberal times that suspicion on its own was no longer enough. Still, he thought, the truth would surely out with the simplest of prompting. Looking at his son sat there with a frown, he knew the little marica would not be troubling this girl. She on the other hand hadn't flinched when he'd held her gaze, introduced himself as Javier's father. El Papá. El Hombre con los Bigotes. The boss man. The Caudillo.

'Javier didn't mention he was bringing a friend home,' said El Profesor, fingering his moustache.

'I'm sure I did, P.'

Javier's objections were dismissed by a cursory wave of his father's hand. 'So who did you say you were again?' he asked, looking more closely this time at the girl, whose mere presence seemed to have cast lines on his son's forehead.

'Laura.'

'Laura?' he repeated, as if rehearsing the name for future reference.

'Sí, señor, Laura. We were studying for an exam.'

'I see,' said the boss man, by now faintly amused by the whole charade. 'So where are your books?'

'He was about to get them when you came in,' said Laura, already sensing Javier's presence shrinking away right in front of his father. 'But we thought it was best to test each other first, see where there are gaps, and then look at the books.'

'Ah, I see,' said the boss man, genuinely enjoying these young people's discomfort at the difficult situation they found themselves in. 'Let me see if I understand you properly then. From what I'm hearing I take it you must have a very good memory, Laura, because I know when I ask my son to do something as simple as switch off the television he seems to struggle with that. Or are you telling me my son is secretly a genius? Is that what you're saying, Laura?'

Javier muttered 'gilipollas' under his breath. His father stopped, gave him a look whose only ambivalence was whether the consequences should be immediate or deferred. Laura saw that look too, felt it would be better to redirect the father's attention back to herself.

'No, señor. We were studying for an exam, and now we're not,' said Laura, annoyed at how El Profesor appeared to relish humiliating his son. She again held his gaze, but this time without too much conviction. Why bother, she thought, when the 'boyfriend' wasn't capable of defending himself, let alone anyone else? All that shit about the heat. He couldn't even bring himself to say, 'No, I don't want this, Laura. I don't want to pretend I'm interested in having sex with you. I'm only with you so the other boys won't think I'm a little marica.' And, of course, she could see now, even his father thought he was just that.

'And what is this exam in?' he asked, still a bit surprised at encountering a young person in his house who actually tried to offer some resistance to his self-styled authority.

Laura, who had been expecting the question, made sure to briefly survey the shelves in the front room groaning with professorial tomes on military history, before answering, almost as a reflex, 'Engineering, señor.'

'Study' sessions were somewhat different after that. They rarely, if ever, took place at Javier's house now that his mother was back from Segovia. The other key change was that they no longer involved Javier.

The boyfriend. What a strange concept! Neither boy nor friend, really, but a little big man trapped in the language of his own oppression. She felt pleased with herself the day she came up with that, sat on the steps leading up to her colegio watching a group of Javier's classmates pestering two younger girls. The way she saw it, everyone knew their role and played along accordingly, from the girls themselves with their mock outrage quickly giving way to conspiratorial smiles, to the boys, unsure of every step but carrying on as though they were veterans.

As she watched their bravado inflate and inflate, the banter less and less playful, she was suddenly struck by the unhappiness of the scene. All that noise and blather when they'd surely be happier free of the expectation? And for what? Such a brittle exchange, little big men, stilts made of sand. She took in the loudness then the speed of the whole thing, how quickly it all fell apart. A withering put down, perhaps not even that, maybe something as simple as a look deflating the bubble, and then she noted how the sounds were instantly muted, a charade built of glass, so very thin, nothing really but little boys ground up in its fractions. She watched the missteps of this dance, promising herself that when her time came *those* would not be her rituals. She vowed that when she finally met a boy who she really liked, rather than the pijos she'd already grown to despise, it would not be like this, squeezed into a gap between learning and desire. And looking at their faces, the faces of these young boys, she saw nothing so much as their terror. So young and already something stricken in their rictus, braggarts made of sawdust.

'I think she likes you, tío.' (Boy 1)

'Claro. But the only question is, how much?' (Boy 2 indicating an obscene length with his hands.)

Laughter all round, a hollow sound, fooling no one, least of all each other.

Right at that moment it came to her. Yes, these boys were trapped, and would continue to trap one another in the language of their own oppression. And to think, these were the boys whose approval Javier was constantly seeking. She'd made the right decision to end things between them. It was the wisdom of what she'd done next that she wasn't so sure about.

The colegio was less than five minutes' walk from the university, and in her boredom at the antics of her peers, Laura had begun spending any free time she had or study periods in what she hoped would be the more joined-up environment of the main square adjoining several of the university faculties.

There was a fresquito that day, and she had in any case been considering a first venture inside the buildings, partly out of curiosity but mainly to escape the cold, when she spotted him. Though they'd met only the once, it was unmistakeably him. Moustache, briefcase, a green overcoat which was all business. It had been an instinctive decision to follow him, up a flight of stairs and down several dimly lit corridors. And without really knowing why, there she was, suddenly knocking on the door with the grandly titled nameplate: Miguel de la Fuente Escudero. Profesor.

THE DREAM AND
THE LIE

'Sí?'

He only looked up when she didn't respond, her nerve for once deserting her. When she continued to stand there, silently, in the doorway, an air of mild irritation came over the man. He lowered his reading glasses and took a longer look at the source of his aggravation. There was something familiar about her, but he couldn't quite place it.

'Look, I'm a little busy right now, and this isn't an office hour, so I'm not seeing any students,' he said, still trying to figure out where he'd seen that face before.

'Señor. You don't recognise me?' asked Laura, more in hope than expectation.

Señor. Of course! The girl who made his boy frown. Who'd looked him, Miguel de la Fuente Escudero, Profesor, in the eye and lied without blinking, holding on to the lie even when he'd given her the chance to come clean. And now this little whore was somehow at his place of work, in his office, standing there at the threshold of knowledge, once again desecrating the sacred pupil/master relationship with her insolence.

Though he tried, unlike his wife, not to get too caught up in the ongoing drama of his son Javier's adolescence, even he'd noticed how withdrawn the little marica had become these past weeks. And at the urging of his wife, now back from Segovia, he'd finally managed to extract from Javier the confession that, *no, they hadn't been studying that day, yes she's my girlfriend, or at least I thought she was, but now we've split up, and I'm so unhappy, I've been wanting to tell you for so long, Papá,* and he'd felt disgusted then,

El Profesor, thinking this is no way for a de la Fuente Escudero to behave, like a little marica, and he'd been grateful for the chance to cut the confession short before anything *really* damaging was said, holding his boy's tearful face to his chest, allowing his own feelings of contempt to dissolve into the snot and mucus patch the boy was creating on his, El Profesor's, brand-new shirt from El Corte Inglés.

'You know my son, Javier?' he asked, placing his glasses back in their case.

'Sí, señor. But that's not why I'm here,' said Laura, making sure to maintain eye contact.

'He's very upset right now. Do you have any idea why that might be?' he asked, less from any great feelings of paternal responsibility than because he sensed it was the right thing to say. It was, he felt, what would have been expected from a man of his intelligence and good breeding at a moment like this.

'I'm very sorry to hear that,' said Laura, 'but, as I was saying, that's not why I'm here.'

El Profesor spread a thumb and forefinger the length of his moustache, taking in the girl who still hadn't moved from the doorway and at the same time absorbing the contents of the shelving directly to one side of the door, neatly packed with a roll-call of military tacticians and the just plain shrewd: Confucius, Sun Tzu, Machiavelli, Mishima, though he had mixed views on the latter, at one and the same time admiring his devotion to a political cause yet repulsed by the homoerotic excess which seemed to underpin his faith in fascism. El Caudillo had been different, he was sure of it. There was none of that degeneration into sexual depravity that he felt characterised your typical Oriental. The Falangists were of good stock, pure stock, like him, and they'd shown how to deal with the depravity. Lorca and the other faux-Gypsy cocksuckers, oh yes, they'd been dealt with alright. Order and authority, they were the only things people really wanted. Sure, they said they wanted freedom, but to do what? Jugando parchís, like Javier, while the real men, like his father, went out to work. His son. The little marica, who he'd caught out more than once playing with himself looking straight at the Real Madrid pretty boys on his wall. In the searing heat of summer opting to shut himself away with two-dimensional fantasy rather than ever play the game or, in yet another sense which stretched way beyond football, be part of the game, of boys and girls and youthful ambition. But no, in his house, this little senator fiddled while all around him Rome burned.

'Go on,' said El Profesor, finding his eyes drawn, in spite of his good breeding, to the generous profile of Laura's breasts under her sweater.

'I wanted to ask you something,' she said, growing a little bolder now that she saw she had his full attention. 'I was talking with Javier one time, and he mentioned that you are a military historian.'

El Profesor looked at her face again. He motioned to her to take a seat, and she did so without closing the door.

'Well, anyway, we have to do a history project, and I want to do mine on military engineers and their role in transforming modern Spanish society. How they have helped build the Spanish economic miracle. Something like that. So I was wondering if I could maybe ask you some questions about that. I'm interested in the links between history, science and economics. But my teacher thinks I'm being too ambitious. That's what he says. So anyway, I hope you don't mind, but that's why I'm here, señor.'

This girl was the same age as his son, but it was as though they existed in entirely separate worlds. The way she spoke, the ambition in those sentences, those ideas, he'd never encountered anything of the sort with his own flesh and blood. And how she held his gaze, that, too, was unfamiliar. Where the marica would obsess about the tiniest details, the ephemera of a half-life, *he said, she said, no but you said, but you did, this is what you said, I know because I wrote it down* (what kind of a coño kept a diary, anyway?), it was clear that this girl was concerned with bigger questions, of structure, context, outcome. Engineering and economics, form and content. It was all there in her proposal. How are things actually made and then how do those constructions alter what a society can be in terms of its own sense of its possibilities? As far as he could tell, the role of military engineers in all this *was*, of course, their traditional one as scientific soldiers, but he felt she was intimating something more than that in how she had chosen to describe them as 'transformative' figures. Yes, there was an implication there, perhaps even an invitation, to unscramble the text which had somehow formulated itself in her head.

She had clearly been reaching out to someone of his breeding, his expertise, to help her decode the message. A snap analysis, honed over many years of departmental infighting, suggested to his professorial mind that this was an enquiry of two halves. First, a conceptual framework of engineering and economic miracles, achieved by the limit figures of science and military planning, but, underpinning that, a concern with aesthetics and form. With the imposing of scientific order and an unsentimental authority on chaos and thereby with the attainment of progress. That, surely, was the unspoken in all this, he thought, as his mind wandered again to her breasts.

Señor.

He never heard that word at home, and, to be honest, it was rare to hear it any more even in the cloistered environment of his work. Every now and then perhaps from one of the largely silent army of cleaning ladies who he'd occasionally encounter for an awkward moment if he had reason to be in the department exceptionally early. But other than that, not from anyone who actually mattered. So, *never* from colleagues or graduate students, and, come to think of it, not even from first-year undergraduates, who he seemed to recall being more deferential in the past. Of course, he knew that this was partly also due to the limited engagement he had with such minnows now. A fringe benefit of his rise to profesor and the well-received monographs on the historical foundations of modern Spain, was the option, when he eventually returned from handsomely funded research-leave sabbaticals, of cherrypicking which courses to teach. Which inevitably resulted in greatly diminished contact with undergraduates in favour of the less easily cowed but clearly also less imbecilic postgraduates. Though he'd be lying if he said he didn't occasionally miss the stupefied deference to authority which still persisted with a dwindling minority of the undergraduates. Profesor was fine, but in these corridors little more than a job description really.

Señor on the other hand, now that actually meant something. That was the country of the permiso marital, of respect for authority, when the word of a man like himself carried a certain weight. And his wife would have needed to seek his permission every time she wanted to run away to her sister in Segovia, to bitch and moan about her unhappy marriage and her unhappy son who, by the way, never seems to leave his room even when the weather's good, and the life she should be enjoying but can't, *not with that man, he's a monstro, thinks he can do what he likes just because he has money*. That's right, cariña, my money, my rules. Not quite boss man, jefe, and definitely not at the level of Caudillo, but not bad anyway, a gravitas in the designation. She'd never really understood. All he'd asked for was some gentle indulgence. Instead, she'd presented him with a little marica and the nagging sense that life was passing him by.

El Profesor provided Laura with books and a work schedule. They would meet once a week in his office to discuss the progress she was making with her project. She learnt about the tripartite elements of combat engineering, strategic support and ancillary support, which was the lot of military engineers during wartime. She learnt of the crucial role that engineers played in the development of hydroelectric power and of contingency plans to deal with pollution control. And if it came as no surprise to learn that they were crucial in nurturing road and rail communications, as well as in the construction of airfields and depots, then the role played by military engineers in coordinating disaster relief was somewhat at odds with the picture that Laura had been building up of a tribe of cold, dispassionate technicians. El Profesor noted that discrepancy, too, sitting back in his chair with a satisfied look then, apparently taking an exaggerated pleasure in telling her, 'No man is purely made of steel, Laura. Sometimes you'd be surprised at how much humanity is washed up inside of those men. They are the ones who have to carry everyone else's weakness, so they have no time for their own, Laura. If you knew you wouldn't be surprised at how much those men feel. If you only knew.'

It sounded good to his ears, and he knew she enjoyed listening to him when he was in this kind of expansive mood. In its own way, he speculated, this had to be as exciting for her as learning about the Manhattan Project, about the pioneers of the H bomb, or the early-warning radar systems had once been for him. Personally, though, he had more of a hard-on for the original 1960s intercontinental ballistic missile bases. The vision, the planning, the sheer chutzpah of it all. Ah, they did things differently back then, there was no doubt about that, he thought wistfully, another long-forgotten memory beginning to stir below eye level.

Laura sensed a shift in the conversation then, from content back to form. Men built of steel and dreams, the move away from pylons to particles. In El Profesor's sentimental analysis she heard that these men carried a lot of hidden depth within them, that they shouldered everyone else's burden, and for what? So that the peasants in Murcia, in Andalusia, in every other godforsaken backwater of this nation, could finally stop clicking castanets and calling it culture. So that they could enjoy clean water and decent roads and, these days, *Miami Vice* on their colour televisions, too. Just below the surface of all that cabling, she considered the interconnectivity of this new place, its logic finally joined up. Wires and cathode rays the holy sacrament. The new high priests swapping cassocks for overalls, and what she heard, right there, in El Profesor's words, was that he saw himself as belonging to *this* tribe.

She saw, briefly, as El Profesor wanted her to see. Him, one of those visionaries, a man of steel, but made of dreams, too, the metal bent out of shape by the pioneering weight of history. She saw the statement moustache and the tomes on his shelves, and in his plaintive words she heard a plea for the enduring power of those dreams. In their filter she saw dust particles suddenly fusing into a giddy mosaic, El Caudillo vanquishing the rebels, Morocco just the dress rehearsal for dealing first with the Asturian miners and then with everyone else who stood in his way. But through this filter she saw how it was not really *his* way, how there was no choice, how it was, in fact, the way of history, of progress, of the future. *He* was just the instrument, and yet there were people who still refused to see that. She saw Guernica, but this time not as a crime scene, rather as art and as staging post for the inevitable triumph of superior air power. The Dream and the Lie, as with all men of dust, drilled through mountains and across valleys, connecting the body parts, the bellic canvas and the artist's studio, the Murcians and the Basques. She saw in the way she was required to see, this country, where she would sit her school finals, or rather she saw its dispersed clans arrayed before her like a collection of unruly spectators. And the only one providing them with a vision, stretched to breaking point to cover their vast expanse of doubt, was a man just like El Profesor, shouldering their burden because, well, someone had to. She saw that, too.

Something Less
Than A Man

IT HURT. WHEN El Profesor finally entered her, he did so from behind, his breath damp and heavy on her neck, the thrusts growing more rapid, a *Ribera del Duero* halitosis supplying its own twisted commentary, the emphasis rising and falling with each stroke.

'And *now*, like the engineers, I'm assisting a less developed region with its power needs. And *now* I'm searching out new territories. And *now* I'm immersed in exploitation of the seabed, and now, yes *now*, finally, I-I-I, yes me, *El Señor, El Jefe, El Caudillo*, I'm exploring the moon and deep space. *Immerse*, and explore, and *immerse*, and, and, and ex-pLOOOOORE!'

She felt sick, a rumour of stale grape clinging to her skin. But by the time she'd put her clothes back on, after they both had, and she saw him standing there, a recently engorged example of Catholic morality, not really sure what to do with the evidence of the sagging and contradictory condom in his right hand, it wasn't really sickness she held on to.

She knew she ought to be angry, or at any rate angrier than she was. The entire experience had been unpleasant, if not entirely unexpected. In truth, she'd known from the start that this was a possibility, and it hadn't deterred her. He had taken advantage of her, but then again he wasn't the first. She'd been with boys before, well, maybe not with his marica son, but there had been others, guapos, too, though they hadn't gone all the way. She knew what a cock looked and felt like, that wasn't the first time she'd seen or touched the throbbing vein or the bulbous head. She knew alright, but they hadn't gone all the way because they were boys, beach kings, and if it was night she could still see that they were scared, even more scared than her, in the muted quickness of their breathing, though *they* were the locals and she was the vallisoletana on her own and out of her depth next to the sea. Whether that was fear of getting caught and of what might happen then or fear of the thing itself, she couldn't be sure. But they *were* scared, and she could almost sense their relief when searchlights started to pick out the upturned boat so that their scramble up the beach to freedom could no doubt credibly be replayed at some later date (at least for one another's benefit) as a heroic act.

This cagón, though, with his caballero fantasies. She knew the play, had read it in translation last year. This was no *Pygmalion*. He was no Higgins. That professor didn't have a marica for a son, and she doubted he was a fascist. No, this cagón had shown no fear. But he would, she'd make sure of that.

The third, or maybe the fourth, time that he fucked her, he insisted on the missionary position. She made herself look at his face, despite every instinct telling her to keep her eyes shut. As he entered her and found his rhythm, she made a slight adjustment which travelled up from her diaphragm into her expression, but the boss man was already lost to his reverie. Some mierda this time about the rewriting of history and the ingratitude of the surrealists, and though his eyes were open she could see they weren't really looking at her. Enrojecidos, full of the blood and fury of history, of life, of the moment and the peculiar burden it exerted on a man of action, a man of vision, a man of good breeding and thwarted ambition. A man in other words much like himself, El Señor, El Jefe, El Hombre con los Bigotes, Profesor de la Fuente Escudero, Caudillo, Hombre de Díos. His rhythm grew more intense as he decried the disloyalty of the artists. Barefaced treachery! Picasso only ever breaking free of that Slavic whore to pour scorn on the men with true vision. Dalí fooling no one with those disgusting scribbles and that pencil moustache. Un francés! And Buñuel, este hijo de puta, the worst of the lot. Pornografía!

Laura felt physically sick. She felt the weight of El Profesor inside her probing around to no great effect. His cock was surprisingly big, and it was fat, fatter than those boys on holiday, and now she felt it redoubling its efforts to leave an impression. El Profesor reminded her of the mandrill she had recently seen on a nature documentary, engorged and swollen and, in that moment, oblivious to anything but its own needs.

His breath was fetid, worse than before, and when he spoke the stagnation hit her full in the face.

'The Basque country, and the Catalans. Those hijos de la gran puta with their Gaudí and their false memories,' he rasped, and that was definitely the word he used, 'falsas', yes, she remembered that, because he kept saying it over and over, impervious to the look of growing nausea on her face, senses battered by successive waves of stale, each one the prelude to El Profesor thrusting ever more spitefully into a silent void.

The man of good breeding took her silence to signify that she had been rendered speechless, and it came as no surprise to him, given what he assumed must have been, for her, the sheer ecstatic communion of his actions. But, in truth, this thought was barely even fleeting. He paid little attention to anyone but himself; occasionally, if he felt his desire waning, willing images into his head of El Caudillo in full military regalia on horseback. The effect was immediate, staving off any unwelcome feelings of doubt about the wisdom of what he was doing, and the ambivalence that that might otherwise have instilled in his magnificent cock, which he felt sure that even a non-believer could see was a gift from above. In his mind's eye he saw El Caudillo at the top table, doing deals with the most powerful men in Europe, and then back in Madrid, implacable, adored, a father figure to the whole nation, firm but fair, and so firm, firm, firm.

Then he saw the sash fall from El Caudillo's shoulder, and just as quickly El Caudillo was an old man, increasingly distant from the gibberish of the spectators who stretched back as far as the eye could see from the old man's balcony. More concerning, however, he could see the pylons, his project, those dreams of order and progress, suddenly corroded by rust, all the old doubts resurfacing, and such little gratitude from the masses. Where once there was steel, now only dust. And no respite to be found anywhere. Even the spaces of leisure sinking into filth. El Retiro full of queers, among them his marica son. The girl, too, she was there some- where, another corruption, another ingrate. His project, her project, blending into a shapeless mess. A loss of form and order and all the old doubts resurfacing. When he tried to picture El Caudillo again, all he could pick out this time was dust, a hazy, indeterminate blanket of dust. Men made of dust. Hecho polvo. Echar un polvo. Form dissolving before his very eyes, blood and bone withdrawing their conviction. He saw the girl looking at him through the particles, really looking at him, as though he were something less than a man. An unfamiliar form, perhaps, or even some kind of a primate. She spoke then, and, as she did so, he realised she hadn't made a sound throughout.

'¿Ya estás?' she asked in a tone he hadn't really heard before and didn't much care for.

He looked at her, and even in his post-coital state of delusion, was disturbed when he registered what could only be described as the contempt virtually dripping off her. He nodded silently, remov- ing his cock with its spent furies.

The bigger shock, though, was when he looked up again and saw that they were not alone. His son Javier was standing in the doorway, and this time El Profesor noted that the little marica had no problem making full eye contact with his father.

Arrangements

THINGS MOVED QUICKLY after that. Laura was amazed at how efficiently the wheels of industry could be made to function with the right sort of prompting. In a city where she'd grown accustomed to the endless delays, the lost paperwork and a hundred other reminders at the municipal level that she was one of the little people, she wasn't really prepared for this. The change in fortune first hinted at by the sudden approval and installation of not one but two telephone landlines in her parents' flat. The work completed by the engineer with the kind of courtesies rarely expected of workmen in that neighbourhood. And not only that, but completed with a fulsome apology that it hadn't been done earlier, the 'hasta luego, señora' blending well with the 'usted' this and 'usted' that of the installation.

Still, if those were the smaller changes, they nonetheless transformed her home life, the effect most fully felt when she came back from classes and was no longer bombarded with questions about when she intended to find a job or, as had previously been the case, walked in holding her books only to be met with a resentful silence in this house of few books. Suddenly her parents wanted to know all about her studies and the mysterious benefactor. They asked about El Profesor who had taken such an interest in the academic abilities of their daughter, to the effect that he had written personal letters of recommendation on her behalf to various powerful people and scholarly institutions. And when they asked, she answered as she always did, that she had only come to the attention of El Profesor because his son Javier was a classmate of hers. She guessed he must have mentioned something in passing to his father about the excellent grades she had been receiving for some time now, and then one day when El Profesor came to the colegio to see Javier, he spoke to her, too, as she happened to be waiting with his son at the time. She made it clear to her parents that *he* was the one who insisted on helping, that *she* had never asked, and though that line initially stuck in the craw, she found that the lie grew easier over time. But the bit she always came back to, because she knew how well it would resonate, over and above her imputed academic abilities, was the telling detail that she, Laura, was now 'known' to 'powerful people and scholarly institutions'. Her parents seemed disproportionately impressed by this, and it made her despise them even more than she already despised herself for letting that disgusting man put his disgusting thing inside her. Or long before that, for never saying anything when faced with her parents' silence, their sourness never really about the books but about whatever else she might have been getting up to beyond the neighbourhood. Rumours starting to spread about a wayward schoolgirl and the depraved goings on in a pijo flat overlooking the Pisuerga. She'd wanted to scream so many times, 'But Papá! You've always been fucked by fascists, too. At least I'm getting something out of it.' But the words never came, perhaps because she could taste how weak and hurt and helpless her parents felt in the silence. Her father the clerk, her mother the dressmaker, their faces worn down by the classificatory logic of this place. El Caudillo long gone but here the Falangist circuitry still the only one that mattered. And if you were one of the little people, which her parents undoubtedly both were, then you learnt to make no fuss even when repairs were shoddy or goods and services non-existent. Within the higher echelons, franquismo still burned bright in this city, and she had always known, even before she experienced it, that this was also something to do with knowing your place. Learning to live with disappointment while others flaunted their entitlement. To goods, services, gratification of every kind. Retired colonels and their highly active pijo sons. Senior municipal figures, highly respected academics. El Profesor had helped her to see things differently, or at least that was the impression she let him have. Then again, she also let him believe that he was her first, her guide, her salvation. And once she had forced herself to look at him in the throes of presumed ecstasy and seen that his eyes were, in fact, closed, she knew then that he would never really see what was actually taking place right under his nose.

Arrangements would be made and a scholarship would soon follow, but for now she knew that as far as her family was concerned, proof enough of their newfound status rested in two immaculately installed landlines.

Never Really
Understood

D WOKE UP not long before the train pulled into Chamartín station. He saw Laura looking at him and wondered how long she had been sat there like that.

'How long was I asleep?' he asked her.

'As long as you need,' she said, an indulgent smile playing around her lips.

'No, I meant have I been sleeping all this time?'

'I know what you mean, D. It's OK, we nearly there now.'

She was beautiful, anyone could see that. Dark hair and dark jeans and no need to dress any of it up. His eyes moved from her face to her neck and down to that collarbone which he loved to trace with his fingers. He didn't feel embarrassed around her, about letting her know *how* he liked it and where. And if she was at all embarrassed by any of it, then D certainly wasn't aware of that. He was so glad they'd made this trip. They'd really connected, and she was right, this place was nothing like campus. He could see now why people said what they did about travel broadening the horizons. He'd never really understood that up to now, beyond a vague sense that he desperately needed to get away from the place he'd grown up in, but this was different. They'd shared something special here, and he felt in no small measure that that was down to the change of scenery. Other than southeast London, where everyone largely talked nonsense, he'd never been somewhere before where people spoke a different language, where they listened to different music and, yes, where they even drank beer and watched football in a different way. And it surprised him how much of a weight seemed to be lifted from his shoulders by being around those simple changes. Yes, he was a foreigner here – what was the word they used, oh yeah, guiri. Yes he was a guiri here, but not in that dank, oppressive way that he had always been a guiri, even back among the natives in Bermondsey. Here he just didn't know the words, but that needn't be a permanent state of affairs. People were more open here, unless, of course, they were kicking you in the head, but he still wasn't entirely sure why that had happened, and a part of him felt it could have just been a case of mistaken identity. He'd not seen those responsible since, and, in fairness, those boat pumps were a far cry from fifteen-hole lace-ups and the kinds of kickings dished out all over Britain for as long as he could remember. Frankie Beverley was right, he thought, as he checked on the extent of the bruising around his mouth. These were the joys and pains of existence, something he felt he was finally starting to embrace with his belated devil-may-care approach to life. That other cliché, too, about the birds loving a bit of impulsiveness in a man, that seemed to be true as well, he thought, his first journey abroad happily coinciding with the best sex he'd ever had.

She dumped him almost as soon as they got back to England, the last leg of the journey, from London to Coventry, spent in stony silence. Spring was over.

PART TWO

SOAK

London, 2008

WHAT THE HELL happened? How did I end up here? Why is there sawdust in my hair? The big philosophical questions in other words, as I'm strongly 'encouraged' to leave the premises before further action is taken.

'Get that soak out of here,' says the landlord as though I am not really there, or at any rate not sufficiently compos to follow the simple instruction.

Further action?! What do these people take me for? Some kind of a social problem, like a leaking pipe, which can be fixed with 'further action'? Cunts. I'll give *them* a leak, I think, only half managing to unzip before the system malfunction ends in a warm background torrent liberally soaking my strides. And then I *am* being forcibly ejected, laughing all the way as my impromptu movers are greeted by my urine shaker. The movers, both volunteering themselves from the landlord's favoured inner circle of daytime drunks, take just that bit longer to react than less seasoned types. The first, attempting a grip near my shins where the trousers are flapping wildly, initially seems puzzled by the difficulty of this manoeuvre. His digits, struggling then slipping, eventually process the liquid data and the look of wanton bliss on my face.

'The dirty bastard! He's only gone and pissed himself,' he observes, more in sadness than reproach, but I can tell he's still hoping for something more than the agreed free pint from the landlord for his troubles. I've been seeing that look more and more of late, and it usually follows some relegation of me, myself and the other bit to the third person.

That soak, dirty bastard, him.

I know how they think.

The invisible man, *if we can't see him, then he's not really there. And how can someone who doesn't really exist have feelings anyway? But Jesus, he stinks! How long do you reckon this one's been dodging the soap?* But at least those complaints still register some kind of presence even if it is a bit remote. The worst occasions, really, are when I overhear strangers muttering 'It's a shame' or just shaking their heads as if I'm some kind of a charity case. That's the only time it really gets to me, makes me want to turn around and, and, and, what was that thing I once read and would then wheel out at the drop of a hat? Ah yes, of course, I remember now. Those words. I don't even have to go hunting for them. They must have been there the whole time, hardly buried at all, perfectly pickled along with everything else. It makes me want to spin around and *really inspect the virtues of their theories and methods.*

'Now look here, squire,' I might open up with, making sure to keep the body language under control. 'I don't make a habit of public disputation, but you, sir, are an ass!'

I'll try not to point, and hopefully the requisite three-foot gap between us will be sufficient to parry the all-day-drinking fumes in the direction of Professor Anthony Giddens and his much vaunted 'Third Way', now more commonly known as the gutter. That's right, Giddens, the dustbin of history. But I know I'm right about this. Kingsway is just over there, and the London School of Economics, where he came up with all that shit, is but a stone's throw from this hostelry.

'Oh yes, you heard right, my friend, I was indeed referring to the Emeritus Professor of something a little bit private, a little bit public. AC/DC, which I bet you know all about, don't ya?'

And, of course, now I'll be jabbing and pointing at the roundly appalled liberal interventionist who wished he'd never shaken his head in the first place. By this stage he'll be looking away, pretending he can't hear me, hoping that if he carries on as if I'm not there, then I really *will* become an invisible man. But even I know an invisible man doesn't carry this level of reek, so I must be here, because it's true, oh *bejesus*, so it is, my stink is so out of control it might even be described as having an 'artistic' temperament. And if *I'm* here, and my skid-row aroma would strongly seem to suggest that I am, then the interventionist isn't getting off quite so lightly.

'Hello, hello. Hello! Yes, friend, that's right, I'm talking to you. No, don't look away. I know you can hear me. I can see your ears twitching. Don't be scared, I only want to talk. It doesn't bite. I just want to talk!'

Did I really just refer to myself as 'it'? Surely not, but of late it's so hard to tell. Everything's a bit of a *tontería*, it's all just so *unheimlich*, if you get my drift? Don't get me wrong, the special DVD extras with running commentary aren't my bag either, but the pause button's a bit fucked these days. Actually, come to think of it, the play's not too clever either, *but don't run away, friend, they're just buttons. They can be fixed. It can all be fixed. Trust me, I just want to par-lay avec vous.*

By now, he'll be wrinkling his nose and praying I don't notice, but he's not been paying attention: I said I was invisible not blind. I'll tease him that way, oh yes I will, because I *am* a little naughty, and besides, I've rediscovered the taste for this kind of thing, him nodding away, diligently agreeing with all and sundry, no matter how steeped in bullshit; by this stage I can see he'll agree with anything really so long as it makes the reek go away. And I'll seize upon this weakness, of course I will, because the other thing it transpires that is also perfectly pickled along with my liver is some primal attachment to a row (only an intellectual one, mind).

'Are you saying I'm not really here?' I'll ask the appalled interventionist, and he'll wonder what he needs to do to make this nightmare go away. 'Because my stink begs to differ, friend. I'm here, it's here, and you better start getting used to us. Oh yes, friend, here's the good news: we ain't going nowhere!'

I'll never reach the bit about Freud or sexuality (his, appalled interventionist's, rather than the good doctor's), and I'll never get to tell him how I could have been a contender, how, briefly, I was. He'll never get to hear about the first-class joint-honours degree and the campus-bred culture wars. He'll be deprived of the knowledge that I was once a risk analyst par excellence, that all the money bags would wait for me, like the man from Del Monte, to give them the signal before acquiring or dumping stock. And all of this right here in this City, just up the road, in fact. And if I was one of the first, then I was far from the last to be frog-marched off the premises. He won't get to hear that either, how these eyes, like Laura Mars, can see disaster ahead. How it's all happening again, the collapse at Lehman Brothers and the domino effect everywhere else. All he sees is a soak, a paraffin, and like so many others he's fooled by the surface. The elasticated waistband, the highly niche bodily ferment. And even if I were to tell him, he'd never believe me. I'm a soak not stupid. I see what's happening here. Faye Dunaway sees, and so do I. All this money, these stone gargoyles, their finances, all of it built on castles of sand. I talk to Faye about this sometimes, Laura, too. Laura Mars, a voice from the past, from space, not from Howrah. Ah, fuck it, that'll be pause and play again. That voice, those eyes, they're so familiar. But from where? Mars, Howrah, the past. They snuck in unnoticed sometimes, and it makes me sad. Like Laura, these eyes have seen plenty. Too much even, lives boxed up and discarded, the only figures that seem to count those on a screen; decimal points and futures heading east and then south. Or is it the other way round? But none of it matters because he won't be listening anyway. By now his nose will be wrinkling, and he'll be hoping, praying, that the reek, of failure of loss of precisely that life that went both south and east, will soon leave him in peace. *We come in peace, we leave you in pieces!* But that's not it either. Never was. Mythopoesis easier to grasp than safety nets or bottles. For this soak, here and now, for me, myself and I, for the father, the son and the other fella, it's no use at all. We just want to shout, 'we've seen things, my friend, things no mytho-poet, or perhaps every mythopoet, should see. Fraud and ambition and hubris and greed. And we've tasted the lust and the

130

pointlessness of it all. The lies and the love that turned out to be lies. And you know what, my friend? We're still here, but those boys at Lehman ain't. So what does that tell you? We're spirit made flesh. Duppies, djinns rising from the ashes of remaindered stock. They tried killing us off before, but it never works. Once, twice, three times a lady, but you don't really see me, do you? This is just a fever dream, and we're the clowns they never sent in. It's soulless really, the executive function, and in the end that's why they'll never succeed. In one shape or form, duppy, djinn, *D Train*, we'll still be part of this place long after their monuments have evaporated, as though they were never really here at all. The executive function, never learnt how to play, how to be playful. Always so brittle while we morphed south of their disdain. Soulboys, sticksmen, sharp tongued and seekers. We were always learning to play dead, you see, from the bombsites to the class-rooms to the trading floors. Even when we fought, we played, and then we fought again. And if money came and went, then style, my friend, was permanent. Oh, I know what you're think-ing. You ain't so stylish now. But this isn't really me, squire. You see that, don't you? Please tell me you see that much. No? Don't give me that look, squire. We speak this way, tongues loosened by drink. But we've always spoken this language, my friend. South of the drink, all mixed up, free of your stink! He'll start to physically move away then, ears still stinging with my Babel. So he'll never really know what we knew all along. The Mithraic temple, subsiding once more under the weight of its own lies. He won't spare a thought for the cracks in the system that no one could have predicted and ...

'Oi, fella, careful! That's my pissy Lois you're manhandling!'

I land heavily on the pavement, but an impressively high Guinness intake cushions the blow. I lie there and laugh, woozy but unbowed. It's a good joke, I think, the one about my urine soaked trousers, but even in this state I can see that it's lost on the landlord's pet, bloody teacher's pet, with his free pint in the offing. A nice play on words, I think, 'my pissy Lois', before I remember that these are not Lois. Far from it. These have an elasticated waistband. And then it hits me: the only things which will be fraying today are my nerves. I stop laughing. I am lying in the street soaked in my own waste. How did this happen? How did I get here? Like I said, the bigger questions.

POTTY MOUTH

South London, late 1970s/early 1980s

THEY MADE LISTS, him and his brother when they were both still
living at home. But D never really took them seriously, never
actually wrote anything down. Not like his brother. He remembered him sitting there, pen and paper at the ready, making notes
during the Wimbledon final. Borg v McEnroe became Fila v
Tacchini. Fila Bj tracksuit top, Diadora Borg Elite trainers. And on
the other side, Tacchini top, Nike trainers. Though the one thing
they could both agree on was that the third spoke in the wheel, the
other left-hander, Connors, was a bit of a wally. Whether or not it
was true, he came across as a typical brat in all that 1881 Cerruti
clobber, and if the telly was anything to go by, it wasn't just them
who thought so. The flame-haired New Yorker with the potty
mouth didn't seem to like the other left-hander much either. In any
case that wasn't the point. Not round here.

Nobody from this neck of the woods was about to sign up any
time soon for the good ship Fauntleroy moored all the way down
in SW19. It wasn't about that, dipping strawberries in cream and
happily paying through the nose for the privilege. No, the same
notepad which faithfully recorded which, and whose, items were
Fila or Tacchini already had a page dedicated to golf – Pringle, Lyle
& Scott, Braemar jumpers – with a footnote concerning Harrods.
Namely, that it was good for Pringle and Lacoste (crocodile),
whereas Lillywhites was better for all the tennis gear, including
Nike Wimbledons on its fabled fourth floor. There were detailed
entries about Ellesse ski jackets and Burberry macs. A whole
section given over to Adidas Tenerife and Trimm Trabs, the ones in
blue with the orange stripes, with the witty ascription next to it,

highlighted in red, 'rare as rocking-horse shit'. And somewhere, tucked away in this book of earthly delights, was the shocking inclusion of a name he'd never expect to find shrouded by the hallowed company of deerstalkers and Kangol hats: Pogo Paterson. Yes, *that* Pogo. *Grange Hill*'s very own flame-haired potty mouth, and next to that name three simple words which left D in no doubt about the attention to detail in this manor.

Fila velour tracksuit.

When the long arm finally caught up with his brother, the only surprise was that they didn't conduct a more thorough search of the premises. Else they might also have discovered the notebook which D had been 'looking after' for his brother – '*keep this somewhere safe and don't let anyone know*'. And the consequences would almost certainly have been more serious. What he remembered most about that day, though, wasn't his brother being led off by the uniforms or even the smug looks of 'I might have known' on one or two of the neighbours' faces.

No, it was something a lot easier to miss.

It was afterwards, the three of them sat wondering how to break the silence, the rare beauty of early-spring sunlight largely wasted on the scene. *That* was when he noticed his dad's arms rigidly tensed, fingers clamped around the tea mug like a drowning man with the last life raft on the ocean. The mug was full, yet the old man barely seemed to notice. Nobody spoke the entire time the tea just sat there, Dad's knuckles virtually popping out of his flesh. Only after the brew had finally gone cold did his Dad torment his lips with the tepid murk, expression unchanged. *That* was the moment he knew. D took the decision there and then that whatever else he did from here on in, French and Italian sportswear in their illicit transactional form would not be his Achilles heel.

SHORT, SHARP SHOCK

THE OTHER BIG surprise round about this time was that Conrad turned out to be, in the immortal words of Ian Dury, a 'right clever bastard'.

In between taxing people for their lunch money and generally being an all-round menace in and out of class, he clearly also had a head for figures and numbers, and that seemed to have translated into several shockingly good O level grades. Not even CSEs but O levels, the proper ones, the ones he, D, had busted a gut to get through. Like D's brother, Conrad had also kept some kind of a ledger, but in his case it was purely in his head, as in mental.

As in *that mental cunt knows exactly how much he's owed and by whom, as well as how much he's already taxed them for.*

And it being a mental inventory, there was never really any proof, or at least not of the kind that could end in borstal. No chance, in truth, of him enjoying a short, sharp shock at Her Majesty's pleasure with the other apprentice crims. The upshot of which was the unhappy presence (for D, at any rate) of Conrad in his sixth form. That first day, when he showed up, it was definitely a shock. (What's *he* doing here?) And it must have shown, Conrad for once not saying anything but making another mental note, this time concerning the anxiety all over the white boy's boat.

Still, something seemed to have changed for him over that summer when they got their results. He was no longer D's (or any-one else's) tormentor-in-chief. It was as though the mere achieve-ment of outlasting everyone's lowly expectations of him had imbued him with a newfound respect for the learning environment. This revamped Conrad contributed in class, often quite eloquently, and every time he did so one or other of the loathsome hairies who seemed to have made it their life's work to masquerade as LEA teachers, acted as though *this* was the summit of their ambitions, the kind of case study that made it all worth while. This. A gifted black pupil from a troubled background thriving under their tutelage, proof positive, as if it was required, of what they'd been saying all along. That it was nurture not nature, something those politicians, the evil ones now giving the orders, would never understand. And they'd stand there at the front of the classroom, moral righteousness oozing from every unwashed pore, lecturing the rest of them about the credit crunch and the dangers of supply-side economics.

D often thought about countering their arguments with some of his own, but an instinctive sense that his thinking, the logic under-pinning his scepticism, was still a little too vague stymied his desire. Even so, the thoughts persisted, centred on a basic unease about the welfare state, which he shared his dad's misgivings about, and the kind of people who seemed to depend on it, and not because they were injured or sick. He thought about all the chancers pouring out of the towers, and not just the suicide one either, and he recalled how often he'd see them down the Post Office cashing in their dole chip and then, far from guarding the spoils, heading straight for the bookie's or the offie as if without a care. Then there were the ones who stepped straight back into a smart pair of wheels brazenly parked right outside. He wondered what kind of complicated personal financing or supply-side economics underpinned what to his eyes appeared to be an economic miracle. He knew the money from those cheques barely covered the price of a hubcap, and yet these motors, not all of them destined for the breakers' yard, kept appearing just outside the Post Office, regular as clockwork, on the same given day every fortnight.

There was that other thing, too.

He couldn't help but notice that an awful lot of these punters, the flashier ones, were black. Kitted out in a slightly different uniform, too. They seemed to favour Adidas, Puma States and the really heavy-duty wool-rich body warmers which to his *London-and-the-southeast* eyes looked like they really would have been better off staying put in the Bronx. He also started to notice the Gabicci knitwear with the suede trim around the neck and the collar. Not only that, the chaps who wore those often accessorised the look with something a little more sophisticated, say wide-brim hats and dark glasses, even in the middle of a London winter. Nothing D had so far experienced by the good graces of the LEA led him to believe that this type of punchy social observation would be welcomed in the lower-sixth learning environment, so he bit his tongue instead and prepared to endure yet another hippy sermon.

Things *were* a little different, though, to how they'd been before, there was no denying that. He noticed it first when Conrad sidled up for a general studies' class in a bright-red body warmer. Not only that. A thick gold chain and those sought-after Adidas with the shell toe. The whole look topped off with a chunky bracelet, appropriately enough customised with a giveaway 'C'. Gone were the bulging pockets of lunch-money loot, the mental inventory, the rapid calculations as to who owed what and where today's revenue stream could be optimised. Absent, too, that look of near-permanent envy which, in truth, was the hallmark of nearly all the suicide-tower residents. In its place an expression D had never previously associated with Conrad. Relaxed. Also, his accent had changed. That much became clear during the classroom discussion, predictably enough initiated by the hippy, on what he described as 'the social unrest' which had gripped the country just a couple of years back when everyone else was gearing up for the Royal Wedding of Big Ears and that Sloaney bird.

'Wha'? You mean the riots, star?' Conrad asked, the request for clarity delivered in some newfangled brogue which D suspected had something to do with the red romper suit.

'Yes, that's right – Conrad, isn't it?' said the hippy, pretending he didn't have nightly wet dreams about precisely this kind of 'social interaction'. 'The riots. Brixton, Toxteth, Handsworth, St Pauls, and not too far from here, Lewisham. On the one hand, the inner city in flames, on the other a lot of people more concerned about Diana's wedding dress. So what do we think that might be down to?'

All the way up to sixth form that sort of question would have been met with silence, like an upside-down Stalinism, no one wanting to be the first to outwardly demonstrate intelligence because that just wasn't the done thing around here. It used to drive D spare, was what made him blurt out 'thirty-two' that one time in class. Was in no small measure why he knew he had to get away from this place. Now, though, the very source of much of that earlier Stalinism was magically transformed into a pillar of Socratic wisdom, embracing the discursive possibilities of being a 'thinker'. Conrad was on a roll.

'The people, them rise up against the shitstem. Cyan only be downpress' by Babylon fi so long, and then wha' bubble up from below unleash the fire of the oppress' above.'

'Go on,' said the hippy, barely able to contain his excitement. *This* was why he taught in a tough inner-city school. He thought how he could just as easily have gone to Godalming, how badly they'd wanted him there, down in Surrey, but, no, he'd insisted on taking this position instead. He was proud of himself for sticking to his guns. Here he could actually make a difference, and to kids who clearly didn't have anyone else fighting their corner. And, of course, he was aware of the problems with discipline (as in a lack of) and attainment, but if anyone could turn that around... Besides, every time he went back to see his parents and was met with the pitying looks on their faces – which, come to think of it, was something he also encountered on a more regular basis with his girlfriend – it simply redoubled his desire to get back to south London and the red-hot crucible of ideas he was helping to foster there. Which, for all its innovation, somehow never seemed to translate properly beyond the school gates.

Conrad, as ever, was very aware of his surroundings. The reified atmosphere of sixth form had filtered out most of the other blacks. Now it was basically just him, a couple more, but the quieter ones (Africans, probably) who he'd never had much to do with and who definitely didn't come from any of the towers. Other than that, some Chinks, or maybe Vietnam, he couldn't tell. A Paki, just because there was always at least one in any given classroom, and the rest of them white as his fresh shell toes.

'Well it might have surprise' some people, but if you downpress' fi four 'undred year it no surprise fi you, na mean?'

But you've only been here ten minutes, D thought. What's all this four hundred years shit? And what is it with that accent? The closest you've ever been Jamaica, my friend, is a jaunt up to Peckham, and I know for a fact that you're banned from all the African shops up there for being a half-inching scrote. So give the fake consciousness stuff a rest, eh? He didn't actually say any of it though. Just sat there and sulked while a blonde girl called Sarah who'd only recently moved to the area pitched in with something about the 'white establishment and racism'.

Bedroom Eyes

'THERE'S A PATIENT by the name of Con-er-raddd,' whispered the eponymous artist to Sarah as they shared the headphones on his brand-new Walkman.

It wasn't exactly a whisper though, the decibels sufficiently out of sync to alert anyone else in that classroom who possibly cared that the white girl was being hipped to the exotic delights of the 'Cool Ruler', Gregory Isaacs, and to a whole heap more besides. Romper suit had recently taken to wearing Farah trousers and Bally shoes, and his hair was beginning to grow out into little picky locks, all of which had left his teachers (and Sarah) in little doubt that there was also an organic political shift taking place here, marrying the primal scream of Rasta with the materiality of Babylon shitstem.

Actually, it wasn't his teachers or Sarah whose poise was unsettled. Of late, D was frequently annoyed by his trains of thought, more often than not supplying an unwanted inner commentary on the flowering classroom romance. He had no idea whether the teachers even cared or viewed things, as he did, through the narrow prism of guilt and opportunity, where whitey was always presumed guilty and darkie, in this case, Conrad, made hay with the resultant opportunities. For sympathy, attention, girls.

'Only you alone can quench this-ah thirst,' they hymned in unison, fixing each other with knowing bedroom eyes which certainly invited comment, though none, of course, was forthcoming. Instead, they were left to it, a certain indulgence afforded these multicultural pioneers in an otherwise self-contained, largely inbred environment.

If his threads were anything to go by, money was clearly no longer a problem for Conrad. That came as something of a relief for D. In that respect things had definitely changed, and for the better. At least now the shakedown could be confined to a past, albeit not so distant, of dinner money skittishly tucked away down the socks and a near-pathological fear of the lunch bell. Indeed, the way Conrad had been carrying on, all ticket-tout flash in his Burberry overcoat, no one would ever have guessed this was the same boy who barely a calendar year previous had a certain skill with a compass that always seemed to have the desired effect, the unlucky target forced to dig deep into their own pockets for whatever shrapnel and, in some cases, notes lay buried there. And yet here he was now, a cut-price south-London approximation of a Natty Dread, cooing sweet nothings to the object of his affections, no compass required. The latest Japanese technology at his fingertips and no hint of the tower anywhere in his clobber.

Over time, though, bedroom eyes seemed to lose a bit of their lustre. While D and the others wrestled with unfamiliar concepts like 'citizenship and good governance' at the hippy's behest, Conrad and his muse appeared to withdraw into a more private world of heartache and despair, or whatever it was that the Cool Ruler crooned into their ears. On a couple of occasions D sensed that the hippy was on the point of losing his cool. He could see him thinking about it, the vein next to the hippy's temple suddenly making itself known the way it had so many times in the past for D himself before he would sink back into resigned silence. In the hippy's case it was no different, some bizarre attachment to decorum getting the better of him when every instinct in him must have been screaming, 'Cheeky little fuckers! For God's sake, man, give 'em both barrels!' D felt a renewed sense of disgust then, not so much for Conrad or his muse but for the so-called authority figure in the classroom. This scruffy cunt with his pencil neck and misplaced sense of priorities. Good governance. What a joke!

An Obliviousness To Deepening Recession

EVERY NOW AND then, once he'd paid for the subscription, D would catch the postman giving him a quizzical look whenever he delivered *The Economist*. It was less a 'not for us' dismissal and more an expression of genuine confusion, as if the cellophane-wrapped magazine he held in his hands was the result of a mailing error, so D would let it slide in the manner to which he'd now grown accustomed, which meant *without* comment but *with* a fizzing sense of resentment lagging not far behind. Still, as his grasp of the deflationary pressure exerted on the economy by oil-price rises and of the subsequent tightening of fiscal and monetary policies strengthened, D found himself paying less and less attention to the crusading Marxist in the classroom.

Bedroom Eyes also appeared increasingly lethargic and listless, more often than not without Conrad now. His presence in class had become intermittent after the first few weeks, the euphoria of those red-romper-suit days already a fading memory. Besides, *Rasta nuh work fi no Babylonian shitstem*, everyone knew that. At least everyone in this classroom did now, Conrad's theatrics sealed with the sound of teeth being kissed and then the blakeys on his tasselled loafers clicking a diva-esque path back into a wider culture which barely even cared, and, if it did, might have taken issue with Conrad's self-description as a 'Rasta'. Those were still baby locks, and no self-respecting Dread would be seen messing around with blakeys this many years after 2 Tone had departed the scene.

When Conrad failed to return after that, Bedroom Eyes briefly perked up. Her appearance improved to the point where it was possible to imagine her as someone who might even have a future outside of this classroom. Minus the privatised instincts of Japanese technology, she started to pay attention again. And it wasn't just her, though, of course, the change was most pronounced in her. It was as if a gloom had lifted from the rest of the group, too. Not only that but replaced by something very rare. Levity, or what that fraud junior Rasta would have called 'livity'. D overheard him say that once, as if he, as if any of them, had the first idea what it meant. The neck on him (admittedly not pencil, but still). Anyway, he was (hopefully) gone now, so no need to feign indifference any more. No need to keep pretending they weren't all swots.

Round here, no one else made it this far. Everyone understood that. So where previously there might have been silence, hands would suddenly shoot up now and questions or answers fill the air. It was strangely exhilarating, being freed from the obligation to demonstrate indifference. And D knew it wasn't just him feeling this way, drinking in the heady atmosphere of learning. Anything and everything from North Sea oil revenues to inflationary pressures suddenly became fascinating, the enquiries flowing in a mixed-up-mongrel mightily relieved brogue.

But where the shift really made itself known was in Sarah's case. Gone were the lovelorn manipulations of Mr Isaacs, or worse, on those days she used to be locked out of Conrad's reverie, when he decided that no, the Walkman was his, that look of mournful forbearance which recognised that, yes, this was the burden that she, a white girl, would have to shoulder if she wished to be with a proud black man like him. None of it needed saying either. It was writ large in those eyes that withdrawal. So the relief now felt in this classroom by all and sundry was truly mighty.

Yes, Conrad was gone, but luckily so was she, that girl, or that version of her at least who used to sit with him. To all intents and purposes the original one was back, except now what used to be irritating about her – the way she, as a recent arrival to the area, had paid little attention to the unspoken local rule about never publicly demonstrating your intelligence – was most welcome.

Every so often she would ask a question about long-term unemployment or the radical monetarist policies of the Thatcher government. When she did, the Marxist scruff would wax lyrical about high interest rates and the public-sector borrowing requirement, as if that would make everyone forget how he'd let the fake Rasta completely usurp his authority right up to the long overdue moment that he'd finally challenged him, which was what had led to Conrad's outburst.

The preamble had been the by-now-routine flouting of LEA rules. Headphones on, legs splayed out, no hint of anything scholarly anywhere in the pose. While the scruff went on about the wider threat to the economy caused by a downturn in domestic consumption, there was no sign of that tendency right in front of him. Conrad looking at him unimpressed, whatever sounds he was listening to suggesting an obliviousness to deepening recession.

'Conrad.'

No answer.

'Conrad.'

Still nothing.

'Conrad! Will you turn that bloody thing off, I'm trying to talk to you!'

The scruff was practically yelling now. Everyone else was quiet, probably all thinking the same thing. What's junior Rasta going to do now?

Several seconds went by, and nothing happened. Finally Conrad slowly removed one headphone then the other, rising to his feet with all the ponderousness one might expect from a member of the lost tribe of Israelites in Southwark. Sarah said nothing the whole time, a resigned look on her face which hinted at the weary familiarity of the scene. D picked up on that, the Marxist, too, so by the time Conrad had stormed out a certain amount of residual sympathy had already begun to form for Sarah. Those weren't bedroom eyes at all. They were just disappointed, hurt, a little sad like more or less everything else in this economy.

Stylised
Indifference

ABOUT THE TEACHER. D knew this man's word, like his 'authority', was not to be trusted. Yes, he liked to go on about the retail price index and inflationary bias, but D had already noticed something. Whenever he raised the question of how to reduce public expenditure, instead of answering the question, the scruff would go off on a tangent. The same if D asked about the reduction of the tax burden on the private sector. Never a straight answer at those moments. The scruff would process the enquiry in a slightly panicked delay between data input and feedback loop. A couple of times D actually thought he could see the cogs slowly turning behind the teacher's implacable mask. But once they had, he'd come back with some guff about the post-war settlement between labour and capital, whatever that meant, and there'd always be something thrown in about the working class, which made even less sense to D when the people being described sounded just like the ones he would see stepping in and out of fancy motors outside the Post Office. Also, on a simple point of order, D noted how shyness suddenly seemed to get the better of the teacher if D so much as mentioned those burgeoning North Sea oil revenues or the significant improvement they'd brought about in the balance of payments, which surely even he, a scruff, could see was a good thing?

No, this man was not to be trusted. Besides, he thought, what kind of responsible adult organised an economics field trip to the Bank of England and then disappeared from sight the moment they'd got off the bus? And what *had* he been wearing that day? A cord jacket and camel lambswool crew neck. What sort of an idiot goes to the bank looking like that? For those reasons as much as any other, D realised, from now on he'd have to get his fiscal knowledge from a more reliable source. That was where *The Economist* came in.

Round about this time, the scruff's appearance started to change. Whether or not the two events were directly connected, the chronology was telling. At least it *was* to a discerning eye. And to one raised on the exquisite contest between Fila and Tacchini, the pleasing symmetry of Forest Hills (Adidas) in Forest Hill (south London) or the enduring appeal of those particular Trimm Trabs, in blue but with the orange stripes, it was as if the sartorial changes were being announced by a foghorn. It also left an impression, because the first time the teacher came to class wearing a pair of grey Farah trousers roughly coincided with an early look of confusion on the postman's face. No one mentioned it in class. Conrad's departure seemed to have rung the death knell for that old atmosphere, the largely pre-sixth-form one of fear and predatory loathing.

This new classroom, as D had already noted with some relief, was a place where debate was encouraged and participation viewed as a badge of merit rather than the preamble to a break-time shakedown. Its curative properties had already begun to take effect on the residents. For the first time D learnt that he was in class with a couple of Africans, a Turk (who he'd thought was Asian) and some Vietnamese as well as the standard complement of English boys still feigning a lack of interest in the learning process but now deprived of the black totem around whom they might previously have rallied their stylised indifference.

Fucking hell, thought D, what is wrong with me? Why can't I just be happy? Everyone else seems to be. Why do I have to overthink every last thing? And what the hell is all that crap about 'stylised indifference'? Rejoice, man, like Thatcher and Bono keep telling you to. He's gone. That cunt Conrad is gone. Your lunch money is safe. No one here's going to be taking what you said about the trade deficit personally.

Sarah had definitely brightened up, too, more or less back to how she was before the interlude with Conrad. Without his brood-ing presence looming over their classroom Walkman sessions, she was a lot friendlier now. Often when D would walk in, he'd see her enjoying a conversation with Nguyen (which he learnt was pronounced 'win') or Ercan, though rarely with any of the English boys. Still, at least she acknowledged him, usually with a smile, and in his world of pathetic micro-competitiveness, that set him apart from the other English boys, a fact which in some indeter-minate way pleased him.

Stop it, man, stop it! 'Micro-competitiveness'?! What the hell is wrong with you? thought D as the teacher launched into an impassioned defence of central planning within the economy. The problem, and confusion, of course, being that D's question could just as easily have been applied to the teacher as himself. *Indeed, Mr Scruffy, what the hell is wrong with you?* All he could think of as the teacher ploughed on was how as recently as 1980 the current account deficit for nations with centrally planned economies was estimated at twelve billion dollars. He'd read that in a recent issue of his subscription. At least, unlike the scruff, *The Economist* pointed out that these economies were not impervious to oil-price rises and the adverse effect of those price hikes on the balance of payments. He knew there was more, much more besides, but his attention was suddenly diverted by the realisation that, good grief, there was some kind of a sovereign ring on the scruff's index finger.

'I don't understand why we can't do that here,' said Sarah, interrupting the teacher. 'Everyone can see how much people are suffering under this government. And there's no jobs either. The government should do something.'

The scruff smiled without saying anything. He looked pleased with himself, as if he was genuinely making progress with his young charges.

'Yeah but they ain't going to do nothing round here,' said Bradley, one of the English boys. 'I mean, when's the last time you saw any ministers come up the Old Kent Road?'

Somewhere in D's mind a light flickered on, in its dim glow a Kangol Spitfire hat and a twin-stripe Fila Terrinda top sauntering away from the Post Office with the fortnightly clutch of lifestyle readies. It didn't really look like suffering to him. In fairness, he wouldn't have had a clue where to get hold of one of those velour tops himself, and that was *with* the benefit of his brother's secret notebook. And when he thought about it some more, he remembered how on other occasions he'd also seen Diadora Borg Elites and those niche Fila Bj tracksuit tops hightailing it with the loot. No, not exactly his idea of suffering.

This time, though, there was none of that hollow laughter he'd come to expect from every classroom he'd ever known, including this one, right up until Conrad's departure just a few weeks earlier. Instead, when the rest of the group just looked at Bradley and then back at Sarah, before Nguyen put up his hand and said, in an accent more south London than Saigon, 'That's 'cause, believe it or not, they've got better stuff to do than piss around in bandit country,' D felt his spirits soar. The teacher didn't like it, that much was clear from the frown spreading out across his face, but he limited himself to a, 'Hmm, do you want to say a little bit more about that, then, Win?' Which, of course, he pronounced with the kind of flourish that so desperately wanted to suggest he'd known boys with silent Ngs at the start of their name all his life.

Sarah didn't seem to mind too much, though. D, who'd been considering asking the teacher about credit controls and inflationary pressure after class, had second thoughts when he saw that Sarah had also stayed behind once the buzzer had gone. He held off, thinking it would make him look a bit of a tit in front of her, and then wondered why that should matter anyway. They weren't exactly going to be breaking bread any time soon. She'd barely said two words to him the whole time they'd been in class. The fact that, unlike with Bradley or any of the other English boys, she *did* at least acknowledge D's presence, hardly made them friends. Better to nab a quiet word with the scruff when no one else was looking. Old habits die hard, he thought, as he walked away, struck by how focused Sarah appeared to be on whatever it was the scruff was saying to her, and by that sovereign ring which at one point seemed to hover surprisingly close to Sarah's face.

Out Of Order

THE NEXT TIME he saw Sarah was not in class. D had been running an errand, picking up his dad's suit from the dry cleaners nearest the suicide tower. Though this wasn't the dry cleaners nearest their home, it was nonetheless the one they used. Mrs Tran, the owner, had previously worked with Mum in the Peek Freans factory, and they had become friendly, if not exactly good friends. The upshot being, whenever there was a suit needed pressing or a dress cleaning, *this* was their family's chosen establishment. 'You've got to show loyalty, son,' said his dad, handing D an extra note for his troubles, but clearly delighted that he himself wasn't the one now tasked with traipsing up to New Cross and back with a suit in tow.

D's brother, for over a year now presumed 'reformed' in the eyes of society, had made the surprise announcement the last time he'd popped round for one of his increasingly rare visits. Their dad, as he seemed to during all key family moments, had been sat in the kitchen drinking tea.

D was upstairs when he'd got the shout to come down. At the time he'd been poring over a longer article in the latest *Economist* examining inefficiencies in the public sector and making the case that slowly but surely the overall economy was getting fitter if leaner. The monetarist medicine was working even if the patient wasn't yet fully cured. Amen to that, thought D as he unhappily found himself fixating once more on those Fila Bj tracksuit tops. As far as he could tell, the patient was still prone to taking the piss on a fairly regular basis. He found himself getting quite wrapped up in the tone as well as the substance of the piece. He liked the confidence with which the author put forward his views. There was no hint anywhere in the article of the kind of muffled, stifled, thwarted intelligence which D knew all too well from his own experience. He couldn't imagine this author running the gauntlet of classroom Conrads wherever he'd gone to school. And the thought just made D loathe his own peers all the more.

For a moment, when he'd heard the knocking on his door, he thought he might be in some kind of trouble. Had the old man found the secret notebook? But then a moment later the door burst open, and there was his brother leaning in all nonchalant as if this was just like any other Saturday afternoon.

'Alright?' D asked, taking care not to look up too quickly from the mag, though he was excited to see his brother. They definitely got on better since he'd moved out. (Well, Her Majesty had taken care of that bit, after all.) And since he'd moved in with that bird he'd been seeing, Angie, he'd become all grown up, getting a job as a trader that her old man had helped him to find. Proper shoes, a suit and an office to go with it. Not bad for a little herbert who'd had a very different routine only a year or so previous.

'Yeah, you?' his brother replied.

'Yeah, can't complain,' said D, aware that his brother was looking at the mag D was holding in his hands.

'What's that you've got there?' he asked D.

'Oh, nothing much. Just for my own interest.'

'It doesn't look like nothing,' said his brother. 'Dad says you're doing well with your studies. That's the way to go, little man. Don't make the same mistakes I did. It definitely ain't worth it.' Looking him up and down with the ex-hoister's practised eye, he went on, 'You still dress like shit, though. Glad to see some things never change.' Flicking his wedge in the direction of the door, he continued, 'Anyway, if you can tear yourself away from your Mills and Boon, I've got some news. Come on, Mum and Dad are getting the hump waiting for you downstairs.'

Which was how he heard, how all of them heard, that his brother was getting married, that Angie was the luckiest girl in the world (they had a good laugh about that) and, *oh by the way, you're going to be grandparents, and you're going to be an uncle* (not so much mirth this time).

Anyway, coming out of the dry cleaners with his dad's suit draped over his shoulder, D spotted a familiar figure waiting by the intercom for the suicide tower. He called out, as he hadn't seen Sarah in class since she'd stayed behind that time to talk to the scruff. That was several weeks back, and the inevitable talk among the others in class was that she had got herself into some kind of 'trouble' and had had to drop out. As usual it was a consensus formed exclusively on the basis of rumour, but everyone seemed happy enough with that. The scruff, who'd taken to wearing an occasional Burberry polo shirt to go with his sermons on the evils of capitalism, seemed oddly uninterested as to the whereabouts of his missing student, but this being England and a thoroughly buttoned-up culture, no one thought to mention it again.

It *was* Sarah. She momentarily looked up, saw D, but this time didn't acknowledge him as she headed into the tower block after being buzzed in. He wasn't sure what made him follow her inside, slipping in just behind another resident whose hands were full with the weekly shop and who seemed grateful for the young man who courteously held the door open while she juggled her key with the fob and the shopping. Though she audibly sighed when confronted moments later with the four most dreaded words in the English language. Lift. Out. Of. Order.

'Don't worry, I'll give you a hand, where are you going?' D said to her, hoping he might be able to spot Sarah on the way up.

The lady with the shopping, who he guessed was West Indian and in her fifties or possibly sixties, appeared a little wary at first. Then she spotted the suit bag he had over his shoulder and this seemed to settle her nerves.

'Well OK then, young man. That's very kind of you,' she said as D picked up several of the carriers with his one spare hand and they began trudging up the dimly lit stairwells. After the first couple of flights, she turned to D, and asked him, 'Which floor did you say you were going to again, young man?'

He paused for a moment, pretending he was a little out of breath, even though he was the junior in this pairing by at least four decades.

'Oh, I'm just here to see a friend, but it's no trouble. I'll drop your stuff off first.'

She looked at D again, this time more intently, as if that might clarify things. He did his best to give her a reassuring smile but felt sure he'd come across as less chancellor of the exchequer and more Stan Laurel. The lady seemed unconvinced, too, but allowed D to trudge up several more flights of stairs with her shopping in tow. Eventually, just as she was saying, 'I can take it from here, young man,' and gesturing for D to hand over the bags, a familiar voice entered the stairwell from above.

'Nan, I was just coming down. Sarah said the lift was broken.'

It was Conrad, not even a hint of Rasta in his diction.

JUST ANOTHER
RACKETEERING
STATISTIC

THE MADEIRA CAKE came out when Mrs Lascaris, Conrad's nan, heard that the nice young man who had carried her shopping was studying for his A levels and was already thinking about university. She seemed less thrilled by Sarah's presence in the flat. The looks she gave both her grandson and this white girl he appeared to have taken up with were laced with far less sugar than the cake, of which she offered another handsome slice to D.

'Educayshun,' she repeated, fixing Conrad with a withering look. 'I grow tired of telling this one to study. 'Im always want nice ting but 'im never want fi work. An' I tell 'im, there's nothing in this life comes for free. But he won't listen. After all, who am I but a lickle ol' lady from Jamaica. Wha' could I possibly know? Tek some more. Young man, yuh all skin an' bone. Mus' keep up yuh strength fi them studies.'

D was enjoying the cake and the discomfort his presence was clearly causing both his former classmates. Conrad still seemed a little stunned that D was sat there drinking in the adulation from his, Conrad's, nan, while he, Conrad, was being berated. And sat there in his, Conrad's, flat! His nan's, to be totally accurate, but the fact remained. This was where he, Conrad, the legend behind that specially embossed 'C' on his chunky bracelet, this was where the legend lived. He didn't mind the white girl knowing that, though his nan never seemed overly keen on her coming round. Still, he could put up with a certain amount of disapproval on her part when he sensed Sarah's approval at where he lived. And its fringe benefit of a hungry mouth around his dick. Though it was never quite as intense as the first time she came up here, when she'd taken in every last detail like one of those contestants on *The Generation Game* trying to remember all the items on the conveyor belt, he saw how her attitude to him always seemed to soften when they were in the tower block. He knew that somewhere, deep down, he was a 'project' for her. A challenge for the girl from the nice residential streets closer to Camberwell. He'd sensed it that first time she'd ever spoken up in class, some dreck about racism and white-people system. When no one had pointed out that the maximum prejudice round this way was white and black together, and it was directed at Chinky or Vietnam (he never could tell), he knew then that it was going to be business as usual. Follow the leader, with him, Conrad, as the boss man calling the lower-sixth shots, while whitey fell in line around him, boys like Bradley always keen to bask in some reflected glory. And when no one called him out on the bone-idle fakery of those picky locks and that cartoon Rasta style and patter, he just did what he'd always done ever since he'd been at school. He simply pushed it some more and kept pushing until the point that even the hippy teacher had had enough. And then he'd got up and left, not even allowing that teacher the chance to throw him out first, and *still* that white girl kept coming up here to see him. Even after how he'd treated her, in and out of class. There really was no accounting for taste, he thought, or perhaps it was just that he truly was befitting of the legend 'C' specially engraved on the bracelet.

Anyway, having the girl up here was one thing, though he could have done without the way his nan was looking at her now. This 'D' on the other hand, now *he* was quite a different proposition. *He'd* also taken a good look around the flat once Conrad's nan had insisted he come in, but it was clear he wasn't so easily impressed. For one thing, the place was immaculate, the mantelpiece and sideboard neatly lined with family photos, quite a few featuring Conrad and a smartly dressed woman with straightened hair who D guessed must have been Conrad's mum. Also a number which, judging from the light and the smiles, clearly hadn't been taken in England. Jamaica, probably, and this time a young Mrs Lascaris, he guessed, looking shyly at the camera but with a hint of laughter.

In the living-room, where the three of them were sat, the only thing that surprised D was that the sofa was still wrapped in its original plastic sheeting, as pristine as the day it must have first arrived. Other than that, what stood out was the neatly lined bookcase to one side of the large Grundig television and the boxy, metallic video recorder just beneath it. The bookcase was stacked high to low with all manner of encyclopaedias and a number of atlases. Incredibly, too, there was a stack of *Reader's Digests* on a small side table near the sofa. He didn't know what, if anything, he'd been expecting, or if indeed he'd ever even imagined he'd one day be up here, but it wasn't this. Neat and homely and with a lot of learning packed into those shelves.

Conrad watched D drinking in the details. This was probably the first time Conrad had ever felt himself tense up around this white boy. He'd known him for years, in the sense that they'd been in the same class at school. It's not that they'd ever really spoken. He vaguely recalled saying something to him in class and getting a good laugh from the rest of the sheep. Couldn't remember what it had been about, but he was fairly sure he'd had the last word. He must have done, otherwise he'd surely have remembered? Nah, they'd never really spoken, and that must have been because there'd been no need. The white boy was obviously just another racketeering statistic. Which was why he *did* now remember taxing him many, many times for his dinner money and the little pussy just handing it over. No doubt he was also cowed, like so many of the other quiet boys, by the great, presumably righteous inner-city unknown they saw stretched out across the black faces they tried to avoid at lunchtime.

Yeah, he remembered that alright, remembered how after a while it was hardly even money with menaces. Resistance was futile, and in any case almost unheard of. Word must have got around. He was the Conrad with the compass. All the 'C's. Everyone knew the drill, and their role in this little drama, and, yeah, he remembered, this D was no different, always opting for minor pecuniary humiliation over a smack in the mouth. Just handed it over like it was the most natural thing in the world, part of the scheduled timetable between double geography and English. Yet here he was now, sat with his,

Conrad's, nan, and sat in his drum (tcha! the neck on him) bold as anything with a couple of slices of Madeira cake in his belly.

'This really is a lovely cake, Mrs Lascaris,' D said, making sure to look over at Conrad as he did so.

Pussy-arsed, fake-Rasta cunt, he thought, if he could have stabbed him in the neck with a fork right then he'd have done so in a heartbeat. Stubbed out a Marlboro light in those picky locks, set fire to the romper suit, too. He began to smile, sensing how deeply his presence was starting to freak Conrad out. Yeah, that's right, mate, I'm sat here nyaming fruit-based afters with your nan (oh, that's right pal, I'm as 'yard' as the next man who happens to be a fake-arsed Rasta) and making you look bad in your own home, and there ain't a damn thing you can do about it, because I now know, from all these books and photos and encyclopaedias, that you're even more bogus than me. *I'm* just pretending to be a product of the neighbourhood, the better to remain inconspicuous for as long as I have to be here. Just biding my time is all. But *you*, you're far worse. Not only are you a fake Rasta, but you're middle class. At least I'm only trying to slip under the radar of other people, but you, you're hiding from yourself. And I'm not even sure why. If your nan's anything to go by, you're from proper people, it's just you that's rotten. To be honest, even your mum (assuming that is her) looks alright from those photos, so it is just you. What you've always been, no matter how many sob stories you get away with in front of those teachers. And I know if you so much as think about reacting badly to that revelation, your nan will beat you with a belt, and even that poor, deluded white girl I actually came up here to check up on will finally be able to see you for what you are. Bullying, thieving, fraudulent, parasitic scum.

Amazing what detail a single look could convey, he thought.

'You're very welcome, young man,' said Conrad's Nan, performing the full Janus beam at the English boy and scowl at her own blood.

Sarah, who'd sat there quietly the whole time, finally spoke up. 'School's not everything,' she said. 'Maybe it just takes some people longer to work that out.'

Mrs Lascaris looked at her, unimpressed. It was bad enough her blood had taken up with this harridan, but now she could see who'd been putting ideas in that fickle head of his. She *had* thought when he finally buckled down and got those results last summer, that he might start to listen to this lickle ole woman more often. How many times had she told him, yuh a lucky boy, yuh surround by all these books, all this knowledge. Now yuh mus' read and learn. It the only way up. Or yuh think yuh jus' step in lift and it tek you to top. Tcha! Yuh should know better than that. Yuh see what it like roun' here. Lift bruk up t'ree day in every five.

And incredibly, it seemed he had listened. She'd been so proud of him then.

Or that other time when she found all those bags of change in his room, and he'd confessed to her that he'd got a job doing a paper round and he'd been meaning to tell her but he wanted it to be a surprise, Nan. What a sweet chile. Pristine, too. Yes, that boy was always very clean, which must have been why he never had any newsprint anywhere near his hands. But ever since this Sarah pop her lily-white face into the area, the boy change. She see it first in the hair! That horrible *dutty* serpent twist falling all over his ears. Maybe that would explain why he stop listening to any good sense for some time now. *Garvey this and Babylon that*, and all the while they stuck up here in this tower a thousand miles from any redemption. *Back to Hafrica indeed! They beat him with stick if that fool ever set foot in the bush. That hidiot boy, always a follower. She say, 'Jump', he go, 'How high, missy?'*

'This boy,' said Mrs Lascaris, indicating D. 'He don't look particular foolish to me, and 'im still in school. This boy have prospects. And what about yuh, young lady? Yuh think y'have prospects? Yuh even know what that word mean? It doesn't seem so. From where I sit, I see someone who already achieve the summit of her ambition. And it not a pretty sight, I can tell yuh that. Oh, Lawd, it not a pretty sight.'

Sarah found herself wondering how the old lady knew. It was still only a question of days, nothing was showing, surely nobody could tell. She *had* thought Mr F— would be happy when she told him, but the look on his face, the way he spoke to her, that wasn't happiness. And after that she'd stopped coming to class, couldn't see why she should bother, especially when he'd suddenly lost interest in her. *That* was when she started coming round here again.

At least Conrad would understand, she thought, when she eventually got round to telling him. That could wait, though. For now she was still trying to take in the news herself. Besides, judging by what he'd been telling her, she guessed he must have had enough on his plate anyway, what with the SUS laws and the endless pressure of Babylon weighing 'pon that nicely locksing-up head. But his nan, that old bat had had it in for her from the start. *Those looks!* As if it was her, Sarah's, fault that Conrad had dropped out.

It wasn't her fault if Conrad's nan couldn't see the grief a proud young black man had to go through every day just for the crime of being himself. But how she was being looked at now, that went way beyond disapproval. From now on, she'd have to make a point of only coming here when she was sure the old bat was out. In any case, that would give her and Conrad the chance to talk, and goodness knows, a little more conversation might have prevented any of this from happening in the first place. Right now, though, she wasn't even sure what she was going to do, whether she was even going to keep it. But after how Mr F— had reacted, something in her had closed up. She couldn't understand why he was suddenly so distant, those things he'd said about it not being the right time for either of them, and, of course, he'd help her, but it wasn't the right time. At least Conrad hadn't turned her away. He'd been gentle with her, and though she hadn't told him everything, he'd sensed she'd been reaching out to him, and he'd reached back, all softly spoken and sweet like Mr Isaacs. Well, to start with he had. Then, as with the Walkman, the mood shifted. It wasn't Mr Isaacs crooning in her ear for long. No it was something more nasal, quicker, unkind, like one of those fast-style local em-cees Conrad had been going on about. Yes, the mood shifted between them, Conrad's eyes always darting around beyond her shoulder whenever she came up to see him. Less and less got shared, and the taint of business crept up on what she thought they had. The first few spliffs gratis. Then ever-stronger weed, tiny fractions to a prime number, but never for free, and suddenly she was necking diazepam with the weed, thinking that might help her decide what to do. She should have known, just from how he pronounced 'barbiturate', *bah-bitch-urrat*, she should have known then what he really thought of her. But she kept necking the pills and the weed, all the edges blurring, even the bitch tone growing faint. Until she could hardly hear anything, least of all the sounds of disapproval.

Before long barely thinking at all, just making her zombie way up into the tower and trying to act normal in a system that she heard was so cruel, that it made a proud black man like him depend on the revenue stream of the drug economy.

Was that what she heard?

She couldn't be sure, all tribulation and reparation. Always money. Always the economy. Nothing for free. Supply and demand. Bloody Mr F— with all his fancy theories! He'd really got inside her head, well, a lot more than that besides, and now she remembered, *that* was where the trouble had started.

Threadneedle Street, the Bank of England.

She'd never forget that place now. *Fiscal discipline.* He'd made it sound so attractive, was it really only her that could quench this ah-thirst? No, that wasn't *him*, that was Conrad. Or was it Mr Isaacs? She couldn't tell any more. In her weed, barbiturate, loneliness haze, lights kept flickering on, some hint of Rasta, some supply side, before she was pitched right back into a high-rise darkness. The only remedy.

D remembered now. It was never actually known as the suicide tower before that. People only started calling it that after Sarah's body was formally identified, the watermelon smash on the pavement only briefly inconveniencing traffic in and out of the tower, or damsels (and chaps) in less distress picking up or dropping off their dry cleaning from the thriving business next door.

Unspoken
Grievances

Home Counties, early 1980s

RUKHINI HATED HER name. Hated it when anyone called her that. It was Roxy, that was how she wanted to be known. *The Roxy, Roxy Music*, whatever. Not strictly what she'd had in mind at the time, but the name had stuck anyway. There was no way she was going through school as Rukhini. Couldn't her parents understand that much at least? It was bad enough being Asian without drawing attention to the fact every single day at morning register.

'Rachael?'

'Yes.'

'Rhiannon?'

'Yes.'

'Roo-kinny?'

Snigger, mumble, grunt.

'Roo-kinny? Has anyone seen Roo –'

'Yes.'

Teacher looking up, not exactly delighted, and her just sitting there, a reluctant witness to her own name.

If this stuff was so important to her parents, why had they ever come here? Why not just stay in India where everyone had weird names, and with a bit of luck, girls called Sharon or Tina were the ones who got laughed at during register? That's what she'd find herself thinking on a fairly regular basis before picturing her mum butting in with the kind of reply she just didn't want to hear. 'But, sohni, in my class there *were* girls called Sharon and Tina. And nobody minded at all. The girls there, in that English-medium school, we all knew we were from good families, even the Catholic ones.'

It would have been pointless to try to argue with her. Only so many times a sane person could bear to be told, 'But you have such a beautiful name, sohni. I don't know why you get so upset. How many girls do you know who can say their names actually mean something? Have you thought about that? Maybe you should from time to time.'

Which, of course, she had. Her mum was wrong. The English girls' names *did* mean something, too, just not the endless *my*-thological (how her mum said it) stuff the harder-to-pronounce Hindu ones were wrapped up in. The number of times she'd wanted to tell her mum she couldn't care less about Arjuna's bow, she just wanted to see whether he had a nice straight arrow. And she'd wanted to ask her mum how much she thought the English girls had the *my*-thologicals in mind when they called her slim Gujarati classmate Manisha 'Boney M'. She never did, opting instead to nurse long-term and unspoken grievances. Against the school, against her fellow pupils and, to some extent, probably against her mum as well.

At least that way she could explore moodiness as some kind of a personal statement. In the absence of any other viable role models – Fatima Whitbread and Sheila Chandra didn't count, especially Fatima, who, aside from not being Asian in the first place, was also way too muscular and just not, well, very feminine – she felt that striking a pose might be the way to go. Charlie's Angels in silhouette. Except this time without that old perv Charlie fiddling around with his moustache. Yes, moodiness, that could be her signature dish, the special skill she'd bring to the triumvirate. Emily, the sporty one (as in, 'yeah, she's a good sport'), Victoria, the friendly one (no explanation required), and Roxy, the moody one.

Actually that's what she'd wanted to say to her mum in the first place about the English girls. Their names might not be wor-shipped in the temple, but everyone knew what they meant. And when she became Roxy, which, as far as she was concerned, couldn't be soon enough, then she, too, would need the signature detail. Some things were more important than being an acceptable puja statistic.

If she had her issues with her mum, who always seemed to know exactly the right thing to say to get under her (admittedly very fair) skin, the same could not be said about her dad. Everything about him just screamed 'reasonable'. From his balding pate to his solidly 'company' moustache to the affordable high-street menswear he favoured when out and about. More than any of that, though, he just never came across like any of the fabled arranged-marriage patriarchs she'd hear about from time to time, who were supposed to be making the lives of girls like her into a living hell.

You know what they're like.

Well that was the unspoken in all of this. The great danger of invisibility, that aspersions could be cast and no one would ever be around to challenge them.

You know what they're like.

Actually, that was one of the many things about school that annoyed her. The rest of the time she, Manisha, any of the other Asian girls she knew, were more or less invisible to the rest of the school. But the moment some story came out in the news about an arranged marriage and domestic abuse, which was also about the only time, as far as she could tell, that domestic abuse seemed to be considered 'newsworthy', then the next day in class there'd be endless questions and looks of temporary concern on the faces of her classmates.

'Is that what it's like at home for you, Manisha?' (Curiously, no sign of 'Boney M' on those days.)

'Did your parents have an arranged marriage? That must have been really hard for your mum. I mean, did she even know your dad before they got married?'

'What do you speak at home?'

And, best of the lot, 'Are you allowed to answer back at home. Is that allowed in your religion?' with the time-honoured punchline, 'Do you speak Hinduism then?'

She wanted to ask them, these freshly compassionate white girls, 'Well if I'm not allowed to answer back, how do you think I got to be such a bolshie cow then?' but she didn't, because, of course, their questions, that concern, were never directed her way. To them she was just 'Rukhs', which annoyingly enough they pronounced 'Rookes'. But in the designation some kind of recognition, too, that she wasn't from Manisha's tribe even if she didn't quite belong to theirs yet. And while she was grateful to not really be lumped in with the other undesirables, that was also part of her frustration.

She felt she had no real identity here, not even an unpopular one. But she knew she was different to the white girls. She somehow doubted these girls in her class had brothers who'd been tormented in school, who even as a little girl she remembered sometimes coming home with bruises and swellings. Actually, that was just Rakesh, her eldest brother, who'd gone to the local comprehensive back when there wasn't so much money around, when things weren't quite so comfortable. He'd never spoken about it directly, but she still remembered how all those years back he sometimes found it hard to look at her when she asked him in her cutest five-year-old way how school was. He couldn't look at her and tell her straight, even though she was just a little girl, and in fairness he could have just made something up, and she wouldn't have minded. He could have told her he'd been to the moon and back, or south London, and she'd have believed him because he was her Dada and his world seemed so much bigger and impossibly exciting to her. Anyway, that kind of detail wasn't so easy to forget. And she remembered his kipper tie as well, and the missing buttons on his shirt and the scuffed shoes. Back when their dad was still just getting started, when they lived in a narrow terrace where no one's dad was an accountant. Before this house and the cars and the holidays and the ability to pay school fees.

But yes, her dad. Not exactly a brute, and definitely not someone who she felt was oppressing her on a regular basis. She knew he was an accountant, and he'd obviously done alright for himself if their house and those cars in the driveway and the regular foreign holidays for all the family were anything to go by. And why not throw in her school, for that matter? It wasn't exactly shabby. Lacrosse, its own tennis courts, Latin, Greek, a highly regarded debating society and a list of alumni that included several prominent politicians, actors and that newsreader her dad always seemed to perk up for, even when the news itself was rarely anything to write home about. Why not throw all of that in? It's not as though she was on a scholarship. Someone had to be providing those fees, and it definitely wasn't her mum.

Both her brothers were considerably older. The eldest, Rakesh, had for some years now been working with her dad, was already married and seemed happy enough in a paunchy, receding kind of way. They – Rakesh, his wife, their two young children – lived just a couple of streets away but were already semi-detached ('a good investment' according to her mum). Maybe it had something to do with how unhappy he'd been at school and how helpless their dad had felt about it, but as soon as he could he had taken Rakesh on in his own firm. Had sat with him night after night, helping him prepare for his accountancy exams. Had celebrated with a bottle of Bombay Sapphire the day the results came through. 'One of the best days of my life,' he'd said, pouring himself another tumbler while Rakesh looked a little guilty for being the source of all this fuss.

Suresh, who was still six years older than her, had gone into the City. He'd once tried to explain what it was that he did there but became so frustrated by the constant nitpicking ('so how do you speculate?') that he'd given up. And the question didn't arise again, their mum quickly getting back to fawning all over him once it became clear that whatever it was that he did paid handsomely. It certainly helped her overlook the fact that not once in the whole of his adult life had Suresh ever mentioned girls, or a 'friend', let alone brought one home. Presumably he was too busy with his life in London, where he'd also bought a small flat 'near the Barbican'. (It actually turned out to be Old Street, which, though it was physically close to the Barbican, wasn't exactly their – the family's – idea of an 'artistic' community.)

The hectic pacing of that life must have been why he often looked drawn on his visits home, as though he hadn't slept properly for a while. But their mum was always pleased to see him, even if their dad tended to spend less time with him than with Rakesh. Or would find a reason to bury himself in a Sunday supplement or discuss business with Rakesh or potter around with his grandchildren in the garden without doing very much at all with the secateurs.

After a while everyone made a conscious effort to steer the conversation away from anything personal and more towards the generalities of politics or sport. Which was something of a revelation for all of them really. After all, they weren't Bengalis, it's not as though they did this kind of thing for fun, instead of putting in a shift or making money or, at a push, playing cards in some pretence at recreation when really everyone knew it was all about learning how to make money. Everyone knew.

Anyway, that's how she found out that her entire family, Suresh apart, were staunchly Conservative.

Aaj-ke Labour Party ek nombor joke hai, was pretty much the only thing they could all agree on. Even her mum, who'd never really expressed any strong political opinions, seemed disgusted by the mere mention of Her Majesty's Opposition. She had a few other things to say as well.

'And just dekho at how they live in Brixton-frixton. *So* many children, and drugs, and just no discipline.' (This from the same woman who, as far as her own daughter could tell, had never lifted a finger in anger at her eldest son's school, brimming to overflowing as it turned out to be with drugs and indiscipline as well as a lot more than the occasional unruly child.)

As for Suresh, she sometimes got the feeling that the only reason he disagreed as he funnelled yet another pakora into what appeared to be his permanently hungry mouth, was to shift the conversation back into the realms of the personal, where he could finally say whatever it was that was *really* bothering him, which rarely seemed to be about what his dad was actually saying to him.

'I don't see what else they can do. What do you want from the government? You can only lead horse to water, Suresh, beta, that's all you can do. If people don't like it, they can vote for someone else,' said their dad, wondering why these young people couldn't see that without tight fiscal discipline there was only chaos. *And why the hell did his son look as though he hadn't slept in days?*

'But it's not about that, is it?' said Suresh, irritation once more creeping into his voice. 'It's not always about numbers. There are real people behind those figures, and you just don't want to seem to acknowledge that. There are people who are struggling out there, and they're getting shafted by the people in charge. They're just trying to live their lives, but people won't let them. That's the problem. It's just a pity you can't see that.'

Rakesh always looked uncomfortable at moments like these, and to be fair there'd been a few of them of late. He saw his wife and children looking to him for leadership, and far from feeling like a breadwinner, the sensation he actually experienced was irritation. Primarily with himself for having always lacked the sort of courage that seemed to come so easily to his brother, sat there now, holding court, happily disrupting what should have been a nice family get-together. No concern whatsoever at what effect his words might be having on their dad, on all of them really. But especially on their dad, a lifetime of ghee and sedentary activity not exactly the best counter to unexpected stress.

When he thought about it like that, his anger at his brother climbed several notches. Besides, he just couldn't see what the little fucker's problem was. Suresh was good looking, successful, the apple of their ma's eye, but he always had to have the last word, could never just sit there and make nice like a normal person would. Plus, his, Rakesh's kids, always seemed far more excited at the prospect of meeting their uncle than they ever were when their own dad would come home after another long day of number-crunching. They didn't climb all over *him* when he got in, yet here they were now, looking to him, their father, for some kind of guidance, a sign, anything at all to provide reassurance. Rakesh tried to find the words or the pose, but the truth was he couldn't find anything. He was about as much of a leader as that Welsh ginger in charge of the Labour Party. *Leader of the Opposition*, what a joke! Forget politics, he thought, running his fingers through his rapidly receding hairline. If things carried on like this he'd soon have his own comb-over, except in his case without even the minor consolations of tabloid interest. What a joke!

Suresh went on, 'People are really struggling out there. You've got no idea. It's not easy thinking differently in this climate.'

'What do you mean by that?' asked their Dad.

No answer.

'Yeah, what are you talking about?' asked Rakesh, patience finally sapped by his brother's petulance.

'Look, I'm just saying in my line it pays to think differently. And it's not easy, not with everything else that's going on out there.'

'Everything else?' asked Rakesh.

'Yeah, I wouldn't expect you to understand,' said Suresh, indignation spreading out across those handsome features.

'Try me,' said Rakesh, bored but also pleased that he'd managed to shoehorn the phrase into a lunchtime domestic. It was mostly a phrase he only ever heard on American legal dramas, yet here it was, right at home with the mittai in a comfortable suburban British Indian setting.

'Alright then. I have to speculate on what goes up and what comes down. So I have to have a fairly good sense of what people are prepared to take a risk on as well as what makes them shy. If the only thing you're ever concerned about is "fiscal discipline" then those parameters rapidly shrink. No one would ever take a punt on anything, and we might as well all give up now. But, you know, the funny thing is, people *do* take a punt, and they carry on taking a punt long after they've been told by the good and the great that that's risky. And the strange thing is, some people are happier risking everything, especially when they know what the alternative looks like. You know what I mean?'

The even stranger thing being, though no one actually understood what it was that Suresh did, everyone sitting round this table, with the possible exception of his twin nephews, *did* know what he meant. Everyone knew.

THE SIN ON HER BREATH

AT LEAST SHE was light skinned. There wasn't a day went by when she didn't thank her lucky stars for that much. It could have been so much worse for her, lumped in with all the other undesirables. Poor old Manisha, of course, but also Mythili (a little too close to *my*-thological for comfort) and even Saira, who in spite of her relatively light skin and user-friendly name seemed to get marked down for never being allowed by her family on any of the school trips. Parental consent was the name of the game in which Saira, for reasons as yet unspecified, never seemed to prosper. More than once Roxy had overheard other girls from her class saying, 'Well, you know what they're like.' But on those occasions their conversation had trailed off when they'd seen her, and there was usually a moment or two of awkward silence before Emily, good sport that she was, would change the subject, and they'd be back to whether that singer, the blond one from The Beat, was more of a dish than what's his face from Duran Duran.

She knew full well, though, *that* was just one of many conspiratorial huddles which probably took place on these grounds every day. And it was the only one she was even partially privy to. No doubt elsewhere her name, or perhaps the name of one of the officially ranked undesirables, was right at that moment being dragged through the mud by another cabal of Imogens without any need for circumspection.

Thank God she herself was light skinned, Roxy kept thinking, the ambiguity it afforded her its own kind of protection. She'd heard other girls describe Manisha as a 'Paki', but that was rare, and only among themselves when they thought no one else was within earshot. Far more often it was that 'Boney M' nonsense, which no one could reasonably object to – after all that *was* her initial, and she was skinny – or the 'brown girl in the ring', and there'd frequently be things said about her hair, especially on those days they had swimming. Also, any time the word 'smelly' came up in class, say in chemistry in relation to one of those gases, she'd usually be able to spot at least one of the white girls looking Manisha's way through her goggles. Anyway, she was just grateful that though things could get tense from time to time at *their* family get-togethers, no one would be objecting to *her* upcoming geography field trip, particularly as they had no idea that there would be boys going from the other local public school, the one Suresh had attended.

'Rookes? Is that like Arabic or something?'

She didn't say anything. Sat there playing with her hair, but when the boy – dark haired, very good looking and every bit as pleased with himself – leaned in for the expected kiss, she turned her head away.

The boy's expression changed again. He looked hurt, a poor wounded animal trying to understand why this girl with the exotic name was immune to his charms. They'd been sitting a few yards from the rest of the group who'd gathered in the main square of the pretty little town they were staying in.

The trip was to the Loire valley, and would involve exploring the limestone plateaus of Touraine as well as the crystalline plateaus of Anjou and Vendée. At least that's what her parents had been told, and after some umming and ahhing, which was mostly just for show, they'd agreed to let her go. Had they known the boys from Suresh's old school would also be tagging along, they might not have given their consent quite so readily.

'What's the matter, Rookes? Don't you want to?'

Right at that moment she wasn't sure *what* she wanted, but she knew it wasn't him. It had been a mistake to sit separately with him. She could see that now. It's just that she was so bored with the rest of the group. Emma and Victoria seemed more interested in the boys than in collecting any kind of field samples, and the three of them had barely spoken since they got here. Not much of a triumvirate at all when she thought about it.

'Let's go back over there,' she said, indicating the cluster of tables and well-appointed English faces outside the bar, which seemed highly relaxed about serving alcohol to possible minors.

'Yah, no problem. I'll get you a drink then,' said the Wounded Animal, relieved that it was a liquor rather than personal-attractiveness issue. By the time he came back, holding two glasses of red wine, she'd already left, accompanied back to their shared room by the other angels who, it turned out, had also been quietly bored with the male attention they'd attracted. It was only when they got back to the room and began swapping notes that any of them actually started to enjoy the trip.

'I barely even know him, and he's already invited me to go skiing with him in December.'

'But you don't know how to ski.'

'Yah, I know, he says he's going to teach me.'

'No?!'

'Yah.'

'But what if you're no good?'

'I doubt that, Rookes. But even if I am, then I suppose we'll just have to stay in the chalet the whole time.'

They all laughed, none of them with any real intention of seeing these boys again once the field trip was over.

She was surprised at just how easy it was to get the boys to do her, to do all of their, bidding. Money, drinks, compliments, suggestions floating around in a gilded fee-paying bubble. Drifting idly from one set of untroubled eyes to the next, just waiting to be plucked. Or burst. And she found that all it took to set the wheels in motion was something as simple as a hint in the eyes or allowing her hair to fall a certain way through her fingers while playing with it in an otherwise distracted fashion. Some tiny adjustment, and they'd be hopping around, fetching and paying, even while they stretched out their rugby-honed physiques and feigned nonchalance. And though she was loath to admit it, they (and that meant all of them, not just the Wounded Animal, Casper) did seem to pay *her* more attention than her two roommates. With Emma and Victoria it was all familiarities – Aches (which she later learnt was Aix), Newquay, *and, oh yah, the next big bash at Jezza's, yah, his parents are away for the summer and, yah, get this, they've left him in charge! Jezza?! Yah, I know. Mad, right?* – spoken across the table, to no one in particular, just left hanging in the faintly Gallic night air. But if they spoke to her, then she noticed how the words suddenly became specific, directed, targeted.

'What are you doing over half-term? A few of us are getting together and going down to Cornwall.'

They were so weak, these boys, that it was simultaneously pathetic and thrilling. She'd look at them outside the bar, in their pink polo shirts and cream chinos or tennis shorts, so eager to please, thinking the ability to get served and pay for things somehow made them into big men rather than the fawning adolescent boys they actually were. She saw how they'd pretend to be laughing and joking about something else whenever her little triumvirate was nearby. But how the more uninterested they tried to make themselves seem, the less convincing they were. All nudges and elbows and changing-room humour, as though the sheer amateurishness of it would somehow remain hidden. She made a point of not drinking as well, rightly suspecting how fascinated they would be by that as well as how uneasy it would make the others, including her roomies.

'Rookes, is it against your religion?' Emma had asked her.

'I just can't,' she'd replied enigmatically. 'I promised not to. He'd kill me if he found out.'

She knew she had their undivided attention then, all of them, the boys who turned out to be friends of Wounded Animal, and the other angels.

'Who, Rookes, who'd kill you?' asked Emma, looking genuinely surprised as well as concerned.

She thought about it for a moment, thought how much she was enjoying being the centre of attention for once and not just for being part of the triumvirate. It was thrilling, the thought that these goras were hanging on to her every word, were finally being made to reckon with the fact that she wasn't quite like them, even if she could lie every bit as well.

'He'd just know. He'd know if I was lying. I think He'd smell the sin on my breath,' she went on.

'Who, Rookes, who?' Emma implored her.

'Look, it doesn't matter,' said Roxy, only now feeling properly like a Roxy for the first time.

If she'd known how much fun lying was she'd have taken it up years ago. And she seemed to be good at it, a natural, knowing just how far to go. Exactly when to leave it. That last bit probably something to do with her mum, she felt.

The number of times over the years that she'd seen her mum gently manipulate her dad, a hint here, an implication there, and next thing she knew there was a new car in the drive, or a new appliance in the kitchen, which seemed to get upgraded every year or so, even though the old appliances weren't exactly old. Or they would be looking out of the porthole or from the window seat at some exotic foreign destination. Were those lies, strictly speaking? She wasn't sure. What *was* clear to her, though, was how productive these little manipulations were, a word or a stance or even just something as simple as a culinary work-to-rule. Those endless days of gastronomic abandonment, 'convenience' the new byword for her casually attired mum, sari and salwar temporarily discarded into a nostalgic realm of home cooking and a happy (sort of) husband. The gradual ascent of the instantly micro-waveable in a kitchen which used to boast fresh ingredients. Food 'to go' even though it was only her dad who actually had a job 'to go' to. Her mum, so clever clever, always rushing rushing around the house in her casual trouser/sweatshirt combo. No concession to domestic harmony until the hinted-at appliance or holiday would materialise. Or the expensive feat of German engineering purred its way into their gravel drive. At which point some semblance of wifely duty would push past the kohl-lipstick-light-skin triptych and the normal state of passive-aggressive equilibrium would be restored. But, yes, lies or just as-yet-unstated truths, Roxy knew from what she'd already observed at home that it was all about what was left unsaid. She'd seen that first hand. And as a strategy for self-advancement, she knew it worked, if her parents were anything to go by.

'Look, don't worry about me,' she said, knowing that's exactly what they'd be doing for the rest of the evening. 'Get yourself whatever you want. But don't worry about me, I'm OK. I don't want to be a damp squib.'

Casper, the Wounded Animal, sprang into action.

'Rookes, you're starting to worry me now. You're scaring all of us. Now listen up, and I think I speak for all of us, you're with friends here, there's nothing you can't tell us. We're all here for you, Rookes. Whatever you need.'

Roxy thought for a moment that she might have pushed things too far. What *was* all that garbage about sin on her breath? What on earth had inspired her to come out with that? Then she looked at the empties on the table in front of her. And from there to the eager, yet freshly troubled faces of her newfound friends. She could see what had happened here. Nothing ever touched their bubble. To be honest, very little happened inside it either. Smooth, unflustered progress from prep school to big school with every encouragement imaginable. *Amo, amas, amat.* From nappies to chinos in one high-achieving whirl. Field trips, foreign travel, the au pair. But for all that activity, nothing disruptive ever happened. No downs to go with the endless ups. So she'd invented one instead. If only to see what they really thought. In that cryptic sentence, with its capitalised 'Him' and the 'sin on her breath', Roxy had effectively outed herself as one of the undesirables. *You know what they're like.* And now she wanted to see how they would respond.

Casper's little speech, though. What a trooper! He genuinely cared, she thought, a little surprised. She'd need to be a little more careful from here on in, else she ran the risk of these people *actually* becoming part of her life. No more random capitalisations, though the apocryphal phrasing could stay.

'I didn't mean to do that,' she said. 'I really didn't want to say anything. It's no biggie really. It's just that I've got a cousin who gets a little over-protective sometimes. Before I came here he made me promise that I wouldn't drink. And I want to honour that now.'

Honour. Good word that, she thought, highly unfamiliar in the context of a Home Counties private education in this year of Our Lord 1983. Ha ha, 'cousin'. Well, she could hardly have indicated her dad as the brooding, sinister patriarch, especially as both Emma and Victoria had already met him at various school sports days, and if there was one thing that man was not, it was sinister.

Actually, the first time they'd seen him he'd been in a particularly jovial mood. That was the same day that Mythili had surprised everyone by winning the long jump, and she, Roxy, had done unexpectedly well in the relay when the girls in both the outside and inside lanes had dropped their batons during the always-tricky handover. Her dad was delighted by his daughter's default triumph, and later, after she'd got changed, she overheard him telling another parent in the car park, how his daughter had won a gold medal.

'But she's an all-rounder. Not just sporty,' he'd been saying as she sidled up to the new Audi estate. 'She's a big help at home, too, and she study so hard.'

The other parent turned out to be the father of one of the girls who'd dropped the baton, but he still managed a weak smile and kept whatever other feelings he might have had in check. All in all that counted as a good day.

Her dad might have been many things that day. Jovial, proud. But sinister? That wasn't one of them.

Anyway, she thought, why not give the people what the people want? Especially when they've never heard this stuff before, or at least not first hand, sitting around in a French town square, drunk on the sheer beauty of their carefree lives. Besides, she thought, everyone knew that all Asian people were the same, basically. Some even said it, though luckily not in her class. She understood the basic premise, though, that what was good enough for one of them probably applied to the rest as well. And it didn't take a genius to figure out what the hermetically exclusive army she was at school with were thinking any time an Asian made the news. *Illegal immigrants, dodgy solicitors, weird religions, pervy family doctors, pervy families.* God knows what happened behind closed doors, but if those tabloid stories were anything to go by there was always at least one dodgy cousin or uncle in every Polaroid family snapshot. And now there was one in hers, too.

That trip bonded them much closer together, she and Emma and Victoria. The phantom cousin definitely helped. They made a pact always to tell each other everything, which, of course, she knew they'd never be able to live up to even as they were taking the vows. But it was something far more significant that she'd really learnt from the trip. She now knew that as Roxy at least, she could have whatever she wanted provided she just knew how to ask. As Roxy, she was far from invisible. She registered as a lot more than a blip on the hormonal Home Counties' radar. And all it took was a pose, a minor adjustment. Not quite white, never quite right, and for the time being that suited her just fine.

The bharatanatyam was her mum's idea. A bit late in the day, and around a decade after the early starters, the little goody-two-shoes the wider 'community' appeared to specialise in at a time when the rest of society was going pleated skirts and Lady Di crazy.

'Sohni, it will be such a good thing for you to learn. Everyone should have some kind of fine art in their background. Painting, drawing, bharatanatyam. Nobody just wants sporty and study.'

She'd had no idea what her mum meant at the time and kept wondering why sporty and study was judged perfectly OK for her brothers but not for her. But mainly to keep the peace (as she had Jezza's do to sneak out to in the next few weeks, in spite of how they'd promised back in the Loire, she and Emma and Victoria, not to follow up with any of the boys they'd proved so irresistible to during the field trip), she agreed to go along with whatever it was that her mum had arranged.

At least it wasn't just her who seemed unhappy during the private lessons. The other girls who had assembled in what was clearly a modified living-room in a fairly large house several streets away also carried that surly, resentful 'You as well? Me, too. I'm only here because it's easier than arguing' look into the sessions. Of course, it wasn't easier than arguing, far from it, and the intensity of Roxy's unhappiness was probably only matched by the searing pain in her calves, her hips, pretty much everywhere from the waist down.

The one thing she did gain from those painful lessons, though, was a newfound respect for the dancers themselves. For instance, when they performed at the various community 'functions' which seemed to go hand in hand with this puja or that festival, and when the best of them was invited to showcase their skills at London-based cultural institutes, Roxy frequently found herself in the audience, dragged along by her mum, who always seemed more interested in what she was wearing and what other mothers (and daughters) were wearing. She'd find herself in this sartorial huddle, a sari never quite right on her, simultaneously loathing and admiring the dancers. Some of them went to her school, and she'd never seen them as animated there as they appeared to be during these performances.

At school there was barely even a hint of their presence. These were the quiet girls whose work was always on time, who never seemed distracted. And if Mythili's long-jump success was a rare moment of physical triumph for one of them, they never seemed that bothered. Lunchtimes they'd be together, the same for mid-morning break times, and the only occasions they ever spoke in class were when they were spoken to. The mere thought of volunteering an opinion seemed not to have occurred to any of them. Yet here they were, in a prestigious cultural institute, delighting the audience with intricate hand and eye gestures, suggestive of all manner of intimacy. On stage, as though they were born to it, a place where no one would likely have guessed their seething contempt for everything around them. The dim-lit community halls, at least half the audience, and the idea beneath that unhappy adolescent skin that somehow *this* constituted an identity. Being told what to do, how to do it, every step of the way, with the ultimate accolade arriving in the form of another dodgy Polaroid uncle and the throwaway remark, 'Oh, Mythili, you've really grown up now,' eyes flitting beyond the costume or the perfection of that 'turnout' and landing upon a pair of surprisingly muscular, training-hardened thighs. Perhaps that long-jump success shouldn't have come as such a shock after all.

Or was that just in her, Roxy's, head? She couldn't tell. All she did know was that these girls from her school, set fair for careers in biochemistry (medicine was still seen as something of an 'English' preserve), never seemed more confident than when they demonstrated what they'd learnt to the rest of the community. Or, come to think of it, more surprised when they became aware of her in the audience.

'Oh, hello. I didn't think you were *into* this sort of thing,' said Mythili the first time she spotted Roxy at one of these events, and, not just that, but spotted her wearing a sari that no amount of safety pins could ever quite fix. The pinning and the awkwardness with which Roxy shuffled under the garish folds, all noted in one faintly amused eye sweep.

'You're really good,' said Roxy, in spite of herself and that fucking look Mythili had given her. But also because, though it pained her to say so, it was true.

'Oh, thanks. But I'm still learning really,' said Mythili, cross with herself for her earlier snap judgement. Maybe Rox wasn't so bad when you got to know her, she thought. Nothing like the coconut the other girls made her out to be.

'But you are. You were brilliant up there,' said Roxy, 'like you were born to do it.'

After that they were joined by a group of girls who Roxy didn't know but who were clearly friends of Mythili's, and it was while they were standing around, Roxy looking for an excuse to leave, that she spotted her mum deep in conversation with Mythili's earlier admirer. This same Polaroid cut-out now fixated on the woman in front of him. Roxy's mum, with her specially imported Banarasi-silk sari, the one with the gold threading, looking more animated now than Roxy ever remembered her being around her, Roxy's, dad.

She tried, she really did. Tried to fit in, get used to the pinning and the small talk. *So and so's girl off to Cambridge, and so and so's to the other one. And, you know, that's just not done in our culture. Let them study first then we can worry about everything else. At least that way they will always have an education to fall back on. He's working for the UNO now.* The 'O' always pronounced 'oh'.

But there were only so many times a year she could bear to spend an evening around her mum. And in the end if only to put a stop to all her mum's shrieking and squawking to virtual strangers in function halls about her daughter's Oxbridge ambitions, she took the decision to withdraw her name from that process. In spite of her predicted grades, she applied to Warwick University instead. And four others, including Leeds, which could be described as many things, though the idea of dreaming spires wasn't necessarily one of them.

'Warwick?'

'That's right, Mum.'

'Why Warwick, sohni? I've never heard of it,' said her Mum, helpful as ever.

'It's a good course, and it's where I want to go,' replied Roxy, sticking to her guns.

They were sat in the living-room, Roxy, her parents and their twin grandsons, who were engrossed just then in a game of battleships in one corner of the thick shagpile carpet. Rakesh had dropped them off earlier en route to whisking his wife away for a 'short break' to Paris. 'That's so romantic,' Roxy's mum had said at the time, but the look she'd given their dad spoke less of longing than envy. *Our own son, who's barely been ten minutes in the door at your firm, and already he treats our daughter-in-law better than you treat your own wife. Paris in the spring. I've always wanted to go.*

'But why set your sights so low, sohni?' asked her mum, knowing as usual precisely which buttons to push. 'Oxbridge. You can do whatever you like there. But that name, everyone knows that name. And then no one will even care what you did.'

She had to admit, there was a certain logic to what her mum was saying. But, of course, that didn't take into account the strong feelings of revulsion that word 'Oxbridge' conjured up for someone like Roxy. Someone for whom the prospect of spending another three years in an institution, and a city, with the same people she'd been wanting to get away from ever since she'd started school was like a form of punishment. Also, she didn't want to be anywhere near such and such's daughter and definitely not so and so's son, who she'd heard had got a place there to study law.

'It's not low. She can study wherever she like. As long as she happy, that the main thing.' Her Dad had spoken, taking everyone by surprise. Roxy had just assumed that this would end in some epic battle of wills between herself and her mum, one or the other eventually buckling under the sheer drabness of it all. But at no point had she expected her dad to suddenly enter the fray, a mild-mannered Solomon briefly breaking off from his ledger. Yet, now that he had, it was clear that this would be the last word on the matter. She would go to Warwick, and her mum would have to find some other material to shriek and squawk about at those 'recession, what recession?' social functions she favoured.

Roxy looked at her dad sat there in his mustard-brown slacks, poring over the accountancy details in some requisitioned book that Rakesh would later tell her had been 'cooked'.

For months he'd put up without complaint as his wife took to wearing ever more garish costume jewellery to those functions she was always dragging their daughter to. He'd never said a word about what to his eyes seemed to be the needlessly expensive perfumes and overly elaborate preparations she would undertake for what was, after all, just another standard 'cultural' evening in the suburbs. Never mentioned how it made him feel to come back to an empty home with an empty fridge. Entire days spent holed up with clients and calculations and grimly detailed bankruptcy proceedings, and yet, when he came back, no lights were on and more often than not he'd find himself ringing for a takeaway. Or watching a video, some Hindi classic which felt even more melodramatic than usual, with his old friends Jim Beam and Bombay mix. But he hadn't said a word about any of that.

Yet here he was, sufficiently angered by the misunderstanding of what that word 'low' actually meant, to finally speak up.

His wife said nothing, for once completely at a loss, and Roxy understood that silence. She knew it was something to do with disappointment, of life not quite lived as high society. She knew it began with her mum's light skin and green eyes (which she'd inherited), and the capriciousness which went with being born pretty, and fair, and wealthy into a culture which prized those accidents as gifts. To those eyes her husband, her dark, honest, plain, non-lantern-jawed husband, was little more than a beast of burden, a coolie whose labours were the only useful thing about him. She felt he was beneath her, and they both knew it, but for a price, a sweatstresshypertension premium (for him), the maharani's silence could be bought. And how did Roxy know this? She knew because some of that high-born, light-skinned, nak ucha stink had rubbed off on her as well. Her mum's gift to her daughter, a permanent sense of unease around her own people, aapne lok. The reason her friends were called Emma and Victoria; the reason she never had any trouble, unlike the other Asian girls, gaining parental consent for fancy school trips abroad. Above all, the reason she found herself regularly repulsed by brown skin and a decidedly post-punk use of safety pins to hold up a sari.

Roxy looked at her Dad, and as she did, she could have sworn that her dad, fully taking in that his wife had finally been stunned into silence, gave his daughter a little wink before getting right back to that complicated ledger he'd been studying.

A Boy Like You

South London, late 1970s/early 1980s

1978. THAT'S WHEN he'd decided. Well, not so much decided as have his hand forced by external events. Blondie, to be precise. That bloody tune, so damn catchy, and as soon as he heard it for the first time he just knew, in the way that kids do, that it would create all kinds of bother for him. Mostly it was the chorus. All that 'do be doo' carry on, he knew that wouldn't play well in the towers or in class. Come to think of it, the 'boy like you' bit, or that detail of the 'eyes so blue' didn't exactly do him any favours either. And near Jamaica Road it went almost without saying that all sorts of people, not just limited to his classroom, would take a particularly dim view of the French verse. Foreign, continental, wrong. His first inkling that something was awry coming before he'd even reached the school gates. Not far from where he lived he'd overheard some workmen talking about the song on the street, and even then, late for school, the tune climbing the charts, he somehow knew his own fortunes were wrapped up in the fate of this instant new-wave classic.

The bigger of the two workmen appeared to be doing a merry little jig on the spot as he serenaded his colleague with the line about it being like a dream when he smiled. To his eyes, the smaller of the duo was deliberately acting a bit camp, how D imagined one of those fellas filling up bathtubs in his verbal-reasoning puzzles might have behaved, batting away the bigger man's compliments with a Frankie Howerd-ish élan and an exaggerated wave of the hand. They both laughed, paying no attention to the schoolboy who'd stopped to watch and was taking in the whole scene with a look of appalled fascination.

By the time D got to class, the standard pre-registration paper fight was already threatening to boil over into something a little weightier, and, of course, there was no sign of the teacher. The scrunched-up ring book cannonball pinged off his cheek before he'd even had a chance to sit down. And *that* seemed to be the cue for the morning singalong, the rest of them in his class so lucky and grateful to have found a boy like him, though in their version, directed at him, it was 'a boy like *you*'. And he wasn't exactly being serenaded.

That's when he'd decided. He wasn't going to be that boy any more. No, that pretty blonde singer from America had made sure of that. No more Denis for him. From now on, just D.

'Dee? But that's not your name, love. It's Denis. Like Denis Compton. You know, love, that cricketer your father likes.'

His mum was looking at him quizzically. He'd just informed her of his decision, hoping that would be that but not entirely surprised to find he was now being made to scramble around for a reason. He felt unexpectedly worked up about the whole thing. Conrad had really gone to town with the 'doo be doos' earlier. He'd been right up in his face with those blazing eyes and that fucking Pan Am bag, which in any case wasn't his, as if that cunt had ever gone further than the Jamaica Road on his travels. And typically, at least half the class, that half which spent a good portion of each day desperately trying to avoid eye contact with the class bully, suddenly felt able to look and laugh now that Conrad's focus was no longer on them.

No surprise either when the teacher finally walked in and didn't say a word, clearly enjoying the 'musicality' of the scene, the gently indulgent look on his face more suggestive of a delighted bystander taking in the sights and sounds of an after-dinner crooner rather than those of an apprentice crim. The hairy seemed to enjoy the spontaneity of it all, the black boy giving form to his exuberance (so 'musical' in spite of everything), and the white one pretending to be shocked (such wits, these cockneys). Yep, the hairy had just let them get on with it in that very Inner London Education Authority way of his that D and the rest of his cohort was already wearily accustomed to. And no, no way was he going to be that boy any more.

'But that's what I want you to call me. D. It's mysterious, Mum, and everyone loves a good mystery.'

'Mysterious? What are you talking about, love? Your father won't be happy, I can tell you that right now. I don't want my son to be a bleedin' mystery, I want him to be my son. And last I checked, his name was Denis.'

'Look, Mum, I've made my mind up. I want to be known as D. And I want you to tell them at school an' all. It'll be for the best. I promise. And you'll get used to it in no time. Plus, it'll save time. Think about it, all those extra seconds saying "Denis" when one sound will do from now on. More time for you, less time spent running after me. You see, Mum, it makes perfect sense when you think about it.'

She didn't say anything, pondering what her son was trying to tell her. He took the silence to mean she was wavering. He thought perhaps he hadn't made the strength of his feelings clear enough.

'Seriously, Mum, who else do you know who's called Denis?'

As it was a largely rhetorical question, and because he was trying to make a point, he carried on before she could even mention Denis Law the footballer, who, for some reason, she seemed to quite like. Maybe it was that backheel that had sent his old club down? They'd all had a good laugh about that, including Dad, and *he* barely had any interest in the football, least of all when it didn't concern any of the local clubs.

'Denis the Menace, and Denis Healey, with those mad eyebrows, which ain't exactly great, Mum. But D, well, no one's going to think "mad bloke on the telly". And it's just to the point, Mum. You can see that, can't you?'

It was a masterstroke. He didn't know it at the time, but in that telling detail about the abbreviated name being 'to the point', he'd unwittingly appealed, not to his mum but to her younger self, who'd always been attracted by a bit of style and no little purpose.

That's what she'd first noticed about the man who would become her husband. The knitted polo shirts, the mohair parallels and just how 'to the point' that look was. He couldn't possibly know, she thought. Then again, he is our son, and everyone knows what they say about fruit and trees.

'Well alright, love, if you're sure? I can see you're dead set on doing this, Den –'

'D, Mum, it's D,' he interrupted her.

'Dee. OK then, Dee,' said his Mum, her voice softening, faintly amused and even mildly impressed by her son's line of argument. 'But I tell you one thing, love, your father definitely isn't going to be happy about this. You can tell him yourself when he gets home.'

Of course, he knew if he'd told her the real reason, that it was to do with some pop record and a bit of teasing at school, she'd have been anything but amused or impressed. And it's likely that D would never have got out of the blocks. To be honest, it's why he never had that conversation with his dad. His mum, bless her, had had it for him. That evening there'd been lots of to-ing and fro-ing across the kitchen table, the old man's incredulity matched by his mum's implacability. *I know it sounds daft, but the boy really has made his mind up,* the point at which his dad more or less threw in the towel, wiped his mouth and asked his wife what was for tea.

In the manner of these things, there was one other detail that was left unsaid. And for good reason, too, as he knew both his folks would have taken a dim view of it. Meanwhile, though, it hadn't escaped D's attention that many of the rogue elements in his class, who also happened to be black, had for some time now been adopting 'street' names. Lloyd became 'Sticks', Michael resurfaced as 'Daps' and Conrad, well, everyone knew he was just a big 'C'. It was never actually clear why these specific names had come about, but that was beside the point. The main thing was, as D noted to his regret, that the girls at school seemed to love it, as much as the teachers hated it. The lads who went by these names appeared to puff out their chests a little more than anyone else when it came to lunchtimes and the mass skirmish on one side of the playground which passed for the main game of football taking place. A couple of passes strung together, and the usual suspects would be carrying on like they were Brazil.

'Sticks, man, on your left!'

'Seen.'

'Sweet as a nut, Daps.'

'Safe, man. To your right!'

'Seen. Soon come.'

None of it really made any sense to D, but even a blind man could see the confidence and cachet visibly growing around these boys. And while the LEA hairies didn't much like it, they also made sure to tread carefully around this newfound confidence. That big punch-up in Lewisham just before Elvis took the count was still fresh in most people's minds, and D had already heard plenty from other people around his way about the mouth and manners on the younger blacks, though not from his folks. But *that* wasn't the bit he paid attention to anyway. What interested D was how a simple change of name, with a few stylistic tweaks, had evidently opened up a whole new world of possibility for these lads. The birds loved it, and they got a free pass from everyone else, so they could more or less spend the average school day doing and saying as they pleased. The other thing was, they never got bullied by anyone, especially not by Conrad, and for that reason alone it suddenly seemed a worthwhile proposition.

Besides, it had been a long time coming.

He'd never really been happy just being himself in this place. A boy like him, Denis, bored and unhappy, constantly harbouring thoughts of doing a John Stonehouse. A disappearing act which would allow him to escape this classroom once and for all. To leave behind its myopia and self-appointed stupidity – *thirty-two, motherfuckers, thirty-two!* – and revel in whatever else was out there beyond these LEA walls. Perhaps all that was missing was his own little stylistic tweak, from Denis to D, and some other place, or at least some other experience of this place, could be his.

He couldn't help but feel that the shortening of his name would in some indefinable way lengthen the odds of his remaining stuck here, and there was something pleasing in that for a boy who already mapped out his everyday life according to a crude cost/benefit analysis. Hide the lunch money in his socks and risk a more severe shakedown upon discovery, or spread the risk between socks and pockets and possibly get to hang on to at least half of the money. Also, in that simple initial, 'D', he could see a hiding place for himself, the anonymity he'd craved ever since he'd set foot in this school. Plus, he just knew it would get under the skin of Conrad, and perhaps Sticks and Daps, too. So maybe in the end that blonde bird everyone fancied, Debbie Harry, had done him a favour. The name change was always on the cards. She'd just speeded things up a bit. Else the decade might have run out with D still unhappily answering to Denis.

In the end, though his Dad still thought the boy was being daft, he went along with his son's wishes. It wasn't just that his wife had asked him to, though that also played a part. He had to admit, albeit a little grudgingly, that in the abbreviation 'D' there was a certain economy of style. No waste, a minimum of fuss, but the point still being made, and made forcefully, that a phoenix had risen from the ashes. D just an initial, yet behind it, he sensed, a whole lot of thought. And, to be honest, it wasn't the worst thing. It's not as though the boy had left for school in the morning looking like his son and come home at night looking like something else entirely. He'd heard about that kind of carry on, not so much around here, but he knew it happened. One of the chaps from work had been complaining just the other day about his own son dressing like a 'queer' in safety pins and dog leads, and when he thought about it like that, what *his* boy wanted was hardly outlandish. Ultimately he offered no objection because he could see that the rest of his son's character was solidly there, still intact, perhaps more so than before, when it had just been attached to a name not of his choosing. It was clear to him then that yes, this time the boy had made his own choice, and like the great man himself, Denis Compton, he'd put his front foot forward. There was no arguing with *that* in his mind, so he put away whatever misgivings he might have had and, like any true modernist, made his accommodation with the new.

SENT TO THE TOWER

CONRAD HADN'T ALWAYS lived in the tower. He'd started off a few streets down, with both a mum and a dad, and a communal playing area that wasn't overrun with dog shit or tinfoil. He'd been happy then, played with the other kids. When his mum, Eunice, was back from her shift working as a nurse in one of the local care homes, she'd often see him, bright-eyed and lively, bouncing around near the swings on his space hopper. Though they didn't have much, she felt pleased that things seemed to have settled down for her. Nursing college had been a hard slog, and there were times when she'd doubted her own ability to see it through; usually when she'd overhear a stray remark from one of the doctors on the wards she'd trained on. Though sometimes it was from one of the other ladies in blue, who rarely smiled her way even if they seemed less spare with their affections when it came to her fellow trainees. Sometimes it was just the sheer damn cold of it all, bearing the pitch-black mornings through gritted teeth. Shivering away in that uniform which seemed ill equipped for the smog-filled, rain-soaked gauntlet. But she'd persevered, knowing the one thing that was worse than any of that would be to remain trapped up here with her mother.

Her cussed, beloved, mule-headed mother, who said she'd never really wanted to come to this godforsaken place, but once she was here had never shown any inclination to be anywhere else. Her father long gone, barely even present in whispers. Officially driven mad by the cold, the cold of it all, the spit-snarl-fuckeries of the locals. Colour bar and its unsmiling small print just too much for a proud island man who never paid much attention to how things were supposed to be. Bespoke-suited at a time of rationing, the brim on his hat almost as wide as his Kingston pearly whites. A mechanic at London Transport when such jobs were the preserve of a particular kind of local. A time before mangoes, or even garlic and peppers, in the local markets, when tempers would fray over a lot less than the presence of a black man in the white man's refuge. Especially one who remained steadfastly dapper through every provocation.

Unofficially, though, enduring it all with customary good grace until the day something snapped, and this handsome man in his Huntsman suit just upped and left, trailing a distant set of island curses. Driven away in the end by something even more corrosive than the colour bar, something no kind of law could get round. The barrage of complaint from his wife, which began more or less the day they arrived in the towers and never really stopped until the day he finally decided to walk away from all that cloud-capped disappointment. Just packed his bags and left to start over who knows where, or perhaps not even to do *that* much. Eunice never knew because she was never told. Her own mother so consumed by grief and rage that she barely even noticed when *her* daughter started to question this life they had in the tower. Started to see things in her father's absence. Started to hear things in the silence. Beneath the whispers, a shrill lament for the cussedness that had already driven one husband away and was now threatening to do the same to her only daughter.

Her mother had never warmed to Clement. It was as though she'd decided that if *she* couldn't be happy, then happiness should also elude her daughter. That way at least she'd never be truly alone. So when Eunice first showed up with her fancy man, her mother made a point of ignoring the flowers and the fruit bread he'd picked up on the way. She acted as though he, Clement, had quite some nerve even being here with a girl like Eunice. *A respectable girl, a nurse no less! She's from learning, young man. Yuh hear that? Learning.* And she'd gestured at all the books and journals, encyclopaedias and atlases that her departed husband had left her with, as though Eunice was from a long line of scholars whose current location here in the tower was just a temporary state of affairs which would soon be remedied once their housing case file landed on the right desk.

For the most part, Clement had ridden out the barbs, fore-warned by Eunice that her mother could be 'difficult' and knowing better than to ask what had happened to Eunice's father. But there was often an underlying tension whenever they visited, Eunice sensing her mother's hostility to the man she felt had spirited her daughter away. In reality, where she and Clement had set up home was less than five minutes' walk from the tower, but the second-floor perch and neat, communal areas felt a world away from the endless stairwells and pinched faces she was more used to in the high rise. One time she even remembered complimenting Clement on his 'natty threads', and her mother, making out as though she had wax on her eardrums, screeching, 'Wha'? You tek up with Natty Dread now? Rahtid. Filthy, nasty man. The shame of it.' It might even have been funny if her mother hadn't kept up with the 'dutty man' curse the whole time they'd been there, poor Clement silently absorbing the blows, though he'd never even considered having dreadlocks. His nattily altered threads just another inanimate victim of neglect during that painfully awkward encounter.

By the time Clement went to bad, Conrad was already a little boy. A happy one, too, his first years outside playing with the other children on the grass. Contentedly bouncing around with his space hopper and his friends. Fortunate, too, that he missed the worst of Clement's rages, reserved for indoors and for Conrad's mother.

'HOPEC, Eunice. Blood clart Harabs and all that blasted hoil! And now they talkin' voluntary redundancy. Voluntary! Is wha' kind of stupidness this? I don't give up my job voluntarily. They want me gone, they have fi tek it from me! I swear, Eunice, I won't go quiet. Yuh jus' watch.'

Later when the full effect of what those 'Harabs' had done was being felt in the council, where Clement had previously felt secure, respectable even, in his job as an accounts clerk (more like a glorified office boy, even though his qualifications put him far in advance of the pimply faced Englishman, barely out of school, who was his manager) with the aftershocks rippling out way beyond, Clement found his voice again. But only at home, simmering and resentful, where this time Eunice was the shock absorber, and more than once, hidden from his parents, Conrad had stood in the hallway, cowering away behind his space hopper.

For a while after Clement had left, Eunice had tried to hold on in that flat. But it was hard, the work drying up and the little boy no longer hiding away. Answering back, sounding each day more and more like the little English urchins she'd pass on the way to the shops. The ones with smart mouths and no fear. She could see what Conrad was becoming, those eyes which used to be so playful now aflame the whole time. Perhaps because he'd never really known him, he missed his father, and she could also see that in some distant fashion he held her responsible for his father's absence. Whenever she'd tried to explain to him that his father had had to go away because he wasn't happy any more, Conrad would fly into a rage. He screamed and shouted and threw things and made it very clear that he blamed her for everything. And as she had always done in the past with her own mother, resuming the habit once Clement had started to give voice to his rages, Eunice carried on absorbing everyone else's shock, a one-woman buffer zone for their myriad unhappinesses. The day she stopped was when she spied her little boy in one of the communal areas, using the space hopper as an offensive weapon, repeatedly bringing it down on the head of a much smaller child and laughing but with no particular joy as he did so.

Not long after, in the manner of a bad fairy tale, he was sent to the tower to live with his grandma. Conrad, like Rapunzel, was in distress, but unlike the fictional heroine, he had no tresses. Far from it. This little boy didn't even have locks. He'd be in that tower a while yet.

BACK OF THE NOSE
AND CORNER OF
THE MOUTH

AT SCHOOL THINGS took a turn for the worse round about the same time that Farah trousers became the big thing. D had watched the shift occur some time earlier, when that big tune by Freeez, 'Southern Freeez', started to climb the charts and push past the 2 Tone bands on their way down. The MA1 jackets and skin-tight-bleached-jeans brigade had, in any case, started to taper off once they ran into a bit of proper resistance, which in this manor usually meant from blacks. They'd still have something to say, of course, whenever more middle-class-looking kids, usually from Dulwich or Camberwell, strayed into their flight path, but those occasions were rare, and in the absence of anything better they'd make do with abusing the local Asian shopkeepers and stealing their stock. Sweets, fizzy drinks, all the standard trappings for an Aryan stormtrooper.

In general, though, they tended to avoid D, and that suited him just fine. At least a couple of them knew he had a brother with some sort of rep who worked the markets, but that didn't stop them giving him the occasional snide look on the evermore infrequent days they actually bothered with school. For the amount they went on about mates and cousins in various detention centres, D often got the impression they wished they'd served time in these institutions themselves. Parade-ground nonces, really, without much grasp of the finer points of style. Short, sharp shock written all over their barnets, but the way they carried on, it wasn't as though there was much else going on up there. The scowling and cackling, the occasional muttered 'jungle bunny' (only ever around the more bookish African kids, mind, never in the vicinity of Sticks or Daps), the aversion to all things disco.

From D's vantage point, skirting the edges of every other tribe, it was somewhat predictable. A little bit obvious, nothing left to the imagination. White boys as ever trying a little too hard not to fit in. They made it their business to hate the hairies, even though the teachers largely avoided them, but the way they hung around, these skins, always in a little group, circling the wagons in one corner of the playground or a classroom, wasn't lost on the smarter kids, even if the hairies remained as clueless as ever.

Sticks, Daps, probably Conrad as well, for all he knew, must have seen something in that corner positioning. It was defensive, rope-a-dope, but these skinheads were no Ali. The smarter kids would have spotted the tell-tale signs in how the peanuts just had to be near one another, their crew cuts and MA1s like a high-visibility mating call. And in that playground and those class-rooms, that could only mean one thing. They must have been scared. And this was even before that fire a few months later just up the road in New Cross, the one that killed all those black kids at a birthday party, after which they possibly had good reason to be.

To D's eyes, though, the MA1s just looked silly, all puffed up like Popeye. It was supposed to be a new decade, yet here they were imitating a bunch of Dickensian glue sniffers. And once they'd recognised its popular, cross-party appeal, the fact that more or less everyone liked The Specials, they'd made a point of moving away from the half-decent music, the 2 Tone stuff, and nailing their colours to a much more antisocial mast. All that Oi! rubbish, which at least spared them the embarrassment of having to share its dubious pleasures with straightforwardly square classmates. It just sounded like angry noise to him, even the better stuff – the two-chord thrash, having a good old shout about the life and times of the neglected white man. Small town chronicles devoured by the glue sniffers and the ex-punks, the skins and the suburbs. Straight-arm salutes and brittle sounds, which seemed about right, D thought, if the local playground contingent was any kind of benchmark. Plus, that accent so many seemed to adopt, what was that all about? Cartoon cockney, the sort that was rarely spoken in London itself any more. Again, D thought, it was as though they were all trying just a little too hard to be authentic. The accent, back of the nose and corner of the mouth, doing its best to remain undiluted by whatever it was that they'd been putting in the water. A losing battle south of the drink, though, where a little bit of everything already flowed downriver.

Somehow, the jitteriness, the shouting, the silly look was all connected in D's head to the playground and its relative hierarchies. Swots to one side, usually the bit nearest the class-rooms and what he guessed was their relative safety. Footballers in the middle, taking up the main stretch. And then the tribes, plotting and scheming in various corners, or in the case of Sticks and Daps and their little crew, cutting a distinctive, patois-patterned swathe closer to one of the boundary walls. The skins more or less opposite but attracting fewer comments, and defi-nitely fewer girls. Himself, he was bored with the whole set-up, but at least, since becoming D, he had found some wary acknow-ledgement from Sticks, though Daps was still keeping his own counsel. But he was pleased that lopping off a couple of syllables had imbued him with some kind of presence. At least he registered now, even if it was just as 'the off-kilter one'. (After he'd nodded to Sticks one lunchtime, the boy Sticks had been talking to asked him who D was, and D had hung around just long enough to overhear Sticks answer, 'Who, him? D. He's alright, but he's a bit off-kilter.') Oh yeah, and there was always Conrad, of course. That cunt was still everywhere taxing everyone except, of course, Sticks, Daps, the skins and now himself, which, in its own way, he guessed, counted as progress.

Even so, that jitteriness surrounding the skins, he knew it was something to do with Sticks and Daps and the other boys who hung around with them, sporting the red, gold and green wristbands or carrying Head holdalls customised with badges in what he learnt from Sticks were the Rasta colours. With the girls they had no problems attracting. Above all, with the hairies who clearly loathed them (the blacks) but had no idea how to deal with them. They must have known *they* were the main billing, these burnished rebels, with the skins barely even making it on to the undercard. And when he observed their pinched expressions, D was left with the sense that the skins knew it, too.

One thing for sure, the skins spent far too long with each other, and he sometimes got the impression from how they'd forever be eyeing up the other tribes, that what they craved above all was a bit of recognition. The problem, of course, being the antisocial vibe they'd spent so long cultivating and now positively reeked of. Most of the other kids were either scared of them or disgusted by them, so by and large they were left to their own devices. But Sticks and some others, they'd already picked up on that scent, and though nothing was explicitly said, everyone knew who really belonged here and who didn't.

For D, though, things had definitely improved since he'd retreated behind the initial. With Conrad no longer on his case he was able to concentrate more in class, and his teachers were pleased, putting him forward for half a dozen O levels. In the process reaffirming his sense of difference from most of his peers. As ever, there was a balance to be struck, though. Overdo it with the freshly minted academic status and he'd risk being lampooned, or worse, at the hands of the CSE woodworkers. But underplay his (genuine) enthusiasm for his dramatically improved academic prospects, and it was the newfangled attentiveness of the teachers that he would be jeopardising. So he quietly got on with it, using the initial as a shield. Implacable behind the mask – not really a scholar, just D. And making friends in that anonymity with his old friends Pi and Algebra, which sounded to his ears less a curriculum requirement and far more like one of the daily specials down the local caff.

Still, most of that year, 1980, was spent quietly slipping under the radar of classroom priorities. So while the vast majority of his class seemed to have already decided it was that slightly chubby blonde who'd shot JR, D cracked on with past papers and isosceles triangles. He hadn't exactly made friends here, so there was effectively no one around to notice the change in him. His way of listening while feigning boredom, but then following up on his notes away from the scrutiny of the tribes, out of sight in his bedroom with CliffNotes, pass notes, whatever else he'd managed to squirrel out of the teachers. There was no one to tell him how pleased he seemed by where he sat in class, away from the other white boys but only a desk or so removed from Sticks. And definitely no one to warn him that the anonymous sticking plaster, D, could be ripped away at any moment to reopen that festering sore, Denis. Perhaps he should have known better than to expect a lasting peace around here.

The Dread colours had really taken over after they showed the Marley gig on the telly, the one he played for that new African country that had just got its independence.

Even as he was watching it with his folks, D knew there'd be an upsurge in the playground fashion stakes. It was just how things worked. Some band would be on the box, and everyone would be talking about it the next day. Depending on what got said, it wouldn't be long before the look itself walked through the school gates. It happened with the black kids and Michael Jackson, that natural looking 'fro after *Off The Wall*, and then with the white kids and 2 Tone, suedehead crops, Sta-Prest and blakeys, though there were always moody Lonsdale and Adidas crew neck tops doing the rounds as well. (Through his brother's ongoing exploits in the hoisting business, he had privileged access to much of this gear but never really saw it, as some others might have done, as a business opportunity.) Though he loved that particular Michael Jackson album, D tempered his enthusiasm with the bitter memory of being held up more than once during this period by Conrad, hair now grown out in the appointed fashion, and armed with a 'fro comb as his new weapon of choice.

Sure enough, the red, gold and green started to appear everywhere, on folders, bags, wristbands, tracksuit tops. And there was little the LEA could do about it, overtaken as usual by events beyond the council chambers.

When it kicked off in Miami less than a month later, D knew he wasn't the only one from school who'd be watching the plumes of smoke and the burnt-out buildings with a certain amount of interest. And no matter how much the news went on about the rioting itself and the damage to property, it was also wrapped up in other statistics. Dead bodies, numbers of National Guardsmen and of people arrested. Black people, really angry ones, bricking white motorists, then chasing them from their cars, sometimes catching them. He knew Sticks would be watching this, Daps, too, and, if he was really unlucky, Conrad as well. This was just the kind of story he dreaded, because he knew it would nourish the very worst instincts of these boys, the ones which fed off any kind of rivalry. Instincts which were probably digesting the details, feeding the resentment right at that moment. Another country in the high rises. It may as well have been Miami.

Though they all lived nearby, D never saw them out of school. Perhaps it wasn't that surprising. The authorities had merged together several schools from neighbouring areas to make up one giant, experimental cohort in the school he attended, which at times made it feel more like a holding pen. Some of these kids were from Bermondsey, but many, many more came from Peckham, New Cross, even Lewisham. The school itself was located in that part of the borough, much closer to where the NF had tried to march than where the Great Fire of Tooley Street had once raged. It was another country that end of the Old Kent Road. Evidently a blacker one, too. All he knew was that the moment they stepped outside of those LEA borders, it was as though the black kids disappeared into some parallel universe he knew nothing about. Only to reappear some time later with pigment-specific accounts of hostility and harassment (which they always pronounced 'arras ment, as if it was two words, compared to the 'harrisment' which rolled around, largely theoretically, on *his* tongue). Even though the bodies, the arrests, the original offence, had all taken place an ocean away, he knew the aftershocks would be processed far closer to home. That distant city on fire licking away at this localised baby black consciousness. The heavy-handed response over there somehow mirroring 'arras ment grievances right here. The bad looks from shop assistants or store detectives, even though the vast majority of hoisters were white. Worse looks outside cab offices or near the snooker hall. And nothing cuddly whatsoever about police pandas.

Still, he envied the blacks what he saw as their sense of kinship, how they felt connected to distant events just by virtue of being black. Or at least that's how they carried on at his school. Marley in Africa, Rasta accessories left, right and centre. *Off The Wall* burning up the charts, 'fro combs at the ready. It just wasn't the same being white. Well, everyone was white, except for the blacks, that is, so what did kinship even mean under those circumstances? Relating to JR, or to the bird that everyone thought shot him? Or to the LEA hairies or to the other kids? Or maybe to the skins? To be honest, D felt virtually no connection to anyone around him, less still because of a pigment issue. On the contrary, he'd been trying to avoid tribal affiliation for about as long as his brother had been hoisting sportswear, and that was a long time. The way he viewed it, no useful purpose was served by the appeal to some primal longing he just didn't harbour. Better to trim the fat – Denis to D – and then just sit out the tribal disturbances under the cloak of anonymity.

What really lit the touch-paper, though, wasn't the usual lament about police brutality or racialism or the SUS laws, but a bloody boxing match! Not even local, or one of the fight nights at York Hall near those other docks. This was all the way up in Wembley. But it was seen as a grudge match, black against white, even if most people were careful not to describe it in those terms. Everyone knew, and that included round this way. It was a bit of a tinderbox anyway, but the fight didn't help. Nor did the timing of it.

Maybe it was because this was D's O level year, which also

meant the last year many of his classmates were actually required by law to be in school. Maybe it was down to *that*. They knew they were leaving anyway so felt they had nothing to lose. *He* fully intended to stay on for sixth form, but all the chatter at classroom level was about getting a job, making some money, moving on, as though by repeatedly mentioning it the work would magically materialise, as would the council flat and the girlfriend. Maybe that was why. They were all little big men now, just looking for a stage on which to prove themselves. The tribes in unison wiping their mouths, moving on and never once stopping to check whether anyone else even cared.

Things had been a bit tetchy anyway ever since the Miami tear-up. Curses flying across the playground from one tribe to the next, then scuffles, then back to geography. But given how temporary any calm in this place was, hardly anyone seemed to notice. And at least they had all taken the summer to defuse, spending their time antagonising shopkeepers or store detectives instead of one another.

Of course, the fight was scheduled for the end of September, by which point all the tribes had been forced back together again for over a month at the start of what would indeed for many prove to be their final school year.

Things certainly were bubbling away in that month, the brief summer respite already feeling like a long time ago. That was probably the one thing everyone could agree on. Those classrooms had never felt so cramped, growth spurts and animosities jockeying for position in a collective act of denial. The smart mouths still talking up their chances in spite of every unfavourable indication just beyond the school gates. No one mentioning those snaking queues outside the dole office or the fact that every other shop was boarded up. As befitted the image they'd been trying to cultivate, the skins forever going on about getting jobs as welders or, failing that, about their mates with borstal tears. As if anyone fucking cares, thought D, though, of course, he kept that to himself and did his best to stay aloof from the simmering tensions. There *was* one other thing the skins seemed obsessed by, beyond the welding and the dodgy facial tattoos. The army got mentioned more than once and then kept cropping up, once the skins worked out that it wound up Sticks and his crew something rotten. On the surface, D could see that they were talking among themselves, though only a fool would miss who they were really directing their comments at.

'Ian. You know Ian, Frank's cousin? He's off to Belfast again. Second tour of duty, says he's going sort out those Micks good and proper this time. Might join him. He says they're always on the look-out.'

'Which Frank? The haulier?'

'Nah, the other one. Frank the plank. You know, the geezer that was in one of those dirty vids.'

'Oh, *that* Frank.'

'Yeah, him. Anyway, it's his cousin Ian who I ran into. And he was saying the army's always on the look-out.'

'For what?' asked Sticks, who'd been listening, unable to resist the urge. He knew the whole charade was being staged for his benefit. *Frank the plank!* What kind of idiots were these people?

'Bal'ead chichi bwoy. Is that what the British Army is trying to recruit now?'

And though the skin didn't really know what a chichi bwoy was, he knew he wasn't happy being called one, so punches were already being traded long before the regulation fight.

Things carried on that way for the entire run-up to the fight itself.

Jab jab jab, nip and tuck, Cannon and Ball.

Every day, like bickering couples, the tribes squaring up at school, feeding off the well-documented nonsense everywhere else. That other celebrity couple, the fighters themselves, one white the other black, the English title holder, the American challenger, well, there was no love lost there either. The Englishman popular among the skins, generally among the white locals. *One of us*, though he was from nowhere near this place. Still, *one of us* in the cut of that jib. Jaw jaw jab jab, something shown, something snide, a bit like this place, its rep, the markets. *Bought as seen, one born every minute.* Jaw jaw jab jab. *No intention of losing to a black man. Nah, nah, mate, that's not what I said. Seventeen years getting to the top and no intention of losing to this black man. Get it right, mate. This is England. Bought as seen. No refunds here.* Jaw jaw jab jab. *Soldier boy from UK. Island race, yeoman fighters. Sort out the Micks once and for all. Have a straightener with the nigger while we're at it.* Jaw jaw jab jab. *I've got a job. How about you, jungle bunny? No? Never mind, here's some bananas. Now, fuck off back to the jungle. Nah, nah, that's not what I said, mate. I just said I got a scoop for you. I've got a job, and you ain't. Cheer up, Sticks, it might never happen. Have some of these, my old son. Plenty of potassium.* Jaw jaw jab jab.

D thinking, not now, fellas, not with my O levels coming up, and hoping, praying that his self-imposed distance from his own name, from the other tribes, might just spare him from this fracas. But it's ongoing, and there's no great love anywhere in that sparring for booksmarts or caution.

'*I don't touch white flesh*'. (Allegedly.) '*No intention of losing, not to a black man.*' (Misquotedly.) '*He'll pay for saying that when we meet...*' (Definitely.) Jaw jaw jab jab. *Soldier boy, they'll have fi weld your arsehole back on by the time the Micks are through with you. Na mean? Soldier boy from UK. I shit 'em.* Sticks throwing in some Harold Shand to really wind up the English boys, the ones who are supporting the English champion. The die-hard loyalists in their MA1s. *Welder boy, don't make me laugh! Chichi bwoy, more like, chichi bwoy in army beret.* Jaw jaw jab jab. Another clinch, but this time a cut eye and more curses. A right hook, too, Daps piling in, the supply teacher nowhere to be seen. D just thinking, work the angles, stay out of trouble. Under the radar, behind the initial, the hidden line between the warring factions of the isosceles.

Plenty of people from the area heading off to the fight itself or talking up their chances. *Yeah, he's got tickets, he knows the promoter. How? A friend of a friend, they go way back.* The usual trappings of local bullshit. Of course *no one* they know is actually there. Everyone's at home or sat around a transistor, waiting for the highlights. D breaking off from fractions, needing to know how this will play itself out.

He doesn't have to wait long. The Englishman, draped in the flag, the challenger not messing around. Jersey. *Newark*, that is, before the relocation to Brockton. Riot-strewn eyes unimpressed by the Union Jacks, the St George's Cross, by the crowd baying for blood. His. And he knows the Englishman's cut history. A bleeder. A bleeding Englishman. And he knows what he's been saying, how he's been mouthing off. And now he's in the ring with him, and that Englishman, stripped of his pageant, with nowhere else for the big talk to go, just looks, to his Brockton eyes, well, that English-man just looks worried. No more jaw jaw. Now just jab jab.

Cut eye within one minute. Jab jab. Then claret pouring out of the nose. Jab jab. Then a cut below the right eye. *Not to a black man.* Brockton eyes narrowing, homing in on their target. *These colours don't run! Oh yeah, Englishman, well they're running now.* Brockton and English doing their little dance, Brockton closing down the space, no more line between the factions. One punch knocking the gum shield clean out of the champion's mouth. The challenger making good on his promise. *He'll pay for that when we meet.* Blood streaming out of the nose, from the other gashes. 'He can't keep the man away!' screams Harold, but this time it's Harry Carpenter not Shand. And the ref's stepping in to stop the beating. It's hard to make out on the radio, but Harry's shouting about chaos and being covered in beer. And it's only later when he sees the footage on the news, Brockton being pelted with bottles and cans by the Englishman's crowd then bundled to safety without even receiving his belts, that D gets the feeling that this fight has yet to fully run its course.

Typically, back at school on the following Monday, there was no sign of any of the skins. That particular tribe appeared to have gone temporarily Stonehouse. But Sticks was there, Daps, too, and for once even Conrad was in, bright and early, with his 'fro comb poised at a jaunty angle.

*

The skins more or less stopped attending after that. Which meant it was left to the remaining white contingent in class to mop up the residual fallout from the fight. With one half of the isosceles triangle gone, D soon realised there was little to be gained by being an invisible buffer any more. What *did* help, though, was the navy-blue Puma kagoule he'd managed to acquire through his brother's ongoing business activities and which he proudly strode into class wearing one morning not long after the fight. At a time when the best his peers could come up with was a black Harrington jacket to go with their school uniform, D's prize acquisition did not go unnoticed. And it wasn't long before he was passing on wish lists from some of Sticks' crew to his brother.

They seemed to heavily favour Puma and Adidas, tracksuits and trainers both, those being Marley's labels of choice, though he didn't know that until his brother pointed it out. Anyway, it was a good trade, cloth for security, though it didn't extend as far as Conrad, who claimed he never had the money for the cloth even though his pockets were regularly bulging full of everyone else's change.

The bit which really stayed with D, though, wasn't so much about cloth or labels. Rather it was the personal equation between risk and profit and what he could now see was a finely balanced juggling act. Walk the wrong side of that line and a shakedown was headed your way. But get it right, have a commodity worth trading, and the benefits were obvious. Just for starters, money in your pocket and no 'fro comb in your face. And at this time, in this place, those were no small mercies.

Close, But No Cigar

'ALRIGHT, STICKS,' SAID D by way of a greeting. 'My brother says he can get you the Clydes, but you'll have to wait.'

Sticks looked at him, unimpressed, but didn't say anything.

'I mean there's a bit of a waiting list, is all. But don't worry about it, he can definitely get 'em for you.'

Sticks kissed his teeth and turned back to the conspiratorial huddle he'd been sharing with Daps and one other boy. His reaction surprised D, particularly given how enthusiastic he'd seemed in the run-up to Christmas when D had first mentioned that a consignment of the sought-after Puma Clydes, immortalised by ladies' man and basketball hero Walt 'Clyde' Frazier, would soon be fetching up on these shores, and if he, Sticks, just gave him the nod (and the readies, of course), then a pair of those beauties could be his.

He'd more or less repeated verbatim his brother's sales pitch, the one he'd been perfecting for some time now on the markets or on his slightly-too-easily wowed younger brother, and every now and then in front of a bedroom mirror as well. But Sticks had seemed enthused by the prospect of owning some cult footwear, the more so when D mentioned that this was the brand of choice for the Black Power athletes back in the day. *Always works a treat with the Schwarzes*, his brother had told him with a wink, as if they were East End Jews and not umpteenth-generation English quite possibly from a diminished gene pool somewhere near the docks.

But now Sticks didn't seem quite so excited by this timeless piece of classic design and D found himself walking away a little confused. *These were Puma Clydes.* They didn't come round that often, especially not in this neck of the woods. *Rare as rocking-horse shit*, his brother had said, as if the point had even needed making. Rare as rocking-horse shit, D thought to himself, and yet here was Sticks, acting like he'd just been offered a pair of plimsolls.

Later that day, after his companions had dispersed, Sticks caught up with D in the corridor outside one of the classrooms.

'So, yes, D. What's the damage for those Clydes?'

D felt relieved. It had been nearly a month since the fire. He was beginning to think no one round here was ever going to get past the events of that terrible night. Daps had barely said two words to him since, even though he'd gone out of his way to get him that bowling shirt. And Conrad's face was almost permanently enraged now. Sticks was the only one who made any kind of effort, and even *he* seemed unwilling to acknowledge D unless he was on his own. But if there was one thing that D knew from his rudimentary playground observations, it was this. Kissed teeth, screwed-up faces, curse words would always dip in intensity the moment any female attention was drawn their way. The number of times he'd seen that, the instant shift from a scowl to a smile, some need other than vexation suddenly on display. Without warning, everything recast as fun. Boys who two seconds earlier had been talking about 'knocking heads' reinventing themselves as charmers in more or less the same breath. And so it was with the Clydes. Ladies loved Clyde Frazier, he'd spun that one out specifically for Sticks' benefit, knowing there was a new girl on the playground scene and correctly guessing that right about then the only thing on Sticks' mind was very far from the Campaign for Justice which was taking shape throughout this postcode and well beyond. All those dead kids in the New Cross Fire and black people taking to the streets, but the only demonstration that interested Sticks concerned the cult trainers with the leaping cat on his feet. With some people it was style over substance every time.

*

The skins resurfaced not long after the fire, taking up their usual positions in one corner of the playground. Their short, sharp barnets had started to grow out, and one or two had dispensed with the MA1s altogether in favour of Harringtons, but they were still unmistakeably the same antisocial mob that had been so loud all the way up to their previous disappearing act.

There was nothing muted about them now, though.

Taught 'em some manners, fucking jungle bunnies.

Never quite loud enough to carry to any of the areas Sticks' crew had marked out for itself. But D heard them, and the way they looked at him, let him know they were well aware of that. Of other stuff, too, his dealings with Sticks not going unnoticed. And perhaps that was the point. They saw and he heard, though the 'what' always remained just out of view. Tantalisingly close, but no cigar. Never quite enough evidence to convict but grounds certainly for reasonable doubt. He was bound to let slip at some point during his merchandising bonanza with the Schwarzes. The skins were banking on it, *that's* why they said it loud enough for him to hear. And they knew all about hearsay, and reasonable doubt. So many cousins and mates, that mountain of parade-ground expertise to draw from. He'd hear them, and he'd see them, still looking over at the other tribes, looking for a rise but largely without that earlier desperation. As if some kind of a marker, about presence and recognition, had already been laid down.

WHEREABOUTS ACCOUNTED FOR

South London, summer 1981

AND PEOPLE GETTIN' *angry*. Well, that's what Neville from The Specials thought. D wasn't so sure.

Up the road, in Lewisham, from what his brother had told him, it was all about electrical goods. (He'd never fully explained what he was doing there in the middle of a riot, but it made for a good anecdote.) Yep, according to his brother, it was all about the electricals. Shopping trolleys piled high outside the well-known high-street retailer, special attention being paid to the Breville sandwich makers, the recently arrived Walkmans, electric toasters and any kind of VCR. But once they'd run out, the angry people (given their alleged anger) had been remarkably methodical, working their way down the list: MIDI systems, kettles, ghetto blasters, cameras, vacuum cleaners. And only then had their attention moved on to the low-value items, the cassettes and head cleaners (and even at that firesale point with a conscious effort to seize chrome over normal, TDK or Sony over BASF or Memorex), which, as far as he could tell, were mostly just there so that stragglers could grab a memento. *I woz 'ere.* Though, of course, they'd have been a bit daft to advertise the fact. The same way his brother had told D but hadn't breathed a word of his exploits to anyone else, least of all their dad.

D's folks were simply relieved that *he* was indoors the whole time, *his* whereabouts at least accounted for by an unexpected and highly welcome devotion to curriculum learning. 'Displacement activity,' he'd overheard Dad telling Mum just outside his door. They thought he was probably a bit unsettled by the whole thing. After all, he was a quiet lad, and it probably wouldn't take much to put the frighteners on him. He didn't mind too much, though, happy to accept his mum's constant supply of tea and biscuits while his dad occasionally popped his head around the door to make sure he was OK.

He spent so long in his room he even started to enjoy the geography textbooks, some egghead going on about silt patterns and porous rock, and D thinking that everything was patterned and layered, from topsoil to bottom of the pile. Himself, of course, somewhere near the summit, or at least rapidly ascending with the summit about to come into view. The skins, Conrad, probably Sticks, too, with or without the Clydes, some way further down, still too busy grappling with one another to see the bigger picture. The object of the exercise the same as it always was, whether it was a question of book learning or procuring in-demand consumer items. First, not to get spotted and then, the bit which usually followed on from that, not to get caught. No, D wasn't exactly bothered by what was going on outside, but there was no need to let on, spoil the fun while the fig rolls just kept coming. The constant sirens and flashing blue lights, well, it wasn't all that different to Millwall match days. Not exactly like the area didn't have form for this kind of thing.

It's what else was in the topsoil that gave him pause.

Watching the big-eared royal get hitched to that Sloaney bird, now *that* was a bit alarming, and not just because of her dress or the posh inbred look on half the entourage's faces. It was eerie how everything was suddenly so quiet outside. Almost as if people were suddenly busy plugging in their new kettles, preparing to toast the happy couple with a hot brew. And then no doubt getting ready to play back the images on the new VCR, fresh out of the box, this time perhaps with a toasted sarnie to go with the tea. At any rate, *that's* how it felt to D, studying for his exams with one eye, as ever, on the long-range forecast. Sunny spells, Big Ears punching above his weight, romantically speaking, and 'Ghost Town' still the people's favourite.

Not so much an uprising then, more a shopping spree. Something a bit distant (well, a bus ride away) and yet all too familiar (you're better than this, son). He liked The Specials, loved the second album, the weird one that seemed to have alienated most of the skins, but on this evidence he'd be taking another look at some of those lyrics. People weren't getting angry. They were just getting stuff.

SMARTS IN HIS BLOOD

Just up the road, 1980–1

LOOKING UP JUST then, a pigeon might have seen his face in the window. Conrad, looking for all the world as forlorn as one of those blindfolded American hostages in the embassy in Tehran. Bad enough that he had to be here with his nan, who had her ways, though wasn't as difficult as he'd first imagined. The real problem lay in the attention the Old Bill suddenly seemed to be paying him.

That had never been an issue before he'd come to live in the tower. There might have been the odd look, and admittedly there was that one time he'd had a spot of bother with the law, but looking back he could see how that had come about. Just habit, really, answering back, though he should have known better. Even so, he blamed the hopelessly permissive regime at his school, where the habit had been formed, for leaving him so ill equipped to cope with the routine racism of a police stop-and-search in the world beyond the gates. The difference from school, where a blind eye was turned to most things, could hardly have been greater.

Still, what the plod had said, 'Don't get lippy with me, Rastus,' he'd been shocked by that. Rastus?! Where *did* they find these people?

Ever since becoming a high-rise inmate, though, they'd been on his case. The 'why' never even came into it.

'Where are you coming back from?' (The older, bearded one, just because there was always one who was older and bearded.)

'Why? Who's asking?' (Conrad.)

'"Why?" he says. Well hark at him. This little monkey's got some spirit. What do you reckon?' (Beardy.)

'Well he's definitely a little monkey, that's for sure.' (Beardy's younger colleague, warming to the task. 'Monkey'. This is great, he thinks, I'd never have got away with that at Hendon.)

'That's right, a little monkey. Mouthy little so-and-so. I think he's got something to hide, that's why he's being all chirpy. What do you think?'

'I think you might be right. A bit too chirpy for his own good.'

'Anyway, what you got in the bag there? What are you trying to hide?'

Conrad instinctively drawing the bag closer, knowing what's coming next but with little else to fall back on but muscle memory.

'Let's have a look then, shall we?' (Beardy.)

'Why?' (Conrad.)

'He just doesn't learn, does he?' (Beardy, to colleague.)

'How about this then? Your behaviour has given me reasonable grounds to search your person. Your chirping and the way you're holding that bag right now and your failure to answer any of my questions properly, well you have to admit it's all highly suspicious. And that's all I need to stop you. Suspicion.'

After they'd looked in his bag and found nothing more offensive than the fruits and pumpkin his nan had sent him out to buy, they laughed. Though on other occasions the jollity had been absent, the hint of observational comedy – 'What *do* we have here, Fanny Craddock?' – replaced by something more robust. Gloved hands a little too eager to pat him down, feel him up, or fit him up, for stash.

Merch. Fractions. Eighths, halves, ounces.

None of it ever on his person, though that rarely seemed to trouble them. The first, the second, even the third and fourth times it happened, the stop, the verbals, the embarrassment of it, meant that Conrad remained agitated for days afterwards. But by the time the faces of Beardy and his apprentice had hoved into view for, say, the seventh or eighth time, the jarring novelty had worn off, and Conrad's local experience of the SUS laws were just another mundane feature of his daily circuit.

*

Those bal'eads at school, though. Nearly as bad as the plod. In some ways worse, stomping about with all that parade-ground 'rights for whites' nonsense. Once, while he was being patted down by the local constabulary, he'd spotted a couple of their ringleaders haring it away from the corner shop, more or less in full view, without raising so much as a pulse from Beardy or his colleague. He remembered feeling particularly aggrieved that day, especially when moments later one of the older lads from the tower, well known at the football and at certain local menswear outlets that had yet to invest in worthwhile security, sidled past making little effort to conceal the packed holdall he was carrying with a price tag peeping out of the top where the zip had failed to close on his misdemeanours.

Later that day, when he'd mentioned it to his nan, she'd initially gone very quiet, putting down her *Reader's Digest* and heading for the kitchen. But when she'd returned, it was with two cups of tea and a very stern look on her face.

'Conrad, mek me tell yuh something. And yuh 'ear me out, alright?'

'Alright, Nan,' said Conrad, wishing he hadn't said anything now. Experience should have shown him by then that it was always better to let her find things out in her own way or not at all. Like the time she discovered the fruits of his lunchtime revenue collections during a random inspection of his domestic cell. (His regime had basically boiled down to 'tapping' the more timid play-ground elements for their dinner money.) And though he'd been loath to see that money go, he also understood it was a small price to pay for Nan's ongoing goodwill. Besides, from that moment on she'd been entrusting him with ever-increasing amounts of petty cash to pick up fruit or pumpkin or the special hard dough bread she liked from the West Indian bakery near the market. And he felt good about having the responsibility, even if the plod's unwashed hands rooting around among the groceries always left him with the slightly queasy sense of Nan's homespun lilting around just above the intrusion.

Dutty white people.

She was probably right, too.

'Now listen, Conrad. Yuh is a special boy, y'hear me? A special lickle boy. Yuh jus' have fe put yuh mind to it, and then anything yuh want to do, yuh cyan do. Cyan do it, y'hear me? So if those dutty people hevah put dem hand on yuh, mek sure fi remembah that, y'hear me? Mek sure fi remembah who yuh are. Yuh mudda, Lawd bless her, she mek me promise her one thing before that terrible hillness tek her away. And is only now that I tell yuh, becau' it pain me right 'ere,' she said, pointing to the wrong side of her chest, where her heart wasn't. 'Yes, it pain me to 'ear yuh say how dem dutty people dem look at yuh. Well mek me tell yuh, Conrad, yuh bettah than dem dutty people, fah fah bettah than dem hevah know. And now yuh mus' prove it. Mus' do bettah than dem in hexam. Total Knock Out, Conrad, it's the honly way dem hevah believe yuh. Nevah leave it to the judges,' she stressed, reminding him of the old community adage whenever there was a boxing match where one of the fighters was black and the other white. A bit like the recent Minter v Hagler bout, he thought, though on that occasion he remembered being disappointed when the ref stepped in before the black man could really dole out some punishment. The bal'eads at school hadn't liked that either, but he suspected for very different reasons. In their eyes, Minter wasn't supposed to lose, not to a jungle bunny. And the funny thing was, however chirpy they'd all been in the run-up to the fight (and they *had* been chirpy), once it was over and the white fighter's ill-advised pre-fight boast laid bare, there was no sign of any of them. They just melted away, recognising in some primal way that Minter's humiliation was also their own. But unlike the vanquished English fighter, Conrad suspected even then that these fairweather 'fans' were just regrouping.

'Conrad?'

They *had* regrouped. He knew he'd seen something.

'Conrad?'

He almost wished he hadn't. But it was true, he *had* seen something. Up in the clouds with his books and his revision. That's what you got for being a swot, he thought ruefully.

'Conrad! Yuh even listening to me, bwoy? Two shugah already plenty. Yuh want fi kill yuhself before yuh even get started?!'

He looked up. Nan was glaring at him or, more precisely, at the endless teaspoons of sugar he kept stirring into his brew with the gormless look of a boy who'd already travelled miles from the moment. He stopped stirring, tried to focus on what he was being told.

'Study harder, twice as hard. And even then, dem only give yuh half di chance. But is bettah than no chance. Mek dem see yuh no tief. Mek dem see who real tief is.'

She paused for a moment to wipe something away from her eye. Conrad listened, sensing the sermon had a way to travel yet.

'Lawd, as I tell yuh dis, I can even 'ear yuh mudda speak. So from 'ere on in, yuh stay 'ere, yuh work 'ere, yuh study 'ere, yuh na budda wid outside. Whatevah book yuh need, I buy. And yuh 'ave whole library up 'ere anyway. Remembah that, Conrad. Yuh is from learning. Yuh mudda, too. From now, all yuh worry about is school and hexam. No more herrand fi yuh granny, and that way, no more dutty man haccost yuh in street. Now, drink this tea. It help yuh study.'

It wasn't quite what he'd been expecting. Then again, he never could tell what his nan was actually thinking. It was still unclear, for example, whether she'd bought his backstory of a secret paper round as the explanation for all that loose change she'd found in his room. All the same, the thought of being boxed up here even more hours of the day filled him with foreboding. Doing his solitary like some lifer in Parkhurst. Perhaps she was right, though. About this being the moment to prove his doubters wrong. Besides, how hard could it be? He'd barely even been awake in maths, and he was still light years ahead of the rest of them. All those lunchtimes nursing complex accounts in his head, and he'd never been wrong once. Always knew exactly who owed him what, as well as what level of pressure needed exerting to bring about the desired result. Crucially, too, given his chosen sideline, it also paid to know precisely who was hiding out where, so geography was unlikely to present too much of a problem either. His eyes that bit sharper than his peers, quick to read cunning, the more so when it came to fear.

*

The night of the fire he'd been looking out of the kitchen window, taking a well-earned break from the Mitchell Beazley *Joy of Knowledge* volume he'd been poring over, the one he'd taken from the middle of his nan's groaning shelf. He liked the maps at the back, countries he'd never even heard of, like Taiwan, as well as the more familiar-sounding ones which tended to be in Europe.

Actually, to start with, he'd been disappointed that Jamaica, where Nan was from, didn't seem to merit its own entry in the book. In fact, the whole of the West Indies, which it was grouped under, barely got a mention. However, once he realised the island did, in fact, have its own entry and he'd simply been looking in the wrong place, his enthusiasm was rekindled. Then again, even after he'd located the individual entry for Jamaica, sandwiched in between the Ivory Coast and Japan, he was disappointed to read about the Caribbean island's comparative poverty and high unemployment. It didn't sound at all like the place Nan had described to him. That said, without knowing who this Mitchell Beazley was, Conrad suspected, just from the name, that he was one of those melanin-deficient devils he'd been reading about in another of Nan's books, the kind who was always trying to put the black man down. Or, at any rate, the type to use some spurious pretext to harass him when he was on his way home carrying nothing more dangerous than half a pumpkin.

It was a clear night, and though he was high up, Conrad knew he'd seen a couple of figures pulling something out of a car and then moments later jumping back into the car before speeding off. Of course, it wasn't until later, the street reporting sirens and flashing blue lights, that his thoughts went back to just what it *was* he might have seen.

The black boys in his class from nice homes, proper houses, boys who gave themselves names like *Sticks* or *Daps*, yeah, right, they were always giving it that 'junior Dread' large, but when it came down to it, what were they actually doing about any of it?

Thirteen dead, nothing said.

The New Cross Fire, within a spit of the tower, and he'd definitely seen something. All those boys and girls, just like them, like him, burned to a crisp, and what were the fancy boys doing about any of it? Petty scuffling with the bal'eads, but they'd been doing that anyway, ever since that English boxer got his face *bruk up* by the black American. He sometimes got the impression it was all for show, scuffle but no risk, the real pay-off being that new girl in class who Sticks was sniffing around.

Sharp eyes, never missing a trick.

Oh yeah, he'd seen them all lovey-dovey in one corner, him in his fancy new trainers, her thinking him some kind of sportswear Garvey. Yeah, Sticks man, junior Dread. As if! Daps no better, thinking just because he shun that English boy, D, the one Sticks get his trainers from, that he somehow the conscious Dread of the two of them. What a joke! This pair, Sticks and Daps, they belonged in *Smash Hits*. Pop Dreads without even the locks. Just pop. The whole thing about *gyal* and look *fi dem*. *Fi dem!* Funny, right? Evah since Nan give him the pep talk, this voice just kept popping up in his head. One thing for sure, though, there was nothing pop Dread about it. This voice was *his* now, the voice of the recluse, the seer. And he'd seen alright, he'd seen something that night, something he wasn't supposed to.

He couldn't shake that image, of the figures and the car, and whenever he tried he'd hear the sound rumbling up through his gut. Crawling up his chest until it was yowling like the lights, blue bloody murder. No, he just couldn't shake it, though it made him shake. A serious voice emerging from a high-rise library. By the time it had spoken to him, Conrad's head was already ablaze with the unfairness of it all.

The illness which took away his Mum, a registered nurse, far too soon.

How they could only watch on the Victorian ward as it ate her away from inside, this proud, fierce woman reduced to skin and bone, barely a rumour. And then not even that. When the remnants petrified in a blank look and some distant promise shared between a mother and her daughter.

He should have kept his blubba mout shut. A rookie error, thinking he was on nodding terms with Beardy and his colleague on account of his excellent performance as a SUS statistic. Then again, to start with at least, it bore all the hallmarks of a routine stop.

'Well, well, well, if it isn't our old friend, pumpkin.' (Beardy.)

'Busy day then?' (Conrad.)

'Listen, son, there's two ways of doing this.' (Beardy, who'd taken to using the more familiar, some might even say affectionate, 'son' after the first half a dozen stops.)

'Yeah, yeah, yeah, keep your hair on.' (Conrad, sailing close to the wind but still just the right side of 'banter'.)

'I won't tell you again, son. Speaking of, what *is* going on with your barnet?' (Beardy again, this time focusing on the more natural *Off The Wall* 'fro that one of his favourite IC3 collars currently seemed to be favouring.)

'Glad you like it. I think you might struggle to grow one of these, though.'

'Right, son. Let's get this over with. Hands and feet apart, and then we'll take a little look in your bag.'

They'd been amused to find *The Merchant Of Venice* in there but seemed more interested in the tin foil which Conrad must have forgotten to throw away. The foil his nan wrapped his sarnies in.

'And what do we have here then?' (Beardy.)

'What does it look like?' (Conrad, irritated by the way they were now looking at him, as if connecting the dots in what must have been fairly basic minds to form a picture which somehow linked him, 'from learning', with the lowlifes he'd occasionally see shooting up in the stairwells.)

'Don't get lippy. Just answer the question.' (Beardy's colleague, for the first time today.)

'It's what my lunch was wrapped in.'

'I'll bet it was. And how long did it take you to smoke that?' (Beardy's colleague.)

'What?! No, that's not what I meant. I swear to you, it *was* my lunch, as in sarnies. If you don't believe me, have a look. You won't find anything other than crumbs.'

'Alright, son, but you can't blame us. You have to admit, it does look a bit suspicious.' (Beardy, using his experience to dial down the tone.)

Once his colleague had satisfied himself that the only traces on the foil did indeed belong to the remnants of a ham-and-cheese sandwich, Beardy adopted a more conciliatory approach.

'If the contents of your mind are anything like those in your bag, then you're obviously a smart lad, barnet notwithstanding.'

They both laughed at that, the older man clearly pleased at his shoehorning of the fancy word into an admonitory speech. Conrad not entirely sure where this was headed but doubtful it was anywhere good.

'The point is, you must see a lot of things going on up there in the tower that we can't down here. There's definitely a problem with the foil, and that can't be very nice for you living next to that. So if you see or hear anything about that, just let us know, and maybe something can be done. You help us out a little bit, and perhaps there's some way we can help you.'

'Oh yeah, how's that then?' asked Conrad, thinking he probably shouldn't have said anything but unable to resist anyway.

'Well, you let us know about the skaggies, the foil merchants, and I'm sure we can turn a blind eye to whatever it is you've got down your socks right now. What do you reckon, son? That sound like a plan to you? Or are you still keen on giving me hairdressing tips?' asked Beardy, tapping his nose and smirking.

Shit! How had he known? Conrad thought he'd got away with one there, the little cellophane package tightly wedged in his Bally shoes. Just a sideline to keep on top of the books really. School was

217

largely devoid of them, and he'd been amazed at the price of text-books when he'd made the enquiry at the local library. They only had a few of the ones he needed, and, in spite of the pep talk, he'd be damned if Nan was going to have to dip into her pension just so he could learn about Shakespeare. Anyway, Daps as well as a couple of the white boys with the new wedge haircut that was becoming popular, had in no time become regular customers, as had several of the younger kids who lived in the tower. Besides, he was saving up to go to Jamaica. Wanted to do it under his own steam, find out all the bits Mitchell Beazley had left out. And for that kind of trip, he knew the lunchtime shakedowns would barely even get him to the airport.

Anyway, that's when he'd blurted it out.

'Yeah I'll keep my eyes peeled then. There *is* one thing, though. Been meaning to say something ever since. Seeing as though you're here now. Anyway, it's about the night of the fire...'

He told them everything, about the men and the car and the fact that they were carrying something heavy when they left the car but the same thing, perhaps a petrol can, seemed lighter when they returned. And though he was some distance away, he was sure, thinking about it now, that it was a petrol can. He should have known better when they just let him speak without inter-ruption, occasionally glancing at one another but otherwise not saying a word. Not when he described the fire engines and the noise and the wailing, which he could hear even from so far away. Nor even when he carried on, in spite of every instinct in him suggesting otherwise, telling them about reading the news reports and hearing about the bodies and the smell of charred flesh and the sleepless nights he'd started having and what a relief it was to finally be able to tell someone about any of it. And now that he had, he hoped it would help with the ongoing investigation, and, and, and why are you looking at me like that, officer? Why isn't your colleague writing any of this down? What's wrong? Was it something I said?

*

If a pigeon had looked up just then it would have seen his unhappy face. It might have settled on a high-rise perch, peering in at the gloom which stared right back. The pep talk from his nan, even the stench of his mum's illness, the grotesquery of all that prim hospital Victoriana surrounding a woman who could no longer eat or breathe or evacuate, it wasn't really any of those things which was the problem. What really troubled Conrad was how, when he looked out, he saw nothing but himself reflected back in the panes. Just a rumour, another high-rise statistic, destined for nothing much beyond the expected dysfunctions.

Nan was right, though, he had smarts in his blood. *From learning.* He liked that. Nan believed in him, even if no one else did. Still, the fact remained, he *had* seen something that night, but, as with all the knowledge he was gleaning from those books, the impression Conrad got from the evident lack of interest of the plod was that he should just forget about it. That type of knowledge, those kinds of visions, *well, listen son, take a tip from the pigeons. That kind of unsubstantiated rumour just doesn't fly around here. Now, be a good little monkey and get back in your tree. Oh yeah, and try not to scratch your arse on your way back up. It upsets the neighbours. Like I said, though, when you're ready to tell us some-thing about the skagheads, you'll find, my fat-lipped old china, that we're all ears.*

Conrad's unhappiness came from the one thing he'd already learnt long before he delved into any of those books. Black boys like him weren't supposed to see or hear anything that could actu-ally make a difference. Yeah, wearing a tam, sporting the colours, like Sticks and Daps, even talking the talk if it meant gaining a competitive advantage in the flirting stakes, all of that was just about acceptable. But under no circumstances was he supposed or expected to replace this locale's gutter expectations of him with something born from on high. Sound and visions, albeit unhappy ones, up in the tower, but all they had for company now was the indifference of the pigeons.

BRUK UP LIKE PUMPKIN

STICKS AND DAPS, a right pair of jokers really. When he thought about it, Conrad was hard pressed to recall even one instance when they'd done anything other than hedge their bets. Even the times they'd ended up scuffling with the baldies, apparently over some difference of opinion, he could tell it was largely for show. Knowing girls would be watching them, licking their lips, thinking they were all so grown up, them and the girls. Fucking lightweights. *He* was the one who kept getting his collar felt. Not them, going back to their families in their fancy terraced houses. Mummy Sticks and Daddy Sticks, and Mummy Daps and Daddy Daps, making sure junior was always fed and watered and never short of readies. Fancy trainers, wristbands, headgear, specially customised tracksuit tops and Pan Am bags, all of that cost money, he knew that, so did they. And for all that junior-Dread rubbish they'd spout, he'd spotted them doing business with that white boy, D, the one who'd shaved off half his name. Yeah, in the end they were all talk.

Even the bal'eads seemed comfortable enough with that. So long as they got to throw the occasional insult, or punch, everyone acted like that was enough.

But those kids had been burnt to a crisp. A minor scuffle wasn't going to bring them back. Sticks, Daps, they couldn't see that because they always had one eye on the girls, the other on each other. Smirking and joking and just too comfy. Good homes and the latest gear and a hollow sound under every sentence which grated to well-tuned ears. He saw how they looked at him every now and then, when they thought he wasn't paying attention. He'd catch the tail end of that disgust then, the broadened nostrils, the rolled eyes. But always a bit snide, never direct, because for all the stuff they had no idea about, they certainly *did* know what he was capable of with a compass or a 'fro comb.

The more he read, the bigger those views were from the kitchen window. Conrad quickly learnt to see beyond the snatches of conversation that occasionally floated over from an adjacent flat. Those concerns, the gas, electric, rent book or, on a bad day, raised voices and duller sounds, were soon absorbed in a wider diatribe on unequal development and reparations which he'd found in a pamphlet tucked away inside one of Nan's encyclopaedias.

Reparations.

He liked the sound of that. It made him feel that there was a purpose behind all the lunchtime taxations. If any of those bloody teachers ever asked him, that's what he'd tell them. He was collecting reparations.

He could just picture their faces, if they even knew what the word meant, that disappointed look they seemed to specialise in whenever they were dealing with any of the black boys in class. Or at least the ones like himself who'd made an art form of feigning lack of interest, having long since convinced themselves that what they were being offered within these four walls was not for them.

Not for them. Not for us.

Sticks, the bal'eads, every other comfy rascal in that classroom closer to each other than they'd ever care to admit. But, in truth, that wasn't how he viewed things.

The point was, he read the pamphlet, but it was the book the pamphlet was hidden away in that really interested him. And the more he delved into it, with its detailed entries on science and technology and breakthroughs in home computing, the broader those views became.

Sometimes he felt that those books were like the carrier pigeons of yesteryear, carrying secret messages from one excremental coop to another. What made it particularly enjoyable was the knowledge that, should he wish, he could immerse himself in all this learning more or less in plain sight without being labelled a swot and paying the penalty that automatically went with the label. And he knew that because, unlike Sticks or Daps or the bal'eads they claimed to despise, he already came from somewhere a bit sad.

No terrace, no Mummy, no Daddy. Which, of course, meant he carried that weight around with him, pressing down on his tongue when the friendly local constabulary would squeeze him for tips.

'Cheer up, son, it might never happen. Now, about those smackheads on the fourth floor, or is it the fifth? Refresh my memory, son.'

'What you asking me for? I ain't got a clue, officer. Anyway, what about that stuff I was telling you the other day?'

'That's very rude, son, answering one question with another. Didn't your father ever tell you that? Oh, wait a minute. Whoops.'

The weight would really jam down on his tongue then, burying his desire to confess all. About the fractal patterns and the soon-to-be-affordable home computers and who *di' rass you think supply them with the smack? Dutty people, junky scum.* Yeah, that's right, officer, all you're seeing is a boy with some out-of-date *Off The Wall* stylings, but if you only knew where to look, you'd see that under all that natural, there's a 'fro comb and a compass and a comprehensive knowledge of the human body and pressure points, where to cut and how deep. And from where I sit, officer, the fourth floor is down, deep down into the vaults, into the bowels of this thing. *This shitstem of yours, Babylon, sah.* Oh, why so surprised? You think I'm stupid? You think I don't read, I don't know? No, sah, it's you who have no idea. You'd be shocked, oh yes, you would, to see Nan's shelves groaning with tome after tome of anti-stupid. *Not for us. Fuck you. Not for you maybe, but don't drag me down into your happy-to-be-categorised IC3 gutter.* Do I look like some comedy Dread from a proper house? Exactly. And the funny thing is, even if I told you all of this, you still wouldn't believe me. Because all you ever see is something familiar, a bit scared, some might say out of date, but at any rate, tucked away, out of sight, where he can't upset the neighbours. Mostly, though, during those moments Conrad just wanted to tell them about the encyclopaedias and the fractal patterns.

Something was bound to snap, though. It didn't take a genius to work that out. Once even boys from nice houses, and 'good' families, started to find themselves on the wrong end of the local constabulary's 'suspicions', then it was only really a matter of time before the powder keg exploded.

Conrad found it quite funny, the giveaway looks of surprise and outrage on the faces of boys like Sticks and Daps, coming on to the Dibble's radar as if for the first time. Fucking lightweights. No doubt they'd go home and blab and cry about it to their mummies and daddies and anxious girlfriends. But yeah, he'd be lying if he said he didn't find it even a little bit amusing. Welcome to my world, he wanted to tell them, though on reflection he didn't really have anything to say to them other than, 'Now do you see?'

He couldn't even remember what the trigger was. That wasn't really the point. By that stage it could have been anything, from a stray look to some throwaway remark, perhaps not even that much, and the whole shambolic tinderbox would have gone up. Anyway, the *real* point was not to get nabbed, and the best way, of course, to achieve that – *not* being nabbed – was to head out with a plan, or at least a list.

Later, once the toaster, kettle and Walkman were safely stored under the false bottom in his chest of drawers, Conrad allowed himself a celebratory cuppa, but then it was straight back to the books and whatever the next instalment of the Mitchell Beazley *Joy of Knowledge* was. He'd give it a while, he thought, before he'd present Nan with the toaster and kettle as a nice little gift set, so for the time being he brewed up using the old Kenwood, which seemed to be gasping even more than usual.

As he looked out of the window nursing his PG Tips, he could just about make out two lads matching the description of Sticks and Daps being hauled off in one of the many meat-wagons he'd seen doing the rounds that day. They didn't seem to know the drill or understand that now was not the time for surly. That would have been *before*, in the absence of any prima facie. He laughed. Fucking lightweights. Hopefully, though, someone would have told them to pack a toothbrush?

'Nan?'

When she didn't move, Conrad drew his face closer to where she appeared to be slumped in her favourite armchair in front of the television. She seemed peaceful enough, and he was pleased to note that she had bought herself a new cardigan, presumably with some of that money he'd given to her on the pretext of a phantom paper round. He was glad. She rarely treated herself to anything, especially since placing herself in charge of supervising his studies. He saw that she'd opted for a very natty lime-green number, the Marks and Spencer label still showing. It looked good on her, too, a nice change from the more sombre colour schemes she generally opted for.

'Nan? Are you OK?'

She woke with a start, wide-eyed and scanning his face for signs of recognition.

'Why yuh do these ting? Is why, yuh mus' tell me?'

'Sorry, Nan. You had me worried for a moment there. I wasn't sure if you were asleep.'

'Well, sure as can be, I'm wide awake now. Anyway, why yuh creep up on me like that? It like havin' duppy in the home. Yuh want to scare yuh ole nan?'

Though he was being chided, he could see she was smiling now, the momentary fear in her eyes gone.

'I'm making a cup of tea, Nan. Milk, two sugar?' he asked her, testing the water with the deliberate syntax error.

'Two sugars. What is this two-sugar nonsense? An' after I tell all an' sundry what a clevah boy my grandson is. Two shugah. Tcha!'

He laughed, sufficiently reassured that Nan was back to normal, and went off to eke more favours from the Kenwood. By the time he came back, the tea and a pleasing assortment of biscuits balanced on a small tray, Nan seemed ready for sleep again. He gently helped her to her room and waited outside until he was sure she'd made it safely into the bed. Then he went back to the living-room and systematically worked his way through the biscuits, making an effort not to slurp his tea.

The late-night film had just started on the television, and though he'd been enjoying the Mitchell Beazley entry on 'war reparations' in an essay on twentieth-century history, he found himself a little distracted by the strange images beaming out from the box. Either dream-like and hazy, as in the opening robbery and double-cross sequence, or sun-bleached, bright and shiny, all the qualities, Conrad reckoned, southeast London singularly lacked.

He liked the central character, though.

Walker.

Lee Marvin in a tasty whistle, bottling and battering his way through this parched landscape. And he laughed at the bit when Walker repeatedly shot a telephone for not delivering the correct message. As far as he could tell, this bloke was hardcore, not some fucking lightweight who blabbed to his mummy. And he just kept going, like one of those Tonka toys. Wasn't bothered by what anyone said or how they looked at him. Just kept going. Yeah, he was relentless. No way he was going to stop until he got his money. What a chief! Mainly, though, Conrad just liked how everything in California looked really neat or plastic. Or just excessive, all that sunlight, the only shadow to be found in the underpasses of huge motorways the likes of which he'd never seen. Vast concrete structures nose to tail with endless lines of massive American cars. Great big wood-panelled houses, or steel and glass. And he could see why they called them skyscrapers over there. Nothing at all like the tower or the Old Kent Road. Suddenly everything around him just felt a bit closed in.

When the exam results came through, they celebrated, him and Nan, with a trip to the pictures. The new James Bond film, showing up at the Odeon. To be honest, he thought it was a bit pony, but Nan seemed to enjoy herself anyway. Mostly, though, she seized any and every opportunity to tell all and sundry about her clever clever grandson. Conrad couldn't help noticing one thing, though. No matter who she told or how enthusiastic she was in the telling, no one actually seemed to be listening to her. Their eyes mostly glazing over once she mentioned the A grades and the full set of maths, English, science.

'Hinglish. This boy so clevah, 'im quote Shakespeare in 'im sleep. And 'im some kind of maths genius. All frakshun, long divishun, store up in 'im head like reference library.'

No, they didn't want to hear that. He wished Nan could see, but he understood, she was just excited at having some good news for once. Mind you, some things were best left unsaid. Like the little detail Nan insisted on sharing with her already bored looking friend, Hortense, outside the West Indian Social Club.

'And did I tell yuh, 'Ortense? Not only that but this sweet lickle pickney, 'im still find time to give his granny present every now and then.'

'Present?'

'Oh yes, 'Ortense. Did I not tell yuh, then? 'Im present me with brand new kettle an' toaster. "Gift set for yuh, Nan," 'im say to me. What a sweet chile.'

It was a hard thing to never be believed. Just for starters, no one else taking him seriously when he tried to tell them that. The teachers, oh they made a show of listening to him, but deep down he sensed they were no different to the plod really. Just more white men covering up their nerves with something pretend. Like any of them gave a shit what he'd seen that night. All that 'when you're ready to tell us' crap when the truth was he'd been telling them all along. And just like Hortense, and everyone else with his nan, no one ever listened. If they had they might not have acted so surprised when he resurfaced in the sixth form, but this time minus the familiar *Off The Wall* trappings.

He knew from all that Mitchell Beazley he'd been poring over, that wherever there was a void there was a power vacuum. Didn't matter whether that was post-Weimar Germany or more or less any of the LEA schools he'd ever attended. He rightly suspected the Dread-lites, as he'd taken to calling Sticks and Daps, would no longer be present. And, as far as he could tell, that left a gap in the market for some false prospecting. He could be every bit the fake they'd been, and then some, except in *his* case recent memories of compass or comb should, he reasoned, keep the finger-pointing down to a bare minimum.

Anyway, when he showed up that first day, all junior Dread with the picky lock an' ting, sure he'd had some looks. But they hadn't said anything, not even when he started with the vocals. Testing the water with sounds he'd never dare around Nan. *Two shugah. Tcha!* And when the new teacher looked at him with those eyes he'd seen a hundred times before. Those *talk to me, bredrin*, eyes, full of longing and pleading and the whole panoply of Babylonian teacher-training college bullshit. *That's* when he'd known.

Talk to me, Dread, unless it's about something which actually matters, in which case, don't bother.

Right there, in that look, he'd spied weakness, and he fully intended to exploit it. If they wouldn't listen to anything serious he had to say, then he'd just make stuff up. Besides, ever since that film came out, the one with Brindsley Forde set in south London, he'd viewed it as a bluffer's guide to this season's inner-city Dread. By which, of course, he meant himself. Ha ha, it was funny really, the more he pushed it with the adopted mannerisms, the style and patter, the garishly coloured romper suit, the less people called him out on any of it. Typical, he thought. All complete horseshit, and *now* they're listening.

It was different around that girl, though. Sarah, from class. She was nice. Actually listened to him from the get-go. He'd liked her from the moment she'd spoken up for him that first time in sixth form. He'd never really had girls show any interest in him up to that point. Mostly what he remembered were smirks hidden behind group stares. Safety in numbers. Whispering. Or nothing at all. Blank expression, like that tune the bal'eads went on about from that first Specials album. But this girl, Sarah, she wasn't like that at all. And it wrongfooted him, really. Nan was the only one who'd ever made any time for him, but she was his nan not some girl from school, so it wasn't the same thing.

Sarah let him talk, even as he just made more and more stuff up, getting carried away with himself, with the novelty of having an audience who actually seemed to care. That's why he'd fucked it up. She should have told him then to put a sock in it or rolled her eyes or kissed her teeth or employed any of the other standard devices by which a girl round here communicated to a boy that he was talking shit or being an idiot or, as was more usual, a bit of both.

But she didn't, so he just carried on, Babylon this and black man that, surprised that he was being allowed to indulge every half-cut Dread-lite fantasy he'd been harbouring probably his whole life. And, of course, the more she let him, the worse he got. What began as a stylistic tic, Mykal for Michael, one kind of black (Uhuru) for another (Jackson), was now a full-blown delusion. Moodswings and capriciousness, just to keep that poor girl on her toes, no point going all lovey-dovey now. That was the type of sub-sidised thinking he fell victim to round about that time. Rationing her access to the Walkman, and Gregory, and feeling that he was somehow 'schooling' her, when the truth was he was a half-cut fraud himself. A two-bob. Pop Dread, 'Night Nurse' on the Walkman, though his heart still belonged to the former Motown prodigy from Gary, Indiana. A two-bob.

First time at sound system in that red-romper-suit stupidness, and he knew he'd always be out of place. Saxon Studio, a freebie down the park near Goldsmiths College, the one they said was full of arty girls, whatever that meant. Heading back towards Lewisham, but still south London, a whole heap of black face, and yet all he could think about was 'Rock With You'. Hated the way they kept stopping the records, picking up a mic, chatting some shit he didn't understand over the top of rhythms he didn't care for. Hated the sound box, the Pac-Man effect his fellow revellers seemed to go wild over. Wild but no joy, no joy anywhere in this miserable five-man-to-one-woman ratio. And even in the sunlight that one woman still finding time to look at him with disdain. He felt it even if he couldn't prove it. The feeling exaggerated in that moment when the DJ lifted up the needle and dropped yet another tune he didn't know. This time the whole crowd shouting their approval then singing along with the rewind. And when he looked at them then, all toothy grin and Ratner jewellery, singing, '*Oh, Mr DC, don't you touch my collie,*' he hated them, too. Smiling and happy and properly part of some community. A boy not much older than him talking on the mic about *Shugah. Shugah Boogah.* (But not two shugah.) And that crowd laughing and cheering as if any of that was supposed to mean something.

Yeah, he knew what he was. A two-bob in a red romper suit, and well away from the dance, there he'd be chatting shit with the best of them. *Dutty Babylon*, four hundred years, which, of course he recast as '*four 'undred ears*'. But Sarah let him, so he carried on, and when she let him do other stuff, too, he saw no reason to stop then either. Actually, he couldn't. He knew if he stopped she'd see how scared he was, how inexperienced, how brittle. If he stopped there was a danger she might really listen. And then she'd hear the sounds of his uncertainty. She'd hear the dry in his mouth before those teeth were kissed. She'd hear the empty under all that cursing, behind all that smoke. Spliffs and pills and then something stronger, something, anything to take away the dull sounds of defeat. Of a life in the tower looking at nothing much. Even when that nothing turned out to be a something, the tower a somewhere, a vantage point, a look-out post. Perhaps especially then it was a defeat, because, *eejiut boy* that he was, he told the wrong people, uniform and blank face, and they knew not to tell anyone. So what he said, what he saw, simply disappeared, a bit like his daddy and then his mummy. Eaten away by prim Victoriana, the *hillness* of just being here. Sarah would have listened, but he didn't know how to tell her. And now she was gone, too, just because he couldn't say.

Didn't know how. She'd reached out to him, and he'd shown her a blank face. Shared spliffs and a lot more besides, when really all he'd been doing was passing on the poison. Making her carry his toxic on top of everything else she was already carrying. A lot of weight, a lot to carry, and maybe that's what unhinged her, he thought. Peering into the void, Conrad was suddenly struck by the clarity of his vision. That should have been him down there, but no, it was her, the only person other than Nan who'd ever given him a chance. Her face not even a face any more. *Bruk up* like pumpkin. Should have been him. Fucking lightweight.

PARTY ANIMALS

JEREMY – 'JEZZA' – LIVED in one of those massive houses not far from the common. They'd known each other since prep school, him and Casper and the other boys Roxy had met in the Loire. But Jezza had been expelled from senior school the previous year for trying to steal a computer from one of the technology labs. And now he was having to make do with being privately tutored in this huge house, which, as Casper might have mentioned more than once, came with its own games room.

She'd lost Emma and Victoria not long after they'd arrived, but Casper, bounding over, had made sure she didn't feel neglected.

'Rookes, I –'

'It's Roxy,' she corrected him. He looked a little hurt, as if being accused of something he genuinely hadn't done.

'Oh, yah, Roxy, sure,' he said, trying his hardest to sound blasé, though the confusion on his face said otherwise. 'Rox, I'm so –'

'Roxy,' she repeated, beginning to enjoy the pedantry of it all.

'Yah, Roxy, right. Got it,' he said, as if people around him were always changing their names on a whim. 'I didn't think you'd come. Actually, I was trying not to think about it. Part of me didn't want to get my hopes up. I've really missed you, you know. I think about you a lot, Roo, erm, I meant Roxy.'

Oh, God, she thought, he was already going all puppy dog on her, and she'd barely been here ten minutes. She'd been hoping to at least meet a couple of new people first before the inevitable tête-à-tête, probably in the kitchen. Just her luck she'd picked the one teenager in the country who seemed to have Trevor Howard as a role model. Too bad for him she was no Celia Johnson.

'Anyway, now that you're here, you may as well have something to drink. Jezza's a bit of a whizz with the old cocktails, but I wouldn't be at all surprised if his cellar's stacked as well.'

'Cellar?' Roxy repeated.

'Oh, yah, it's like the engine room for these parties, Roo, Roxy. Come on, I'll give you the guided tour,' said Casper, gesturing to nowhere in particular. Not long after, in the cellar, when he leaned in for the expected kiss, she surprised herself by how forcefully she pushed him away, especially as she had no strong feelings about it either way.

'Roo, Roxy, I, I, I'm really sorry,' he stammered, mortified by what he'd done, which, in truth, was very little. 'I, I didn't mean to, I mean, I didn't erm –'

'What, you didn't want to?' Roxy asked, enjoying the panicked look on Casper's face in lieu of actually feeling anything. The whole charade was just so predictable, she thought. If he'd given her any reason to forcefully resist, that might have been one thing, but this, this pathetic little performance worthy of an RKO picture, it just made her cringe. She couldn't care less if this boy wanted to stick his tongue down her throat. But he lacked conviction, and that was not attractive. Still, not reason enough to burn bridges while they were both secreted away down here.

'Look, Roxy. Can we start again?' Casper asked, more than a hint of pleading in his voice. 'I think you're a great girl, and the last thing I wanted was for you to feel pressurised. There's no rush. I'm sorry if I gave you that impression. Truly, Roxy, I'm sorry. I hope you can forgive me.' He waited a moment before holding out his hand. There seemed to be genuine remorse in his eyes. 'Friends, Roxy?'

She made him wait just that split second longer before accepting the olive branch. 'Friends, Casper.'

'I promise you, Roxy, you won't regret it,' he said, the puppy-dog look already returning to his face.

'Is that a Dom Pérignon?' Roxy asked, fingering the fat belly of the offending bottle, one of several peeping out of a huge wine rack.

'Yah, Roxy. I'll get us a couple of flutes then.'

'It *has* been a while, hasn't it, Casper? You've already forgotten that I don't drink,' she said, noting the crestfallen look on Casper's face and savouring how easily her white peers seemed to be wrongfooted by the non-alcoholic detail. Best of all, it wasn't even true. She'd been sampling her dad's bottle of Bombay Sapphire at home for some time now, topping up the remaining liquor with water, and so far, at least, avoiding the cloud of suspicion, which seemed to have settled squarely on her mum, which as far as she, Roxy, was concerned, was an unexpected bonus.

'Oh, yah, Rox, of course. I didn't mean –'

'Roxy,' she corrected him again, wondering what it was with these Trevor Howard types that made it so hard for them to say a name without making it sound like a pet or a destination. 'Rookes', 'Rox', but never actually the name they'd been told.

By the time they'd got back upstairs Emma and Victoria had resurfaced and were sitting in one of the lounge areas with the other boys they'd met during the field trip. There were no cocktails but plenty of bottles in evidence. Roxy watched as Casper's friends hovered around hers, rarely allowing a glass to remain empty for more than a few seconds. She looked at the labels, Pernod, Cinzano, Bacardi, and they seemed vaguely familiar from her dad's well-stocked cabinet. But what really struck her was the speed and efficiency with which the lounge crowd were devouring the contents. It was as though they needed to achieve a particular level of saturation before feeling ready to reach out for anything other than a bottle. No one really seemed to be listening to anything that was being said, and Roxy sensed that the details were largely for effect, as if preamble for the boys in particular to engage in some joshing. On the face of it, for the girls' benefit, but Casper's friends did seem unduly pleased with themselves, given that all they were doing was talking out-of-date rubbish and drinking someone else's liquor.

Royal Wedding, yah, I bet that was a gig they were all trying to get. I mean, why wouldn't you? Did you see what they were doing to the rest of them down in Brixton? I know if that was me getting pelted I wouldn't be hanging about.

If that was you, Hugo, you'd have still been in bed.

Yah, you're probably right, except I'd have been waking up to a nice Tuscan sunrise. They'd have to throw that brick an awful long way to ruin my day.

Oh, stop it, Hugo, you're incorrigible.

If you say so.

Of course, Emms, Vicky, I need to choose my words carefully here. Those weren't normal people like us doing the pelting. That was a mob, and they were out for blood. Is it any wonder some of the boys in blue are angry? I know I was, and I wasn't even there.

Oh, that's right, Hugo, you would have been in Tuscany, non?

Indeed. Still, no biggie. Refill, ladies?

As their stomachs became increasingly lined with the contents of the distillery, Roxy noticed how her friends barely seemed aware of her presence any more. One of them might occasionally look over, but without any great recognition and even less interest. Then they'd look back at the boys and at each other, and something purposeful would pass between them.

Casper dutifully fetched her an apple juice and made sure her glass was constantly replenished. He still seemed slightly embarrassed by his earlier faux pas in the cellar, and she made no attempt to reassure him, even though she'd long since forgotten whatever it was he was supposed to have done. She was grateful for the music when it finally started up. As soon as the first few notes of that big Queen hit, 'Another One Bites The Dust', filtered through from wherever the stereo was hidden, she found herself gravitating towards the sound.

The second lounge turned out to be moderately busy with people she didn't know, slightly muffling the funky stylings of Freddie Mercury. Looking around, Roxy saw that the skirting boards were lined with a number of empties, though this time limited to wine and beer. Several of the boys were smoking, and there was a strong, stale smell which lingered in the air. She wondered if she was the only person who was bothered by this, as the smoke rapidly started to cloy her nostrils, cling to her hair. No one else seemed to mind, or if they did they were handling it far better than her.

'What are you doing? Oh no,' she found herself saying aloud, involuntarily, as Casper began to do what could only be described as a Home Counties' limbo in the middle of the room. He'd been joined by another boy, also sporting the tell-tale Brideshead haircut, which went well with the drink-sozzled face, and they carried on with the competitive contortions for another few seconds while the rest of the room looked on, laughing and clapping. When they returned to being *Homo erectus*, both the 'dancers' high-fived each other and hugged, before Casper turned to Roxy with a broad smile on his face.

'Rox, this is Jezza,' he said, as if introducing her to the cure for crippling shyness.

'Rox. What an interesting name. Is it short for something?' Jeremy asked her once they were sat together, the three of them, on his bed upstairs.

'You could say that,' Roxy replied, shooting Casper a resentful side glance. 'It's actually short for "Don't you ever listen, cloth ears?"'

Jeremy, smirking, fired up the tip of what she assumed was a joint which he'd just withdrawn from a small money box kept in one of the drawers by the bed. He looked over at Casper, who appeared to be staring at his shoes.

'Feisty little filly you've got there, Caz,' he said, as though Roxy was not also sitting on the same bed with them firing daggers with those green eyes he'd not been able to properly place. Middle Eastern, Spanish? Definitely not a Paki, though, not with those eyes. He took a deep drag on the spliff, passing it on happy in the knowledge that there was a lot more where that came from. Ready-mades, part of the airtight deal he'd got going with his dealer, who also happened to be one of his English tutors. The supply chain of virtually no interest to him, other than that the end product was just that. The finished article. He didn't have time to faff around with Rizla papers and saliva and that delicate process of actually building a spliff. Far better, surely, to pay a bit more and receive a deluxe service? After all, he was a Fairbairn, and he knew this clan didn't get where it was today by wasting time on the little jobs. That's what the help was there for. So yah, ready-mades, as easy as slipping on a johnny.

Casper looked surprised when Roxy accepted the spliff, taking in a lungful and holding it down for a few seconds before coughing out the smoke.

'Don't worry, it's not against my religion,' she said to no one in particular, though instinctively looking over at Jeremy and making a note of the sly smile playing around the corner of his mouth. She wasn't even aware of Casper getting up and sloping away or at what point it was just her and Jeremy left in the bedroom.

By the time they'd rejoined the other party animals, something rancorous had occurred in the smaller of the two lounges. Casper was sat on the floor with blood still oozing from his recently bandaged right hand. Next to him were several fragments of glass, remnants of the tumbler he'd crushed in his hand. Emma was trying to comfort him, sitting next to him in some act of solidarity, cradling what Roxy had to admit was his very handsome head in her arms. Hugo and the other one whose name she couldn't remember were looking at her strangely, and Victoria seemed slightly embarrassed when Roxy finally made eye contact with her. Jesus, these people were such prudes! It's not like she'd had sex with the host. All she'd done was wank him off while he sucked her tits.

The other lounge had emptied out a little, but music was still playing. It was that ABC tune she really liked, 'Poison Arrow'. Casper gave her a suitably offended look as she wandered into the second lounge. The sound was less muffled than earlier, and this time she was able to pinpoint the stereo, tucked away in one corner well away from the empties.

Actually, she was quite surprised by the musical arrangements.

It was a MIDI-system, much like her own or perhaps not quite as good. Nothing Japanese or German – 'As a rule of thumb, when it comes to a hi-fi, always trust the Axis powers,' her eldest brother Rakesh had once advised her – and not even particularly new. Then again, she was the only one who seemed even to notice the disparity between the tinny sound and its expansive surrounds. Still, as Martin Fry belted out the lyrics, she couldn't resist shaking a leg. Jeremy, flush with what he clearly regarded as his latest bedroom 'exploit', joined her in the middle of the room, all elbows and angles and every bit the Fairbairn scion in his expensively tutored lack of co-ordination.

When the results came, they were more or less as expected. An A and two Bs. Her predicted grades had been exactly that, except that she got the A in French and not English. Anyway, they were good enough to get her out of here, she thought, and that was the main thing. A clean slate, a fresh start, and this time *she'd* be setting the tone, not helplessly sitting around like one of those Jane Austen heroines she'd reluctantly studied, constantly reacting to events beyond her control. No, well-bred martyrdom was not for her. She'd already seen enough of that in her dad's stoicism to cure her of the habit for an entire lifetime. An A and two Bs, and even if her mum wasn't over the moon – it's not Oxford, sohni – she knew her dad would be more than happy to drive her all the way up to campus. Warwick University. No more Home Counties hangdog for her. In other words, plenty good enough.

PART THREE

NOT EXACTLY BELLE ÉPOQUE

London, 2008

It wasn't supposed to be like this. Me, kissing the concrete in the middle of the day while other fellas are out there somewhere, busy making money. That was never the plan.

There is still defiance, oh, don't you worry about that, my friend, but it would be a push to call it a stance. I'm a soak not a fantasist, so don't write me off just yet. Yeah, I have my moments. Dribs and drabs, mostly, but take it from me, friend, there are fleeting glimpses of something older mixed in with the more recent decline. I can feel it sometimes, the old me making a comeback, though I'm not kidding myself. Only on a good day and rarely for very long. It's hardly a policy statement. All the same, I know when it's happening, usually outdoors by any tuft of green where this city suddenly remembers to breathe again, to take in a great lungful of me, the whiff of numbers and hedged bets fighting their way past the more obvious reek. Or sometimes in the queue for free food supplied by the Hare Krishnas outside the London School of Economics. Yeah, fuck you, Giddens, I often think during these moments, picking the third way out of my nose or somewhere lower down. The students never seem that bothered, though it wouldn't hurt them to say 'please' and 'thank you' to the Hare Krishna once in a while. He's white but not English, some kind of European, Italian, I'm guessing from his accent. Nice kid, never lets on about the reek, always gives me a little more than he does the budding young economists, piles my paper plate high with bread and lentils and rice.

'Thank you, sir,' I say to him, and I can tell he's surprised. The lunchtime crowd is many things, but courteous ain't one of them.

I sit a little distance from the students, take my time mopping up the last of the lentils with the slightly sweetened bread. It is healthy scran, better than the gruel they hand out in that kitchen I sometimes frequent, though only when I am truly desperate and can't think well enough of myself to make the trip to Kingsway and Giddens' old stomping ground. *Third way*, my arse! No two ways about it, the man was talking shite. Anyway, I'm here now, and he ain't, so yeah, fuck you, professor!

The lentils and rice taste good today, but even so I can hear some students complaining about it. Cheeky so-and-sos, I think, they wouldn't know a credit crunch if it jumped up and stuck its income-starved dick in their mouths. Suck on that, you little cunt, and while you're at it, read some Hayek. *The Road To Serfdom.* That's it, all the way, make sure you get every last drop. Waste not and all that, my future masters and mistresses of the universe. And when you're done, how about a nice coffee from that global franchise across the road where they won't serve me because of the reek?

They are looking at me now, the masters and mistresses to be, so perhaps I've been thinking aloud? No, it's nothing, I decide. One of them just happened to turn my way when he put his can of fizzy pop down on the wall. I hope he's not just going to leave it there. Oh no, he is. Oh dear. I wish he hadn't done that. Now I'm going to have to go over there and remonstrate with him about the ecology. And I know, I just know he's going to wrinkle his nose and smirking will be going on, all the while the ecology, the economy just degrading before my very eyes. I know this because he should have been me. *Was* that me once? On second thoughts, maybe not. I never left rubbish for someone else to clean up after me. Don't ever remember doing that. No, I wouldn't have done that. Was never a litterbug. You don't shit where you eat, as the old gentleman's club saying goes. No? What do you mean, I've just made that up? I can see you've no experience of the type of high-end establishments I favour. *Me, moi, a dedicated follower of ze eye-end fashion, meine Dahmer und Heron. Don't poop in ze loop, I believe was how they described that particular faux pas. No pasa nada, tenemos Arconada. Yeah, I know, surprising, non? On the surface a soak, but get below the fibres, the wet viscose, the three-week reek, and there, my friends, is the real ich. Yo, je, i. Better than plant extract, you know the one I mean, our old friend haw haw bah and definitely better than this.*

'Excuse me?' says the litterbug, trying to absorb what I've just told him.

'Actually, friend, I'm of no mind to do that,' I say to him, the import of the words spreading out across his face in a puzzled expression. 'You seem a bit confused,' I carry on, pressing home the advantage. 'That's a mighty puzzled look on your boat, son.'

I see it now, the smirk. It's not him, though, it's Lady Muck to his right. Still, I don't blame her really. After all, I've thrown her a bone there with the old rhyming slang. How quaint, she must think, last of the Mohicans and all that. *And you know, Mummy, I actually met one. One what, dear? A cockernee. A what, dear? A cockernee, Mother, you know, apples and pears, when I'm cleaning windahs. What are you talking about, dear? I'm afraid you lost me at 'apples'. Are you OK, Lucy? Is everything OK there? You sound frightfully peculiar, dear. A cockernee, Mother! You know, jellied eels, Gawd blimey, is that the time? I'd best be getting myself down to the gin palace. Fancy a spot of cider with Rosie? You haven't been taking drugs, have you dear? That's not why your father keeps sending you money, dear. He'd be, we'd both be mortified if that was where all those cheques were going. You know you can talk to us, dear, if you're having any kind of difficulty. I hope you know that, dear. Now, Lucy, what's the matter? Have you met a black boy? No, mother, even better than that, a cockernee. And he's not even a student. What? Lucy, you're breaking up. I can't hear you. A cock on your knee?*

The litterbug has another go at clarifying the position. 'No, I mean excuse me as in "What did you just say to me before that?"'

'Oh, that,' I say. 'That stuff about Hayek. Don't take it to heart, son, but it's true.'

'What's true? What *are* you on about?' he asks me, and I can see he's getting a little agitated.

'You must be the cream of the crop then?' I ask, changing tack.

'What? What are you talking about?' comes the definitely agitated response. I know about these micro-aggressions. Honestly, I do. It's not just the drink talking. I can taste them, smell them before most people even know a line has been crossed. A connoisseur of the socially awkward moment, moi. Et vous, what sort of a cunt are you?

'Crème de la crème, n'est-ce pas?' I say, with all the Gallic flair I can muster from a land beyond my two-day-old smell of cheese and sweat. Or is it three weeks? I really can't tell any more. How frightfully Proustian of me, I think, but it's not that time, not even the century which followed. There is no reply from the young master, and Lady Muck isn't smirking any more.

'Cream of the crop, and you've no idea what I'm on about, do you son? Hayek, son, Hayek.'

A flicker of recognition crosses his boat. I sense relief. He looks at me, an indulgent smile playing around his lips.

'Oh, I get it, you mean, Salma,' he says, turning to Lady Muck and their two other companions. 'Our friend here is a fan of the lovely Ms Hayek,' he says, pointing my way as if I'm Exhibit A. 'I think he's got quite a thing for her. Well, he must do, he came all the way over just to share his little crush with us.'

They laugh but hold something back, especially as I make no attempt to leave. Lady muck definitely isn't smirking now, not when I pick up the empty and place it in the young master's lap with a cryptic and phonetically varied explanation.

'No, son, lovely though she may be, *that* is not the Hayek to whom I refer. The Hayek to whom I reefer is Freddy, Daddy Freddy, Friedrich. And the point which I wished to highlight was this,' I say, indicating the lap-dancing empty with recently sweetbreaded fingers. 'The road to serfdom lies this way, son. Mark my words, fail to take individual responsibility, and chaos this way lurks, son. Chaos,' I say to him, emphasising the anarchy under the cheese breath. He flinches, just as I knew he would, and I deliver the punchline, 'Crème de la crème, I shit 'em!'

It's more or less all for Lady Muck's benefit. I can tell she's a seeker. I've known her sort before. No, really. She'll tire of the young master, and when that happens, my friend, when that happens…

What do you mean by that? So what if you're right? So what if when it happens I'll be nowhere near. You don't know that for sure, none of us does. It's all a game, a bet, a calculation, a risk. Always was, always will be. Nothing ventured. What, what are you laughing at? You want some? Outside, now! Except we are outside, and it can only be now. It *is* now. It *must* be. Well, I'm here, aren't I? It's an ontological thing, son, you wouldn't understand.

There's dirt under my nails and filth in my head, and I don't really know which shows up more. I eat what the Hare Krishnas provide, and I find remnants of my old self in the post-prandial environment. I gather them up in my dirty hands and make a supplication to my unexpected benefactor. *Hare Krishna Hare Rama.*

What's that look for? You don't know. Like I know.

I can hear the squelch near my midriff. I can feel the shame once again. Leaden footed, unable to move, not like the others. You don't know. A squelch, an electro squelch. I can hear it. Like I know. The fibres leaking, burning into the flesh. I can hear it, I can taste it. Like I said, a connoisseur. Serious Intention burping out of the tannoy, but this time the threads are dry, the thoughts clean. Soulboys and sportswear. I can see the flicked wedge haircuts, I can taste the joy not quite unconfined. It's not here, not even now, but who cares? You want to make something of it? No, well fuck off then, you cunt! I'm trying to tell you something here, and I thought this was supposed to be a place of great learning. So you can take that London-and-the-southeast smile, and you can stick it right up your harris, son. Think of it as a fiscal stimulus. Surprised you don't already know about those kinds of things, son. Thought it would have been the first thing they taught you here.

Show me the money, son, show me the money!

Why the wounded look? Oh, do behave, son. What, the penny's

only just dropped? I'm not the man I used to be, a half-cut, pastiche, cardboard-cut-out cockney. Barely rhyme and nearly always out of time. A two-bob. Yeah, that's me, son, that's me alright. Bang to rights, guv'nor. Just a game really. Nothing to get upset about. Just a game.

I shouldn't have said that. I should never have ripped off Harold Shand, the words forming an instant command. Lady muck is giving me a strange look as I attempt to excuse myself. I can already tell, that nose will wrinkle as I shuffle away, but that's no longer a priority. I just need to get past security in reception, and then there is a male khazi on every other floor. If I can just get past reception. So long as it's not the Somali gentleman, I should be fine.

This is the least glamorous of all the buildings here, Sociology, and the Somali must resent his posting. He must know this is the poor cousin to Accountancy and Finance. He must loathe its daily parade of hoorays experimenting with social conscience and worse, much worse, the clearing-house detritus who didn't quite get their grades for Political Science. And I can't say I blame him, but still, why take all of that out on me? What have I ever done to him? What's that you were saying? How do I know he's Somali? Oh, do grow up, son. He's got the beak and that narrow look in his eyes. Almost looks like a P–, erm, I meant like an Asian. And he's really got it in for me. You do one lobby fart, you get judged for it till the end of days.

It's not him. My relief is palpable. At any rate something is.

I amble past and upstairs, into the cubicle. Wind turns to mud, and something Darwinian evolves from my gut. The deposit is tribal, a Mameluk waving goodbye to the Pharaohs. That world, ancient Egypt, flushed down the pishadoo along with any semblance of dignity. Hopefully, outside there's a professor hopping from foot to foot who's waiting to ablute. I spray the seat using my own instrument of mastery. It's not exactly belle époque, but I know Friedrich would have understood.

In my own way, and given the limited room for manoeuvre inside the cubicle, I feel I've just delivered my own devastating verdict on command-and-control economies. I hope Freddy would have understood. I think he would. After all, this was a man who became interested in modern economics while trapped in the trenches during the First World War. I still remember reading that way back when. It's one of those remnants I scooped up with the blessing of the Hare Krishnas. He had his trench, I've got my cubicle. I open the door. There is no professor, but miraculously, tragically, there *is* a Somali standing just outside, and he looks annoyed.

Whaddya Say, Whaddya Know?

'DON'T TOUCH ME,' I tell the Somali. 'I'm going. Just don't touch me.'

I'm sensitive about these things nowadays. Ever since that desk clearance and the walk of shame all those years back. What matters most to me is the impression of free will. I know this with every fibre in my being, including the ones which are sozzled. They humiliated me that day. Paraded my sacking in front of everyone like a naughty kid. Never again, I vowed, and I like to think I've stayed true to that. Every building I've been told to leave since has been exited with head held high and hopefully with the impression given that it was always my idea anyway, and no, don't be fooled by my chaperones. Even that hostelry, to the untrained eye that might have looked one way, but the truth is, I was in control all along there. It might have looked like I was being manhandled, but really, it was still me calling the shots. I'd had enough of that place anyway. My decision was made. They just gave me a helping hand.

This cunt, though, he must think he's secret service or something. Why else would he be on a walkie-talkie with that narrow look on his boat just getting more angular by the second? We're not in the movies, I want to scream, but I fear irony's not his strong point, so I watch quietly as he gathers reinforcements. They are pointing my way and nodding to each other in some dismal secret code. I'm no Alan Turing, but even I can tell what will happen next if I don't go into full compliance. The Somali takes a step closer to where I am stood, embodying (me, of course, not him) one of Hayek's key theories. I can see he doesn't care for my rendition of the economics of the whole. He just wants to see whether I will back off so that those narrow eyes can once again proclaim themselves the victor. I want to tell him, I really want to tell him, there *are* no victors in this, that in the end we will all lose out, no matter how much he believes that my personal currency has been devalued. But I don't bother; I can see it's pointless so long as he imagines himself to be 'Smokey' and me 'the Bandit'.

'You stay away from here,' he tells me, the other tried-out-for-the-filth-but-failed-the-interview suspects forming a protective phalanx around him. I say nothing, and he takes my silence as a challenge to what he must clearly think, poor deluded creature, is his authority. Yep, he's giving me that look, the one that says, 'Do not defy me. I am the law!' But he's not. I know that, so must he. Can't he see he's no Stallone? He's not Dredd or Rocky or even Butkus. *Yo, Butkus, old buddy, whaddya say, whaddya know?* That's not him either. The carousel spinning faster, the old mastiff, Jimmy Cagney, or was that Butkus, looking out at the speakeasies and at the dwindling opportunities. Even Rocky, sparring with the silent slabs of meat, hangdog but resilient. All jowls and dignity. And there's another face on the carousel, too. Whose is that face? A little more jowly but still some resilience in there. Resistance. Not. Futile. It spins round one more time, and that's when I realise it's me.

For now, though, I'm not saying anything, and I can see how little this pleases the Somali. Those eyes are narrowing, really narrowing, silence and something else looming up in the sightlines. As residual defiance. I'm no betting man, but even I can see the anger in those slits. Like I said, I've got a gift for this type of thing. Micro-aggressions. I've known them all my life, ever since a stray 'thirty-two' amused my bouche but no one else's. This stuff I know, perhaps the more so with the reek and the disappointment. The stench of failure which should probably be hanging about me but which for some reason seems to have transferred itself to the Somali. He feels I am embarrassing him in front of his colleagues. As far as he's concerned, this isn't over.

'You stay the hell away from here,' he repeats. 'Next time we take you to lock up. Don't let me catch you in here again. And don't try to hide. Your stink, it give you away every time. Now, get out of here, you tramp!'

It's not a zero-sum game, I want to say. Devaluing my currency, putting up these barriers to my entry and full participation in the common market of clearing the pipes, might restore *his* wounded pride for now, but in the long run it will hurt us all. Perhaps he subscribes to those older theories, I think? The ones that have been disproved time and time again. Maybe it's that. He genuinely believes that clamping controls on capital outflows will not only reduce balance-of-payment deficits but will uplift government revenues by preventing gold from leaving the economy. Perhaps he believes that the Treasury will no longer be deluded of its precious bullion and all will be well once more in this land of milk and honey? It's hard to say, as the Somali still seems to be basking in the afterglow of the takedown.

'You're wrong,' I say, surprising him into looking back at where I am standing and away from his colleagues' glad-handing. 'You're wrong about that, friend. Clamping down on my capital outflows might present me with a problem for now, but it's all of you who'll be waist deep in it later. Mark my words. And then you'll regret it. Then you'll think, I should have just let that gentleman shit where he eats. But it'll be too late by then. You don't know, squire, like I know. I know that building right there, I know how it works. Don't you worry about that, friend. I know all about it. How the pipes work. You should have just let me shit one floor down from where the Emeritus Professor of Social Thought once sat. Shat where he sat. Oh, wait, that's me, not him. But you didn't. You had to louse everything up, didn't you, friend? You just couldn't resist sticking that beak in. I guess you're used to the smell, though, eh?'

He looks at me, shocked. I can see I've got this cunt's full attention now. Some students have started to gather, attracted by the commotion. I spy Lady Muck in among them, so I clear my throat and keep going.

'Think about it, friend. If everyone restricted everyone else's capital outflows, all the pipes would just remain blocked. And blocked pipes can only mean one thing. Disease, poverty, death.

Oh wait, that's three, but indulge me, if you will. Indulge me, squire. You've got to keep free enterprise functioning or the pipes get blocked. What goes in must come out. It's how stuff works. I'm guessing, and tell me if I'm wrong, friend, but I'm guessing you don't know too much about that, do you? Never heard of Hayek have you? Or Keynes or Schumpeter? Or the Musketeers?'

'What?! You talk like crazy fool,' he says, possibly feeling a bit self-conscious with so many students now gathered around on the steps.

'All for one and one for all? No? Didn't think so. What's good for one is not always good for all,' I tell him, noting how Lady Muck still hasn't departed the scene. 'What's good for you now will eventually be bad for us all,' I say, gesturing to the students, hearing what I think is a vague murmur of approval ripple through their ranks. When the expected altercation doesn't materialise, though, the students start to drift away, back to whatever it was they were doing before raised voices and the promise of conflict briefly distracted them. That's when the Somali makes his move. But yeah, Giddens, the Somali, the third way, I shit 'em.

I C 1

I WAKE UP in Lincoln's Inn Fields. I can hear birdsong, and it distracts me from the pain I feel shooting up from my ribs. It takes a moment for my eyes to adjust, squinting back at the sunlight which, for now at least, is a comfort. There are little clusters of students dotted around the fields. They seem happy, carefree. At any rate they do to me. From where I squint, any cluster seems preferable.

I'm not the only overage NEET in here. Yeah, I know the language. Not in Employment, Education or Training. NEET. But I'm too old to be one of those, apparently. The salvage boat only casts its net out to youngsters. I'm one of those beached whales, the tragic type who fetches up an ocean away from where they began. But in my case there won't even be any frantic efforts to revive the beast. I've known this for a while now, in the downward looks and wrinkled noses, in the way that I always find space in this most crowded of cities. How it miraculously appears wherever I do, an exclusion zone permeated by the stink of failure. I am the stain on the surface, a public embarrassment. A public failure. No one likes to see that, not here in the cradle of democracy. I am a white Englishman, an IC1, and this was never supposed to be my fate. Not here, not like this.

'Are you OK?'

It takes a moment to register the question. Am I OK? That's a difficult one to answer. As long as the sun offers its caress and the park stays open, I guess I am. OK, that is. Don't really want to go the *cogito-ergo* route just yet. So yeah, I'm OK. Who's asking?

'I wasn't sure you were going to be OK,' she says.

I try to focus. My eyelids are still caked in sleep, and it briefly hurts when I force them open. When they adjust, I'm surprised to see that it's Lady Muck. Happily this time Lord Snooty isn't with her. It is just the two of us and a series of photocopied articles she is clutching with what I can see are slender fingers. I shake the thought from my head. Too old to be a NEET, so most definitely too old to be having those kinds of thoughts. It's the outdoor life to blame, though, I tell myself, it plays tricks on your judgement.

'What do you want?' I ask her a bit too gruffly. She seems a little startled.

'I was just a little worried about you,' she says, and right away I feel ashamed of myself. A public embarrassment.

'No, I meant, why do you care anyway?'

She looks at me, and I see that there is no pity in that look. Just curiosity. 'After the security guard pushed you over, I wanted to make sure you were OK.'

'Yeah, well, as you can see, I'm just tickety-boo here, love,' I say, wondering when exactly I turned into such an arsehole but all the same largely unable to stem the flow of idiocy.

'That's a relief,' she replies, 'because when you staggered into here and then collapsed it didn't really look like you were OK, if you don't mind my saying so.'

If I don't mind her saying so?! What is this, some kind of costume drama with full period etiquette? I want to feel outraged somehow but know I've got no reason. I'm just a soak who's fucked everything up. I've fallen through the cracks, and even then it's been a soft landing, on the grass, with my very own Florence Nightingale to watch over me, though God knows why.

'Don't I know you?' I ask her, pretending only *now* to have recognised her from earlier. 'I know you, love. You were laughing at me before. Yeah, that was you alright.'

'I wasn't. Honestly I wasn't,' she explains. 'He's alright, really, my friend. It's just that he sometimes gets carried away with himself and comes off sounding insensitive. But he's not like that, really. He doesn't mean any harm. It was all just a misunderstanding.'

I've only the vaguest idea that she's referring to Lord Snooty but nod my head sagely as though I've been thinking the exact same thing and was just waiting on her for confirmation.

'What's your name, love?' I ask her.

She pauses, sizing me up with what I can now see are steely blue eyes. Once she's satisfied herself that I pose no legitimate threat either to her being or to those papers she's holding on to, she tells me, 'Lucy.'

She's right, too. I pose no threat. I am the soak in the undergrowth. Yesterday's man, though even then I got the feeling that I belonged to the day before. All the same, it hasn't deterred her. From what, I've no idea, but the fact remains, she's still here.

'What were you talking about back there?' she asks me.

'Back where, love?' I reply, happy to play along with the 'harmless' label.

'Back on the steps, next to the food queue. That was really interesting what you were saying, though I didn't manage to follow all of it. But I'm sure you mentioned Schumpeter as well as Hayek. How do you know about them?'

Again, I want to feel some righteous indignation, but it won't come. *How do I know about them?* Well, love, I want to tell her, I only studied them as though my life depended on it pretty much every day since my bollocks dropped, but hey, other than that, what do I know? Someone like me. An old fashioned, inner city IC1, yeah, what do I know?

I try to summon up the requisite anger, but it's just not there. That's not what she's saying, and I know it, but it's still a game. To me it is anyway, even if no one else is playing. Like David Byrne said, 'the same as it ever was', but I bet he's never been to Bermondsey. The thing with this game, though, is that there's no time limit on it. No bandy-legged ref blowing on a whistle and half-time oranges. No, this game just goes on and on until every foul, every offside, is siphoned back up into the whistle's pregnant middle, along with each player and their misplaced sense of injustice. So that the only things left standing are the goalposts, which I can see now aren't posts at all but jumpers, so later who'll even believe that there were posts or a game or players, that any of it ever existed? But there *was*, there still is, I want to shout. The game goes on long after the final whistle has blown. Everyone's got a number, and every number comes with its own performance. Midfield general, pacy winger, hatchet man in defence. Though the truth is, I never really found my role. For all the good it did me, I was the quiet one, slipping under the radar. The Category Unknown.

So I think, should I tell her? Should I show her who I really am? Or will that blow the mystique? Will that ruin everything? Turns out I've got quite the talent for spoiling things. Careers, marriages, prospects. What about olive branches, though? That's what this is. I'm fairly certain of that.

She's a seeker. But if I tell her the truth, she might not like what she finds. She's definitely a seeker, though. Why else would she be here?

I'm an IC1, white English, like her, but the grub under the nails, the freeform row with security, *that's* my shtick. That's what caught her eye, why she's sitting here now taking a genuine interest in my well-being.

I'm the chap who reeks and rows.

Yes, it is I, the outdoor economist, high priest of 'the big society' – *Hare Krishna, Hare Rama* – and a certain neoliberal rigour – 'you don't shit where you eat'. But it's not organic, none of this is. It's been finely honed over a lifetime of underachievement. Waxed and polished and rubber-stamped with institutional approval.

University.

The City.

A whole new tax bracket. I'm no rebel, barely even an outsider. An IC1, albeit not quite in the manner of Lord Snooty. Still, an IC1 rather than an IC3, 4 or a 6. If I told her, would it spoil things?

'I've seen things,' I start to tell Lucy, already knowing which way this is headed. 'I've seen things you wouldn't believe, love,' I continue, any doubts about the lies which will follow already being dispelled by the look of eager anticipation on this young woman's boat. Still, I have to remind myself, no one's looking for the truth, least of all those who claim to be.

PARSING THE
SLAGHEAP

NOW I KNOW what the reek is. It is habit which clings to me like
disaster. The problem with habit, of course, is how hard it is to let
go of. I barely even try any more. I've got used to being alone, but
that doesn't mean I'm happy about it. Most days I tell myself I'm
OK. A little porkie to go with the bigger ones, and who's counting
anyway? But they're habitual, the porkies. The half-truths, the
embellishments, the outright fabrications. And we cling to each
other, myself and the lies, because it's what we've always done.
They're a shadow and a cloak. They cover me when I'm cold and
feed me when I'm hungry. It's not really me in that queue with the
other supplicants. *Hare Krishna Hare Rama.* No, it's not me, that's
just habit lining up. And I'm OK with that. I've learnt to accept
that man. He's not the man he used to be, that's for sure. That
man, he used to hide behind anonymity, thought that gave him an
edge. He shaved his own name to the bone just to be alone. And
back then in that horrible classroom, doing that made him feel so
free. Now, though, he wants those letters back, wants to forget
about being alone. It's true, I tell her, I just want to stop hiding. I
want my name back. I'm not him, and he's not me. We don't even
get on. Plus, *he's* a smelly cunt.

I didn't realise before, but I'm so lonely. I thought I was doing
OK, but no. Turns out it was just habit standing between me and
the abyss. And now even that's falling apart. It doesn't take much.
This young woman's company is enough to make me reach down
into the slagheap for something, anything, some little scrap that
might keep her interested. I don't want those steely blue eyes to
dim. I can't bear to think of her just getting up and walking away

because the stench has become overpowering. The numbing reek of boredom. My reek. I know she will eventually. They all do. But it's been so long since I've even spoken properly with another citizen. Rowing with publicans or two-bob security doesn't really count. This girl, Lucy. She's a little different, though. She's kind and she's clever and she's, oh no, I'm doing it again. It's the same thing all over. I never learn.

I start to rap my knuckles against my forehead, moaning away like the Hasidim at that wall of theirs. I'm trying to break the habit of a lifetime, knock some sense into what ironically transpires is that risk-averse skull of mine. Each time I do, I call myself by a fresh expletive. Those blue eyes look genuinely troubled, as though she is somehow moved by my plight. This makes me want to try all the harder, fail just a little better, as the great Irishman would have had it. I'm like poor old Tom, popping back into the third dimension after his head has been flattened by a frying pan. That fucking mouse! Still, the point remains, I can feel something shift inside of me, so I keep rapping, and cursing. And it's only when I've run out of the local favourites and am forced to think beyond these shores – *cagón, hijo de puta, marica* – that I work out what it is that has changed. *It is me!* I've grown bored of my own stench, of its rhythms, its pacing, its conventions. It is just dull. As if swallowed up by the whistle, the reek has suddenly gone. So, too, have the jumpers and all evidence of the game.

So I tell her everything, from the fish knife to the audition but leave out the bit concerning the well-known pizza franchise. I tell her how I lost everything, the marriage, the job, the house and then something even bigger. The sense of hope that life could ever recover its interest for me. And I tell her it's *that* way round. I insist upon it. It's not me really. It's life.

She listens to me without interrupting. The lunchtime crowd has melted away from the park, so I lower my voice, suddenly self-conscious in the empty space. People are my background noise. I draw comfort from that, I tell her, and those eyes really soften then. Even an old soak like me can tell she's looking at me differently now. I'm the outdoor philosopher. Life is my library. Ah, fuck, that's bollocks, I think. What sort of a cunt says that? But she's not put off, not in the slightest. This probably still counts as cutting edge in her world. So I soldier on, parsing the slagheap for more snapshots of my own genius. I tell her about the name change and the reason for it. I wonder if she even knows the singer, but it seems she *has* heard of Debbie Harry.

I try not to make any lewd comments, and it is surprisingly easy. To not make them, that is. No trouble at all since I took up with the great outdoors. That was never me anyway, that was those boys who never made the change, who hung on to every syllable they'd been handed on a birth certificate. Hung on and did what was expected of them. Hurly-burly and wisecracking seeing them through the boredom of school and straight into whatever it is that boys like them fell straight into. I tell her I was never like that. Tell her how that was never going to be enough for me. Explain that's why I shaved the letters and bided my time. I leave out the bit about my brother and the long arm, and still she listens, whatever earlier plans she had for the afternoon now second fiddle to this grand confession.

The bigger surprise is how easy it is to tell her. I've hoarded these thoughts like Scrooge. Hoarded them for so long that they just became part of the reek. The foundational element, constipation. Blocked pipes. My very own control-and-command economy. Yet once I unlock that dusty old trunk they waste no time bolting for freedom. Yes, I unlock the trunk, and out they pop. I parse the contents and find there's a lot stored up in there. This is an ancient blockage. It needs release. I need release. I sift through the contents. It is a visual pun, starting in the back of my throat and ending in birdsong. When I look up again, the girl is gone. The only signs of life are next to where I'm sat, blinking into the sunlight. A small spillage on the grass. I am definitely alone, but it's not me really.

NOT HIS FAULT

'AND DON'T COME back!' yells the manager.

'Fuck you!' That's what I try to say, but it comes out as 'far queue'. I am slurring now, but the deed is done. A floater in the khazi. The manager saw this as an unspeakable liberty. And yes, he did see it. The unspeakable liberty that I've taken deriving from my status as a non-customer. And not only that but a crapper to boot. For the use of paying customers only. Oh, far queue.

I slept near the bridge last night. Don't ask me which one, but I've found a little pitch nearby. It's not too bad. There's a couple of us, and we take it in turns to watch over the pitch, which means some guaranteed shut-eye without the usual histrionics. He's a foreigner, the other chap, and I think he likes the fact that I'm English. A proper IC1 to lend a bit of credibility. That must be it. I doubt it's my witty repartee. Of late there's not been much of that to share around.

But I like coming to this fast-food outlet to unblock my pipes, so to speak. I feel no way about not flushing or washing up afterwards in this type of establishment. It's not at all like that underground café linked to the church, the big one near Trafalgar Square. I'm always very meticulous when I'm there. Much more my milieu. Literary types, I think, absorbed in their books or their conversation. Either that or there's quite a few who don't exactly sound local, if you know what I mean. But they're a classier crowd, never give me those looks which are virtually guaranteed in the fast-food outlets. It's true.

Something else I've noticed, how basic manners seem to have left the building the moment neon strip lighting and meat of indeterminate origin came in. These managerial types. I can't see what their problem with me is. They make shit, and so do I. We're not so different really, though I somehow doubt this manager could provide the kind of risk-weighting analysis of his business assets that a trained eye like mine could achieve with little more than a visual sweep of the premises. (Insider knowledge of the floater in the khazi notwithstanding.) So yeah, mister manager, far queue.

He attacked me last night, the other man. I don't really care. Perhaps I should. He ran off with my valuables. But he'll find nothing in there, nothing he wants. The weight is all the waste paper I've been collecting from the bins outside the London School of Economics. Some of it is headed notepaper, but for the most part it is made up of timecoded photocopying remainders. He might hang on to the biros, though. I've picked up a few of them in that area by the bookshop, where the Hare Krishna pitches up, bless him.

I've been thinking for a while now that I need to throw my hat into the ring. It's no good carping around the edges any more. That just won't do, not with my explosive insider knowledge. It's true. I've been meaning to put it all down on paper just so the burger munchers will know one day how their lives were briefly touched by genius. By the virtuosity of a former insider. A real rogue trader. Something to tell their kids, if that processed dog meat they swear by hasn't already shrivelled their bollocks to the size of a raisin. But yeah, if it's not already too late for the next generation of wee burger munchers, then let my words wean the little cunts off their attachment to the gold standard. The bullion in the khazi. The stench of raw capital. It's the low-end theory I favour, but the claret is filling up my mouth now, and I'm finding it hard to think. Clearly. About. Anything.

The men in uniform speak softly. They even help me gather up my papers which, just as I suspected, the foreign gentleman had discarded along with the biros not fifty yards from where I have been discovered.

'Foreign, you see. Not his fault,' I tell them. They are not impressed. It's the kind of comment I'm not expected to make, with or without a bump on the head. Though when I consider it some more, which in my state is about all I can do, the ambiguity is writ large. Are they unhappy with me because they feel I'm attempting to excuse this man's fiendish actions, worthy of a foreign national, or is it that I've crossed some sort of a line by even drawing attention to the fact that he is, lo and behold, foreign? I don't know. I just can't tell any more.

Every so often the rules change, and what was OK a moment before is suddenly the equivalent of leaving a floater in the swimming pool. I'd never do that, of course, not while there're still fast-food outlets the length and breadth of this green and pleasant land. And I'd like to think Burt Lancaster never left a floater, not while he was swimming across all those private pools in that old film *The Swimmer*. Great film, too. Remember seeing that with the missus, a special screening I think it was, in that lovely little rep near the river, Hammersmith way. She was impressed when I mentioned the John Cheever short story it was based on. I don't think she was expecting that. IC1, but yeah, I've got varied interests. Always have done. Anyway, that's not the point I was trying to make. It's just so confusing. Yesterday's girls are today's young women, like Lucy. The lovely Lucy. She just disappeared, though. Ah, well. Or blacks. Didn't they used to be Afro-Caribbeans? Or was that Schwarzes? Anyway, now you've got to call them 'African-Caribbean' apparently. The black lady at the soup kitchen told me that. I think she's only being half-serious though. I think she probably likes me. It gives her an excuse to have a natter. African-Caribbean. What, even a cunt like Conrad? I wonder what happened to him?

*

They are keeping me in for observation. That's what I'm told by the lovely African-Caribbean nurse who turns out to be no such thing.

'I'm from Mauritius,' she tells me, when I ask her which bit of the Caribbean she's from.

'You must get that a lot,' I say to her, hoping it sounds like a compliment, but never really sure in this day and age, what with the shifting boxes of virtue and vice.

'Not really,' she says, 'You're the first.'

But they want to keep an eye on me. I've had a nasty bump on the head, and they want to make sure everything is as it should be before they release me back into the wild.

'Try to get some rest,' she tells me. 'You've been talking a lot in your sleep. I'll bet you didn't know that?'

I dread to think what I've been saying. It's been so long since I had a proper bed and some clean sheets. Or someone to make a fuss over me. I take whatever pills she gives me with the little plastic beaker of water. There's neon strip lighting in here, too, but I'm hoping the meat they serve up later for my dinner is not of indeterminate origin.

I see an African-Caribbean gentleman sitting on his own near the window, so I slowly shuffle over and ask him if he knows Conrad. He looks at me without any malice. So I repeat the question. For a moment it appears as though he does indeed know my old tormentor. But then the light fizzles out, and his face is blank once more. I look around. Many of the inmates are African-Caribbean gentlemen – of a certain vintage, I might add. At least we're not neglected, though. The nurse comes round regular as clockwork to give us our water and our pills. And she's very diligent, always waits until she's sure that I've swallowed, that we've all swallowed. She certainly wasn't joking when she said they wanted to keep an eye on me. Gawd bless her and her exotic island origins.

It's a funny kind of hospital this. Sometimes the nurses seem larger than normal. Burly even. If I'm going to be honest, they don't look like nurses at all. They remind me of match days and Millwall, but then again, what do I know? I've had a nasty bump on the head, and they just want to keep me under observation. They always seem to appear quite suddenly, though, when you least expect it. *Surprise!* Except they rarely speak, and I've noticed they only respond to the doctors. Yesterday I tried to ask one of them if he knew where Conrad was, and he just looked straight through me as though I wasn't there. I'm glad they haven't found the pills under my pillow. I think they might notice me then.

Last night I tried to go for a walk, but everything was locked. I don't like being locked in. I just want to take my constitutional. I'm an IC1, and I demand to be let out for my constitutional. But when I tell the duty nurse she just looks at me like I'm an IC7, or was that 9, I can never be too sure about that one? Anyway, she gives me that 'category unknown' look and tells me I've had a nasty bump on the head and why don't I get some rest, it'll be the best thing for me. *The best thing?!* How can she possibly know what will be best for me? She doesn't even know me, she doesn't know anything about me. But here she is telling me who's who and what's what. If she knew anything, then she'd know about the pills. But she doesn't. None of them does. I want to tell her about the Hayekian discipline it takes to trim the fat from your own name, to shave it to the bone, to make it work better in the deregulated environment of the Thatcherite classroom. Or at the heart of the fiscally restructured economy. But I can see she's already lost to her nails or makeup or crossword or whatever it was she'd been doing before I came along, so I don't bother. An IC1 in the land of my birth, and I can't even access fresh air.

In some ways it reminds me a bit of school. Not the screaming, though eventually you get used to that as well. Which isn't to say it doesn't bother me, of course it does. I'm not a monster. But I need my rest the same as everyone else, so I just put it down to first-night nerves now, even the ones like me who've been here a lot longer than one night. That's the other thing. I've lost track of time here. I can't feel the bump any more, but I'm still here. I don't know how long it's been. But yeah, the school thing. Not in the way time stands still, though come to think of it, that's another similarity. No, it's more the semi-structured approach to the learning environment, if you know what I mean. No? I take it you're not from round here then? Student centred, before anyone even knew what that meant. In practice, lots of time milling around trying not to make the wrong kind of eye contact. Huddles and cliques and plenty of sniggering. This tribe and that tribe and a profitable sideline in 'merch'. Fags, porn mags, trainers. About the only thing the tribes could agree on, though even then...

Two of the African-Caribbean men here don't seem to like each other very much. They clash sometimes when they think no one's looking. The older of the two, who I'm guessing is around my age, has started receiving messages in his food. That's what the younger one objects to. He can't understand why his sausages don't also contain instructions for warding off evil spirits. I am guessing he feels left out. He tells the older man he is a 'crazy old scarecrow', and his rival – for what, don't ask me that, I don't know; I'm just an onlooker, I'm not really here – tells him he is the 'devil spawn'. When they fight the younger man quickly gets the upper hand and pins the older man to the wall with one hand while the other rapidly transforms the left side of his face into a mass of blotchy-blueblackred. It is odd, though, how long it takes the oversize nurses to appear on these occasions. They are normally so prompt, but not when these two fight. The old man is wailing by the time they pull his assailant off him. Even so the nurses like to make a show of strong-arming both combatants as if they were meticulously observing the principle of joint liability.

But the school thing. Mostly we're just left to our own devices, a bit like school. Here I am the ape with the crayon in between my toes. They don't know that I can draw. I have started to call the

Schwarzes by their correct denomination. My head hurts. It is full of diagrams, flow charts, demand-and-supply curves. It tells me to buy low and sell high. I can see the crop report in there, and Eddie Murphy and assorted African-Caribbeans leaning in to have a look at the pie charts. Pie and mash. Pi and algebra. Pythagoras. The crayon draws a stick man under a sunny sky. Perhaps it's one of the Dukes, the Dukes of Hazard? Or maybe not. The man is too skinny. Well, like I said, he's a stick man. Eddie Murphy seems interested. Oh, now I get it! It's one of the other Dukes. I think it's Mortimer. He thinks he's cornered the market. He doesn't know yet. Not about the crop report. I do, though. I know it all. The long-range forecast, scattered showers but with dry intervals. A mixed bag.

I'm gasping down lungfuls of the stuff. They gave me the all-clear. It must have been a mix-up. I don't think I was ever supposed to be there with all those IC3s. Me and the Schwarzes, or should that have been the Schwarzes and I? Something else they never taught me at school. Anyway, they say I can go now. They don't seem so worried about the bump any more. Which can only mean one thing. That guy, the patient, the one with the bump, that wasn't really me. *This* is me, a bona fide Englishman just filling his lungs with the taste of freedom.

SOUTHBOUND

London, 2008

THIS STUFF USED to wake me up in the same way as a bracing walk. The pick-me-up of fiscal crisis, ballooning public deficit, the need for austerity. I read the headlines in one of the many free papers which are strewn all over the seats. I am on a train southbound. It is more or less empty as I move through the carriages. Just for fun, I say, 'Tickets and passes, please. Have your tickets and passes ready for inspection.' A young man looks up from his mobile phone, sees that I am far too dapper to be a ticket inspector and silently mouths the word 'cunt' at me. No doubt about it, this one's southbound.

London, 1982

In the end all roads led south. 'There'll be prizes, surprises and a best-dressed competition,' teased the voice on the radio. An early-eighties, London voice. Not Greg Edwards but invitingly seductive all the same.

The reception this high up in the towers was crystalline. Conrad briefly marvelled at the network of antennae and transmitters which made any of this possible. He knew there were people clambering around up there in all weathers, fixing, mending, planting the flag for their little piece of sonic Antarctica. By rights a good percentage of these fearless explorers would be the self-same high achievers he'd been at school with, who'd sooner stab themselves with toothpicks than show some initiative during P.E.

He couldn't place the announcer's voice. The man sounded

black but not strictly local. He sensed the effort going into making that voice sound vaguely American. There was a mid-Atlantic twang about it even when it was introducing something more exotic.

'This next one is for all the serious dancers. From the land of the rising sun, Ryuichi Sakamoto, "Riot in Lagos".'

Chances were it was someone who'd never strayed further than the barber shop round the corner, but he admired the neck on the guy. Chutzpah. That was the word he was searching for.

Nan was out with Hortense and some of the other ladies from the social centre. They had clubbed together to hire a van and a driver to take them to Brighton for the day.

'Fish an' chip an' a lickle view of the oh-shan,' Nan had said by way of an explanation.

He was glad she wasn't here. One less thing for him to worry about. Besides, if anyone deserved a break it was Nan. It would do her good, the tang of sea salt in the nostrils and crazy golf on the pier. At the last minute she'd panicked, seemed to have a change of heart. 'I feel a terrible dread in my bones,' she'd told him. 'Someting is tellin' me fi stay 'ere with yuh. Let me jus' call 'Ortense an' –'

'Nan, don't be silly,' Conrad had interrupted. 'You go and enjoy yourself by the sea with the ladies. You deserve a day off, Nan. You don't need to worry about me. In case you hadn't noticed, I'm all grown up now. Anyway, I'll be busy all day. You just keep an eye on the other ladies. I know what you're like when you get together,' he joked.

She laughed, reassured by her grandson's growing maturity, and seemed visibly excited when she received the phone call from Hortense a few moments later to say the man with the van had just pulled up and that they would soon be 'on their way'.

He waited and watched until he was sure the van had left for its coastal jolly. Then he double-checked the items he'd pulled out from under his bed. The petrol can, a bundle of rags and a book of matches, the latter filched from that wine bar which had recently opened just up the road. His feeling when he was in there that it was the kind of place he'd probably come back to with a fat wedge in his pocket and a white girl on his arm. He'd had a couple of sidelong glances but nothing out of the ordinary, and, to be fair, the bar staff hadn't missed a beat when he ordered a 'club soda'. The music had been a bit predictable, though. Shalamar, Kool And The Gang and some tune he'd heard being plugged by the guy with the fake mid-Atlantic drawl. It wasn't much good, but, in the way of these things, he taught himself to enjoy its smoochy interiors, if only because it was a tune he kept hearing, and one the ladies seemed to like. On the plus side, no one had mentioned anything about his Tacchini top or the way he kept slipping the customised match books into his cavernous jacket pockets. He'd been struck by how white the clientele was, though there was a smattering of blacks (all men) with white women. In his head they were still 'blacks'. He just couldn't bring himself to call them 'brothers'. It was one thing reading up about Garvey and the Bull Bay Dreads. Quite another extending the hand of brotherly friendship to total strangers. Anyway, he was going to need some proper money in his pocket before he'd even consider a return visit here.

Though he had things to do and places to be, Conrad yawned. He hadn't really slept properly for a while. Last night was no exception, the djinn pulling its usual routine, picking away at whatever sticking plaster he'd placed over that memory. Always around the same time, too, before the psychotropic birds shat their fury on the window panes. Always in the early hours, a ghoul forcing his lids open, inviting him to toss some meat on to the open grill. Then watching and laughing as Conrad reached in to the plastic container and pulled out a fresh body part.

A hand, an ear, one time even a whole head, all Funkadelic 'Maggot Brain' but with the eye sockets hollow where the flames had already had their fun.

That bit always got to him. He would scream and thrash around, fists punching air until the apparition had passed, and it was just him and Nan's blessed snoring once more, vibrating through the paper-thin wall.

Thirteen dead, nothing said!

The djinn was laughing as he whispered it, and Conrad could see that in his hands the djinn held some barbecue tongs. He was also wearing an apron, and when the chef turned around to check on the party guests, only Conrad flinched at the sight of his lolling tongue, unfurled to virtually his knees, then shooting back in like a retractable coil past his fleshy lips. It gambolled around his mouth, occasionally flicking out debris from behind the gaps. A ring, a finger, half a foot served up in its own squid ink, where the rubber from the trainers had melted.

Pan fry, pan fry! The djinn kept repeating, flames starting to leap from the grill where his tongue had drizzled the grate.

Pan fry, pan fry! The djinn handed Conrad the apron and tongs, tongue still carousing with body parts and police statements. Every now and then a piece of flesh would land on the grate to no great fanfare. The djinn was helping himself to a Dragon Stout, opening the bottle with his teeth, stained red from some time before. And all Conrad could do was turn the offending item over before the heat and the jerk seasoning had too much of a say. It would stink, and he'd wail, and the djinn's wasn't the only tongue he would see.

Nothing said?! It wasn't for want of trying. He'd tried to tell Beardy. *Had* told him. But nobody wanted to hear what he had to say, not unless it was about the skagheads. What did he care about them, though? Even on those days when the lift was broken and he had to pass that flat on his way down, they never said anything to him. He'd barely see them, but on the rare occasions that their paths had crossed on the stairwell, no words had been exchanged. So why was he supposed to care about them? Because Beardy said so. Fuck him. As far as Conrad was concerned, so long as they never troubled Nan in any way they had nothing to fear from him. There were much bigger fish to fry round here, not that Beardy or his mob ever showed any interest.

*

Conrad placed the items in his holdall, making sure to hide the rags inside a pair of baggy Lonsdale shorts. He wrapped the can in another plastic bag first before propping it up in one corner of the holdall with a butternut squash and a copy of *The Merchant Of Venice*. The matches went down his socks taking the place normally occupied by the draw. But so as not to unduly arouse any more suspicion than was standard, he made sure to include a tiny little wrap in his other sock, a sixteenth, and a packet of Rizla in his trouser pocket. He figured there was nothing to be gained by disappointing Beardy on the off-chance they bumped into each other on the street. And if it wasn't exactly random, then all the more reason to have something to show. Better a ticking off than a full-blown search of his person and property. Typically, though, today, after all the necessary precautions, the meticulous preamble, there was no Beardy anywhere to be seen. Nor any of his colleagues. Conrad slung the bag over his shoulders in the approved local fashion and followed a familiar route along the high street.

It felt strange bowling up to the sixth-form college where he'd been enrolled until fairly recently. Though in the wider scheme it was barely ten minutes since he'd left the place, it already looked small to him.

What Conrad saw as he hung around near the entrance was a linear parade. Kids his age, seventeen going on seventy, filing in, ready to punch in their time cards.

Yes, sir, no, sir, homework ready, sir.

Actually it wasn't that at all. No one called anyone 'sir' here. It was probably a bit of jealousy on his part. He envied these kids their routine. There was no reason other than himself, of course, that that shouldn't also have been his routine. It *was* his routine for a while, and he'd been doing OK, charming the hippies with all that sub-Garveyite nonsense. But then he'd met that girl, Sarah, and she'd really got under his skin. The first time, really, any girl had shown any interest in him, and he just hadn't dealt with it very well. Sticks and Daps, they'd have known what to do, but not him, not Conrad, the big 'C'.

He'd gone all moody, playing at being conscious Dread rather than party Dread, and because she was nice, she'd let him. She should have told him there and then to pull his picky locks out of his arse (not that they'd reach anyway), but instead she'd put up with him. SUS this and Babylon that, though the SUS bit was fair enough. No need to let on Beardy was about as close as he came to a friendly face on the high street. At least a familiar one. Had been for a while.

And he'd just kept pushing it and pushing it, seeing how much he could get away with before this girl, someone, anyone, set him straight. That was the thing, though, they all let him. So he kept larging it, kept pushing and pushing that poor girl until eventually, as he must have known he would, he pushed her away from him and into the slyly receptive arms of one of the hippies. His fault really. Party Dread would never have let that happen, but Conrad was inexperienced, and, unlike his more seasoned peers, he tried to veil his greenhorn with bluster.

What started off as a joke – the body warmer, the accent – had rapidly become part of his persona, his shtick. And he'd found it a lot harder to discard than what might well have been a promising academic future. Sadly, he thought, it was just the way with black men round here. Once they worked out which bit of the fantasy appealed most to the white girls, they were wedded to it. And he had to admit, most of them played the part well. It's why the area was full of those kind of hook-ups, but rarely the other way round. Plenty of Errols and Lloyds with Sandras and Tinas, but hardly any Spensers or Bradleys with Micas or Lornas. He wasn't even that, though. He'd fucked up the role play, getting confused halfway between Marley and Mandingo. Idiot. And she must have felt that, too, so that by the time a man with true authority, a teacher, had shown her something other than confusion, it was already too late.

His fault. The weed, and worse, just another way of avoiding responsibility. His.

If he'd been any kind of friend to her, he'd have listened, and he'd have heard what it was she was actually trying to tell him. Which was, 'I came back to you, Conrad. *You*. Doesn't that tell you something?' But he couldn't hear her. Instead, under the distortions of his own self-pity, all he could make out was that she'd been with another man. A man, not a lickle boy like himself. That she was only reaching out to him now because that man had rejected her. He, Conrad, was a sloppy second, a bit like Hull or Keele or any of the less vaunted institutions on those UCCA application forms she'd also been telling him about.

It wasn't him she wanted, as much as the minor narcotic consolations he could get hold of. *That's* what he heard, though she never actually said it. So when he built those first few spliffs there was already resentment in his saliva. Strictly business just his way of accounting for it. The problem being, underneath it all, past the bluster and resentment, the failure to live up to his role, one thing remained constant. She was sweet, even when she was damaged. After all the wailing and regrets, the disappointment and rejection, she still found it in her to somehow reach out. She still had that openness, and if he'd just been a little bolder, if he'd just made that leap of faith which would have allowed him to take off the mask as well as the wool-rich body warmer, then she might still be here, he thought. She may never have taken her own leap into the dark.

His fault, and maybe he deserved those nightmares. That was his penance. Purgatory more like. Cold sweat and a cackling djinn.

Still, as he spotted Mr F— coming out of the main building to light up a fag in the car park, Conrad suddenly thought of that film he'd been watching the night he found Nan asleep in front of the telly. Lee Marvin and that suit, wingtips and royals. *Somebody's gotta pay*.

Adam F— put the kettle on. He felt happy, saw no need to rush. Time enough for a cuppa before he'd head back and break the happy news to his girlfriend. The promotion, to head of department, had taken him by surprise. He'd only been expecting contract renewal talks that morning with the deputy head and someone from HR. So when the offer was made, he'd been somewhat blindsided. There was a delay before his body language processed the euphoric signals being transmitted from his brain, but this only served to heighten the impression that he was a young man who wasn't so easily impressed. At which point the deputy head threw in some extra perks concerning the parent–teacher association and upcoming bid proposals and gave him that look, which even he, a young man not long out of teacher-training college, couldn't possibly miss. *Say yes, Adam, and these won't be the last sweeteners you get to taste here.*

'You've been a breath of fresh air since you joined us, Adam. Don't think we haven't noticed. A young man like yourself, with ambition and talent, well, the sky's the limit, really.'

'I couldn't agree more,' said Adam, trying not to sound too giddy but at the same time hoping to convey just the right amount of enthusiasm. Flirtation rather than fellatio. 'I'm really excited about this. Thanks again for putting your faith in me.'

'Don't make me regret this then,' said the deputy, enjoying the opportunity to introduce an element of unnecessary drama to the proceedings. 'Of course, we're still going to have to advertise, but just between ourselves, that's a bit of a formality. In general we prefer to promote from within, and I'd like to think that you're part of our little community now. I wouldn't be wrong about that, would I, Adam?'

'Not at all,' replied Adam, immediately understanding the question's true implication. The need for discretion, especially in an otherwise challenging environment. 'You can count on me.'

'I do hope so, Adam, I really do. Once the formal interview process has been concluded, Chloe here should be able to answer any further questions you might have regarding terms and conditions. Or, as we like to say here, "rights and responsibilities". Anyway, if there's nothing else, I'm sure you'll be wanting to crack on, Adam.'

*

Perhaps he shouldn't have been so surprised. The vital signs had been there all along. He just hadn't gone looking for them, but they were there alright. Public recognition in the form of a letter from the parent–teacher association about how sensitively he'd handled the fallout from the tragic suicide of his former pupil. Glowing testimonies from the rest of his class about not just his crisis management but also his innovative teaching methods, and the added bonus of a definite spike in university applications from this cohort. He was clearly popular with the other members of staff, too. That's partly why he was here, in this house, he reflected. Mr Charteris from geography had been called away at the last minute by a family emergency somewhere up north where he was from, and he'd entrusted Adam with the keys to his house and the responsibility for keeping his beloved tabby, McKoy, fed and watered. Yes, Adam thought as he squeezed all subtlety from the teabag, in a few short months he'd gone from teacher-training upstart to valued and respected staff member. Maybe now his girlfriend, or even his own parents, might start to take him a little more seriously. Other people recognised his talent, why couldn't they?

If his girlfriend just paid him a little more attention, he thought, all the unpleasantries could have been avoided. He held up his end of the bargain, finished college, went to work and now, it seemed, genuinely had a career to look forward to, the one he'd been enthusing about all along while her only response had been non-existent or at best, 'What about Godalming?' Which in some respects was even worse than if she'd said nothing, because he took that to mean she didn't think he was up to it, not Godalming, but the inner city. She didn't think he had the balls to make a go of it so far from where either of them, or anyone they knew, had grown up. She thought this was just a phase, another little stop-gap while they plotted their way back to the Home Counties.

It was a mystery to him sometimes why he still put up with her, but maybe it was because he was a principled man, and being cut from that cloth never meant an easy path. After all, it was his principles which had drawn him to southeast London in the first place, to this challenge which was turning out to be quite the opportunity. And, to be fair, though she might have struggled to see it that way, that girl, the tragic one, had ultimately run four-square into his principles. Perhaps she was a little young, and that's why she couldn't understand that it was his principles that left him no choice but to oblige her to assume responsibility for her own body. That surely was what any good feminist would argue? In time he felt sure that she would have understood, and that was the real tragedy, he thought. She would have got there eventually, and all the recriminations, the tears, the cursing, would have just dissolved at that point. She would have seen them for what they were – the understandable outpouring of grief by some-one who hadn't yet attained the emotional maturity to take responsibility for her decisions. And, though he doubted they could ever have become friends, she might even have thanked him one day for helping her with her personal growth. Well, he'd certainly done that, though maybe not in the way everyone imagined. It was unfortunate, of course it was, but hardly that surprising when her lack of foresight regarding precautions was factored in. Anyway, she'd clearly not told anyone. That was obvious just from the way her family treated him during the grim aftermath. He'd even been invited to say a few words at the funeral, and his principles meant that he'd obliged, stressing her love of books and learning and sidestepping altogether her unwillingness, or inability, to take even the smallest amount of personal responsibility for her actions.

As McKoy came up to Adam with a slightly wary look on his face, the freshly appointed head of department wondered why he was even bothering with these thoughts on such an auspicious day. He stroked the cat absentmindedly, and for a moment thought he saw a vaguely familiar figure walking up to the front door holding something in his right hand. He dismissed the thought as the cat made itself low and squirmed away from him. Where was the gratitude? McKoy was only getting fed because of him. Some acknowledgement of that might have been nice, he thought, vaguely hearing the letterbox snap shut.

The tea, a standard Yorkshire brew rather than one of the fancier Chinese efforts he'd been hoping to find, tasted a little smokier than he expected. He looked around. McKoy was gone.

'The victim, named locally as Adam F—, was treated at the scene but later died of his injuries. Police are treating the blaze as suspicious and have appealed for witnesses. In particular, they would like to talk to a young male, described by witnesses as Afro-Caribbean, who was spotted hanging around in the street in the moments leading up to the fire. The suspect, who at this stage the police cannot rule out of their inquiries, was seen carrying a holdall and appeared to be alone. The victim, Mr F—, was a much-respected local teacher who, sources close to the college where he taught can now reveal, was on the point of being made one of their youngest ever heads of department. He himself was also no stranger to tragedy and was praised just earlier this year for his sensitive handling of the tragic suicide of one of his own pupils. One line of inquiry that hasn't yet been ruled out by police is that this might also be a case of mistaken identity. In a shocking twist, it turns out that Mr F— was only at the address because he was feeding a colleague's cat. We tried contacting Mr Charteris, the homeowner, but he was unavailable for comment. At this stage, though, police are keeping an open mind. The only silver lining in this tragic blaze, it seems, is the cat Mr F— had gone round to feed. McKoy, pictured here being comforted by the one of the neighbours, luckily managed to scramble through the catflap Mr Charteris had only recently had installed before flames engulfed the property. He will be staying with neighbours until such time as Mr Charteris can be contacted. So, to recap our main story tonight, one dead, one missing, after a deadly blaze in a quiet residential street in south London.'

'Poor man,' Nan said. 'An' wha' will 'appen to that poor lickle pussy?'

Conrad tried to stifle a laugh. Nan was not long back from Brighton. She'd clearly enjoyed her seaside jolly and only had the news on as a bit of background while she regaled her grandson with tales of home-smuggled hot-pepper sauce to go with the fish and chips on the pier. Apparently, the ladies had made quite an impression on the locals.

'And 'Ortense, she carry on like it her first time at seaside. It like she nevah see the oh-shan before. Can yuh imagine it, Conrad, two minute out of Jamaican country parish and she hacting hall hup-town like she city slicker. 'Ortense we talkin' about now. *'Ortense!* An' she hall smiley face an' chuckle when Hinglishman come ovah fi ask 'er 'ow yuh are, my dear? It shock me to my very core.'

In truth, she didn't seem all that shocked, and Conrad thought it best not to point out that Hortense had apparently spent one winter more than his Nan in this country, which he knew because Nan had once mentioned how kind Hortense had been to her when she, Nan, first arrived in Britain. Before she knew anyone with a friendly face and endless patience for all her questions. But mention of Conrad's old sixth-form college and one of his teachers had suddenly keened her attention. She kept shaking her head, looking from the images on the television to her grandson, who, to her eyes at least, darting from wreckage to familiar and suddenly fearful for this generation and the next, seemed awfully skinny in those big shorts he was wearing. He was just a boy really, and it was a bad world out there. What did he know of any of it, she wondered, this lickle bwoy as vulnerable and big eyed as that cat?

Much Easier To Play Dead

London, 2008

I SEE THE tower blocks flashing past as the train heads further south. The young man who seemed less than impressed with my ticket-inspector wheeze, gets off at Lewisham, giving me a rueful glance over his shoulder. But he's not so different to me. Just for starters, I'd say from the way he's pushing up behind another commuter that he favours the same discount-travel option as do I. He has the agility of a young man, and I can imagine it's that which will get him through the narrow window of opportunity at the electronically operated ticket barriers.

For my part, I always make a note of those stations without barriers and then plan my route accordingly. It is rarely convenient, but the need for an elasticated waistband has left me with little choice. Back in the day I could have outrun the station Stasi, no problem. But I'm carrying a bit more weight now, and besides, that's a young-man's game. In much the same way as when an older footballer is described as being 'intelligent' what they really mean is that he's lost a yard of pace, so nowadays he has to rely on a clever pass instead. Well, that could be me. I'm playing that longer game, the smarter one. Not for me the shuffle-up-close bolt for freedom. No need. When my stop arrives I'll amble away like a country squire, the Teddy Sheringham of fare evasion, with the railway network as my fiefdom and no one any the wiser.

I see a lot nowadays that I never previously used to notice. Not sure if that's anything to do with the bump on my head they said I was carrying. For instance, the other young men who get on the train at Lewisham and attack one of the passengers in the next carriage. I see them take his phone and then punch him, even though he is already cowering. It jogs a distant memory. Another life, a lunch-money shakedown. The face of one of the attackers even reminds me a little of the chief culprit back then. But when he looks at me his eyes are blank, and he seems to stare right through me, as though I'm not here. There are three of them, but they all ignore me as they head straight for the next carriage and whatever richer pickings lie in wait. I see them working their way through the terrified commuters who must have also joined the train recently, as I don't remember them being there when I boarded. One man tries to defend himself and is set upon by all three. I see the flurry of fists and curses, and I can hear the screaming. I see the Transport Police board the train at the next stop, which is mine, and I say nothing as they file past, though the images of the young assailants are still fresh in my mind. Finally, I see that there is no one manning the station exits, and I am the first to leave, touching an entirely imaginary Oyster card against a very real card reader. I am home.

I sleep on the Common. The locals call it 'the Heath'. It is usually quiet, just the occasional dog walkers or frisky youngsters looking for a place to make out. Generally, though, they don't say anything if they see me sprawled out near the undergrowth. One or two might laugh, but I can tell their hearts aren't really in it. It is nervous laughter mostly, the sound of adolescents trying to act tough. If they are drunk, they might shout out something, but on those occasions I know better than to respond. Not everyone's like that, though. Most of the time people don't even know I'm there, but I remember once a young woman sharing a bottle of wine with me. Her lipstick and mascara was running, and her face was a mess. I felt bad for her. It was obvious she'd been crying, and when I asked her why she just collapsed. That was when it all came out. The boyfriend, with her best friend. It was like something off daytime telly. Poor thing. She'd just been walking round and round the Heath clutching that bottle. I've no idea for how long, but anyway, by the time she spotted me, she was ready to talk. Swig and talk and cry and commiserate. *Lousy bastard, cheating rat, you deserve better than that, love. Is this a Riesling?* She wasn't expecting that, I could tell. She stopped and looked at me for a second or two, and I could see she was trying to work out what kind of a soak I was. It was a right-click moment, all the text shifted from one part of the sentence to another. A soak and a connoisseur. And a good listener, love, a good listener. But the moment passed, the milk whole on the surface crater again. I let her talk and cry, and my shoulder was there for her, though I don't blame her for keeping her distance. Like I said, though, the milk was whole again, and I could see her visibly regaining her composure. We talked some more, and then she left me to do what, I don't know, maybe find her friends again. I didn't mind. I never expected her to stay as long as she did. But she was nice, all the pretension gone in the way of the freshly bereaved. Though other times there have been arseholes as well, usually blokes. I know when it's coming because they're never alone, and it's always a performance.

'Check this out. Darren, you definitely want to check this out! It's a lush!'

'No way. What's he doing?'

'What do you think he's doing? He's pissed.'

'Of course he is. No money to pay the rent but plenty for some meths.'

I want to tell them I'm classier than that. Thunderbird or paint stripper is not for me. More of a Riesling man, actually, but what's the point? They've already made their minds up.

'He stinks, Darren.'

'Sure that's not you? You know what you're like after a ruby.'

'Fucking hell, he's awake! I saw him move. I think he's trying to get away!'

'Don't let that cunt run off! This is England, Dawl. We don't shit where we sleep. Dirty bastard!'

'Fucking hell, you're right. He proper stinks, though. Fuck this for a game of soldiers, I'm going somewhere else for a slash.'

The thing is, if I don't respond, I know they'll go after a while. Just like school, they get bored in the end. The trick I find is in not antagonising them in the interim. Far easier to more or less play dead. That way there's no kudos in it for them. Even a cunt like Darren, he'll eventually fuck off. No need to point out that if I'm a micro-enterprise today then that's no reason to believe I won't be the small or medium enterprise of tomorrow. I won't always be here, not in this form, whereas Darren, well, a cunt like that will never change.

I've tried to throw my name in the hat, stay part of something bigger. That's why I started going to the LSE in the first place. Not the London Stock Exchange, the other one, just off the Strand. In theory at least, more ideas fewer elbows. The free lunch was just a happy bonus. *Hare Krishna, Hare Rama.* And that's the truth, not that anyone's going to believe an old soak like me. I just wanted to be in the firmament again, feel the raw pulse of numbers and concepts roaring in my head.

I told myself that's how it would feel, like sitting in the engine room of my past, observing the gear shifts and crankshafts, the nuts and bolts of an economy. Of style, material and monikers clipped to the bone. And of the flesh beneath, still taught, dead on arrival. Just not so *taut* any more, the many days of obsolescence sagging off the bones. That's why I started coming here, to be as close as I could bear to be to the hallowed moment *before* being overwhelmed by numbers and volume and profit, when a simple subscription felt like the most urbane fact of my existence. I wanted to remember that excitement, postie with the cellophane-wrapped magazine. And the truth is, that first time, I almost made it to the bookshop nestled next to Sociology before all those good intentions were intercepted by a queue which had begun to form on the promise of Krishna lentils. Don't judge me too harshly for that. The Hare Krishnas know their market.

*

It's getting harder, though. Everything's monitored now, the better to squeeze the random from any encounter. Ticket barriers at Waterloo East, that was the last straw. Time was I could just take my chances with the other daytime skivers and still be at the LSE in time for a Hare Krishna special. And if I saw the loathed Revenue Inspectorate as I shuffled up the ramp from the platform, then I'd just turn right round and head straight for the opposite platform, usually A, and hop on the first train going back towards Lewisham or the forbidden zone of north Kent beyond. OK, so it would mean foregoing my lunch and the prospect of a good parlay outside Professor Giddens' old stomping ground, but that was a chance I was prepared to take. Of course, I still had to remain vigilant for inspectors on board for the return leg, but on the rare occasions I *would* see them, they tended to avoid me, focusing instead on easier, less pungent collars further up the carriages. Once my relief had abated, though, I hated what that said about the whole thing. It meant they saw me just for the surface. The milk might not have been whole, but if they'd just bothered to look properly, they would have seen that my collars were, no, scotch that, *are* as white as anyone else's. I'm no soak, that's just impressionistic.

Now, though, it's all different. The barriers have removed that element of the random. You've got to have a purpose and a card, and of late I've had very little of either. They have monetised vagrancy, forced me to look further afield for my escape route. The Elephant and Castle, sometimes left unmanned, is my standard default. It's not as pink and perilous as I remember it being when I was younger, but it's still a complicated route getting there, and even then it's a long, dispiriting shamble from there to the bridge, and over it into Giddensville. I'm already exhausted by the time I arrive, and it's all I can do to load up on the kindness of the Hare Krishnas. But I make the effort because I feel it's worthwhile.

I know about derivatives, and I've studied kleptocracy. In

another life I was part of the foundations, and then suddenly I wasn't. Led off the premises, but at least I'm still here, not like some. Take my old teacher, Mr F—, only a few years on me, and he's already been pushing up daisies for decades. *Mr F—!* Where did that come from? I've barely thought about him since, yet here he is snucking in under the guise of memory. A teacher, a bit like old Giddens, I suppose. Both 'A's. Anthony and, what was his name again, oh yeah, Adam. Adam F—. He never liked me much. I always got the impression he'd have preferred it if I didn't read *The Economist*, if I *hadn't* spent so much time challenging his views. But I don't know. He was a hairy and he never fooled me with the Farahs or the sovereign ring. He was just another hairy under all that, and he didn't belong, and then he was dead, and the whole thing meant almost nothing to me beyond the temporary disruption to my studies, which, in any case, was offset by my ongoing subscription to *The Economist*.

That Adam might not have meant anything to me, but when I discovered another Adam, the founding father of economics, well, that was something else entirely. His words electrified me, and even now, in the shadow and spit of the third way, it is to those older words about markets and self-interest that I constantly find myself returning. So yes, I have tried to keep my hat in the ring, or was that my name in the hat, I don't know which any more, but I can see that here I am the rabbit in the hat. They are the magicians, and I am the rabbit. It is a conjuring trick which draws the words from some burial chamber. Draws them from deep and redirects them at the angry Somali who I can see is headed towards me with the usual venom in his eyes.

'It is not from the benevolence of the buggers, the bitches and the bratwursts that we expect our tucker, but from their regard to their own interest. *No, sir.* We will fight them on the beaches, in the bedrooms and the boardrooms, and we will *never* talk to them of *our* own needs but of *their* advantages. *Never* has so much been owed by so many to so few. Friends, buggers, countrymen. Mark my words. We will walk tall, build ourselves up from the ruins. The bitches, the butchers, the bakers. For we are an island people, a proud people, and you, sir, don't touch me! *I said, don't touch me!* Yes, *you,* sir, are an ass!'

I've learnt how to live alone, but I'm not always happy this way. I want to be part of something bigger, but I just don't know how any more. Some nights when the wind is cruel I emerge from my pit and watch the bikers loading up on hot tea from the all-night tea hut on the Heath. It is funny because I know people think that *they* are the outlaws, the closest we get to rebellion on the trunk roads. Yet if they were true rebels, surely they'd recognise a kindred? But they don't see me either. My threads billow in the wind, but all they see spread out before them is the Common. I am just another ghost. Wat Tyler and his peasant army. Black Death cadavers. I'm sleeping on the past, but I don't want to be forgotten. Not yet. I leak into the soil, an alien corroding the surface. My blood is acid, burning through the outer layer. I can feel it seeping into the cadavers, boring deeper into the bowels of this thing, into its greed and insatiability. The plague has blood on its tongue, and I burn a hole through that as well. Past giant worms and lava and into a thick, congealed soup. Primal mud mouthing ohs and every now and then shapes slithering, still looking for spine, hardness, structure. My bones are leaky, and my threads are blending with the weeds. A hostile merger. I'm on my own here, and I can't see the lender of last resort. I can't see any more. I've played this all wrong.

ALL LIP AND SHIVER

London, 1982

THE DJINN KEPT his apron on this time. After the charred mess Conrad had made of the grill and its contents during their previous barbecue, he wasn't about to repeat that schoolboy error. Besides, *he* wasn't the schoolboy.

He looked at his dinner guest, all lip and shiver. *Tremble, tremble* like pretty boy in prison shower. Pathetic really, he thought. After all the effort he'd put into scoring those body parts, massaging every nook and crevice with his expert fingers, bathing the statistics in his lovingly prepared marinade. And then this little chimp couldn't even hold them steady over a flame grill. Hands shaking like a primeval wanker. It had been neither forgotten nor forgiven.

'Wakey-wakey, hands off snakey,' he whispered. 'Pan fry, pan fry, or would you prefer to just off and die?'

Conrad started to cry. He'd done his best to hold back the waterworks but now felt the first liquid drops push past the tremble. It started a torrent, and before he knew it he was moaning, but low like a condemned goat.

'Why so sad? Pan fry special tonight. Prizes, surprises and a best-dressed competition.'

'What?' he asked, the question stirred by some vague memory.

'What? He asks, when really the question is not what but who? Who, who, who?'

'What?'

The djinn slapped him hard with an open palm then quickly followed up with a backhander. His fingers were covered with heavy rings, and Conrad could feel the skin tearing around the corner of his mouth. By the time he was able to refocus sufficiently, the djinn was serenely manning the grill. Every now and then he pulled a fresh slab of meat from a plastic container and placed it on the small table he had set up next to the grill. There he used a paintbrush which he would dip into his special marinade before caressing the meat like a true artist. As the meat sizzled on the grill, Conrad was able to make out the hint of lime and yoghurt muddled in with the flesh. He saw the grill man remove a blackened ring from a lifeless finger. Saw him place it in his mouth, watched it melt on his tongue.

'Eat up, young man, while it's hot,' encouraged the djinn, handing Conrad a plate of fingers served up with fried plantain and a side salad. 'Don't be shy now. I know you don't suffer from shyness. What am I to think if you just sit there looking at your plate? After all the effort I put in, it's the least you can do. Tuck in, young man. Show some heart. Or was that kidney or lung or finger, I forget?'

The grill man was roaring with laughter, tickled pink by his play on words. He was getting better at this, he thought. The more lowlife hauntings he conducted, the subtler his methods were becoming. Kidney, lung. He was quite the raconteur. This little chimp, though, he'd gone right off his bananas. Yeah, that's right, his bananas. Oh, what? You thought just because there's some otherworldly going on here that all that local flavour would have been overpowered by the homemade marinade? Idiot. Djinns make good grill men, but if it's kumbaya, marshmallows in the camp fire you were after, sorry to disappoint. This little chimp did something very naughty. That's the whole point of the nightly barbecue. Lee Marvin said it best in that film. Somebody's gotta pay. Take it from someone who knows, the djinns love that film.

'That's right, every last bit,' said the djinn, force-feeding Conrad the fingers. Crispy skin with delicate citric notes. He fed him one after the other, and when Conrad gagged, he scooped up the debris from its gloopy surrounds and fed him all over again. Resistance. Was. Futile.

'Karma's a bitch, eh?' said the djinn, disgusted by Conrad's weak constitution. 'Never pictured you for being such a gaylord,' he added, relishing the goading element of his work. 'But that's clearly what you are. You sure it's a finger you want to suck? Perhaps you'd prefer a thumb? Do you want your mummy? Is that who you want? Mummy? Well I've got news for you, son. She's fucking dead an' all. Now eat up you little cunt before I really lose my temper with you.'

Conrad ate and wept and vomited and bit into fingers, and by the time the appointed hour hoved into view – 5.40am – his sheets were soaked with more than sweat. He became a regular fixture in the laundrette. His nan never could understand why he needed to change his sheets so often, but when he made a point of including all her items, too, and then starching and ironing the lot however long it took, she found herself suppressing the question. After all, she reminded herself, he always was a very clean little boy. No newsprint on the hands even when he'd been doing that paper round, so perhaps it shouldn't have come as such a surprise that he'd now developed quite an enthusiasm for laundry.

Of course, the djinn found it hilarious, the goat moans and tribulation. Night after night of his faggoty whimpering, trying to refuse all solids like some Russian ballerina. Needing to be force-fed. Reminded, like the suffragettes, that he'd been a very naughty boy or, in his case just as likely, girl. Actually that was a bit unfair. Pankhurst and her mob clearly had bigger balls than this one. Little two-bob Brit Rasta with his comedy locks and ridiculous accent. Fuck him, little cunt. He'd been naughty, and, as the djinn reminded himself reaching for the apron, his work here had barely even begun.

'Why did you do it, monkey boy?'

'I wanted to make things right.'

The djinn smiled. This was progress. Baby steps at least. His dinner guest was beginning to comply without too much arm twisting. Also, none of that hyper-sensitivity he'd sometimes encounter about the pejorative simian reference. Nearly as tiresome as the denial of liability. (Forgive me, I'm a djinn, you mistook me for someone who could care less about equal opportunities.)

'Make what right?'

'The girl,' said Conrad, though, of course, moaning like a goat so that it comes out as 'grill'. The smile immediately disappeared from the djinn's boat.

'Are you questioning my grilling, son? Don't tell me that's what you're doing. And here I was thinking I might go a little easier on you tonight. Cheeky little bastard.'

'No, girl. I meant to say "girl".'

'Oh, so you've finally noticed, have you?' said the djinn. 'I was wondering how long it would take. It's just embarrassing, son, the way you carry on. Look, I'm only the pan-fry man, but I'm telling you, that's no way to behave, not in this day and age. A word of advice. You want to sharpen up before you slip up, my lip quivering friend. Because I tell you what, you won't last a day in the big house. You'll never be lonely, though, I can guarantee you that.'

The lips started to go again.

'Oh, for fuck's sake, not this. Did I not just tell you? What did I just tell you? Pull yourself together, son, you're embarrassing the pair of us. Here, this should help, have a burger. Now, you were saying something about a girl?'

'Yeah, I just wanted to make things right for her.'

'And the small matter of the arson and the dead teacher, that was your way of doing that?'

'Yes. I wasn't there for her before. I should have been, but you said it yourself, I've got no balls. I wasn't going to let him get away with it, though. She was just a girl, she never meant anyone any harm. And he just ignored her, treated her like garbage. She told me everything, you know. Didn't tell anyone else, but she told me. And then I did the same thing. I ignored her because I was still angry about it. She'd been with him, you know. He was supposed to be someone she could trust, and he took advantage. I couldn't let that go. That day when I followed him, I was going to confront him. But when he looked up and saw me, I just couldn't face it. I knew he'd manage to talk me round, and I wasn't having that. She deserved better, from all of us. So I emptied the contents, and lit the rags. And you know what, I felt nothing then. I thought I might feel something, fear, anger, excitement. But the truth is, I felt nothing. I haven't felt anything since Mum went. Actually, that's not quite right. I felt something when I met Sarah, but it didn't last. I mucked it all up. Mucked it up. Let her go. Should never have done that. All that shit I was reading, but it turns out I'm not so clever clever after all. She was an open book, and I couldn't see that, and I'm so, so sorry for that. I'll miss her for the rest of my life, but I know she's long gone. I haven't got anything else, I'm done.'

'Where are you from anyway?' Conrad asked, hoping his admission would allow for some pleasantries to be exchanged with the djinn.

'Why? Who's asking?' came the curt reply.

'No, I was just wondering, that's all. It's not important really.'

'Let me be the judge of what's important and what isn't, eh?'

'Yeah, no offence intended,' said Conrad, starting to think he'd misjudged the mood again.

'None taken,' lied the djinn, still annoyed at the mouth coming off this one.

'So where *are* you from?'

'Woolwich.'

'Woolwich?! That's full of silks, isn't it?' Conrad blurted out, a split second before his brain suggested to him this might not be the smartest line of enquiry.

The djinn gave him a practised look, the boredom barely masking its partisan, enraged interior. 'Silks?'

'Yeah, with all the headgear.'

'In Woolwich? Silks? What are you talking about?'

'You know, the ones with the turbans. I heard the place was full of them.'

'Oh, I get it. Silks. With the headgear. The ones in court,' said the djinn, still only faintly amused, and even then more by his own verbal dexterity than because of anything the youth might had said.

'I don't know about that,' said Conrad. 'I just know there's plenty of them down there. I mean, you must see quite a few if you're from round that way.'

'Can't say I have,' said the djinn, wondering how long he'd drag the joke out for.

'Still, Woolwich, what's that like?'

'Ah give it a rest, blubba mout,' said the djinn, only mildly interested to see how the object of his affections would react. Conrad seemed shocked, though the djinn suspected it was largely for show. When he finally answered, there was something unmistakeably West Midlands about the accent.

'You're a racialist!'

It was just the kind of highly imaginative response the djinn should have expected from a high flier like Conrad.

'Why are you talking like a Brummie?' he asked, noting, not unreasonably, the Smethwick twang in Conrad's protest. 'You sound backward enough as it is, and believe me, that accent ain't helping. *All that 'pan fry, pan fry' crap?* You were fooled by that? You really have got a lot to learn, my ebony friend. I made it all up. I'm a cut-price djinn. I'm from Woolwich. The nearest I've been to pan fry is that Caribbean take away up near the college. What? Don't give me that look, *Jagger* lips, you know which one I'm talking about. Yeah, that's right, the place with all the arty gyal. Anyway, had a jerk something or another last time I was there. Mother misery who runs the place, I think she likes me. Touch of eastern promise and all that. Always gives me an extra portion, if you know what I mean? What? You don't like that? Don't like how I'm talking about her now? Well, I am truly sorry to hear that. The thing is, though, she likes what I do when I take my apron *off*. Yeah, that's right, lippy. Though I'm guessing you wouldn't know too much about that kind of thing either. Still, never mind, eh? There's always the big house, and I like I said, I doubt you'll be lonely in there. Oh yeah, one other thing. That bit about being sorry. I lied. Sorry? To you?! *The neck on you, you murdering little cunt!* You can't even hold the tongs steady. I've seen them tremble in your faggoty little hands. But you weren't so shy when it came to frying that teacher, were you? And that poor girl, you failed her big time, fat lips. What? You think I'm a racialist? So what if I am? *I'm* not the one who pan fried an educationist, so why don't you have a think about that. Give it some thought while I sort out these last few pieces. Now, what *have* we got here?' he asked, reaching into the container and pulling out a well-scored foot. A hoof. Or was that a trotter? 'Do you like what I've tried to do there with the marinade?'

Conrad screamed. The djinn punched him hard and placed a palm trailing the flavours of yoghurt, flesh and onions over Conrad's mouth. He put the tongs on the table, freeing up his other hand, and dug hard into Conrad's eyes with thumb and forefinger, continuing to press down until he could feel the eye-balls about to skid from under his fingers. Conrad's screams were muffled by his other hand, clamped down tightly over his mouth but with thumb and forefinger pinching his nostrils shut. Conrad began to convulse so the djinn gently clambered on top of him, feeling the youth's erection pushing up into his own midriff. It was disgusting, he thought, the lack of decorum that usually attended these moments. At his most contemplative, he liked to think there was something epiphanic about it all, but, looking down now at the thrashing body beneath him, he had his doubts. Faced with his first grilled foot (well the first one he was *directly* responsible for), the boy had caved. Blubbed like a little gaandu, as if that was going to help his cause in any way. Public/private, AC/DC, these Britishers were all the same, thought the djinn. Empire this and smelly that and boohoo, don't say those mean things to me, coolie. Dirty Paki.

'*You're the racialist*, you say. *You can't say that*, you bleat. Well I just did, fat lips. Did you forget? I'm a djinn. What? You'd have preferred a duppy? More culturally appropriate? Not my problem, I'm afraid. Not down to me if they're all on strike. Some health and safety crap, something to do with the tongs and the barbecue. Sounds like nonsense to me, that's why we're affiliated to different bits of the Spirit Union Congress. That's right, monkey boy, SUC. Bet that's not the first time you've heard that line, eh? Anyway, as I was saying about those duppies. No bloody work ethic, not like us djinns. So, that's why *I'm* here, how about you?'

The question, as they both knew, was purely rhetorical, and the djinn allowed a few moments for the distraught-looking youth to absorb what he was saying. Once he was satisfied that Conrad was fully compos, he resumed what for him felt like a pleasing train of thought.

'Did I mention that bit about being a djinn and not giving a shit about equal opps. You think anyone cares about that crap where you're going? If *I'm* here, that's down to you, to what you did. That's right, *you*, hot lips, not me. And I'm not here like one of your teachers – oh, I don't know let's pick one at random, how about the one you burnt alive? But I digress, picky head. As I was saying before your criminality so rudely interrupted my train of thought, I'm not here to listen to your pathetic whining, I'm here for the other bit. Whine and grine. Cannon and Ball. Crime and...?'

He removed his hand from Conrad's mouth, hoping to encourage the desired response, the one which would acknowledge the enormity of what this little scoundrel had done and what now needed to be done about that. Instead, when all he could make out was a whimper, the djinn felt his anger rising to new levels. He let Conrad breathe properly again because he really wanted him to focus on the next bit rather than on what had become an increasingly desperate struggle for air.

'They really didn't teach you much at school did they, monkey boy? Let's give it another go, shall we? Morecambe and Wise, Chas and Dave, Crime and...?'

'Pushman,' came the faint reply.

'Sorry, what was that? You'll have to speak up.'

'Punishman,' said Conrad with a few more breaths.

'Again. A bit louder this time so that something other than your gaandu of an id can hear you.'

'Punishment,' moaned Conrad, eyes streaming where the djinn

had applied the pressure. *Finally*, thought the djinn, some genuine progress.

'That's right, punishment. Glad we got there in the end. Now, that wasn't so hard was it?' said the djinn, noting with considerable disgust the wet patch spreading around Conrad's groin as he dismounted him. Fucking degenerate. A crier and a spiller. This one would be paying a heavy price for his infractions. He'd make sure of that.

Heading downstairs, Conrad paused. He wasn't yet out of the door when he looked back. Nan was still sleeping, the gentle rhythm of her snores somehow sealing her off from what was happening in his mind. Night after night of the same apparition, cursing and pushing down on his eyelids until his whole head hurt. Worse still the taste of something burnt sticking to his tongue. A rumour of flesh and remorse, but the same sick feeling each morning, pillow soaked and shorts drenched. 'Sorry, Nan,' he whispered, closing the door behind him before making the shortest of journeys down to the fourth floor.

A Loss Of Control

BACK ON CAMPUS, most of her days were now spent studying. Laura remembered she was there on a scholarship, not like that cabrona from Burgos. What made it easier was the fact that D had effectively been ignoring her once the penny dropped that his increasingly desperate-sounding pleas for the two of them to just give it 'one more shot' were falling on deaf ears. He'd made quite a point of it as well, making sure to look the other way any time their paths crossed. She understood, though. He was still hurting from how she had ended things between them. There was clearly some need on his part to save face, and this was his way of doing that. It was a little theatrical for her tastes, but she knew where it was coming from and couldn't really blame him. Actually, she was pleased the day she saw him locked deep in conversation with some Indian girl outside the Arts Centre. It came as something of a relief, too, removing any last vestiges of guilt from her daily routine. At last, Laura thought, she could actually get on with her work, with the serious business of being a scholar. She'd been surprised by just how guilty she *did* feel whenever she paused to reflect on how things had ended with D. They'd had some fun and now it was over, and really that should have been that. But for some reason he made her feel bad with his little-boy-wounded routine. Anyway, she was happy he'd met someone else. Now she was free, just her and an immersive programme of study.

She wrote it out on a card like a mission statement, then nailed it to the corkboard just above her desk:

*Engineering is the professional art of employing
science for the purpose of optimising conversion
of the resources of nature to benefit humankind.*

She had slightly modified the original, lifted from a key primer, because she wasn't so keen on the idea that her discipline was there to benefit 'man'. But when she delved a little deeper it all made perfect sense. Her alteration, that is. Once she had established that the words 'engine' and 'ingenious' derived from the same Latin root *ingenerare*, meaning 'to create', she felt pleased with the logical dimension to her instinct. Her gut wasn't wrong. The early-English verb 'engine' meant 'to contrive', and that was what this was all about. Contrivance. Engines of war, newfangled (at the time) devices like catapults, floating bridges and assault towers, with someone like her at the helm. Crucially, the brains behind all this was the engineer, the military engineer. And somewhere like Facha that could only mean one thing. Franco's boy. Fascist poodle.

Still, she consoled herself, at least this figure had a benign counterpart, the civil engineer, who used the same knowledge and skills to devise basic, yet complex, social structures like streets, water supplies, sewage systems and other projects which would directly benefit civilians. This was impressive, she felt, but a bit limiting in its scope. No firearms, and the only violence enacted by diggers on rock or so widely dispersed as to barely even constitute violence. Problem solving, abstract mathematics, an overriding concern with the effect of engineering proposals on not just the physical but also social and economic environment. Yeah, yeah, yeah, she thought, I get it, the engineer's supposed to be the good guy. Deductive reasoning, feasibility studies, performance criteria. Complex decision-making, the talent to conceive vast, well-integrated man-machine-environment systems for the wider social benefit. Dios mío, she thought, these people sounded dull. Materials, mechanics, thermodynamics, transfer and rate processes, information processing and electrical science.

¡Ya basta!

Nice, nice, nice, good, good, good. Worthy and useful and so very dull.

And, of course, she understood that without such skills, and the professionals to implement them, then everything would start to fall apart. Buildings, streets, all those cabling networks bringing light and joy to the peasants in Murcia. The landlines which let her mama tell all who wanted to listen, as well as plenty who didn't, about her daughter's scholarship to study abroad. The television in front of which Papá would sit stupefied as the men in white scrambled to yet another late victory with the mysterious advent of some partisan refereeing.

¡Uuuyyy! ¡Marica! ¡Desgraciados!

Or perhaps it wasn't so mysterious after all? A public secret. Remove the cabling, she thought, and the whole network starts to unspool, the cracks in the plaster, shit in the pipes, the whistle raised to less than neutral lips. Poised to blow, the whole thing poised to blow. Pijos looking around, surveying their fiefdom. The whole thing inherited, fathers to sons, officer class, El Corte Inglés. As for the rest, la clase obrera, well they were there to work, get back in the cracks, down the mines, into the sewer. Nightlights and drills and the weary resignation that if it was the team in white, Franco's boys, then the whistle would blow at a time of their choosing.

She saw the shit surging down the tunnels, racing past the chicane. Saw it rear up and tear down the bricks, the cabling, the plaster until finally it was poised, a great pungent mass of expulsion, outside the gates of the palace. Saw it corrode the metal, walk off with the pipes. Saw this festering tsunami of shit smash against the Guardia Civil, uniforms and holsters carried away by the tide, now sweeping away everything that lay before it. Saw Falangist hands briefly rise up out of the shit, before being sped away back to Galicia, El Caudillo's spiritual heartland, where once again they would be returned to the Atlantic. She saw the shit as their primal soup and watched the hands crumble. Hecho polvo. All those dreams, those neatly engineered dreams, of progress and order, just mud again. Shapes slithering in mud and not a backbone in sight.

Yet she rarely found her interest waning when she would read about military engineering. Not so much the defensive engineering feats of the ancients as evidenced in their hill forts, fortresses and walls. No, the stuff she found exciting was a little less stoic. The Renaissance reappraisal of siege tactics with the development of the cannon and the use of gunpowder, both as a propellant and as a demolition explosive. Breach-loading artillery, high-explosive shells, guns, muskets. Further down the line, torpedoes, trinitrotoluene (TNT), which she liked the sound of, plastic explosives and, of course, El Profesor's personal favourite, the Manhattan Project.

However, the more she learnt about the atomic bombs dropped on Hiroshima and Nagasaki, the less she liked it. Why had the Japanese been singled out for this special treatment in a way that the Germans, or even the Italians, had not? The question belonged, she felt, to that tide of shit flowing out into the Atlantic. She also knew it would never be answered honestly because those hands poking out of the surface, hands which once controlled all the levers, well, she had the strongest feeling that those hands would rather be returned to mud and swamp and dreams of dust than countenance the truth. Falangist hands, or American ones, would never admit that this was about mastery. Of people, resources, history.

She knew the arguments, about how it had speeded up the end of the war, and in so doing had, in fact, saved lives. But she also knew that the Japanese were already exhausted, on the point of collapse. Their surrender and overall defeat was, in fact, imminent when the bombs had been dropped. Those hands just wanted to feel that they still controlled the levers. She knew *that* as clearly as anything she had ever been told. She would never forget lessons learnt about exploitation of the seabed and exploration of deep space. This wasn't so much about the application of science as it was about the flexing of aggrieved muscle. White men reacting to the novel experience (for them) of being oppressed by Orientals in khaki. A loss of control, a lack of deference, and they did not like it one bit. Those were Escudero's soiled mitts discharging the payload as much as the Allied pilots. Those were his prints on the scene of devastation. Miguel de la Fuente Escudero. Profesor.

She probably should have known better. That brief, giddy interlude between her final exam and the results coming out might have been a good time to take a break, explore the countryside, anything really but stay on campus. Yet the tiredness of the preceding months only properly hit her then. The cumulative effect of twelve-hour days left Laura barely able to contemplate a trip to the shops let alone a jaunt in the fields. She slept for more or less an entire day, oblivious to the raft of social events being planned all around her. Summer balls and club nights and one student party after another in the wealthier top end of nearby Royal Leamington Spa.

When she awoke, though, she suddenly felt a sentimental urge to do a complete circuit of the campus, as indeed she had done when she first arrived. For some reason she felt wise as she headed down to the lake behind the tennis courts. Sitting there on the neatly manicured lawn she was reminded of an earlier moment, sat on the steps of her old colegio, observing the faltering steps of sex and ambition. Boys and girls coming together for the briefest of dances, and she, Laura, always a little remote even if the language and moves were already familiar. Replayed over and over along with that fateful decision to seek something a little more advanced at the nearby university. Something a little less secondary.

'Laura?'

She looked up. It was D. She hadn't seen him for months, shuttered away with her copious revision notes. He'd lost a little bit of weight. Probably exam pressure, she thought, but it suited him, the slightly haunted look. Nothing too poetic mind. This was a man-made lake not the Seine. It just wasn't that kind of left bank.

'D, how are you?'

'Better now they're over and done with,' he said, glad he'd actually plucked up the courage to come over when he spotted her.

'I feeling the same way,' she said, wondering how long he was just going to stand there. 'You want to join me for a bit?' she asked, deciding to put him out of his misery.

'Yeah, why not?' came the still slightly too eager reply.

Less predictable was how she rode him outside, and how he let her, near one of the bushes but still more or less in full view of anyone who happened to be passing. She liked that he made no attempt to please her or stop her. There was a confidence about him which felt new. Perhaps she'd misjudged him, she thought. Her impulsiveness for once also reflected in his reaction, none of the usual scrambling around for condoms or lubricant. It felt easier than before, when they'd actually been together. But then when he was done and he wanted to lie there and talk, extend the moment into something it wasn't, *that* was when she was reminded of the gulf between them. So she made her excuses and left, knowing she wouldn't wait until the end of term before heading back to Spain.

POWER ITS OWN
APHRODISIAC

Valladolid, mid-1980s

No ONE HAD even heard of Nan Goldin back in Facha. Laura didn't mind too much, though, as that meant her proprietorial edge was left intact. That was just how things worked, she thought. She didn't make the rules, but far too many days spent skulking around the edges of 'in-group' conversations had taught her *that* much about structural mechanics. Everyone needed an angle unless they were rich or beautiful or both, in which case *that* became their angle, and then all they needed was an audience. Those Corte Inglés bitches and their pijo boyfriends, well, it was so much easier for them, she reflected bitterly. No one ever questioning their credentials or asking who *they* knew and what the nature of *their* business here was.

But at least they didn't make a point of lingering in the university district once their law lectures were over. Quite a few of them had cars, and she would see them driving off, though rarely more than two per vehicle, presumably back to the luxury flats on the other side of town. More often than not they would be alone, and she imagined overpowering them, locking them in the boot before driving towards Medina del Campo or Burgos, where she recalled that puta, Patricia, said she was from, and abandoning the car with its well-bred contents in a ditch by the side of the road or, better still, freighting down the gas with a brick and watching the lot gently subside in the Duero. But something, perhaps a little decorum picked up with her fancy foreign letters, perhaps some other kind of doubt, always intervened at the last moment so that the Renault and its unwitting occupant was able to slip away to a barely recognised safety. And she would head back to the library where she was researching the links between engineering and an aesthetic modernism. The way Spanish cities had been transformed into temples of scientific progress without abandoning a patrician grandeur honed over centuries of global pre-eminence.

This was a project she was carrying out on behalf of none other than El Profesor, Miguel de la Fuente Escudero. The man with his hands on the levers and, as it turned out, the purse strings as well.

Her first-class degree result had helped, as did the fact that they were hardly strangers, but he had seemed as surprised as she was when she had walked in to his office, the day after her return to Facha, and asked for a job. She couldn't quite believe she was doing it either, a long-suffering Nan Goldin heroine, except that she wasn't. Her eyes were not blacked and her face was not swollen. Then again, she *had* been feeling a little out of sorts ever since the random hook-up with D several weeks previously, which had turned out to be the last significant detail of her time in England. But she had put it down to her body readjusting after the accumulated stress of her degree finals. Her taste buds had been a little off ever since, and this too, she felt was something to do with reacquainting herself with a more familiar diet and climate after her stint in the non-culinary paradise of Warwick. But she was certain that the one thing that would really help right now with that process of reacculturation was a job. And so here she was, asking for, and finding, work in the one place where she knew it was unlikely that she would be refused.

Besides, whatever else he was, El Profesor was hardly the brooding animal of a Tom Waits song. No sucking on filterless cigarettes, no swigging from bottles, though sometimes, when he would lie there naked and spent in a less than upscale hotel room, she sensed a vulnerability. Defenceless, infantile, the confidence diminished in a sagging condom. She knew it was an affectation, though, the very first time during this stint when he raised her with powerful hands and lowered her on to his throbbing tool. A tertiary fantasy, the third part of some late middle drama. Parts one and two his rise through the ranks, the 'helpful' (for his career and for the custodians of the nation's 'honour') historical revisionism, the death notices signed, proof of loyalty to the regime. Part three an unexpected renaissance. The man of letters, comportment and, yes, a certain local grandeur, at last invited into the hallowed portals of immortality, of the men with undiminished dreams, on the strength of his convictions. Power its own aphrodisiac, the research assistant his muse. She'd known all this even before surprising him with her enquiry.

'Well, well, well. Laura, what a surprise.'

'A pleasant one, I hope,' she said, maintaining the myth of conviviality.

'And what brings you to my door today?' he asked, genuinely curious but also keen to quickly re-establish boundary markers, of terrain, authority, ownership.

'Well, I was hoping to talk to you about a research idea I have,' she replied, assuming (correctly) that this would rekindle fond memories for El Profesor of the passionate consequences of her previous academic proposal. Yes, it hadn't really ended so well for him, but surely that was a price well worth paying for the conceit that they were lovers in some grand Russian drama? So what if he'd had to make representations on her behalf? Ultimately amounting to little more than a couple of letters and the calling in of a long overdue favour. He'd got off lightly really. She could have made things a lot more awkward for him, though the truth was, by that stage, her mind was more or less exclusively focused on the notion of escape. As for Escudero, the garnering of a generous scholarship had at least cushioned the financial blow, even if some of that money had been diverted from funds earmarked for his own research. Besides, he didn't seem to be doing too badly, she thought, noting the heavily polished mahogany desk (which was new) and what appeared to be a designer armchair in one corner of the room.

That first day, though, she'd tested his enthusiasm by only allowing the most coquettish brush of lip on cheek when he had got up to greet her properly. She knew he would be expecting a lot more than that when they next reconvened to 'discuss' her research findings. But she also knew enough about men like Escudero to understand that a little bit held in reserve was what really excited them. The thrill of the chase, El Profesor dropping the donnish mantle for the cloak of rugged individuality. A conquistador striding out across the pampas to civilise one of the savages. Even one with a first-class degree in engineering from a prestigious foreign university.

'Escúchame, Laura. You are young, you still have so many things to learn, and I have no doubt that learn them you will. Well, I could tell you were smart the very first time I saw you.'

'Really? You could tell? But all I was doing was waiting with Javier,' she said.

She saw El Profesor flinch at the mention of his son, so decided to push her luck. They were sitting in his office with only the occasional sounds of a colleague's footsteps passing by in the corridor to remind them that they were in a public institution. It was summer, and most of the faculty had already fled for the coast or the hills, away from the city's stifling heat. But at least his office was cool, and the skeletal staff presence ensured that they would not be disturbed.

'How is Javier these days? Is he still in Valladolid?'

'Do you mind if we don't talk about Javier?' replied El Profesor, clearly uncomfortable with this turn in the conversation. 'You were about to tell me how your research was coming along. And remember, it is the aesthetic character of the cities which matter as much as the technological developments. I think you already hinted at some of the key issues the last time we spoke. How does the aesthetic change also build character in the people? Is it possible for a nation to transform its entire sense of mission through the onward march of science and technology?'

'Mission?'

'I think so, Laura. After all, what is a nation without purpose?

Each civilised nation must have a sense of its own reason for being. Without that we are just a rabble, no better than one of those African tribes the anthropologists spend so much time weeping for. This is where science plays its part. All the tears in the world won't build a railway or a street grid or grand municipal buildings where the important business of government can take place. And without governance, well, I'm sure even those anthropologists would agree, there is only chaos. We are not savages, Laura. That's why we wear clothes, so even if those communists from the Anthropology Department do finally venture down here, they won't find us sitting around scratching our butts.'

He seemed pleased with the analogy, however spurious its foundations. But there had been a moment just before when the melancholy had threatened to overwhelm him. He'd been having a few of those of late, snapshots of his own decline, in how breathless he would get just going up a couple of flights of stairs or in the way his back slumped into a chair like a blind man feeling for the exits. Go see the doctor, his wife had said, but she hadn't implored him, and he'd felt disgruntled by that. There was no urgency to any of it, no panic or catch in her voice the way there once would have been. He was a joke to her. They hadn't slept together in years, and as for that little marica son of his, well, his absence had hardly made El Profesor's heart grow fonder. In Madrid doing God knows what and with God knows who, yet still their son was all his wife ever worried about. Javier this and Javier that, and *do you think Javier might come to visit us soon? I've left his room just as it was. Do you think he's eating properly? He seems so flaco.* El Profesor scarcely even daring to think what Javier was eating down in Madrid. It made his skin crawl to imagine that was his own flesh and blood, right now probably on all fours with some other degenerate in that perverted sewer. In a way, he thought, the boy was worse than the Africans. They had no choice really, were born into it, rape and cannibalism and whatever else they did at weekends. But Javier, that marica had made the deliberate choice to embarrass him, to undermine a lifetime's good work, and for what? So he could join all the other cocksuckers in Malasaña. Coño. He'd been too easy on the boy when he was growing up.

This was the price you paid when you were one of the good guys, he thought. And the melancholy wasn't even the half of it. He thought of that Mahalia Jackson song he liked, 'Nobody Knows The Trouble I've Seen', and he had to admit that for a descendant of bone-idle apes she had a remarkable amount of insight. It was almost as though she understood the inner dimensions of his pain, the enormity of his loss. The reality that his bloodline was over, that the little marica who bore his name was effectively divorced from every inherited trait, every last slither of conviction or courage or vision that went into the making of a de la fuente Escudero. In that sense if in no other, it appeared that he and the negress were on common ground. Nobody knew the trouble it took. He had only heard the song for the first time some months back at a colleague's house, and the colleague had been both surprised and delighted by El Profesor's emotional response to the record, tears streaming down his cheeks while his (the colleague's) wife scrambled around for some more tissues and another almond tart for their esteemed dinner guest.

It wasn't just the melancholy. Of late he'd been tearing up at the slightest of provocations. Just the other day when he'd been home alone (yet again), his wife presumably out with the other local brujas on one of their regular trips to 'sites of historical interest' (her words), and he found himself watching television nursing a generous glass of port, the waterworks had started up again. The decision to come home early as damning in itself as the distinctly unmanly tears.

In years gone by he would never even have been available during the summer months. This was the time when the professorial perks traditionally came into their own. Handsomely funded sabbaticals, or at the very least a generous allowance to attend prestigious foreign academic conferences and deliver keynote speeches or the occasional paper. These were often little more than a rehash of canonical orthodoxy but with an ironic element which he made sure to include when he noticed how well this went down with the repellent postmodernists, who seemed to just multiply, like cockroaches, with each passing semester. And though he loathed them with their 'dissolution of metanarratives' and suspect political sympathies, there were just so many of them now. Too many not to throw them a little bone once in a while. So, for instance, he would find something positive to say about that hijo de puta comunista, Galván, the wildly popular mayor of Madrid, and when he did he quickly noticed that no one paid any attention to his stiffening body language or a lip unable to restrain itself any longer, curling back in anger to reveal gritted teeth. All these 'death of the author' types filling lecture theatres and banqueting suites, and yet none of them ever seemed to recognise the mortal recoil taking place right in front of them. How they loved it when he spoke of the ironic choice of Malasaña as the engine room for the new people's republic! The proud forebears of anti-Napoleonic resistance looking on from that ethereal History Department in the sky (how they loved that) while the barrio's newest inhabitants renewed the area's dissident vows. Lip drawn back almost like an enraged primate, but no one ever noticed. Not while there was still irony to savour and history to dissect.

This year, though, there had been fewer invitations, and nothing foreign or prestigious. So for the first time in recent memory he found himself shuttered away in his office in the prohibitive July heat, constructing elaborate funding proposals. His radar was a little off, unaccustomed as he was to being in this position, and when that girl, the one who'd caused him all that trouble before, walked in, he felt even more disorientated. He should have made it perfectly clear there and then that he, Miguel de la Fuente Escudero, was no longer involved in any way with her career development, and besides, young lady, the academic year is over. Finished, as in 'ya'. But he just couldn't bring himself to tell her that. Perhaps it was something to do with the formality of the request, maybe it was something else entirely, he couldn't be sure.

The upshot, though, was that he'd taken her on as a research assistant. Money could always be found, and actually, he thought, he rather enjoyed the process. It made him feel powerful, albeit in a very specific, tenured-faculty sort of way. But it was good to know he could still pull a few strings, that there were committees, on which sat powerful men with institutional clout, where his name did not yet belong with the ghosts.

Maybe he was just lonely. His wife rarely seemed to be home any more, and Javier, well, it was probably for the better that he had left. Still, he'd taken the girl on, and now on those days she made her excuses and headed to the library or was nowhere to be seen, he found himself drifting off into a deep melancholy.

He could scarcely even bear to stay in his own office. Its well-appointed comforts and the generous furnishing grant that had helped to achieve the overall look were, as he well knew, a sop for being passed over yet again for head of department. There were younger faculty coming through who he knew to be highly unsympathetic to the historical foundations of his work, recent ironic appendages notwithstanding. And the view had been expressed more than once at fractious departmental meetings that, especially given its recent past, did the department here, at Valladolid, *really* want to be seen as upholding a particular view of history, nationalism and identity? When he'd questioned them as to what they meant by that, there had been vague mutterings of dissent beneath the official line that the teaching and research here needed to be more in line with the 'progressive' dimensions of modern Spanish society, but no one had mentioned El Caudillo by name. It had all been left hanging like a bad smell, just the way these comunistas always left everything hanging. And the worst of it was, they hadn't needed to resolve anything. There were more of them than there were of his people. And both sides knew it.

Modern Spanish society?! The insolence of these people! Not so long back they wouldn't have dared even raise the issue. Now, though, with all the restraints lifted they felt free to question his life's work, and it angered him deeply, the more so when he looked their way and saw that there was barely a haircut between the lot of them. It was a disgrace, the achievements of the past looked on with disdain by people who had risked nothing. And, though he hated the organised-labour activists and the uneducated peasants, even he was prepared to acknowledge that they had paid a price for their ignorance. It was harsh but necessary and, in the end, for the overall good of the nation. But these so-called 'historians', they hadn't even been born while the nation was purging itself of its backward elements. And they had the nerve to sit there and question his commitment to modern Spanish society?! There would *be* no modern Spain, he wanted to scream, but for men like himself.

So there was no real solace to be found any more in the academic community. No conviviality, nothing collegial. Instead, just younger men and some women (was nothing sacred?) who seemed to relish putting his nose out of joint. Whose proposals seemed to garner greater enthusiasm from increasingly remote committees and funding bodies where *his* name had once meant something. During one especially bitter confrontation – *this isn't history, this is revisionism!* – he paused to reflect how the cocky little puta making the extraordinary allegation had looked over at another younger faculty member first, as though this was the opening salvo of an orchestrated attack. Time was he'd have taken some secateurs to those pointing digits, and his fellow Falangist brethren would have ensured no dirt under *his* nails. Her family would have known better than to push their luck, knowing the same fate, or worse, awaited those who stepped out of line. Yet now, not only was there no fear, but the moral righteousness which he had always believed was the sole province of the true Falangist patriots seemed to have slipped from their grasp and somehow fallen into the possession of social degenerates. Couldn't they see that even now, in taking this promising young graduate under his wing, he was still attempting to nurture, or perhaps instil, the truly modern virtues of science, technology and progress in the brightest and best of the next generation? Couldn't they see that?

*

He watched the television with a mixture of incomprehension and regret. The programme, he learnt, was called *Barrio Sésamo* and it was set on a street which was teeming with friendly Spanish actors and kids as well as some unusual inhabitants. There was a Big Bird, 'la Gallina Caponata', always getting into friendly scrapes, but he found his attention drawn to another character, Espinete, a little pink hedgehog, who seemed proud to have spikes on his back and not his front so that he could hug the other characters without hurting them. El Profesor did not feel the need to question why this animal, which walked around naked, needed to wear pyjamas to go to sleep. He was already entranced by the cuddliness of the little creature. He just wanted to reach down and scoop it up in his arms, cradling little Espinete while he rubbed his face against the hedgehog's non-prickly surface. He was an innocent who needed to be protected against the tide of filth and corruption which would eventually, if left unchecked, engulf this street as it already had so many others. In his mind's eye he saw the face of Felipe González appear like a monstrous socialist Kong, looking at the hedgehog with a demonic gleam in his eye. The hedgehog needed to be saved from this deformed socialist monkey. On its own it stood no chance against the simian Andalusian brute. None of them did. The savages had their own ape in power now, seated at the high table dispensing grants and wisdom as though he was born to it. As though ten seconds earlier he wasn't loping through the Andalusian undergrowth, putting one primitive spanner after another in the works of a more advanced breed.

When the sounds of his wife struggling with her key in the door snapped him out of his reverie, El Profesor was surprised to find that port had spilled out across the floor where he had dropped the glass. Less so that his cheeks were wet with tears.

LESS RUGGED THAN
VICTOR MATURE

IN THE END, the decision to have a break in Madrid was a surprisingly easy one to take. Actually, it wasn't even his suggestion. When his wife came home to find him alone and clearly distraught, with ample evidence on show that he had been drinking in the middle of the day, she told him he needed to get his head straight.

'You haven't been yourself for a while now,' she said, sounding almost relieved that there might be extenuating circumstances for his unhappiness beyond what, for many years, had in any case been their marriage in name only.

'I think you're right,' he agreed, perhaps a little too quickly but equally with some sense of relief. 'I've just been under so much pressure from the department. You know what they're like, and especially now with all the new blood coming in. Every other day they want to know about my research and my aims and where do I see my work fitting in with the updated curriculum and the changing profile of the discipline? I can't stand it, Nuria. There would *be* no department if it wasn't for me, but let me tell you, there's no gratitude. And now they want me to take on a mountain of teaching as well. The shame of it! Undergraduates. Sometimes I think they're deliberately trying to make life so unpleasant that I'll just give up and walk away. I think that's what they really want. That's what everyone wants, for me just to go away. Maybe you're right, maybe that's what I should do,' he said, correctly anticipating her howls of *No! No! No! That's not what I meant at all.*

He felt better than he had for some time, though. It was surprisingly good to hear those protests and what he discerned as the sudden desperation in her voice. Those were precisely the same needy, grasping characteristics which had first attracted her to him and vice versa. The time-honoured qualities of mutually assured destruction which enabled them to function, albeit as more of a shell company than legitimate smallholding, no matter what the dysfunction. And sure, he'd be the first to admit he wasn't perfect. He was man enough to do that, yet in the end it was their mutual co-dependency which saw them through. Through his multiple affairs, which, of course, she knew all about, even if she could never quite bring herself to admit it. Through the near total lack of love or affection which he understood as the inevitable hallmarks of the long-term union of man and wife. The necessary sacrifice to ensure the sanctity of that sacred bond. Above all, through the obvious disappointment he felt when he looked at his son and saw nothing so much as an even greater disappointment staring right back at him.

Her expression had visibly softened at hearing her name invoked. She couldn't remember the last time he had done so. An anniversary, perhaps, though even then she was struggling to recall a single occasion in the past calendar year. It had got worse since Javier moved out, happy to slam the door on everything but the monthly stipend which she had practically had to beg his father for. At least while he was still under their roof they had him to discuss: his studies, his friends, his moods, even his unhealthy obsession with that Real Madrid poster on his bedroom wall. Since he'd left, though, that glue had also started to unravel. Trying to raise the subject of his well-being had been difficult enough even while his presence in the house was still a physical one. But with him gone, El Profesor had begun to act as though it had always been just the two of them. No children, no stain on the family honour. Javier little more than the latest casualty of his father's historical revisionism.

Oh yes, she'd heard that phrase alright, seen it hurled as an insult by a handsome young lecturer on the news fairly recently. And she planned to use it against her husband one day, though not just yet. She had barely been paying any attention to the television, which was mainly just there to serve up background noise. She found it comforting these days in much the same way that the tannoy announcements at the station soothed her. Pre-recorded instructions directed at busy travellers, yet what she heard beneath their electronic ring tone was a kindly voice, patrician, helpful. Unflustered in spite of the thousands of little journeys touched daily by its regard. She found that reassuring, to know that there were still men in this land who made it their daily business to care and to guide others.

She found herself wondering whether the young man on the television cared. He sounded as though he did, and from where she sat there was real passion in those eyes, or was it the sensual curl of those lips? He seemed terribly young to be a lecturer, and yet there was a conviction to his words which felt every bit as old as ruins. As though he was the Philistine who had first brought the Roman Empire to its knees. In truth, this Samson was less rugged than Victor Mature, but all the same she kept watching. It turned out to be an in-depth feature on the changing face of Spanish education under Felipe González, and when her husband's name had cropped up she adjusted the volume, though much to her own surprise, upwards.

She knew her husband would be surprised to hear that. Not that she watched the news – he probably thought she sat there in a stupefied trance all day whenever she was home – but rather that she did so with a critical eye. The notion that she might have something other than a purely sedentary engagement with his work would have been anathema to her husband. And he would have been especially surprised to learn that she had long been aware of the mounting controversy surrounding his latest monograph, elements of which had been negatively viewed as a tacit endorsement of franquismo.

But still, he'd called out to her, even addressed her by name. He must be in real pain, she thought, bending down to mop up the last of the spillage. Perhaps she had also been neglecting him and her wifely duties since their son had moved out. She pondered this while sweeping up the fragments where the glass had shattered. It can't have been easy for him, a man raised with austere and inviolable principles, to watch his own son reject everything he himself held dear – comportment, history, culture – and turn instead to complete strangers for guidance. She couldn't imagine how hard that must have been for a man of his bearing to suffer such indignity. And on the increasingly rare occasions they *had* all been together under the same roof, she had seen for herself the looks Javier gave his father. At the time she had just thought he was angry with both of them because he saw it as his job to be. Him and the legions of the comfortably unhappy, who she would hear about from other faculty wives or the somewhat more reliable source of television news; those middle-class children both propping up, with their endless consumption, and beneficiaries, in their parents' unfailing largesse, of the Spanish economic 'miracle'.

'I'm not hungry,' he would say if his father suggested he take another helping of his mother's delicious lechazo, which she had so lovingly prepared for him. And on those occasions when El Profesor persisted, then Javier's mood and tone would grow darker, and he would tell them that 'meat is murder' and that the abattoirs were no different to gas chambers, 'Though I don't suppose you've got a problem with that,' he would add with what she had assumed was an accusatory look at both of them, but which she now realised in hindsight had never really been directed at her.

In Javier's eyes, *she* was just his father's willing dupe. *He* was the evil ringmaster stuffing his greedy mouth with lamb or pig or some other innocent who couldn't answer back. She saw now how much it disgusted their son to be around these rituals. Home, hearth, taste, all of it tainted in his eyes by the association with murder, with ritualised slaughter, a domestic killing field where even El Profesor's favourite cheese was known as 'pata de mulo' (leg of mule). She saw how much he hated it when his father produced a fresh bottle of wine with the prized Rueda Denominación de Origen. As if guzzling courtly wine from the time of the Catholic Monarchs wasn't yet further proof of his father's undisguised authoritarianism. Far from lending El Profesor a certain classical grace, his portentous pronouncements on the verdejo grape or the rosés of the Cigales Denominación de Origen made him sound increasingly desperate, an aristocrat with no castle, reduced to small talk with family ghosts.

That must have been hard for him, though, knowing that his life's work meant nothing to his own flesh and blood. And she hadn't exactly helped, always taking the boy's side against his father, ignoring every warning sign even when they were left lying about as an open provocation. The eyeliner and blusher, the jewellery and those disgusting magazines which, of course, she'd been too embarrassed to confront him over directly and which she'd made sure to put back in the exact same spot she'd found them under his mattress. Yet she'd always defended him against his father, even when the only thing his father wanted to know was what his son's plans for his future were. That must have wounded him, too. She could see now that this man who she'd written off as a 'monster' to anyone who would listen (which, in reality, meant her sister in Segovia who had never liked him anyway) was in fact in terrible pain. He was weak and vulnerable and had been failed in the most abysmal manner by those closest to him.

She was suddenly overwhelmed by the strongest feeling that it was she who needed to make that right. This poor man crumbling before her very eyes, and where had she been in his hour of need? In Segovia lubricating herself with those bloody grapes! She felt ashamed of herself. The least she could do was try to patch things up between them. Her life, this beautiful house, every comfort she could have dreamt of. She owed all of it to him, and so much more. If the only thing he asked in return was a bit of support, then she was going to be there for him now, even if she hadn't always been in the past. Perhaps they could still rekindle those earlier memories, when he'd been so attentive to her needs, gently probing her for the details of her likes and dislikes. *The floorplans* he liked to call them. 'And I'm going to build a palace in your name,' he would say, pushing in a little deeper, quickening his thrust.

She cast her mind back to that time when she would have said they were happiest. Or perhaps it was just *where* they were that made things so special? Madrid. Right at the heart of everything. And in a flash it came to her. *That* was where they needed to be now. They didn't even have to see Javier, though surely it wouldn't hurt to try? The main thing was that they reminded themselves of who they really were and how they could be. For all its aspirations, Valladolid was just too provincial for their particular brand of metropolitan sophistication. This trip was long overdue, back to the epicentre of their romantic peninsula. And it would be what his doubting colleagues least expected of him. The rekindling of passion, the renewing of their vows in the very place they had first fallen in love. And at the exact same time that they themselves, the fashionable snipers on television news bulletins, would be running from Madrid to the hills or the coasts. Running like the cowards they had always been. Men without principle or vision. And right at that moment she felt grateful that these were men who were nothing like her husband.

She hadn't expected him to agree quite so readily. She had only mentioned Madrid as it was a place which had positive associations for her. For both of them, she hoped, though she hadn't even got to that bit yet. The floorplans. Her favourite little bodega just off the Puerta del Sol and the romantic walks they used to take near El Retiro. And then how he used to hold her in the park. She'd barely even finished naming the nation's capital and already he'd leapt in to congratulate her. There were no protests about what she'd said to him concerning his state of mind. None of the expected outrage or defensiveness or intimations of barely suppressed violence. Instead, a brief lament about his profession, and in particular *his* discipline, and then the bombshell, which she was still forensically examining for the existence of a 'we' by the time he reached the punchline: 'You're right, Nuria. I've really not been myself of late. I do need to, how did you put it? Ah yes, now I remember, straighten this head out,' he said, pressing both hands against his skull to emphasise the point and paying no attention while he did so to his wife's mouth, which had suddenly sagged open like the famous Munch painting.

'I think I'll just go to Madrid for a few days, and then you can be the judge of my convalescence when I'm back here in Valladolid. You know it's been so many years, Nuria, mi cariña, but you still understand me better than anyone,' he added, even as his mind was already being distracted by the pressing need to make train and hotel bookings for himself and his recently taken on research assistant.

Razor Sharp

ONCE SURESH FINALLY outed himself, their dad not saying much, Mum doing her best to remain cheerful, Roxy found it a lot easier to act without limit.

'I've also got some news,' she piped up barely a week or so later, the words somehow still unheard even though no one else was speaking. 'I've started seeing someone, and he's older than me.'

She felt very adult with those words. They would, she hoped, finally draw a line under Rukhini, who, though long since abandoned in her other world of parties and art and clever undergraduate conversations, still held sway here, at home. Her reasoning was simple enough. If Suresh could come out as gay then Roxy, too, could almost certainly take her first tentative steps out of the closet.

She tried to tell them.

No, Mum, it's not just about the name, that's a different me altogether. That girl's happy and confident, and she's going places. But they wouldn't listen. *What are you talking about? What is this nonsense? Going where?* And she had to hand it to them. They were nothing if not consistent, as Suresh's grand confession had been met with much the same incomprehension. Even though in his case they all knew, and actually, once the obligatory mutterings (though only from their dad) of 'pitcher or catcher?' had melted away, it was probably something of a relief to everyone, with the possible exception of their mum, whose kohl had started running more or less in tandem with those words, 'I'm gay', and had barely let up since, only pausing every so often to shoot accusatory looks at their dad, who she clearly held responsible in some ineffable way.

She had come home after receiving a phone call from her mum at her hall of residence.

'I think it's for you, Roxy,' said one of her bemused flatmates, handing her the phone still not entirely sure who 'Rukhini' was.

'Sohni, it's your mother.'

'Hi, Mum.'

'Hi, Mum. Hai hai! Your own mother calls you and that's all you have to say?'

There was a pause, both sides weighing up how long an acceptable delay in hostilities should last.

'Everything OK?'

Her attempt to strike a conciliatory note, like so many other things in her relationship with her mum, misfired almost immediately.

'Why does everything not have to be OK for me to call you? Can I not just call my only daughter because I miss her? Or is that something else that you young people don't want to hear nowadays? That yes, we are not monsters, your parents. Believe it or not, *we* have feelings, too. And every now and then it's nice to just share them with those you are closest to. When did you become such a stranger to us, sohni?'

From anyone else that might have sounded almost gentle. But coming from her mum, those words left Roxy with an uneasy feeling. There was something forced about them, as though she was reading from a script, ticking off imaginary boxes which corresponded in her mind to a good parenting guide. Feelings, check. Sharing, check. Spontaneous communication (i.e. an unscheduled phone call), check.

'Look, Mum, I'm sorry. I didn't mean to sound like that. But I'm really busy here. I've got a couple of essays to hand in this week, and I need to get back to the library,' she lied, pointing to the receiver and hamming it up with the long-suffering look for the benefit of the flatmate who had taken the call.

'Well don't let me keep you from your precious library,' hissed her Mum. 'Your own brother of the gay, and all you can think about is books. Hai hai!'

'What? What are you talking about, Mum?'

'No, no, you get back to your books. I can tell I've wasted too much of your time anyway.' This was the tone that had always got under her skin. Even now, hundreds of miles away on the other end of a crackling line, her mum seemed to know exactly which buttons to push, and when.

In the end the 'Roxy' detail was a blessing in disguise. They spent so long fussing over the whys and wherefores – 'it's a terrible betrayal' (Mum), 'easier for the goray to pronounce' (Dad), 'fair play to you' (Rakesh), 'I'm gay, doesn't anyone round here care about that?' (Suresh) – that the other bit of her 'news', the mysterious older man, was virtually forgotten about almost as soon as she'd mentioned him. Her dad seemed less interested by her romantic attachments than her potential deed-poll requirements, as ever thinking ahead to names on wills, which would now need amending, and how best to minimise the legal costs. And would this affect her undergraduate status in any way? *No, of course not, Dad. Sure? Absolutely. Even though they gave the place to Rukhini not Roxy? Yes, Dad, even though the name's changed, the person is still the same. OK then, no problem, but you'll always be Rukhini to me*, he said, giving her a little wink, which, if she'd been paying attention, she would have realised was a hint that Rukhini had never been his idea in the first place. But she hadn't, and the moment passed.

In fairness to him, she thought, he must have still been processing the news that Suresh was a homo. Batting for the other side, he might have said, given that at that point (1984) Indians were still largely new to golf and thus unfamiliar with the concept of 'putting from the rough'. Actually, she had no idea what it meant herself, but it sounded quite funny when other people said it, which they sometimes did in the student bars, though not when any of the militant dungareed lesbians were around, which they tended not to be whenever there were drinks promotions going on and the rugby club was in attendance. Anyway, she thought, he was still clearly in shock about his son's gaandu tendencies (though, of course, the reality – which there was no way he could ever admit to the family or anyone else – was that he'd known all along and was actually quite bored with how long it had taken the gaandu to confess).

Suresh seemed briefly unhappy with her for stealing his week-long thunder. Perhaps he'd been hoping for more drama, harsh words, the threat of violence even. Something, anything that he could take back with him to whoever's cock he had been sucking just outside the Square Mile. Or perhaps she was being a little mean? Perhaps it was Suresh who was indeed being serviced. Pitcher or catcher? So hard to tell, especially when his face, hand-some though it was, appeared frozen in a near permanent scowl.

But he wasn't happy with her.

One week was not enough to constitute real suffering in his book. The ink barely dry on *his* revelation and here she was acting like *she* was the big family rebel. As if her news was the earth-shattering moment when, yes, they would finally realise that as much as pakoras or accountancy exams, it was bigotry that really held them together. She was just so bloody selfish! It always had to be about her, he thought, even though *he* was the one taking all the risks.

The other reason for his unhappiness, which, of course, wasn't so much unhappiness but more akin to a rapid deflation, was the utter lack of a definitive response.

Yes, his mum had cried, but then she was always like a coiled spring with her emotions around him anyway. He could have told her he'd narrowly missed out on a promotion, and her reaction would have been the same. But it was the near complete absence of violence, or even disapproval, in his dad's reaction which had really left him high and dry. He was a fudge packer, a shirt lifter, a windy walker, and nobody even cared.

It had taken every ounce of courage that he possessed to even contemplate having this conversation, let alone actually seeing it through. He had no way of knowing how they would react and he knew he was risking everything by doing so. Yet here he was barely a week later having to endure his younger sister's pantomime antics. And here was his mum's kohl tearing up again, black footprints on the march once more down that easily wounded face. Rakesh not fussed as usual, and Dad more animated than at any time during his, Suresh's, grand performance. He had bared his soul to them, and they had acted as though he had given them little more than a racing tip. What kind of cold, unfeeling monsters were they? Who *were* these creatures he was related to by birth?

She was pleased her family never found out about Dr Thornton. They might have done if they'd even been listening. But they hadn't. Roxy took up all the space. In the end there was no room left for the older man.

Peter.

And she couldn't have been happier about that.

Though he couldn't have been more than a decade, or perhaps a decade and a half, older than her when they first got together, it was as though he was from a different planet. It wasn't long after she'd dumped that idiot, D.

She was sick of boys by that point, and their stupid, pathetic little lies designed to impress girls like her. Well, she had news for the silly cockney twat. *She* wasn't one of those girls. She was Roxy, and Roxy didn't put up with that type of shit. Anyway, Peter had remembered her from those soirées, which he used to draw such pleasure from. This pleased her immensely, especially as she wasn't even a student of his. But when D's name came up and her face clouded over, *he'd* known exactly what to do. He was so sensitive, such a good listener, in spite of what she imagined was probably a huge workload.

He always seemed busy, rushing from lecture to seminar or back to his office carrying a sheaf of papers under one arm and that tatty briefcase in his other hand. Yet still he found time to stop that day and listen to her problems, which must have sounded a bit trivial to him, she thought. And he'd sat with her and listened and then invited her over to carry on their discussion at his house, which she remembered from the soirée and which now seemed a lot bigger without any of the other students in attendance. And when he'd put the wine down and reached for her it hadn't felt forced, or awkward, even when he had had to desist that first night claiming the lack of a condom, though she suspected it might also have something to do with the amount of wine they had both consumed. Still, she forgot all about that when he whisked her off to the Louvre one weekend not long after and they admired the paintings of Eugène Delacroix together, especially the *Women Of Algiers In Their Apartment*, which he explained was part of the 'Orientalist' tradition adopted by many French painters during the imperial expansion of the nineteenth century. And when he explained to her that these paintings revelled in the supposed opulence and extravagance of the Orient, she saw no contradiction between his razor-sharp insights and the way he drew her head to his midriff. Or, later, with how he contrasted the civilising mission of the West with the despotic cruelties of the Near and Middle East, lightly pinching one of her nipples between thumb and forefinger as he did so. When he made her kneel on the bed and entered her from behind, not long after a sermon on Flaubert and Egypt, she appreciated how far he would go to make an aesthetic point. This was true didacticism, and she was lucky to be a part of it.

Within a month, though, things had cooled between them. Peter never seemed to be available any more out of office hours. She left messages on his answerphone, but there was no reply. On the rare occasions she might spot him on campus, he now seemed to be under a permanent cloud. There was no stopping to greet colleagues or small talk with any of his students. Her own studies had begun to suffer, and it was that, as much as the near constant feelings of anxiety she had been experiencing, which persuaded her to follow Peter home one evening, making sure he was inside before marching towards the front of the by-now-familiar Georgian terrace.

Though it was still quite early, she could see that there were lights on in the front room. Peering in through one of the large front windows, she struggled at first to make sense of the scene. A woman was sat on the large oriental-print sofa, which dominated one side of the room. She appeared to be reading a magazine supplement but would look up every now and then to keep an eye on the infant, who Roxy suddenly spotted on the thick shagpile rug running parallel to the sofa, playing with a box of colouring pens and an open book. The woman, who was dark haired, seemed a little older than Peter. Thirty-five she would have guessed, though the light and her snatched view might also have played a part in that assessment. She was wearing one of those dogtooth Cambridge skirts that had been really popular a couple of seasons back, and the child seemed to appreciate her fashion choice, tugging on the ends whenever she wanted some attention. The woman herself didn't seem at all interested in what the child was actually doing. Once she'd satisfied herself that the infant was, in fact, using the pens to colour in the shapes in her book, she drifted back to the magazine and whatever it was that was so captivating in its pages.

For a moment, Roxy wondered whether she'd somehow got the wrong house, even though she'd waited until she was sure it was Peter who was tramping his feet up the garden path and then disappearing beyond the threshold.

Suddenly the infant's entire demeanour changed. She dropped the pen she had been chewing on, and her face lit up as though a sweet, sticky portal had just appeared in the middle of the room.

'Daddy! Daddy!' she yelped delightedly, raising her little hands to anticipate the bigger arms that would shortly hold her aloft.

Roxy looked again. It was Peter cooing away in what she assumed was his daughter's ear. Gently jogging the child in his arms but never taking his eyes off the woman on the sofa who, Roxy couldn't help but notice, didn't make eye contact with him the entire time, not even once.

When she thought about it, her and D, it had always been on the cards. It was uncomplicated, and, for all his feeble fibs, she felt he was a good man. Not particularly exciting or the greatest lover, but good enough. It went without saying that that was also the source of her shame. That this was not some grand passion, Omar Sharif and Julie Christie in the snow. She couldn't pretend that she had known from the moment they'd first met (she hadn't). But he was good around her family, even managing to charm her mum with endless compliments about the food (often catered) and supplying expensive Christmas and birthday gifts without fail. In truth, she had always suspected that her mum would be happier with a gora for a son-in-law, even one with glottal stops, and so it proved with D, whatever reservations her mum might have had quickly dispelled by the perfumes and kind remarks. All this despite the fact that D clearly got on better with her dad and both her brothers, though perhaps for different reasons.

He was adored by her nephews, and that, in turn, softened Rakesh's view of him, the wariness of the older brother giving way to begrudging acceptance. Suresh, on the other hand, felt that in D he might have found a kindred spirit, driven by risk and reward and drawn to the limitless bounties of the Square Mile. No one mentioned the cocksucking, and that suited everyone just fine. And then, of course, there was her dad, who started to call D 'my boy' and made no secret of his desire to be playing with more grandchildren while he still had some energy.

She loved her trips to Bermondsey, too. They spoke to the long-suppressed traditionalist in her, his parents' tea-time rituals and then their gentle mockery of all the ritual. She loved that, especially his dad, the way he always had a kind word or a protective gesture. Through all the spotting and the agony, they'd been there – 'Don't worry, love, it'll all come right in the end, you'll see,' somehow breaching her defences in a way that her own mum's voice rarely could. And even with no kids they would have been alright, too. She was sure of it. She'd tried to hold on to some of that tradition – the sarnies, the socks – and he'd never questioned her, whatever he truly thought of her motives. For her part she'd got beyond the shame of things just being 'good enough', no longer feeling it necessary to excuse what to a certain sensibility might have looked like her barely adequate choices in front of her thriving, big-belly, 'with child' (and career) friends and colleagues who after a while all seemed to meld into one upwardly mobile mind-belly-homemaker hybrid.

They were good people, though, she felt, going out of their way to include her in their expanding social whirl.

Birthdays, fêtes, cake-cutting ceremonies for little Jake, Rosalind, Tara or Hugo.

'You're in charge of decorations/goody bags/music,' she'd be told in no particular order, the idea being to convey how integral her presence was/would be during such moments.

'You know how much the kids love having you around. It won't be a party otherwise.'

But for all the generosity she sensed the pity, sometimes, in how her friends would look at her, an imperceptible gap opening up between the linearity of their lives and the way hers appeared to be stuck. Static, blocked, something wrong in the tubes. It hurt, of course it did, when one after the other her own productions fell flat long before opening night, spotting and bleeding and ectopic leeches her signature style. Yet, paradoxically she thought, so much failure perversely lent some purity to what she and D had. They stayed together in spite of it all. Just them and whatever it was that had first brought them into each other's orbit. Unlike almost everyone else they seemed to know, not bent out of shape to accommodate another life but simply the original nuts and bolts of their construction. Feeling around one another's frailties and cobbling together some kind of structure. And really, she no longer needed to reassure anyone in her circle, *that* was more than enough.

So, after going through all of that, to be undone by a simple lie was perhaps the most painful betrayal of the lot. If he'd just told her there and then she felt sure that they could have worked things out. It was just a job; there would surely be others. And if he'd told her she might even have been able to help him. It wasn't the end of the world. They had already been through a lot more than that. Besides, the work, what did it really feed beyond the lifestyle? And even then, it was just a taste, a method of parading the bland monotony which seemed to go with the industrial furniture. *De rigeur*. She assumed that he of all people would understand, just as she did, the difference between a taste, a certain liking for particular foods or holiday destinations or perhaps stripped-wood floors and exposed brickwork, and a hunger, that keening need for life and dependency and the gorgeous unvarnished mess of unconditional love. She thought that was the one thing he *would* know. But he didn't, his omission, or, more accurately, the cowardice behind it, bringing her right back to that humiliating memory of being outside Thornton's house in Coventry, and of her tear-streaked face tormented in its utter helplessness, Thornton playing her, playing all of them for fools.

She *had* thought that was in the past, though the memory still chafed. But she was wrong. In the end all it took was one simple lie and then the inability to let go of it, for the whole flimsy artifice to be corrupted again. The nuts and bolts were not enough. Perhaps they never had been, she reflected bitterly. And soon enough that face undergoing its own paroxysms of bad faith would begin to thaw, its rictus morphing first into incomprehension and from there into a volcanic rage, even if the lava was a decade in the making. The Specials to The Stone Roses, D might have said, but fuck him. He lied.

He shouldn't have done that, she thought, all the other sounds suddenly muted. He lied, and this time she had a knife. Stainless steel, santoku, Japanese and some way beyond razor sharp. Fuck him.

She at last felt conviction bursting through where so often in the past there had just been ennui. Finally, she thought, this was what it was like to truly *feel*. Such a hollow life up to now, cosseted and validated at every turn. The seamless flit from Rukhini to Roxy. Friends, boyfriends, university and barely a crease on her Donna Karan, the fabric, like her life, draped and somewhat flattering. Family always in her corner, even Mum, never short of a kind word or money or home-cooked comforts, no matter how capricious her behaviour, how lightweight the sounds. Daddy's little girl, and she knew it. I want this, I want that. No, not that, *this*! Though, interestingly, she never carried on like that in front of D's parents. The thought wouldn't even have occurred to her, in much the same way that she'd always found time to listen to her English friends bemoaning the small print of what appeared to be their otherwise happy lives, yet if Suresh so much as hinted at any of the details of his own clearly less than happy existence, she'd suddenly be busy with some imaginary task or on her way out to a prior engagement, 'I can't, Suresh, I'm already late as it is.'

It wasn't so much what Thornton had done as how he'd behaved. That was what really got to her. She was nothing, less than one of Flaubert's houris. In her case her body, its intimate secrets, little more than an extra-curricular appendage. Herself for once superfluous to requirements, Peter the one rushing away to some prior engagement. When she looked in through that window, what she'd really seen was just how small her presence was. This man, who had opened her up to a world of art and poetry, to Delacroix and Hugo, Flaubert and Paris, and then had opened her up again, away from prying eyes, she could see now how little she actually meant to him. For all her willingness (and she had been willing) to play his didactic games, only now could she see that her presence in his life was little more than theory. Against that, D, she thought, had represented solidity. For all the numbers and predictions he would find himself tasked with, he was the one sure thing she felt she had, beyond every other sure thing she'd always taken for granted and so never even acknowledged as such.

And now that, too, had proved to be a lie. After all they'd been through, and he couldn't even tell her he'd been sacked. Fuck him, she thought. It might only have been a limited orbit, but it had been *theirs*. Them against the world, building their own memories against the forces of nature. Fuck D, fuck Thornton, fuck them all. She'd find her own way to the estate agents' promised land, to its middle-class nirvana of Nappy Valley, or perhaps to dilapidation-chic cocktails in the city of the future. With or without a fat belly.

PRIMARY

Madrid, 1986

THE HOTEL ROOM overlooked a courtyard in which there was a steel door, presumably leading down to the cellar. It was located in a part of the city that Laura had never really been to, even though it was close to some familiar haunts in an area she *had* previously spent time in. In the taxi she'd been struck by the sudden reduction in external noise the moment the vehicle had turned on to the wide, tree-lined avenue. Gone was the bustle and frenzy of Chamartín, replaced now with a kind of sedate contemplation. These buildings were old and grand, and even from behind a slightly neglected passenger rear window she felt their patrician gaze settling upon her. El Profesor must have felt something, too, as he looked back at her for the first time since clambering in next to the driver at the station. He'd said nothing from the moment the driver had asked him how long he planned to spend in Madrid with his 'son'. The silence had been awkward but necessary. He now regretted initiating any kind of conversation with the driver. It had been an ill-advised moment of weakness on his part and entirely indicative, he felt, of the new Spain. Yet there had been a time when the driver would not have dared to assume anything about his paying customers. His patrons, at least for the duration of the journey. Irrespective of whether or not they had exchanged introductory courtesies.

Looking at him now, the stubby fingers, the squat physique ill-framed by a cheap, unbuttoned half-sleeve shirt, El Profesor found himself fighting hard to restrain an almost visceral contempt. From his accent and general demeanour, he surmised that the man was an Andaluz, a primate who no doubt had followed his leader, the vile socialist monkey, Felipe González, and the other backward hordes into Madrid.

Sitting next to this creature, El Profesor was assailed by a terrible vision, the strength of which made him ball his fists. He saw peasants flooding in to the Palacio de Santa Cruz or, worse, the Monasterio de las Descalzas Reales, holding guidebooks and cheap snacks in their foul, dirt-ingrained fingers. And it left him appalled. As if anything in their impoverished upbringing could adequately furnish them with a language, a grammar, with which to appreciate the extraordinary history and architecture of this city. He was outraged. What could they possibly know of, how could they possibly appreciate, the 'Madrid de los Austrias'? Of the crescent junction between Calle de Carretas and the Puerta del Sol where Carlos III once sat astride a horse? Or of the Pontificia de San Miguel, with its baroque-inspired basilica? Its flowing cornices and oval cupola? What could they know of the men of science and vision and of the courage it took to realise those visions? Did they even understand what leadership meant? The sacrifices and self-discipline that nation-building required? Of course not. The barbarians were well and truly at the gates.

But this was the new Spain, he reflected bitterly. A laughing stock at its own World Cup only a few short years back. He thanked the Lord above that El Caudillo at least was no longer around to suffer these indignities, to see such humiliations played out on a global stage. The best this nation apparently had to offer humbled by minnows in front of a live audience in the hundreds of millions, perhaps even more than that. *Northern Ireland?!* He didn't even know they had a football team, let alone one capable of this type of feat. When did they even find time to practise in between all those bombings and shootings? Brazil, Italy he could just about accept, albeit grudgingly, but Northern Ireland? A bunch of terrorists! It was almost worse than losing to blacks. Surely that wasn't right? But yes, it had happened, and the whole world had been there to watch.

It wasn't always so, he recalled. Just a few decades earlier, and he could still see, could almost taste in his nostrils, El Madrid, Real, *his* team, whose European coronation had at that time been an annual event. They had strutted to all those titles, inferior foreign opposition vanquished much as the degenerate elements within the nation's borders had been. And that taste, that was the heady scent of victory. He'd been a young man then, but it wasn't so long ago. Everything had seemed possible in those days when he'd moved through a world of order and progress. Indeed, that notion of orderly progression was what he missed most of all. Back then he, and a select few like him, had been favoured by the administration for their ability to take the difficult decisions without recourse to sentiment or doubt. It had needed an unwavering instinct to plough through generations of superstition, of the swarthy degeneracy bequeathed this peninsula by the Arabs. The cartoon emotionalism of the Gypsies, the hypocritical resentments of the Basques and the Catalans and of the peasants, like this fat-fingered Andaluz, all of them speaking at once, the distinct, forlorn babble of primates. And yes, it had taken instinct and a certain amount of determination to break down those howls of complaint, break them down into their regional components from where they could more easily be pitted against one another at a time of El Caudillo's choosing. But he had persevered, they all had, and their rewards lay as much in the vision of the brave new society they were at the forefront in creating, as in the lucrative commissions, the prestigious titles, the crucial land leases or the irresistible 'loan' agreements. They had all made great sacrifices in the service of their nation, and these were but trinkets to recognise their devotion. Yet in a few short years since that terrible November day when the news they had all been dreading finally became official and El Caudillo was pronounced dead, he had seen so much of their good work forced to unravel, the degenerates once more emerging from their caves, emboldened with placards and demands curled around uncultured peasant fingers. Communists and socialists, unionists and women picking away at the threads. Catalan and Basque and Andaluz, united now in their desire to forget. Or, more accurately, to obliterate. The savages picking and picking until the very foundations of the nation's prosperity were in doubt.

Spaniards now cried more easily, he reflected, whether that was the marícas in the Bernabeu or his students, unable to comprehend that without established historical sources their work would never amount to anything more than polemic. There were no shortcuts, he would tell them, and they would cry. Not all of them, and not instantly, but in sufficient numbers to plant the seed in his mind that this was a generation of blubbers, given to histrionics and not the sober discipline of history to which he belonged. His need to even indulge them with an explanation was a source of genuine regret to him, but those were the conditions under which a once proud autocrat like himself was now expected to operate.

'Gracias. Hasta luego,' said the driver as El Profesor handed him a generous tip. But there was still no sign of 'señor' anywhere in the exchange, and they headed up to the room with El Profesor wearing the expression of a man who felt he'd been somehow short-changed. It was all highly unsatisfactory, he thought, the lack of deference from these ancillary types. The lady on reception had been little better, and he had sensed her disapproval as she handed him the key to their double room. He *had* thought about confronting her but then reminded himself of the reason for his trip and was able to step back from the moment. Besides, his secretary had made the reservation, and this was probably just her way of letting him know what she *really* felt. He'd seen her flinch when he'd mentioned that the room needed to be a double, as if the thought of him still being able to function in those terms was too much for her to contemplate. She probably wasn't even aware she was doing it, but he'd spotted her anyway, his uncanny instinct for zeroing in on the dissident fraction as sharp as ever. It pleased him to note that whether it was sniffing out communists or buttoned-up moral prudery, he was still second to none.

He'd insisted it was a 'romantic break' for himself and his wife, but his secretary had just given him a knowing look and silently assented, which infuriated him. These admin bitches probably all knew each other, he thought. One big tut-tutting coven for whom men of vision, men like himself, no doubt reminded them of everything they most disliked about their own lives. Their weak, talentless husbands and spoilt, parasitical children, those of them that even had families. The rest, like this cabrona on reception, clearly embittered by their own unattractiveness to everyone, by the sheer dullness of their appearance, and so prime candidates for the sort of non-existent customer service he was constantly having to endure nowadays but with little recourse to any of the older channels. The official and unofficial avenues that might once have resulted in an unmarked resting spot for a bruja of this sort. And all it would have taken was a phone call. How he missed those days, his name alone sufficient to set so many wheels in motion. A bruja like this, she wouldn't have dared.

Thank goodness Laura wasn't like that, he thought, as the heavy wooden door opened on to a pleasingly spacious room, bay windows admitting the late-afternoon light, much of it settling on the large double bed, which had been neatly decorated with an array of cushions of varying sizes and a crescent of petals fanning out across the middle of the bed. He had to admit that was a nice touch, but he'd be damned if he was going to mention it to the bruja. Still, he briefly felt bad for the way he'd earlier judged his secretary, but, in truth, his thoughts were already turning to the complimentary bathrobes and what he could see was a very well-stocked minibar.

In the taxi on the way over, the hotel had seemed closer to Malasaña. On foot it felt further, sweat beading her forehead as the streets shed some of their grandeur, patrician boulevards giving way to youth. These were the youngsters who couldn't afford to 'summer' elsewhere. No coastal or mountain hideaways for their perennial black-clad sense of rebellion.

She paused at one point, suddenly overcome by sickness, and briefly found herself dry-retching by the side of the road. A young man passing by asked her whether she was OK, but when she tried to answer the words stopped short, held back by the metallic taste in her mouth. It wasn't the first time this had happened recently, and she found herself wondering what else her insides might be saying to her.

She wasn't sure how long she'd been walking, but at some stage the streets had narrowed, clusters of nocturnal revellers generating their own intense body heat on top of nature's cauldron. Some were clutching at, or still swigging from, litre bottles of beer or cider which bore the discount-supermarket brand name. Their evening would probably end here, sprawled out in the loose embrace of neo-gothic camaraderie. No one paid her much attention as she entered the bar. As far as they were concerned, she was just another young person in black rejecting the city's mainstream dress codes.

Once inside she felt good. The outside warmth meant fewer people than usual on the ad hoc dancefloor, though the bar area was still busy. It wasn't actually a dancefloor as such, more a space between the bar and the toilets where the less inhibited would strike poses. She wasn't sure where the music was coming from, but there was no sign of a DJ, so she assumed it was from a tape which was being played over the in-house system. Besides, she'd heard about this place from other people who took great pride in telling her this wasn't that kind of a bar. No one came here to listen to some rich boy from Chueca massaging his own ego. Quite the opposite. The attraction here was its simplicity. Music, drink, dance. The bar and its surrounds little more than a conduit for whatever mood its patrons had brought along with them. That was where the real skill lay, in how the bar staff judged the mood. Get it right, and the till receipts would more than justify the conscious decision on the part of the owner to opt for a low-maintenance musical policy. Though, of course, there *were* times when certain staff (often the newer ones) would woefully miscalculate and the one memorable detail on those nights would be the chorus of disapproval followed by vigorous use of the 'eject' button.

Tonight, though, there were no such problems. Laura paid for her drink with money she'd lifted from El Profesor's jacket pocket and lounged against the far wall, invisible from the street but from where *she* could still see the exit.

The other drinkers were in good voice, singing along to the expected crowd pleasers by Mecano and Radio Futura.

She felt lighter, more at ease, than she had for some time. On the way over her head had still been pounding, but now, bolstered by this beery, new-wave anonymity, she started to relax. When she had first changed back into her standard black T-shirt/jeans combo and then slipped out of the hotel room with her smart travel uniform – suit trousers, a light-blue men's cotton shirt (originally belonging to El Profesor's son but which El Profesor had appeared very keen for her to wear) and the tweed cap which had felt stiflingly hot but under which her hair, tied into a bun, had at least remained hidden – unceremoniously stuffed into a plastic bag, she had been terrified that the receptionist would spot her. After all, she hadn't exactly seemed overjoyed when they'd arrived, though on reflection there was something boyish about Laura's appearance, and perhaps it was that rather than the age gap which she'd found so objectionable. In fact, Laura reminded herself, gathering up her courage, the receptionist had barely looked at her beyond taking in the details of her masculine attire.

When she *was* able to walk straight past the receptionist and back out on to the street without attracting so much as a glance, her thoughts began to reassemble. She looked at her watch. It was past 9pm. She still had time. Skirting the perimeter of El Retiro, she headed towards the Gran Vía. Though the wealthier elements of the city had already fled the summer heat, the streets were still busy, mainly with students and foreign tourists. Laura found this a blessing, as she was sure it would have been the pijos who would otherwise have been the first to seize upon the panic in her stride. But they were largely absent, and though she mainly kept her eyes to the pavement, on the few occasions she did look up there were just the botellón kids with eyes for nothing but their next shoestring fiesta. Near the northwestern corner of the park she spotted Arturo walking towards her in his trademark faded jeans and jungle-green T-shirt. As they passed each other, the plastic bag silently changed hands, and, without pausing to look back, the young man headed away for another late shift at La Paz, where he had been working as a porter for over a year. In less than an hour the contents of the bag would have been incinerated, and Arturo, now changed back into his orderly's scrubs, would be attending to evidence of more regular casualties.

Just as in the past he had never asked her why she had needed to stay in his flat for extended periods back in Valladolid, so now he thought better of enquiring after the contents of this bag. (The flat had originally been his abuela's but was now his after she had taken the hugely controversial decision to bypass her own children, including Arturo's father, in the will for, as she put it, 'being on the wrong side of history'. And, of course, her historical break led to his own from his family, by now too consumed by envy and bitterness even to consider him their son any more.) When they had spoken earlier, Laura had made it clear that she was only asking him this favour because where she was staying there was no question of starting a fire. (Again, he had known better than to ask.) They had arranged a time and place for the handover, to which she'd cryptically referred as being of 'a bag of sweets' (though he'd known there and then that it would be anything but), and even from a distance he could tell she wasn't yet in the right frame of mind to talk. Then again, he thought, that's just how things were between them, how they'd always been. Even when they'd been kids and the only reason she'd got into trouble was because of some suggestion he'd made. Even when the pijo she'd tricked (on his say so) into buying specially packaged (by him) liquorice for what ended up being a perfectly legal high, even when that pijo turned out to have a father who used to be a colonel and who could still count on extra-legal favours. Even then she'd kept her mouth shut, and she'd put up with the disgusting things those policemen had done to her before encouraging the pijo, who they'd brought along for the ride, to do the same. And still she hadn't said anything because she must have known deep down that whatever they did to her, however bad it was, they would do tenfold to him. She'd said nothing and absorbed everything, and for that alone he would forever be indebted to her.

*

When the first gloomy notes tipped out of the speakers, Laura found herself giving a little yelp of satisfaction. Ian Curtis singing of a 'live transmission', and she felt he was talking to her and her alone. How many times had she listened to this with D? And always the same interruption, D knowing exactly when the record would skip and cutting in just before to warn her. As if she didn't also know its every imperfection. 'Salford rain in its postmark,' D would say, though she never knew why. She closed her eyes and tried to imagine a healthy Ian Curtis, and yet she could see that he also had his eyes closed, a clockwork soldier pirouetting ever closer to the edge. Without meaning to, she mimicked his karate chops and tasted his sadness, ground up in some northern dispensary. The song ended, and when she opened her eyes again she was surprised to discover that the dancefloor was packed and that several strangers, ragged-looking boys with spidery legs, were looking at her with something akin to awe. It was the last song on the tape, but the crowd remained patient, the mood interlocking with the hidden spools even when they ran out of space. Deft hands flipped the tape over and the crackle from the original recording sizzled just above room temperature. This time the voice was higher, Ian Curtis' funeral dirge giving way to another singer she knew from her time in England. Robert Smith. And again, though it was a tape, she could almost smell the vinyl, its soldered grooves relentless. She knew the words, and really, in spite of herself, her urgent need to remain hidden, she was singing along, one of the few here who even understood English. She loved this band, The Cure. She'd loved this tune; they both had. 'Primary'. The very first time she saw his face, she knew...

El Profesor appeared distracted. Though she could feel his eyes nominally straying to her chest, for once they didn't linger. Perhaps it was the combined effects of the journey and the heat, she thought. Since changing into his bathrobe, El Profesor had flitted between giddy and listless, depending, it seemed on which bonsai liquor he was busy consuming. That instinct, which would ordinarily have wondered why his companion was producing a pair of surgical gloves from her inside pocket, for once felt dull. He watched her put the gloves on, and all it computed to was a vague frisson near his midriff. It was much the same when she secured his hands to the bedposts, using two silk ties that she had picked out from El Profesor's luggage. He moaned, as much down to being parted from his precious cargo of Osborne whisky as from any kind of excitement, the smell of her breasts close. And when she tugged on the knots to make sure he was properly restrained, a faint smile, born of confusion and the vague rumour of sex, continued to play around the corners of his mouth.

'You'll like the next bit, Profesor,' she said to him, producing a neatly folded plastic bag from her other pocket.

'¿Qué es esto? ¿Estás loca?' El Profesor started to say, but in the instant she saw his eyes change and a quaver enter his voice, she had already straddled him and the bag was over his head. She held it there for almost a minute, gently rocking back and forth in time with the bag's increasingly rapid contractions. Finally she removed it, El Profesor's head lurching forward, eyeballs beginning to rise up into their sockets. He was no longer able to speak, so she took a moment to compose herself, propping up his chin with one of her gloved hands. When she addressed him again, her voice was calm, each syllable speeding the death rattle up his chest and into his brain where all the pylons were collapsing.

'How does it feel to be outsmarted by a primitive, Profesor?' she asked him, pushing his chin up so that what was left of him was forced to look straight into her eyes, which, if he could even tell any more, were calm. 'You know what's happening, don't you? You're probably going into shock round about now, if you haven't already. Bet you wished you'd laid off the whisky now? But let's just make sure,' she added, placing the bag back over his head. This time she kept it there until she was certain he must have gone into cardiac arrest. At which point she removed it again, determined that his last moments should be as appalling as possible, the words necessary even if they were barely registering. She spoke softly, noting as she did so how his earlier jerkiness had now subsided.

'You're dying, old man, and when you're gone, which shouldn't be long now, I'm going to go through your pockets and spend every last peseta on a celebratory drink for myself and a dance. And here's the thing, Profesor, I *never* dance.'

In the chaotic days, and weeks, that followed, the coroner's report made no mention of asphyxiation. The cause of death was rather attributed to a massive coronary episode most likely brought on by a combination of alcohol, fatigue and, as attested to by the deceased's spouse, a vulnerable state of mind in the days leading up to the fatal episode. During preliminary inquiries conducted both by the Municipal Police Force in Madrid and the university in Valladolid, there seemed to be some confusion as to whether El Profesor had indeed been alone at the time of his demise. Conflicting reports (from both his secretary and the receptionist at the hotel in question) of a 'double' room booking and of a young male companion were quickly deemed unhelpful or impossible to substantiate or perhaps both, and somewhere, doubtless behind closed doors, a decision was taken to suppress these (alleged) details from the official newspaper coverage. By the time of his valedictory oration, delivered by a colleague who was the first to admit he hadn't always seen eye to eye with El Profesor on every subject but that they shared the utmost intellectual respect for one another's scholarly output, Miguel de la Fuente Escudero had already been rehabilitated as one of the most important historians of his generation.

Feeling bold, though not especially reckless, Laura decided to take up the offer of one of the spidery-legged boys in the bar to spend the night. The clincher for her was the welcome detail that they shared a flat nearby which was already being sublet from a 'friend of a friend'. And, though it was late and she felt the exhaustion of everything which had passed earlier, her mind was still sufficiently alert to perform the necessary gymnastics. At this moment in time, obtuse was good. Off the grid. A friend of a friend. Three cherries on the slot machine. When he made room for her on their sofa, she didn't argue, in fact, she was delighted that no attempt was made to cajole her into his bed. It would have broken the spell. Besides, these boys just seemed grateful that she had chosen not to ignore them. This girl that knew about Joy Division. In their flat! And when she awoke the next morning to the familiar sounds of The Stranglers and a blur of spidery legs, she didn't complain. Sweet boys really, and they were putting on a show for her. No one even asked her her name, and for now, at least, that suited her just fine.

Random Cruelty Under An Inkblot Sky

London, naughties

I HAVE LEAKED through the cloth many times. It used to bother me, but not now. Like anything else, eventually you get used to it. It just becomes part of the fabric. I think it's something to do with that bang on the head I once took and the strange hospital where I was treated. I blame the bump and my time in that place where they told me how worried they were about the bump, though I don't ever remember them doing anything about it. If I'm going to be honest I don't even know how long I was in there for. No one told me. I don't remember anyone coming round with a calendar marking off the days, or was it months, or maybe even longer? I just don't know, and I don't want to make those figures up. I never used to, so why should I start now? The bit that sticks in my head was that the place was full of Schwarzes, and in that sense it reminded me a bit of school. Speaking of, I remember looking for Conrad in there and being oddly disappointed when I couldn't find him. The devil you know and all that.

Anyway, that whole period is a bit blurred, especially after Mum and Dad passed in 1997 in quick succession. I remember being in the hospital then, both times, all of us crying and pretending we weren't. I remember all the tubes Dad had attached to him. They were sprouting from every spare bit of flesh, and I remember him making a terrible joke about not having any problems any more catching the tube. We all laughed, even Mum, though it wouldn't be long before it was her in the bed stoically enduring a constant stream of visitors. I remember their skin, how papery it felt to the touch. Near the end how fragile they seemed, when all I wished for them was sleep. How angry I felt at all those people who wouldn't let them sleep. Cousins, aunts, uncles and then people I'd never even seen before, filing in with their fake bonhomie. Who are you? I wanted to shout at them. Why are you here? Sometimes I wanted to shout at my brother, too, at Angie and the kids. Why are you so sad now? You never cared before! Or maybe I did say some of these things? I'm not sure any more. The edges start to fray round about then.

Roxy never showed at the hospital. I thought she might. She always got on so well with them. They liked her well enough, too, but then that's how they were with most people. I thought she might have heard from someone. Not me, of course. I wasn't about to say anything. Wouldn't have known where to start. When she left, I let her go. Not like that, that's not what I mean. It's not as though anyone was barring her exit. No, I let her go as you would a discarded memory. I knew I had to. Dad was already starting to get sick, and in a way it was good I lost that job. At least I got to spend that time with him rather than with bar charts and projections and that weird greenish neon haze that bathed all our screens back then. Her brother came, though. Suresh, always liked him. Bit odd, always struck me as a touch over-emotional for a City boy, but then again, which of us doesn't have our little quirks? We had a good cry, even though he barely knew Dad. Somehow I got the feeling it wasn't just about Dad, though.

'Sorry, D,' he said, afterwards.

'No need,' I told him.

'Yeah, there is, D, there is. I'm really sorry about everything,' he said, and that was when I knew it wasn't just about Dad.

'Like I said, there's no need, but I appreciate that anyway,' I told him, and then the waterworks started up again, and we were hugging and he was telling me what a good bloke my old man was, what a good bloke I was, and I knew right then I'd never see him again. I think we both did.

Anyway, the point was, someone must have let him know, which meant *she* must have known, too. But she never came. It was probably just as well. There's no knowing what might have happened if she'd shown up on a bad day, say when Dad was having difficulty swallowing, or his arms, his veins, every bit of desire that once flowed through them, were struggling to lift so much as a plastic fork to his lips. If she'd shown up then, well, it's a good job she didn't.

She always said how much she loved them both. Said that about them a lot more than she did me. But in the end they both passed without seeing her again. I won't lie, I won't say I wasn't tempted to look her up every now and then, but I didn't. It took some strength to do that, not that anyone's noticed. It took some strength to not be the one to crack, breathing quietly and unhappily into the other end of a phone while the supposed love of your life – more the choice you made, actually – waits for you to hang up, dead air and regret the only thing binding you to that choice now. Yeah, that took effort, and I won't lie, I was glad when I got those calls, back when I still had a phone and a place, because it meant that she was suffering, that somewhere in her emotional circuitry a rat was gnawing at the cables and little sparks were flying, splintering their scorch marks just beneath the surface. But honestly, I was such a Toby. She stuck me with a fork, and I just let her go. Good job she never was much good at handling that fish knife. I think I'd have remembered otherwise. At least she came at me, though. That's got to mean something, right? At least it mattered enough for her to do that.

I remember the talk. Tea, Formica tops, the tang of grease. I'd moved by then, a flat, what the estate agents were calling 'purpose built', though having lived there for over a year, I still couldn't work out what that purpose might be. Anyway, this café was nearby, and when he said he wanted to talk, I'd suggested it because otherwise he'd have picked somewhere which didn't look so kindly upon frayed edges. I'd taken to wearing high-backed trousers by then. Held up with the old-style button braces, though my expanding girth meant that I rarely needed to rely on them. I'd picked up a couple of pairs in the local charity shop, and though he'd have never gone second hand, something about them reminded me a little of Dad. He'd been particular, right to the end, to that final admission on to the ward and then the Intensive Care Unit. But even while he was on the general ward, he'd made me bring in his favourite flame-orange gingham check Ben Sherman, holding on to my arm with all his strength and instructing me, his voice barely a whisper now, 'Make sure it's starched and ironed.'

Actually, I thought the trousers looked quite fetching, braces hanging loose like an off-duty droog. But when I walked in to the café that morning, and my brother, who was already there, got up to greet me, the look on his face as he did that thing he'd always done, sizing up the cloth in a quick once-over, suggested anything but approval.

'What *do* you look like?' he asked, adjusting the button on his single-breasted suit.

'What? Oh, *these*,' I tell him, indicating my trousers with the flat of my palm. 'Yeah, I know, *not* high street.'

I remember us both laughing and how good it felt. He tells me about his Kilgour-tailored, one-button single-breasted suit – 'seasonal cloth with a trademark polka dot woven into it. It's for the debonair man about town.'

'So why are you wearing it?' I ask him, and we laugh again. There's not been so many moments like these of late. It's the first time I can recall sitting down with him and talking, really talking, since we were kids, and even then it was more a case of 'Don't tell anyone' or 'Keep this somewhere safe and whatever you do, make sure Dad doesn't find them.' Now, though, it all comes tumbling out.

'You know they were proud of you, don't you?' he asks me.

'Yeah, I know. Both of us, as it goes.'

'I don't think you do, though. I don't think you know just how proud of you they were. I can't remember a single time I ever went round there and they didn't mention you. Even with the twins, they'd always tell them about their uncle D "Your uncle D's so smart, he's so good with numbers, I'm sure he could tell you what the answer is." Would you believe, I used to be envious of you?'

'Don't lie.'

'I'm not. I'm being serious. I used to envy how they spoke about you, how Mum's face used to take on this wistful look any time your name came up. And it was as though, no matter what I did or how well, it's what I did *before* that they'd always remember. They never said it, mind, but it was just a feeling I was left with. Thank God for the twins really. Never thought I'd be saying this about my own kids, but I think we all needed a distraction back then.'

I remember the back and forth, all the people we used to know – 'That silly sod, what was his name, oh yeah, Sticks, you still in touch with him?' – a second pot of tea, a full English. And then I remember him leaning forward, drawing us both into a conspiratorial huddle.

'Look, D, I've got some news.'

'It's alright,' I tell him, 'it's 1997. No one cares if you're gay any more. Just look at Barrymore.'

When he doesn't laugh, when he can barely raise a smile, I know it's bad.

'They're opening a new office in Vancouver. They want me to make sure everything goes smoothly. It's a great opportunity for me, for all of us, and Angie and the kids are really excited...'

I don't remember too much else about that day. The edges really start to fray after that. I tried to pay for the food, but my protests were waved away, and then not long after that he was gone. They all were. I think I was pleased for him, for all of them, but I just couldn't bring myself to go to the airport. I don't think they minded too much.

I can't say too much about what happened after that. The details are vague. All I know is that there came a point when I just didn't want to hide away any more. I couldn't bear the familiarity, nothing but four walls as a purpose-built container facility for shame. The embarrassment of knowing how far I'd fallen, the only consolation that at least none of my family was still around to witness it. No work, no money, my whole life a Plog. Plog? Yes, that's right, a Persistent Large Output Gap, PLOG. I haven't forgotten everything, you know. I still recognise when an economy performs below the level it should be producing at and when this pattern is sustained over an extended period. And I just felt so lonely through all of this. Through the shame of being assessed as a benefits claimant – sorry, Mum, sorry, Dad – there wasn't one second when I felt I could actually tell anyone how it felt to have let everyone down so badly. Mum, Dad obviously, but also myself and even Roxy. Anyone who ever believed in me for the split second that it takes to hear conviction in a voice.

It's hard to think of myself as someone who used to talk about Nietzsche. I must have been a different person then. But people used to listen, I remember that, and we used to talk, argue even, before breaking off into our factions and bad-mouthing each other behind closed doors with no great vehemence. But I could never talk to my claims advisor about any of this. He resented me my failures. As far as he was concerned, I'd had every chance, and I'd fucked every one of them up. And I think he was right to hate me for that. But what I really wanted to tell him was this. *Thirty-two, cunt face, thirty-two! There's no space here, there never has been, for the kid who actually knows the answers. Less still for the one who's brave enough to speak up. And you don't mind that, do you, cunty? So let's have a little less of the moral disapproval, eh? At least until you reach down there and you can actually find a cock and two balls rather than your shrivelled lack of ambition.* I know I said something, I must have done, because the welfare taps were turned off after that, but at least the walls came tumbling down as well. And then it really was just me howling at the moon and the stars, the cloth still just about holding up, and the scent the exclusive aroma of the downwardly mobile.

*

Most days I just want to be left alone, and I think I manage that pretty well. But there are times, I won't deny it, when I want to talk. I know when people look at me that's not who or what they see. Their pity, though sometimes it's also disgust, makes it hard for them to understand. That I, too, once had a home and a wife and a job.

Over the years my style has changed. It's more utility outdoor wear that I favour these days, but I want to tell them, there was a time, fella (I've noticed it's usually a chap when the emotion in question is disgust), when I was the best-dressed chicken in town. To look at me now, they'd be hard pressed to believe that, but it's true. There was a time not so long back when I knew all about dogtooth and herringbone. When I would have regaled you, them, anyone who cared to listen with endless tales of pique trim or braiding or jetted pockets and sugar-pink silk linings. When I knew my Timothy Everests from my Tommy Nutters, my Gilbert and George from my George Dyer. Yes, that was me, all me, and, and, and what's that look for? It's no lie. That *was* me.

I decided a while back I'd had enough. No one seemed to care that my decline was so bespoke. I tried to tell them its foundations were hand-stitched, and they just looked past me. It kept happening. On trains, on buses, just out and about. The blank looks, the uncomfortable silence. But, though they would say nothing, I kept hearing the same words in their gestures. 'Get away from me, madman! Leave me alone, you nutter!' Yes! Yes! I wanted to shout. Tommy Nutter, the best of all the cutters. Checks, tweeds, horizontal pinstripes and velvets, all of which became the grain of his beautiful creations. And yes, those are creations more than they are suits. Bespoke tailoring at its finest. I'm so glad you mentioned him, I might add. He took lapels wide and shoulders high, and he really lived life. But now I'd find they didn't want to listen, didn't want to hear about Tommy's gay trysts and the renegade aristos who went in for that sort of thing. That's when they'd look at me, and then it *would* be disgust. If I was already inside, perhaps in one of my irregular watering holes, that's the point at which I'd be encouraged to leave, though often enough, as with the LSE, I would already be gulping down lungfuls of the fresh Houghton Street air and so would be moved on to where my gulping antics presumably wouldn't upset the locals. And that's when I knew I was no longer me. I was just this husk being commandeered by an unhelpful presence. None of the spokes fit any more. There was too much useless knowledge up there, and none of it was really mine. *He'd* taken over, yesterday's man, trapped in a speakeasy he could no longer afford.

Though funnily enough, once I started thinking of myself at a remove, things began to get a little easier. *He* was still me, and *I* was definitely still him, but in the retelling a little gap had opened up, and that was all he needed really, to carry on.

He snuck under the radar, slunk away into an obscurity which wouldn't be so easily conscripted. Since his family was gone, there was no longer anyone to watch over him, to monitor his movements, make sure that he repaid the compliment of a first-rate education by securing work 'commensurate with his skills and experience' and in so doing make himself known again. Announce himself in a flurry of paperwork: to the proper authorities, to potential future employers, the ringmasters of his nine-to-five, which, in reality, as he well knew, meant at least eight-to-eight, with, if he was lucky, a comfort break for something Bolivian. There was no one to oversee this any more, and he knew he was making it harder for himself with each passing week, with each tactical evasion. Of his responsibilities, or of any kind of work, for that matter. Of anything which might lead to a label once more being put on him. Earner, husband, citizen. But he'd been that person before and had no intention of putting himself through those shop-soiled paces again.

At least by staying off the grid he felt he could avoid the indignity of being processed and fingerprinted with all the other soon-to-be-has-beens, the massing hordes spilling out of Lehman's and failing to mind the gap between the platform and the edge. Boxed up, spat out, discarded, the gap opening ever wider, lives and futures unceremoniously dumped like junk bonds. He knew because he'd been the future once. Though for the novices, he was well aware that that penny would only drop once they'd been truly forsaken, spurned by the very people who'd only a heartbeat ago so willingly swallowed their lies. And they *were* lies, though he didn't like it when the markets spoke, told him so. He'd try to fight them, but the markets always had the last word.

Yes, I'm an analyst. *Wrong.* I'm a trader. *Wrong.* It's a bull market. *Wrong.* Bear, then. *Wrong again.* Well what is it then? *It's your life, matey boy, and it's just a pack of lies. There's nothing for you here, son, just some swift bull/bear moodswing action and then a coronary, if you're lucky. Take it, son, you won't get a better offer until the next round of voluntary redundancies.* It bothers me, though. Why is it always the markets that get to speak? Why not the bulls or the bears? I don't like the thought that the markets can see me, that they can tell me who's who and what's what, so when I get those feelings I let *him* take over again for a bit. It's better that way. It's what we do best. Maybe not lies, exactly, more like miniature dramas.

Take him and Roxy. They'd started on a lie and ended on one. And that was the thing. They weren't even particularly big lies. There *were* no bodies. Theirs weren't grand passions, just tremors which barely touched the surface. Underneath, the tiniest flake from what was already a husk, perhaps offering a muddied canopy for the lowliest worm. And on another day carted off in disgrace by the ants. *That* was their relationship. Less than plant food. They touched nothing and changed no one. And then she left.

Of late he has been given over to dark thoughts. No family, no children, no reason to stay. So much of him has already leaked into this soil, he thinks if he could just find a quiet corner where he could maybe watch the ducks one last time, that might be an ideal time to depart. Crawl into the long grass and wait, either for the earth to reclaim him, absorb him back into its elemental mulch, or for the dog walkers to make the discovery. And, of course, he hopes for a boxer, or maybe a Labrador, anything really but an angry Rottweiler. Though he knows by this point it won't be his choice to make.

He considers the far side of the Heath, but then has to remind himself of the Territorial Army base discreetly located between the park and the lesser-known pond. Once he has ruled out that corner of terrain, his thoughts turn to an ideal stretch on the other side of the park with elephant grass and burrows and myriad (well, at least three) places to hide.

He dips in the bins outside the cluster of restaurants in nearby Blackheath Village. It's a good last meal, NepaleseItalianArgentinianfusion, a glorious free for all of *aloopizzapampaslite*.

He feels very cosmopolitan, quite the gourmand, ferrying his intercontinental cuisine back across the Common to his resting spot, which also doubles as his dining quarters. He tucks in, enjoying the spicysaltyrecentlyorphaned taste he has assembled before him. *Al fresco*. When he is finished, he still has sufficient presence of mind to bin the empties. The pleasingly slim Pizza Express box, but also the tins and plastic forks which have accrued over the previous few evenings. He doesn't mind dining alone; it's become something of a habit. At least there's no need for small talk here. It is not such a bad way to go, he thinks. Soon enough the raw bite of the wind will make a mockery of his defences, but by then the man inside will be long gone, the taste of three continents and the whiff of something reified on his tongue.

He stretches out, the last of the whisky guiding him gently into long-desired sleep. Not such a bad way to go. In one way it is merciful. He doesn't see the two figures approaching him. There's no reason for any of it. Just boredom. Random cruelty under an inkblot sky.

When he finally awakes it takes him a while to focus. Is this what it feels like, he thinks? He doesn't know what he was expecting, but it wasn't this. Hospital white, tubes everywhere. And who *are* these people? Are they here to welcome him over to the other side? He tries to focus but finds he can only half open his right eye. The left is still firmly shut, until recently caked with dried blood. For some reason he has the thought that he must look like Toad of Toad Hall. It is quite funny, but it hurts when he tries to laugh. He sees then that his arms are winched up ahead of him, encased in plaster, as is his left leg. It feels as though every particle of his being is sore, bruised, complaining. It hurts even to try to focus, but he makes the effort, the realisation beginning to dawn that, no, this is not the other side. He hears a familiar voice.

'The mummy stirs.'

It's his brother, for once caught short in something highly casual. Through his squint D can still make out, with a struggle, the pink Lacoste polo underneath a Diamond Pringle jumper. He knows it is for his benefit, the one detail that will definitively persuade him that, no, he hasn't gone anywhere and, yes, he's a proper silly sod for getting himself into this state. He can almost hear the 'Look at the state of you. What *do* you look like?' which he knows must be coming. But it hurts too much to protest, so for now at least he does what he's always done during moments of duress and keeps shtum.

'Jesus, what the fuck happened to you?' his brother asks before he remembers what the nurse had told him, that D wouldn't be speaking properly for a while yet. Plus all the usual guff about needing as much rest as possible, and him thinking, that's all this little bastard's been doing. Resting. That's what's led to this in the first place, though, of course, he doesn't mention this to her.

'You're a very lucky boy, you know that?' his brother continues. 'I doubt you'd even be here if it wasn't for those bikers at the tea shack. Apparently one of them spotted you getting a kicking and alerted the others. Needless to say the two cunts who were laying into you bolted quick sharpish once they heard the bike engines being gunned. The bikers even waited with you until the ambulance came. Christ, D, you should have let me know.'

I wanted to but you were never around, he wants to shout, but the words don't come. He wants to ask him how long he's been here, when he got back. But also how long he, D, has been here, in this place. He has lost all track of time. He wants to ask about Angie and the kids and how he managed to find him and, come to think of it, why did he even bother, but when he looks up and sees that his brother is fighting back tears, again, the words, the questions, recede back into the shadows.

'Hello, D.'

Whose is that voice? He knows that voice from somewhere. It can't be. Surely not?

'Hello, D. You famous now, you made the nooze. Is why I'm here. We both here in London for conference and then I watch nooze, and I hear your name and about Hell's Angels who turn out to be more Angels than Hell.'

Both? Conference? Laura?!

'Is Low-rah, D. I know you probably forget me long time, but we used to…'

'I know. From How-rah,' he says, and it takes all his effort just to squeeze those words out.

She must have known what he was thinking then because at that moment she sat next to him on one of those hospital chairs that reminded him a bit of school. Of the two of them, he had to admit, she'd aged better. Looked after herself. Probably something to do with a Mediterranean diet and the sympathetic lines of Balenciaga, he thought. Then again, everything was soft focus at that moment, his squint removing all the hard edges, those other lines etched into the grooves of uneven lives. But his mind was still processing the shock of seeing her after all these years. How many? Twenty-one, twenty-two, maybe more? He couldn't be sure, but it had been at least that long. Loww-rah. Loww-ra. Loww-ra. Laura. Fucking hell! He tried to remember the last time they'd seen each other. Where had that been? Some place in his other life, the one he'd never really believed in. But where?

'Is someone else I want you to meet, D. Someone very special to me. I hope you feel same way.'

Oh God, here it comes, the 'other' person. Of course, it was too

good to be true. What had he been thinking? It's all these bloody
tubes and drips and drugs. Mind as soft as butter. Silly sod. Lie still
and play dead. You're no good at the other stuff. Remember?

'Hello.'

He looks up. A young man, nervously hovering next to Laura, peers back at him. He looks a little lost, D thinks, though there's something strangely familiar about those eyes and that chin. For some reason he thinks of Dad in his mohair parallels, a stepping razor against the dockside gloom.

'D.' It's Laura again, and this time she's speaking very softly. 'This is Roberto. He's your son.'

The words seem to hang in the air for a moment. If he'd felt in any way normal just then, if his physical circumstances didn't involve excruciating pain each time he tried to speak out of the one corner of his mouth that hadn't recently kissed some Reeboks, he might have paused, asked questions, at least allowed some time for the implications of what Laura had said to sink in. But it's just too painful, even with so many medications. He thinks about what he has just heard and whether the tubes siphoning out the gunk or funnelling in the contraband, the illicit stash to make him well again, have in fact left him delirious. But no, when he looks again she is still there, just behind her the young man. And behind him just a hint in his brother's profile of 1983 sportswear casual. And *that* is when he knows that he really is here. In that instant he wants to howl, for himself, for all the wasted years, the pitiful waste of decades searching, searching for something, for what? Something, anything, a style he can call his own.

A sartorial language, a way of being in the world when nothing else really mattered.

Trimm Trabs and Sambas, Fila Bj trackie tops, Forest Hills, dark Lois jeans. Just a way of anchoring himself when all around the old certainties were collapsing. Family, work, the very idea of a future, all of it crumbling. And he was back to being that restless, unhappy child toiling against the grain of the Inner London Education Authority. Never fully prepared to accept the deathly silence around those numbers. *Thirty-two* hanging over him, indicting that entire classroom like the spectre at the feast. Always wanting something more, another equation, a different result. And finally, after so many years, this, a new set of figures. Plus one. No, he thinks, enough time has already been lost, to all of them. The questions can wait. For once it is doubt, however reasonable, that is put on hold.

Without waiting any longer, he blurts out, 'At least he got his dad's good looks.'

And then they really do laugh, all of them, so much so that the nurse has to come back in and rebuke them, topping up his painkillers as she does so and reminding everyone that the patient needs to rest.

DISCOGRAPHY

Denis – *(Not yet a) Category Unknown primer*
Lewisham, Lambeth, south of the river. Soulboys. Peckham and
Bermondsey, the 'sticksman' look popularised by Gregory Isaacs.
Millwall, always its own thing, hermetic and uncompromising. And
somewhere in the middle of it all, Denis, soon to be D, shaving off
syllables but never dispensing with his own style. A thirst for
knowledge but hungry, too, for sounds, threads, and the sensual
embrace of life beyond the locale. Here's a little primer. Of the
sounds that is. Whatever else he got up to, that's his business.
Anyway, stick around long enough, and he'll tell you himself. Like
I said, this is just a primer.

David Bowie
Fascination
The Secret Life Of Arabia

Local boy, chameleon. The more doom-laden white boys love all
that low-fi Eno/Berlin stuff, but even then there were still traces of
soulboy left in the mix. In among the gloom and depression of
1977, 'The Secret Life of Arabia' stood out, a portal back to the
coke fuelled excesses of a year or two earlier, and its culmination in
the album, *Young Americans*. Bowie as Skeletor on the Dick Cavett
show, and there, right there, a young Luther Vandross on backing
vocals. Even better than the title track, though, 'Fascination', a slice
of pure, synthetic funk. A south-London boy who used to play on
bombsites and then dared to dream a little bigger. Perfect.

David Bowie
Rock 'N' Roll Suicide – 'You're not alone'
Andy & Joey
You're Wondering Now – 'You're on your own'

Both great tunes, though presumably addressed to very different pop
subjects. Bowie doing his best to coax the potential jumper, metaphorically speaking, from the window ledge, while the Andy & Joey

ska original, an early hit for legendary producer Coxsone Dodd, and later covered with distinction by both The Specials and Amy Winehouse, laid things out in somewhat bleaker fashion.

Wham
Club Tropicana

Pop, jazz-funk, gorgeous George. Pure froth, but then again that's just what was needed back in those dog days. Both adjunct and antidote to first term Milk Snatcher. Sadly, though, she ended up outliving Wham, if not the affection in which they are still held.

Maze
Before I Let Go
Twilight

Frankie Beverley and the boys displaying their versatility. The first cut one for the soulboys, the next for the house heads, even before they, or house, had a name. The best thing about the whole 'Back In Stride' tour was always 'Twilight'. Hypnotic, minimalist and just so ahead of the game. An instrumental classic, a slice of black modernism, huge everywhere that mattered in 1985.

Errol Dunkley
A Little Way Different

Big tune down Lewisham market. Back when there was still the 'model market' with its fishmongers, highly spurious Afro beauty products and the record shop (shack, really) with the unpredictable opening hours and constant rumours of weed circulating its signage.

Ennio Morricone
Il Vizio Di Uccidere
Al Foster Band
Night Of The Wolf

Owing money can bring the wolf to your door, and if that happens, you'd best be ready with a signature story or a prime cut. Look, I can't tell you what to do, nobody can, and whether or not you believe George Davis was ever innocent, the fact remains: the mid-seventies in Britain was a grim, dank, mustard-brown time, but for some reason one which was peppered with fantastic summers and even better underground music, much of it nestled away among the uglier stuff, the IRA bombs, police fit-ups and a freshly emboldened National Front. If you listen hard enough, it's not just the bifurcation of Northern Soul into dancefloor jazz-funk that you'll hear in the classic stomper 'Night of the Wolf'. In the distinctive howl of the wolf itself with which it opens there's an older sound of stone-blooded bounty killers and the compositional genius of Ennio Morricone. And by the time scores had been settled, 'Il Vizio Di Uccidere' would be the soundtrack to all that exertion playing in the pop subject's head.

The Upsetters
Live Injection
The Slickers
Johnny Too Bad
The Kingstonians
Sufferer

A triad often held up as 'skinhead reggae' favourites. Yeah, yeah, we get it. The cropped hair, the rude-boy look, the professed English working-class love for all things Jamaican which rang out throughout the land in the 'Paki-bashing' 1970s. The Slickers' rude-boy classic, in particular, a perfect example of the sweetest-sounding vocal actually belying the cautionary tale of a ferocious hooligan. No argument with the sounds, though. Sharp, dance-able, heartfelt.

Culture

Two Sevens Clash
Apocryphal. It's almost as though they knew it wasn't such a plum idea for the Front to go gallivanting round Lewisham after yet another long, hot summer of petty triumphalism. Of course, they were talking about Jamaica, but it could just as easily have been Loampit Vale.

Elvis
Suspicious Minds

Lush, poignant, no kind of age at all. Cheated of his health and his future. Terribly sad, but also highly useful as a diversionary tactic for a certain kind of cynic. The King is dead. Long live, ah, fuck it... Now everyone could refocus their energy and attention away from south London and back onto the distant media circus in Memphis. And events closer to home could, predictably enough, be brushed under the carpet. Cracking tune, though.

Fela Kuti
Roforofo Fight

Hardcore Afro-funk workout. Phenomenal fifteen-minute showcase of syncopated mayhem.

Norman Connors
Once I've Been There

The *real* sound of 1977. Phyllis Hyman on vocal, Captain Connors keeping time. There used to be a chap who lived just off Lewisham Way. He loved his garden, and rumour has it that he'd play this particular cut to distraction with his speakers facing the begonias. Pumpkins thrived in that ecosystem, and whenever he was complimented on this fact (which was often, as he was a popular local figure), he'd always humbly protest that the real credit belonged to Norman Connors. 'Once I've Been There', good for pumpkins, even better for the soul.

Mohammed Rafi
Aaj Mausam Bada Beimaan Hai

Beautiful, just beautiful. Strings, aching vocals, a reminder of elsewheres. A love song and slower in tempo, but there's a homespun thread running through this which connects Rafi to Marvin Gaye and the gorgeous Northern apex of 'It's A Desperate Situation'.

Listen up, he's a shapeshifter, D. But not always so remote, which is why it needs saying here, there are often many lives rolled into one. And they ain't linear. Denis would have liked the next lot of sounds, too, I'm sure of it. There's always overlap. But, Wham and Maze apart, he belonged to 1977. What follows is D's list. And that only gets properly under way in 1978.

D – *A Category Unknown playlist*

He never folded under pressure. Wanted you to know that. But the story he told still wasn't quite what we were expecting. Wham? The Cure? Bauhaus? He made it clear that if the fledgling pop subject of 1977 still answered to 'Denis', then within a short calendar year he was performing his own situationist autopsy on that name. And what emerged from the streamlined shadow of D was a seeker, hungry for more. He immersed himself in the beautiful, baleful vista spreading out before him. Sounds, styles, sexual experimentation. He lifted theory from books with the aplomb of the local hoisters, but in the end it was always the sounds he came back to. And, like any analyst, he loved lists. Produced this one the way other people show their holiday snaps. Said it was rudimentary, but even so that it captured something of that life, from Blondie to the fall of Lehman Brothers. Said he was a 'category unknown'.

Mtume – Love Lock / **Blondie** – Denis / **Joy Division** – Transmission / **The Cure** – Primary / **Bauhaus** – Bela Lugosi's Dead / **Freeez** – Southern Freeze / **Ryuichi Sakamoto** – Riot In Lagos / **Magazine** – Shot By Both Sides / **The Specials** – Stereotype (extended version) / **Linda Williams** – Elevate Your Mind / **Starvue** – Body Fusion / **Milton Wright** – Keep It Up / **Foxy** – Mademoiselle / **Queen** – Cool Cat / **ABC** – Poison Arrow / **The Beat** – Too Nice To Talk To / **Chic** – Open Up / **Charme** – Georgy Porgy / **Smiley Culture** – Cockney Translation / **Barrington Levy** – Under Mi Sensi / **Aswad** – Warrior Charge / **Fabian** – Prophecy / **Tenor Saw** – Ring The Alarm / **The Style Council** – Mick's Up / **Jimmy Smith** – Who's Afraid Of Virginia Woolf (Part 2) / **Prince** – Uptown / **Maze** – Love Is The Key / **Luther Vandross** – Never Too Much / **Jon Lucien** – Listen Love / **Joe Bataan** – Ordinary Guy / **Soul Sonic Force** – Planet Rock / **JVC Crew** – Strong Island / **Prince Charles And The City Beat Band** – Cash (Cash Money) / **Frankie Knuckles** – Your Love / **A Guy Called Gerald** – Voodoo Ray / **The Ragga Twins** – Hooligan 69 / **Gil Scott Heron** – Your Daddy Loves You

LONDON BOOKS

FLYING THE FLAG FOR
FREE-THINKING LITERATURE

www.london-books.co.uk

PLEASE VISIT OUR WEBSITE FOR

- Current and forthcoming books
  - Author and title profiles
    - Events and news
  - Secure on-line bookshop
- An alternative view of London literature

London Classics

The Angel And The Cuckoo *Gerald Kersh*
Doctor Of The Lost *Simon Blumenfeld*
The Gilt Kid *James Curtis*
It Always Rains On Sunday *Arthur La Bern*
Jew Boy *Simon Blumenfeld*
May Day *John Sommerfield*
Night And The City *Gerald Kersh*
Phineas Kahn *Simon Blumenfeld*
Prelude To A Certain Midnight *Gerald Kersh*
A Start In Life *Alan Sillitoe*
There Ain't No Justice *James Curtis*
They Drive By Night *James Curtis*
Wide Boys Never Work *Robert Westerby*

New Fiction

THE SEAL CLUB

WARNER WELSH KING

The Seal Club is a three-novella collection by the authors Alan
Warner, Irvine Welsh and John King, three stories that capture their
ongoing interests and concerns, stories that reflect bodies of work
that started with *Morvern Callar*, *Trainspotting* and *The Football
Factory* – all best-sellers, all turned into high-profile films.

In Warner's *Those Darker Sayings*, a gang of Glaswegian nerds
ride the mainline trains of northern England on a mission to
feed the habit of their leader Slorach. Welcome to the
world of the quiz-machine casual.

In Welsh's *The Providers*, the Begbie family gathers in Edinburgh
for a terminally ill mother's last Christmas, but everyone needs
to be on their best behaviour, and that includes her son Frank.
The ultimate nightmare family Christmas looms,
where secrets and lies explode like fireworks.

In King's *The Beasts Of Brussels*, thousands of Englishmen assemble
in the city ahead of a football match against Belgium, their
behaviour monitored by two media professionals who spout
different politics but share the same interests. As order breaks
down we are left to identify the real beasts of the story.

London Books
£9.99 paperback
ISBN 978-0-9957217-6-0

New Fiction

SHE'S MY WITCH

STEWART HOME

Strange things happen on social media, such as the almost chance
encounter between a London born-and-bred fitness instructor and a
drug-fuelled Spanish witch. At first Maria Remedios and Martin
Cooper share their love for super-dumb, two-chord stomp in private
messages, but when they meet magic happens. Maria knows that she
and Martin have been lovers in past lives, and sets out to convince the
former skinhead that her occult beliefs are true.

The main narrative takes place in London between 2011 and 2014,
detailing riots, rock-and-roll excess, and the times of austerity leading
up to the Brexit vote in 2016. In online messages Martin and Maria
hark back to other eras – his immersion in London's 1970s punk
explosion and her tales of teenage drug-dealing and murder on
Spain's notorious Ruta Destroy party scene. As Martin gets ever
closer to Maria, she constantly surprises him by detailing different
aspects of her life – such as running a bar for a criminal motorcycle
gang in Valencia, her seven-year stint as a professional dominatrix,
and a decades-long struggle with heroin.

She's My Witch is a dark romance with an incendiary conclusion,
written to reflect today's social-media world and a
resurgent interest in the occult and kink.

London Books
£9.99 paperback
ISBN 978-0-9957217-4-6

SLAUGHTERHOUSE PRAYER

JOHN KING

When a boy realises the grown-ups are killing animals and that he has been eating their bodies, he gives up meat. But should he share the truth and break another child's heart? As a youth he wants to believe in the ability of words and peaceful protest to end the slaughter, while struggling to resist a desire for revenge. Now a disillusioned man trying to rebuild his life, he must choose one of two paths. Acceptance means security, but those meat-industry adverts keep taunting him and some familiar insults – *smelly pig*, *dirty cow*, *chick-chick-chicken* – fill his head.

Slaughterhouse Prayer deals in human invention and our treatment of non-human animals, the manipulation of language and the corruption of innocence. Society's pecking order is challenged as the story moves to its margins and beyond. A book of dreams, where visions are more real than reality and sentimentality is a strength, it asks a series of questions. Can a person honestly kill without emotion? Could a vegan soldier stay professional and humane? And will we ever confront the terror that surrounds us?

London Books
£9.99 paperback
ISBN 978-0-9957217-2-2

NEW FICTION

DOCTOR ZIPP'S AMAZING OCTO-COM AND OTHER LONDON STORIES

DAN CARRIER

The London Evening Press And Star is a local newspaper holding its own in a time of fast-moving, celebrity-obsessed, click-bait global news. And the unnamed narrator of this book is one of its reporters, an old-school journalist dedicated to his community and his craft. But with every news item there is a bigger, more complex tale, and drawing on his notebooks he reveals the stories behind the stories, and the journeys he has taken to discover their hearts.

Meet Eddie Roll, karaoke-barge proprietor, and find out how he keeps his business afloat on the city's canals. Hear how Batman and Robin leapt from the pages of a comic book to come to the rescue of someone in need. Discover what links Elvis Presley and meals on wheels, learn of Kermit The Hermit of Hampstead Heath, and spend time in the company of a generous Irishman from NW1. And read about the life and death of the enigmatic Doctor Zipp, a marine biologist and inter-species language expert who believed we could learn a lot from the octopus.

If a city is its people and their stories, then this is London at its warm-hearted, eccentric best.

London Books
£9.99 paperback
ISBN 978-0-9957217-0-8

NEW FICTION

BARRY DESMOND IS A WANKER

MARTIN KNIGHT

Barry Desmond is an only child. He's had a sheltered upbringing by ageing parents distrustful of the outside world. This leaves him ill-equipped to deal with the savagery of school, the trials of adolescence and the reality and politics of the workplace.

At school he is a figure of fun, excluded and picked on. At home he struggles with the eccentricities of his parents and is alarmed and confused as his hormones spring into life. He finds guilty pleasure in self-relief. Later, he follows his father into a career with the Empire Bank, a throwback organisation doomed to become extinct. In middle age, and following the death of his parents and redundancy, Barry ventures out into the wider world determined to live his life and strike up relationships. Unlike his parents Barry believes that people are fundamentally decent. Will he find the fulfilment and interaction he craves? Will society repay Barry's trust?

This novel from Martin Knight, author of *Battersea Girl* and *Common People*, explores and illuminates 21st-century suburban loneliness and the grim reality of having a face that doesn't fit. *Barry Desmond Is A Wanker* is a seductive and surprising book, laced with humour, shot through with poignancy and sensitivity.

London Books
£8.99 paperback
ISBN 978-0-9551851-9-9

New Fiction

MALAYAN SWING

PETE HAYNES

Aidan is different. He is small, awkward and often silent, an easy
man to ignore, mock or exploit, yet on the inside he is intelligent and
thoughtful. He speaks to the reader in a way he can't manage in
everyday life, reflecting on the world around him with great insight
and an almost childlike honesty. This is the internal life of an outsider.

We meet Aidan not long after he has moved into a room in a
shared flat, forced from the home in which he felt secure by a policy
labelled 'care in the community'. But the community is dismissive
and threatening. He becomes lonely and scared, his best friend
the radio he carries everywhere. An old shed offers a hideaway
during the day, while his evenings are often spent in the local pubs.

Aidan's physical and mental state starts to deteriorate, and when
he bumps into Joey from the home he comes to the notice of some
bad people. He wanders the streets and is attacked, his life quickly
spiralling out of control. The story ends in dramatic fashion, but it is
Aidan's decency and a sense of escape that remain with the reader.
Malayan Swing is a moving novel, a testament to those living on the
margins of society, and as such is a brave and important work.

London Books
£8.99 paperback
ISBN 978-0-9551851-6-8

NEW FICTION

THE LIBERAL POLITICS OF ADOLF HITLER

JOHN KING

It is fifty years in the future and the individual nations of Europe no longer exist. New Democracy rules. Elections are considered divisive and a thing of the past, power has been fully centralised, and cheerful Controllers make the decisions for the good of the masses. Conformity means freedom. Big smiles, easy debt and lots of nice words mask a corporate-driven, closet dictatorship. When special police unit Cool come to take you away they arrive with fresh coffee and blueberry muffins. But resistance groups are fighting back.

In London, ambitious young bureaucrat Rupert Ronsberger uses Suspicion software to identify threats to the system, stumbling across a shocking murder just as Controller Horace is about to arrive in the city. At the same time Kenny Jackson – a member of the outlawed GB45 – leaves a free town in the West Country and heads towards the capital. Despite the best efforts of Cool, the three men are set on a collision course.

The Liberal Politics Of Adolf Hitler predicts a time when the internet is embedded in the human body, having morphed into propaganda/surveillance tool InterZone; correct thinking and a denied censorship crushes individual expression; physical books, audio and film are illegal; the people's culture is cancelled or sold back to them in distorted forms; and enforced digitisation has seen history edited, deleted and rewritten, so that even the most wicked of individuals can be reinvented.

London Books
£9.99 paperback
ISBN 978-0-9568155-8-3